FUTURE

HOME

OF THE

LIVING

GOD

FUTURE

HOME

OF THE

LIVING

GOD

LOUISE

ERDRICH

corsair

CORSAIR

First published in the US in 2017 by Harper Collins
First published in Great Britain in 2018 by Corsair

3 5 7 9 10 8 6 4 2

Copyright © 2017 by Louise Erdrich

The moral right of the author has been asserted.

A CIP catalogue record for this book
is available from the British Library.

HB ISBN: 978-1-4721-5336-4
TPB ISBN: 978-1-4721-5335-7

Printed and bound in Great Britain by Clays Ltd, St Ives plc

Papers used by Corsair are from well-managed forests
and other responsible sources.

Corsair
An imprint of
)wn Book Group
1elite House
ia Embankment
n EC4Y 0DZ

tte UK Company
1achette.co.uk
tlebrown.co.uk

To
Gookoomisinaan
Kiizh
Light of my days

The Word is living, being, spirit, all verdant greening, all creativity. This Word manifests itself in every creature.

—HILDEGARD OF BINGEN (1098–1179)

PART

I

When I tell you that my white name is Cedar Hawk Songmaker and that I am the adopted child of Minneapolis liberals, and that when I went looking for my Ojibwe parents and found that I was born Mary Potts I hid the knowledge, maybe you'll understand. Or not. I'll write this anyway, because ever since last week things have changed. Apparently—I mean, nobody knows—our world is running backward. Or forward. Or maybe sideways, in a way as yet ungrasped. I am sure somebody will come up with a name for what is happening, but I cannot imagine how everything around us and everything within us can be fixed. What is happening involves the invisible, the quanta of which we are created. Whatever is actually occurring, there is constant breaking news about how it will be handled—speculation, really, concerning what comes next—which is why I am writing an account.

Historic times! There have always been letters and diaries written in times of tumult and discovered later, and my thought is that I could be writing one of those. And even though I realize that all lexical knowledge may be useless, you'll have this record.

Did I mention that I'm four months pregnant?

With you?

Confession:

Nearly a decade ago and almost two months into my first pregnancy, I had an abortion. I am telling you because it is important that you know everything. My decision came about the instant I took the dipstick test—*no*. I would close this door. In doing so, I opened a different door. If I hadn't had an abortion then, I would not be having *you*, now. This time the dipstick test filled me with *yes*.

So I am twenty-six, pregnant, and I haven't got health insurance.

This would completely upset my parents, who actually have more than they need. It is also, without question, a perilous time in the history of creation. Unless the swirling questions are answered soon, you will be born into this unknown state. But whatever happens, you will be welcomed with eager arms into a family that spans several cultures. There are first of all my adoptive parents, whose lyrical name is of British origin. Glen and Sera Songmaker. They are truly beautiful people, there is no doubt, no question, and although I've given them a great deal to worry about, they've dealt gracefully with me for the most part. They are forgiving people, Buddhists, green in their very souls. Although Sera is annoyingly phobic about food additives, and many years ago Glen had an affair with a Retro Vinyl record shop clerk that nearly tore the family apart, they are happily married vegans. They are the dearest people imaginable, except . . . Except I've never understood how I was adopted—I mean, the legality there is definitely to be questioned. There is this law called the Indian Child Welfare Act, which makes it almost impossible to adopt a Native child into a non-Native family. This law should have, even had to, apply to me. Whenever I mention it, Glen and Sera hum and look away. Even if I scream, they don't look back. Still. They are good parents, they will be wonderful grandparents, and you'll have aunties and uncles and a whole other set of bio-based grandparents, the Potts.

As I mentioned, yes, I denied and disregarded the knowledge of my biological family for a short time, but perhaps you'll understand if I explain how my ethnicity was celebrated in the sheltered enclave of my adoptive Songmaker family. Native girl! Indian Princess! An Ojibwe, Chippewa, Anishinaabe, but whatever. I was rare, maybe part wild, I was the star of my Waldorf grade school. Sera kept my hair in braids, though I famously chopped one off. But even one-braided, even as a theoretical Native, really, I always felt special, like royalty, mentioned in the setting of reverence that attended the study of Native history or customs. My observations on birds, bugs, worms, clouds, cats and dogs, were quoted. I supposedly had a hotline to nature. This continued through high school, but waned, definitely waned, once I went to college and hung out with other indigenes. I became ordinary, then. Even worse, I had no clan, no culture, no language, no relatives. Confusingly, I had no struggle. In our talking circles, I heard stories. Addictions. Suicides. I'd had no crises in my life, besides the Retro Vinyl clerk, so I invented one. I chopped off both braids, then stopped going to classes. I'd been a snowflake. Without my specialness, I melted.

One year ago, perhaps thinking that my lack of ambition regarding a degree stemmed from confusion about my origins, perhaps thinking who-knows-what, Sera decided to give me a letter that she had received from my biological mom. Honorable Sera, she had not opened it. I did. I read the letter twice and put it back in its envelope. Then I put the envelope in a manila folder. I am a very organized person. I decided to file the letter. Under what? I needed a label. I thought about that for a while. *Biological Family? Potts?* How about *Immense Disappointment?* How about *FUCK YOU?* It was upsetting to be contacted, after all. And there was worse. It was a shock to realize that on the reservation I was even more ordinary than I'd felt myself to be in college. My family had no special powers or connections with healing spirits or sacred animals. We weren't even poor. We were bourgeois. We owned a Superpumper. I was Mary Potts, daughter and granddaughter of Mary Potts, big sister to another Mary Potts, in short, just another of many Mary Potts reaching back to the colonization of this region, many of whom now worked at the Superpumper franchise first stop before the casino.

What was I to do? Until this biological confusion, until my pregnancy, until this great uncertainty that life itself has suddenly become, I've hidden the fact that I even opened the letter. I've told my Songmaker parents that they raised me, I love them, and that is final. I've told them that I want no complications; I want no issues of abandonment and reconciliation; I want no maudlin reunion, no snake tears. But the truth is different. The truth is I am pissed off. Who are the Potts to suddenly decide to be my parents, now, when

I don't need them? Worse, who are they to have destroyed the romantic imaginary Native parents I've invented from earliest childhood, the handsome ones with long, both-sided braids, who died in some vague and suitably spiritual Native way—perhaps fasting themselves to death or sundancing to heatstroke or plunging off a cliff for love or being carried off by thunderbirds? Who were the Potts to keep on living their unremarkable lives without me, and to work in a Superpumper?

I wouldn't have had the slightest thing to do with them if it wasn't for my baby. Sweets, you're different! You're new. Things can start over with you, and things need to start over. You deserve more. You deserve two sets of grandparents. Not to mention genetic info, which may affect who you are even beyond whatever is now occurring. There may be hereditary illnesses. Or unexpected talents—one can always hope, though that seems doubtful, given my birth mother's letter. Still, I think you need to enter the web of connections that I never really had.

I embraced Catholicism in my crisis-creating year, at first as a form of rebellion, but also in an effort to get those connections. I wanted an extended family—a whole parish of friends. It was no passing phase and I have integrated both my ethnicity and my intellectual leanings into my faith first by analyzing the canonization of the Lily of the Mohawks, Kateri Tekakwitha, and then by editing, writing, illustrating, publishing, and distributing a magazine of Catholic inquiry called *Zeal*. I obtain funding for my work through private donations, occasional per capita casino payments, and a small contribution from my church. I've got enough to keep the magazine going until your due date, December 25, which also means that I've got roughly four and a half months to figure out how to give you a coherent family as well as be a mom.

It's not enough time.

Your father might help, but I'm trying to keep our distance.

All the more reason to find you an extra grandfather, maybe an uncle or two, a cousin—functional, I hope.

"Cedar?"

I have been writing to you and ignoring the constant ringing of the telephone. I decide to pick it up this time because I have a feeling that your father was calling and now he has given up. I always know when he has given up.

"Mom."

"Look, what's going on out there is making us very nervous, honey, why don't you come back home?"

As always, her voice is cool and capable. Stress calms her.

"I've got to do something first."

Now is the time to tell her about you—I really have to—but I'm paralyzed by those two words *I'm pregnant* and so I tell her the other thing. The family thing.

"Remember that letter, Mom? That one you gave me about a year ago, the one from my biological family or whatever? I'm going up there to meet them."

Silence.

"To the reservation," I say.

"Now? Why now?"

Her consternation is not about jealousy or disapproval. After all, she gave me the letter and left the whole decision up to me. She even urged me to open the letter. She really is worried about the timing— this is Sera.

"Because I have to."

"Please, not now."

Her voice has that decisive I-will-deal-with-this tone I've heard just a few times: when I called her and asked her to pick me up from a party where a drunk boy had tried to rape me but instead had puked on me. When I told her I was getting baptized and confirmed as a Catholic.

I know she's right, and yet nothing *out there* feels as important as what's *in here*. Driving to my house, I saw that the streets were full of the usual number of normal, purposed, smiling, and gregarious Minnesotans, people talking at the bus stops. People carrying their shopping bags and backpacks, walking at an appropriate rate of speed, not looking either shaken or scared.

"I've just *got* to, I can't explain it. I'll come right back, Mom, don't worry. I know things could destabilize."

"I think they are right now. It's coming. Here, talk to your dad."

There is some frantic whispering, shuffling, as she tells him my plan.

"Listen, we'll go with you. There's something . . . baby, listen . . ."

Hearing Glen call me baby fills my eyes with tears. He'd do that when I had a rough day at school or had my heart broken or got Bs. I hated getting Bs. Alienating Glen was hard on me, but I had to try. To my relief, I utterly failed to make him go away or even really lose his temper. Once, he said he was exasperated with me. I had to be content with that.

"Oh Dad, I'm sorry. Don't worry. I'm going to be fine. I just have to do this and it's only for a day."

"Cedar, things are taking a more ominous turn, though I don't think people realize it yet. What we're hearing on the news is, and there's talk of, I know this sounds impossible . . ."

"It's only for a day."

"Listen to the news. There's a lot about . . ."

"What?"

"The president is talking about declaring a state of emergency and there's a debate in Congress about confining certain . . ."

"Dad, you're always—"

"This time it's real, please come back."

Sera gets back on the phone. She has composed herself. One of her deepest tenets—her belief in my autonomy—is at stake. She has warred with herself off the phone, and won.

"Well, we don't know. This could be a new kind of virus. Maybe bacteria. From the permafrost. Use hand sanitizer, okay? Will you call us when you're there and call us when you get back?"

"Sure."

"And fill up with gas first."

"I'll be okay."

"Of course you will."

It isn't until after I've hung up that I remember how Glen and Sera often congratulate themselves on their prescience regarding the tech and housing bubbles, then Iraq, the Mideast, Afghanistan, then Russia, the increasing chaos of our elections, and our first winter without snow, among other things, and how good their track record is on political idiocies and wars and natural disasters. They didn't foresee this, of course—nobody did—but they're excellent at reading the fallout of events. I should probably be more nervous than I am, but I evade all common sense by dialing statewide 411 information and getting the phone number of the Superpumper where my biological family work. Then I even let the automated cheery voice on the information dial automatically for me, which costs extra.

"Boozhoo?"

God, I think, they speak French.

"Bonjour," I say.

"H'lo?"

"Hello."

"Who's this?"

"I'm . . . ah . . . looking for Mary Potts."

"Well, I'm not her. Who's this?"

"Okay, well, I got this letter from Mary Potts Senior about a year ago; she contacted me about the fact that she is my biological mom. Is this? I mean, you don't sound like Mary Potts Senior, but are you maybe—"

"Whatthefuck?"

"Hey!"

"MAAAAAHM! Some INSANE BITCH is on the phone who says you're her mom and you wrote her last year."

Mumbling. A voice. *Gimme that.* A crackling thump as someone drops the receiver. A man's voice saying, *Who's that, Sweetie?* Woman's

9

voice. *Nobody!* First voice again. *Getthefuckawayfromme.* A raging scream that fades and ends abruptly in a crash—slamming door?

"Mary Potts Senior?" I ask the hollow breath on the other end.

"Speaking." A whisper. A croak as she clears her throat. "Yeah, it's me. The one that wrote you."

And I suddenly want to cry, my chest hurts, I can't breathe, I'm breaking. The only thing that could possibly overcome what I feel right that moment is a simultaneous mad anger that bubbles up in me and freezes my voice solid.

"By any chance, will you be in tomorrow?"

"In?"

"Home."

"I'm not doin nothing."

"I am coming up there. I am going to visit you. I have to speak to you."

"Awright."

Who's that, Sweetie? Man's voice. *Nobody!* she says again.

I ignore the awful prickling in my throat, the reaction to the second time that she has said *nobody*.

"Who's calling you sweetie?" I ask.

"That's my name," says Mary Potts Senior. "They call me Sweetie up here."

"Oh."

Her voice is so humble, so hushed, so astonished, so afraid. I feel a sweep of killing rage, but it just comes out in cold, weirdly complicated grammar.

"Well, that's very fitting, I am sure, *Sweetie*; however, I think that I will just call you Mary Potts Senior, if that's all right."

"I'm not senior, though. I'm almost senior, not quite. Grandma's still alive."

"Okay, Mary Potts Almost Senior. Now, might I ask for directions to your house?"

"Sure you might," says Mary Potts, or Sweetie, but then she doesn't say anything.

"Well?" I say, icy voice.

Sweetie gets a little sly now, maybe she can't help it, maybe she's a mixture of humble and heart-struck and shrewd, I don't know.

"You said you *might* ask. You asking?"

Now I feel a stab of what is probably instant hatred, because she is the one who wrote me and she is the one who asked me to contact her and she is the one who originally bore me from her body and then dumped me. But I can handle her petty manipulations.

"Just tell me," I say in a cool, neutral voice. "You can give me your address. I'll use Siri or GPS."

"We ain't on no GPS, and Siri's dead. You don't know?"

"Know what?"

"You'll find out. You coming up from where? Up or down?"

"I'll be coming up from Minneapolis."

"Well, you know the highways up to Skinaway—then you cut . . . ah . . . it's a left. You take a left at the river."

She seems relieved to have thought backward, to have figured out directions from my point of view. She even seems awed with herself, a little, like maybe she has never given directions before.

"What river?"

"The big one."

"That would be, I mean, the name. I need the name."

"It's the only big river, with a bridge. Then right after, there's a road. Not paved. Take a left."

"All right then, take a left on an unpaved road. No name to the road?"

"Skinaway Road."

"We're getting somewhere. Then?"

"We're at the end."

"What's your house number?"

She clears her throat. Somehow I get the sense that she is just about to cry out, that there's some desperation on her end, danger of a hysterical outburst. And it occurs to me that reservations—I don't know about them—maybe people just do not give directions on reservations. Maybe everybody just knows where everything is there. Maybe nobody leaves and everyone was there forever.

"Okay, all right, what does your house look like?"

Relief fills her voice.

"It's yellow, newish, a two-story ranch with white trim and a front porch with a wheelchair accessibility ramp for Grandma. We'll have her here for you tomorrow. Until then, Avis is borrowing her. But you just drive into the yard. There will be a black van with purple detailing, up on blocks, but that's the only car . . . um . . . not operational at the moment. There is also a new pickup, that's mine, and a little brown Maverick might be there, Eddy's, and a sweat-lodge frame—"

"A sweat what?"

"Grandma and Eddy doctored Little Mary. That was her on the phone. Anyway, it's right beside the house, a little back, in the yard."

"I still don't know what you're talking about."

"Yeah, and there's some birdhouses too. And a shrine, you'll see that first of all. Mary."

"I don't go by Mary, naturally. My adoptive name, my *real* name, is Cedar."

Long pause. "That's a pretty name." Her voice is tender again, pained and wistful. "I just always thought of you as Mary. But I was actually talking about the shrine, you know, it has the Blessed Virgin."

"Mary? Mary in an inverted bathtub?"

"Well, yeah, I guess you could say inverted, you must be smart, ha! But I would call it stood on end and half buried. How'd you know? We took the tub from the old house. Eddy put that up. I planted the flowers."

"Wow."

Something hits me then, really just about floors me. It loosens up some of the anger and makes me quietly say good-bye and express the polite expectation of being glad to see Mary Potts. When

I put the phone down I just sit there looking at it, thinking. Here it is—inherited genetic congruence. I became a Catholic before I got in touch with my biological mother; Catholicism drew me, and I was fascinated by it all: the saints, the liturgy, even the little shrines. Now it turns out that the saints and the church are things we have in common. Me and her. Sweetie. Mary Potts Almost Senior.

AUGUST 9

The next morning, I travel the highway north to my Potts reservation home. I'm having flashes of poignancy. Everything that I am seeing—the pines, the maples, the roadside malls, insurance companies and tattoo joints, the ditch weeds and the people in the houses—is all physically balanced on this cusp between the now of things and the big, incomprehensible change to come. And yet nothing seems terribly unusual. A bit quiet, perhaps, and some sermons advertised on church billboards are more alarming than usual. *End-time at Last! Are You Ready to Rapture?* In one enormous, empty field a sign is planted that reads *Future Home of the Living God*.

It's just a bare field, fallow and weedy, stretching to the pale horizon.

I pull over, take a photograph of the sign, and keep driving. A car passes me bearing the bumper sticker Come the Rapture Can I Have Your Car? Oh good, not everybody's getting ready to ascend. I love driving. Thinking while I shoot along. If it is true that every particle that I can see and not see, and all that is living and perhaps unliving too, is trimming its sails and coming about and heading back to port, what does that mean? Where are we bound? Is it any different, in fact, from where we were going in the first place? Perhaps all of creation from the coddling moth to the elephant was just a grandly detailed thought that God was engrossed in elaborating upon, when suddenly God fell asleep. We are an idea, then. Maybe God has decided that we are an idea not worth thinking anymore.

These notions turn over and over until I stop. I go through a typical car entrance at a typical fast-food franchise, and eat an egg-cheese biscuit and drink two cartons of milk. So there is still fast food, and I am grateful. Eating grounds me. My head clears, and a few hours later I am on the reservation. I pass the Potts Superpumper without stopping, though I do slow up a little. Well, there it is, I think as it goes by, my ancestral holding—a lighted canopy of red plastic over a bank of gas pumps, a cinder-block rectangle with red trimmed doors that match the canopy. Big lighted windows, a bony-looking man at the cash-register stand, bent over on his elbows, peering into what looks like a book. Probably the used-car blue book, at best a techno guy-thriller. I hope not porn. Probably the skinny man is the husband of my biological mom. Eddy. He was mentioned in the letter. No mention of my biological father.

I cross a bridge with a trickle of water underneath—qualifies just barely as a river, I think. But no turn for a while. The left turn I do take leads past six houses. Five are neat and tidy, trimmed out and gardened, birdhoused, decorated with black plywood bears and moose or bent-over-lady-butts with dotted bloomers. One yard is filled with amazing junk—three kid swimming pools of brilliant blue and pink plastic, a trampoline, dead cars, stove-in boats getting patched I guess, heaped-up lawn mowers and little rusted-out lawn tractors and barbecue grills. Dogs pop from the ditches here and there, at random, and chase after the car, snapping at the wheels. The last house isn't yellow. I stop the car, pull over. A frowzy tan terrier mix springs up and down outside the passenger window, tireless. I turn back. Maybe there's another river. She did say big. The dogs pop out in reverse all the way back to the highway.

There are two other false-alarm rivers, and left-hand turnoffs, all of which lead back into the same first road with the yard full of kid swimming pools. One pool is filled with a couple inches of water and there is a big woman in it, wearing a long T-shirt, letting a little naked baby play in front of her. *Aw, cute. Fuckit!* Where's my birth home? Where's my family? Once again, a false turnoff, a winding road, the dogs newly thrilled each time by me and my car, the woman in the swimming pool now watching me like I am from the FBI. I decide that I will ask directions of her, and turn into the driveway. The dogs go crazy now, foaming with righteousness. I've invaded their territory and don't dare get out of my car. I roll the window down. The woman looks up at me—she has a flat, beautiful, closed-up, suspicious face. She says nothing.

"Could you tell me where the Potts live?"

The dogs throw themselves at the car now, thumping their bodies on the doors, hysterically excited by my voice. The woman puts her hand to her ear. I'm not afraid of dogs, generally, but one is chewing on my tire.

"Looking for Mary Potts!"

"Dunno!"

"How about . . . Sweetie?"

The woman slowly raises one arm, keeping the baby safe with the other, and points back down the same road. Tears sting my eyes. So it's no use, I think, shoving the car into reverse, pulling out of the driveway. Bitterness rises in me. I'll probably take every left turn off this road and cross every bridge and river—how many can there be? Is it all one river, maybe, bigger and smaller in places, winding through like a snake? Is there some kind of settlement besides the casino? A water tower? Maybe a food store? Some place that people can visit for the education and health care I have read is guaranteed to us by nation-to-nation treaty? I get back on the highway and drive, sorrow welling up, lost self-pity, that awful feeling of loneliness. I'm also getting very hungry, a serious kind of pregnancy hunger, *ravening hunger*, and now I just want to stop the car and cry. I drink some water. Eat a little bag of peanuts from my glove compartment. Compose myself. Back on the road, it occurs to me that I could turn around and go back to the Superpumper and get junk food, then introduce myself to Eddy. I'm about to do just that when I come to a bridge and a big river. A real river. At last, one with moving water. And a left-hand turnoff right after with a promising road I know will end in a yellow house.

And there it is. I turn into the gravel drive that leads to my birth family's yellow house—fairly new, three or four bedrooms. There is the wheelchair ramp and birdhouses out front, the broken-down black van with purple detailing, the well-kept BVM bathtub shrine, and the bent wooden—willow, I think—frame that must be the sweat lodge. And there, about the appropriate age, Mary Potts Almost Senior. She wields a garden hose, an unattached garden hose, and she is beating the crap out of a dusty couch cushion. She grins a sly, lopsided smile as I drive up, and gives the cushion a few finishing whacks.

Here is the woman who gave me life.

"Holeee." She puts her arms out and comes over to the car. She is sweating lightly in a tight black muscle shirt that shows pink bra straps, and a pair of flared black capris. Her shapely, bearlike body is all muscular fat, and she has a pretty face with neat features. She's young. She has gleaming white teeth and shifty little merry black eyes. Her dark brown hair with red highlights is fastened on top of her head in one of those plastic claw clips, a blue one, and she wears pearl earrings. They look like real pearls. I exit the car into the stifling hot air.

We stand facing each other, completely awkward. This is not a hugging moment for me, and I don't know what to do about the tears filling the eyes of my birth mom.

"Pretty," I say, touching my ears. "Pretty earrings."

"Yeah, Eddy got'm for me."

She sniffs and looks away, blinking.

"I think I saw him in the Superpumper, reading."

"That was him. Always got his head in a book."

"What's he like to read?"

"Him? Everything. Everything but the sex manuals." She sighs. "Ha! Just kidding. Aaaaay."

My birth mom stands beside the car with her hands on her hips. I notice that she is chewing on a shoelace. She notices that I notice and says that she does that when she's trying to quit smoking. Then she starts smiling at me, a little, but with the shoelace in her mouth this is strange.

"So, what do you think? How are people taking the news up here?"

I don't know what to do. She's not inviting me in, not giving me any of the usual signs of welcome. I try to make conversation.

"You know, the news? The big news?"

She doesn't react at all and I am desperate to make some sort of impression now.

"You look like . . . ," she says.

"Who?"

"Never mind."

"Who? Really?"

"Well, me."

"I do not," I say instantly, without thinking, just a gut reaction. She looks down, at her feet. Then she turns with a little shake of her topknot and walks away, which makes me notice that she's got a perfect heart-shaped butt. As it is packed tightly into those black capri jeans, she moves with an oiled rhythm that I can't help but wish, for a moment, I'd inherited. I'm tall and big-boned, thin, and my butt is flat. When I do not follow her—I am actually just watching her ass, as lots of people probably do—she looks over her shoulder, jerks her head at the house. I walk behind her, up the wheelchair ramp, through the little porch, in the front door. The house is almost bearable, there is an air conditioner somewhere, I think. The living room is thickly carpeted and smells of wild stuff—bark, maybe, or bird seed, or boiling berries—and cigarette smoke.

"You wanna smoke," she says, "I got a coffee can of sand outside for butts. I don't smoke in here, though."

Somebody does, I think.

I put my backpack and my laptop by the door—I wasn't going to leave them in the car. Mary Almost Senior rumble-walks into the kitchen. I follow her and decide to sit down at the table—speckled Formica. I watch while in silence my BM (having trouble with what to call my birth mother, can't call her that) makes a strong pot of tea. She gives me a mug of the tea, sugared, and sits down across from me.

"You turned out nice," she says, then yells into the next room. "She turned out nice!"

"Who's in there?"

"Your grandma. She's old. She had me when she was fifty-three, no lie, remember that. Use condoms until you're sixty, ha!"

"Hundred and twenty-eight," says a reedy little voice from around the corner. A tiny, brown, hunched-up little lady then wheels herself incrementally—she's wheeling herself on carpet—around the corner.

"Here," says my birth mom, "Mary Potts the Very Senior."

The ancient woman gives a breathy, whispery cackle.

"Pleazzzzzz," she actually buzzes, or hisses, inching closer. I jump up and push her to the table.

"She really might be over a hundred," says my birth mother. "She's not kidding you." She tells me about some other relatives with endless lives.

"Mary Bodacia," says the grandma, nodding wisely. "Hundred and eleven."

"Bodacia. Very funny. Everybody's driving me crazy," says my birth mother, to nobody. "And her"—she gestures at me —"she calls me Mary Potts Almost Senior. She thinks that's funny."

"Well, it's almost funny," I say. "I don't know what to call you. You're not Sweetie to me."

"Hehhehheh." The grandma laughs, nodding at the cup of tea that Mary Almost Senior is pushing carefully across the table. I can't bear this and decide to get it over with. I lean forward and address my birth mom.

"Two things. First, why did you give me up? Second thing. I want to know about genetic illnesses."

Both of the woman are quiet, now, sipping hot tea in the warm room and looking at the top of the table. My birth mom studies the freckles in the Formica like she is divining the future from their pattern. At last, she gives one of her sighs—I'm getting to know her sighs—and then she starts to cough. She's getting wound up to speak. After several false starts, with the kind of helpless lack of verbal skill that came upon her when she tried to give me directions, finally, she begins.

"It wasn't because I was that young," she says, "though I was young." Big sigh again. Restart. "It was because I was stupid. Not one day has gone by, since then, when I have not thought about how stupid I was."

She looks right at me, frowning, puzzled.

"Stupid," she says again, and nods. She curls and uncurls her fingers from the handle of the cup. "Took drugs. Not while I was pregnant. After. Fucked every jackass in sight. Just dumbass stupid," she whispers. "Til I found Eddy. Not one day has gone by, though, when I have not thought about you."

Forget about the practical issues. I'll get those later. Right now I'm struggling. Thinking. Not one day? How about not one hour? I want to cry. I *wanted* you. I *needed* you.

"Well, you thought about me more than I thought about you," I say, shrugging.

Nobody talks after that. Her tears dry up and we sit there in silence.

"You got a good family, yeah, rich as hell," she says, shaking herself up straight. "They sent me pictures the first year. Then I wrote and said no more, I can't take it."

"You couldn't take it?" I feel my eyes narrow, and this thing builds up in me, this thing I know well and which I say rosaries to avoid, this anger. It fizzes up like shook pop. "*You couldn't take it?*"

There's the sound of a motor roaring off outside and footsteps, fast clunking footsteps, the door behind me slams, and I turn around to witness the dramatic entry of the Queen of the Damned—Little Mary. She stalks into the room on five-inch-heeled black boots, in ripped fishnets, too many piercings to list and long hair with short bits spiked purple, though limp from the humidity, not sticking up except for a wisp of bangs. Her eyes are surrounded neatly with red and black paint. Magic Marker? Sharpie? Her pupils are black and luminous. She sways in the doorway, obviously high.

"Soooo," she says.

"This is your sister," says birth mom, "the one I told you about last night."

"Oh, nobody?" Little Mary smiles at us, dreamily vicious. Her teeth look sharpened—could they be? Her canines are a bit longer than her incisors and very white against the black lipstick, like elegant fangs. She's pretty, like her mom, prettier than me, I think, instantly doing that thing girls do. Who's prettier. I suppose sisters compare all of the time and right at this minute I am glad I didn't have a sister, ever before, in my life. I'm glad I didn't have this mom and this family, except maybe the grandma. I think of Glen and Sera and all that we share, and tears now do come into my eyes. I turn to my birth mom and I reach over. I hold her fingers and then warmly grasp her whole hand in mine.

"It's all right, Sweetie. Really, it's all right," I say, with the sincerest note that I can muster in my voice. "Just looking at Little Mary I can tell what a good mom you would have been."

My sister Mary is sixteen and it turns out, after Mary leaves, and we really start to talk, it turns out that Sweetie believes that, although she isn't doing very well in school, Little Mary has no drug habit, she does not abuse alcohol nor does she smoke. Sweetie actually shakes her head, marveling.

"I know you meant your comment as sarcastic, you know, ironic, what have you. Good mom. I know I'm not the best mom. I know that. But Little Mary's really doing good. She's the only girl who doesn't fuck and do drugs in her whole class. She says that she's about to crack."

"Crack? And who can blame her." I swallow the urge to fall down on the floor and laugh and thank every saint in the book, once again, for the life I've had. "It's hard to be the only sober one at the party. It's hard to be the sole intelligence."

We sip tea quietly for a while, contemplating the difficulties of Little Mary's social life. Of course, as soon as I think about a sole intelligence I imagine whoever the last of our species will be . . . that last person contending with all of the known and the unknown; for all I know that last person might be you. Or me. I find that I might be unusually long lived, like Grandma. Or maybe, darker thought, the last of the species will be Little Mary.

"Can she talk to Eddy?" I ask. "Is he an understanding type of guy?"

Sweetie shakes her head, a bunch of shakes, real quick, a gesture I'm beginning to like as it jiggles her messy upsweep in a pleasant way. "Them two had a helluva fight the other day and traumatized us all. Eddy caught Little Mary hauling all the Sudafed from the Pumper storage to the car—she let him catch her, of course. A cry for help. Hey, though, she don't do the stuff, but she was selling it behind our backs to some meth kid."

"Sure," I say, "yeah, so Eddy. What about him?"

"Eddy," says Sweetie, and her face goes soft while Grandma's goes sharp. "My Eddy." She gives that happy shudder. "Meow!" She makes a little claw of her fingers and she and Grandma laugh.

"So what's his life story?" I ask, trying to push things along. I don't really want to picture what that little *meow* means.

"Oh, he's smart, yeah, he's got the brains. He went to Dartmouth for his undergrad and then Harvard for his Ph.D. in education. When he came back, he tried to fix the school system on the reservation, but so, well"—now Sweetie's face turns sad, and her whole look fills with sorrow—"the attempt gave him a breakdown. After he returned to this reality, he decided to open up a business, support his family that way, I mean us. He ran for tribal council, and he's writing a book. He is up to over three thousand pages now."

Sweetie purses her lips and indicates a door in the wall, a closet.

"It's in there. Drafts of his manuscript, which is all about me. He follows me everywhere I go and watches all that I do."

"Where is he, then? Why isn't he here, witnessing this historic meeting? You and me?"

"Well, he's gotta mind the store," says Sweetie. "Besides, I am supposed to, well, I do have something on my agenda today. I'm giving a presentation to the tribal council. After that meeting, we're gonna lay sod." Then, shyly, she says, "Wanna come?"

I'm feeling better now, getting the hang of being here, and although I've got the most awkward part of the meeting out of the way, I haven't got to the part where I pump the family for genetic information. But as soon as I've got that, I'm leaving. Getting out of Dodge, so to speak, the reservation version of it anyway.

"What's the meeting for? And the sod?"

"For the shrine. Not the one in our yard. A shrine for Kateri, you know?"

"Yeah, I do. Really?"

Sweetie tells me about the wayside shrine that she and twenty other parishioners have decided to erect at a place on the reservation where people swear they have seen an apparition three times in the past four years. She says that people think it may be Kateri Tekakwitha, Lily of the Mohawks, patron saint of Native people. Again, here's that congruence. Catholic stuff. After we finish our tea, the two of us put Grandma down to sleep on a little bed stuck in one corner, piled high with quilts. Then we get into my Honda and drive over to the tribal offices.

On the way there, we do not speak a word. We park, and go in through the big doors that open underneath the outspread wings of a cast fiberglass eagle. This is all new to me. I'm interested. The air inside is fresh and cool. I breathe in big gulps. I can't wait to tell Glen and Sera details—fiberglass eagle! We sign ourselves in, and Mary chats with the receptionist, a cousin. Finally, we go into the meeting, sit down at the near end of the table. We are the only ones there without big plastic traveling coffee mugs. We're first on the agenda.

They're making small talk now, ready to start the meeting. Mary opens a file that she's brought along.

A woman says a quick prayer, or gives an address of some sort, in Ojibwe, and then Henry "Bangs" Keewatin, heavy, pale, soft, a smoker and classic heart-attack candidate, reads out the minutes of the last meeting and introduces us.

"Mrs. Potts will be explaining this shrine question," he informs the others. Then Sweetie reads a thumbnail sketch on the life of Kateri.

"Born in 1656 at Osserneon, New York, the daughter of a Christian Algonquin woman named Kahenta. Kateri's mom married a pagan, of the Turtle clan, and died during a smallpox epidemic that also left Kateri's face scarred and her eyes weakened. She converted and was baptized in 1670, and thereafter lived a life of remarkable virtue, even, it is said, in the midst of scenes of carnage, debauchery, and idolatrous frenzy."

"Idolatrous frenzy. Is that something like traditional religion?" asks Bangs.

"Yeah, it is," says Sweetie. "I'm a pagan Catholic. Moving on?"

Bangs nods.

"She took a vow of chastity and died young," says Sweetie.

"That's why I never took one," says Bangs.

Sweetie raises her eyebrows, sighs, and continues.

"Miracles occurred. She was beatified in 1980 by Pope John Paul II and since then canonized. Besides all Native people, she is the patron saint of ecologists, exiles, orphans, and . . . people ridiculed for their piety.

"I'm going to pass out these financial impact statements from a site that has registered several appearances by the Virgin Mary. This place is located on Long Island, New York. You can see for yourselves what an effect pilgrimage crowds have on the local business community."

Sweetie slips the papers from the folder and distributes them to each of the members, who eye the numbers critically and come to the end smiling.

"And that's just a tentative sighting, my relatives. By children. The Blessed Virgin waved her hand over some rosebush. They sell the rose petals from all of the roses planted near the shrine. Here's one."

She passes around a small card containing a laminated rose petal.

"Good move," says one of the members, setting down the figures that Sweetie has written up and copied. Bangs Keewatin smiles. "I'm thinking in light of this world situation we're seeing there could be increased interest in appearances of a spiritual type of nature, and we'd best be ready. We should take advantage of this saint showing up here."

"Yeah, she picked us all right," says Sweetie. "Here's more figures on how much money the average pilgrim spent in the eateries and motels adjacent to that spot in New York. Oh, and here's the description of the first two visits." She hands out sheets of testimony.

"You know, this whole thing would be a bigger deal," says Bangs, "if this ghost or whatever had not just appeared to small-time losers."

"That's always the first caveat most church officials have about the sightings," says Sweetie.

Caveat? I think. Maybe she's been coached by Eddy. Or could it be that I've underestimated Sweetie?

"The seven people who witnessed Kateri's visitations weren't small-timers," she says sternly. "They had just lost big money at the slots or blackjack tables and were in a state of severe financial shock when the beautiful Indian maiden appeared in buckskins, carrying a cross. She wore a circle of flowers around her head, brandished the lily of purity. She spoke. Actually, she wasn't comforting. She was forthright, accusing, and even said specifically to Hap Eagle that he'd wasted good food money and his kids would now have to eat from the commodity warehouse."

"Do they have commodities in heaven?" one of the council members, a guy named Skeeters, asks. "How'd she know about commodities?"

"Saints know everything," says Sweetie, her voice severe. "Apparently our saint has made a sort of decision here," she continues, "and who are we to question it? She has decided to appear to nobody but the feckless. Yes, inscrutable, but it's all we have to work with."

"*Feckless*, you *go*," I whisper to Sweetie when she sits down.

"I didn't know she only appeared to virgins," says Bangs, frowning at the others around the table.

"That's feckless, not fuckless," says Sweetie.

She smiles beatifically at the council, keeps talking. "As in irresponsible. If only they'd been affected enough to quit gambling. Nobody redeemed yet, I'm sorry to say. They keep going to bingo with their Bibles at their elbows. Anyway, we'd like to grass in that place you let us keep clear in the casino parking lot. We got a load of sod coming. Here's the bill."

The treasurer takes the bill and says he'll put the appropriation to the vote, which passes. That is that. We walk out and across the highway to the shrine, which is just out back of the newly surfaced and paved casino parking lot. The sacred oval of earth lies between the north and south parking lots, and the committee has decided to begin by grassing it with sod, which was scheduled to arrive an hour ago. The exact place where Sweetie's saint has consistently appeared is marked by a large boulder, for which a plaque is just now being cast. Behind the boulder, the committee plans to put a statue, though Sweetie thinks that a statue might discourage Kateri from reappearing.

When we get there, a black truck with wooden-slat sides is pulled up and six or seven people are pulling rolls of grass off the back. Someone has dragged a long hose from behind the casino to water the dirt in the oval. Sweetie and I get out of the car and pitch right in. Between the two of us, we carry a sod roll to the site and carefully place it just so against the other strips. It only takes half an hour to do the whole thing. Then the others go, the truck too, and my new mom and I are left with the hose, watering down the grass.

This is how the world ends, I think, everything crazy yet people doing normal things.

Sweetie lights up and sits on the sacred rock while I stick my thumb in the stream of water and spray an even fan back and forth over the instant green lawn.

Sweetie sighs—there it is again—shakes her head in that sexy way, and looks out over the parking lot.

"Right on cue," she says, pointing with her cigarette. "That's Eddy, see? Just like always, he's looking for material, and I'm it." She stands up and slings her lighted cigarette with an eloquent motion into the drain at the parking lot curb. She takes the shoelace from her pocket and wraps it around her fingers. Eddy parks and gets out and Sweetie preens a little. I can see she has this fantasy that her husband is slavishly devoted to her, which already I don't think is quite the case, but which somehow works because she can interpret anything he does as an act of obeisance. For instance, he has a slushie in the pickup's cup holder, and now she reaches right in through the open window and fishes it out with a sigh that says *my man takes good care of me.*

"So this is Cedar," says Eddy, getting out of the truck, walking up to me, shaking hands like a well-socialized person. His attitude is just right, not too familiar, and yet he, too, suddenly has tears in his eyes. He's trying not to stare at me. I sense that he is struggling hard to maintain the right distance, the right balance. And like me, he immediately goes for the abstract and talks too fast.

"I was going to ask what's up, how are you, something of the sort, but we can already answer that, right? Gawiin gegoo, nothing. Well, that's not strictly true, is it, since the world as we know it is coming to an end and nobody knows what the hell is going on or how our species is going to look four months from now."

"Then again, maybe she just wants a slushie," says Sweetie as she hands me the cherry ice soup. "That's enough out of life."

"I couldn't agree with you more." Eddy gives me a surprising smile. I say surprising because Sweetie told me that he never does smile.

"Hey, he's smiling," I say to Sweetie. "I thought he never smiled."

"I don't, as a rule," says Eddy, smiling again at me. He looks like such a nice man, really, a little shy, even sweet. "I'm afflicted," he says, half kidding. "I suffer from a chronic melancholy, the sort diagnosed by Hippocrates as an excess of black bile."

Then he tells me that he elects to believe that he shares his condition only with writers like Samuel Taylor Coleridge and great statesmen like Winston Churchill. He doesn't have the modern sort of depression, he says, the kind that can be treated with selective seratonin reuptake inhibitors. His is the original black dog.

"We're all going down the tubes, the fallopian tubes that is, not to mention the seminal vesicles," he says as he cheerfully throws back his head and lets the sun hit his face. "Ah, that feels good."

"The whole world can go to hell as far as I'm concerned," says Sweetie, "as long as Eddy's in a good mood."

"I'm in a real good mood." Eddy plants a tender little kiss on Sweetie's mouth. She looks at him, dazzled.

"That was unexpected," she says.

Eddy's about six two and has a slender build. His face is thin and foxlike, secretive, worried, and that rare smile is wistful, very tentative. But suddenly he is smiling way too much, grinning like an excited child, and I know that there's something wrong with him. His emotions jump too fast for perfect mental health.

"It's just that I knew it all along." His black, thick hair stands on end like a little boy's exuberant cut. "All my life I've sensed an unseen deterioration, Cedar, I've always known that this was happening. It has colored my mental processes and been the reason for all that I have written. I have waited for it and known that it, or something like it, would come. I just feel an enormous sense of calm. Perhaps relief."

Sweetie did not describe Eddy as manic—that wasn't part of his self-diagnosis—though I've read that depressives may seek out manic episodes as the melancholy weighs so heavy and keeps their thoughts so sluggish. Maybe Eddy is getting his wish. His demeanor right now might be temporary euphoria—an extremely understandable reaction to the strangeness of this disaster, so I am gentle with him and issue an invitation. I am going to ask them to lunch, after which, I decide that I'll drive back to Minneapolis, counting my blessings all the way.

"Let me take you two out to lunch, okay? Come on."

"There's still lunch? Of course there is," says Eddy. "We can probably still sit down and order our usual Cobb salads and wild rice soup. Lettuce is still being shipped here, most likely. Corn is still tasseling. Cows have not stopped giving milk. But then, I think, it won't take long before they give a lot less as they are bred for milk capacity."

He's right, I think as we walk to the casino. I remind myself to lay in a stock of powdered milk right away, to maybe hit a big Cub or Rainbow market before I get back to the Cities. I make a mental list of long-shelf-life high-protein foods. Peanut butter. Durum pasta. Rice, beans, lentils. And salt. I'll get a lot of salt. We'll need salt whatever we become. And people run quickly out of liquor, right? It's good to have it, to bargain with. Walking toward the restaurant, I imagine myself hunkered in my house with a closetful of Morton salt and fifths of vodka, which I can trade for diapers.

"Since you know so much then, Eddy, what's going to happen?" I ask.

"Indians have been adapting since before 1492 so I guess we'll keep adapting."

"But the world is going to pieces."

"It is always going to pieces."

"This is different."

"It is always different. We'll adapt."

We make our way through the jangling gloom, past Treasure Castaway and Bullrider quarter slot machines to the entrance of a discreetly Native-themed grill. Geometric wallpaper, heavily varnished stripped pine, metal light fixtures with eagle-feather cut-outs. The booths, solid Naugahyde, are comforting and cushy. We order our food—everything is on the menu—and it comes in the usual amount of time. I noticed when Eddy got out of his truck that he had a briefcase with him, and I think immediately of Sweetie's description of his manuscript. Sure enough, once Sweetie finishes her food and takes off for the tribal offices, where she works as some kind of special coordinator, a job I'm unclear about, he lifts the brief-case onto the tabletop between us and takes out some pages of what turns out to be his book.

"I'm revising," he says, "not that it's going to matter, ultimately. Short is the time which every man lives, and small the nook of earth where he lives, and short too the longest posthumous fame, and even this only continued by a succession of poor human beings. Marcus Aurelius. Typically up to the moment."

Eddy says that although he quotes the Roman emperors and orators, he also likes Russian novels. Dostoyevsky is a favorite. Eddy lugs *The Idiot* around in an old clothbound edition. That's what he was bent over when I saw him through the big glass windows. He says that people buying gas at the Superpumper some-times catch the title and ask him if it's his autobiography. But Eddy really does feel that Dostoyevsky has used up the only two titles that could possibly work for his own book—*The Idiot* and *Notes from Underground.* He is constantly searching for a title as good as those. He is keeping a list. Eddy tells me that his book is basically an argument against suicide. Every page contains a reason not to kill yourself.

"Some potential titles include the very literal," he says. "*Why Not to Kill Yourself.* There is the more colloquial, *Don't Off You.* The trium-phant declarative, *I Live Yet!* The confusedly academic, *Contra Selbst-mord.* Here!"

Eddy pushes the page he is editing across the table. That page, numbered 3027, is titled "Even Gas-Station Food Can Save You."

I

Today I did not kill myself because of the sweet foam on the top of a cheap cardboard cup of cappuccino. What can I tell you except that it was delicious, swept off the surface of the denser brew onto my finger, which was slightly redolent of windshield wiper fluid. As I lowered my lips to the steaming liquid, I inhaled tones of vanilla, then took a tentative sip. Intense sweetness filled my mouth. I tasted fully. Malt dextrose and a resonance of airplane glue with a scorched plastic finish. My senses fully awakened. Awful and Superb!

2

I had a cardboard tray of nachos for lunch that was slightly flawed in the presentation, as I pushed on the hot cheese pump too forcefully and splattered the edges of the tray and counter. But that failing was made up for by the implacably rich marriage of salt and sodium, corn and hydrogenated grease, vegetable gum and number-five red that lingered in the back of my throat for hours.

3

I ate a postdated ham-and-cheese sub. Then two oranges from the fruit bin. Thusly, tasting deeply of all that gave me life, I made it through another unpromising morning and wholly treacherous afternoon in which between ringing up sales and unblocking gas pumps I attempted to manage my dread. The syncopation of my heart. A willful retreat of my entire mental process as I contemplated the 1 p.m. tribal council meeting which I was scheduled to attend.

Strike that. Endure. *That I was scheduled to endure.*

"I wouldn't change a word," I tell him. And I wouldn't. Even if I wanted to, I don't think that my services as an editor are really required. I'm pretty sure that what Eddy mainly wants is validation. I am happy to give it, although you may think, given the subject of the book, that I should perhaps ask Eddy to report to a psychologist. I do consider it, and then decide not to because even now I believe Eddy's book serves as therapy. Like this book, or notebook, like yours. Also, Eddy makes me promise not to.

But there is something. Something that occurs during that lunch, during my first meeting with Eddy. Something clicks, is what I'm saying. Eddy talks, but Eddy also listens. He is the first person in this newly met family and also, come to think of it, the first person including my adoptive family, who actually sits and just *listens* to me.

"Yes," he says, nodding, or "Hmmm," he says, or "More, more on the subject?" Or even, "What do you think?"

So it is Eddy I first tell of your existence. Eddy whose jaw drops, whose brow knits, whose eyes fill with sympathetic concern. It is Eddy who lets me cry in the booth across from him as I describe my fear—of going to a doctor, of visiting the ultrasound lab. I keep imagining stunned silence and some mystified pronouncement by a doctor. Eddy's face is grave and concentrated as I tell him I fear that we are heading into a lightless future devoid of the written word. I tell him that nonetheless I am writing this long and involved missive which I hope that you will someday read.

"Of course there's the big if," I say. This actually just occurs to me.

"What?"

"*If* my baby's teachable."

"You've got to have some faith," says Eddy. "Everything's in flux right now. You've got to realize how little we know of our ancestors."

"The hominins at Jebel Irhoud looked like us, but their brains were different. It's too much to process."

"Then don't process," Eddy says.

"What?" I laugh a little. "You're actually telling me not to process? I've just met you, but I can tell that you're the original processor, Eddy, you're the one who thinks too much. You're the one who examines your every waking hour. You're the one who's alive only because you process your reasons for living every single day."

Eddy just smiles and orders coffee. He sneaks the bill from the hand of the waitress, but I snatch it from him. He pulls and tugs it gently back, and pays. We continue to sit there thoughtfully as people swirl in and out.

"I know," says Eddy at last, looking at me with a kind of delicate distance. He's being appropriate, but trying to show me that he's fond of me in a newfound, stepfatherly kind sort of way. "I know today's reason I'm alive." He keeps nodding at me. I suddenly want to cry again, but I just keep nodding back at him. There is more stirring of coffee and sipping. I drink more ice water. I am waiting, but Eddy is lost now, perhaps composing pages in his mind. So at last I have to prod him.

"Aren't you going to ask me about the father?"

"Well, yeah," he says, "I was going to, but then I thought, number one, this is all too new. Number two, she's got some reason for not telling me. So I'm letting you off the hook."

Even though I'm disappointed, I notice that he numbers his remarks just the same way I do. I think that I was hoping Eddy would question me until I cracked and spilled my words. I think about your father all the time. I want to talk about him. But Eddy doesn't seem to care. It is really frightening how expendable fathers can be in this culture. I think maybe I am wrong with the secretive thing. Maybe the better course would be to talk nonstop about your dad. Maybe then your father will become someone I can accept. So I do talk.

"All right," I say, "you've twisted my arm enough. I'll confess. The father of my baby is an angel."

"Oh yeah?" Eddy smiles now, thinking maybe I am really in love and even might be happy. "Sure he's not an archangel, just an angel?"

"Yes." I do not smile back at Eddy. I look down at the gleaming cracks in the cubes of translucent ice in the water I am drinking at the table. The water from the vast and beautiful hidden aquifer below us, the gigantic underground source of purity, which we're all sucking dry. I am missing your father, I am seeing his face, I am wondering if in any way you will resemble him or if your features will obscure your parentage completely. I am seeing him, yes, I am flashing briefly on the gorgeousness of the moment of your conception when he laid me down and kissed me deep and covered me with his soft brown wings.

————————

I go back to the house, to say good-bye. The door to the house is open, so I peer in. Little Mary is sitting in front of the television. When I do walk in, she does not acknowledge me, but there is an odd smell emanating from her—more than the wild teas and roots I smelled the first time I entered the house. This time, it's just a feet smell, something slowly going rotten. Behind her, I notice, the door to her room is open. Through that doorway, I can see pure chaos—a shockingly grand mess. It's the sort of spectacle you can't help gawking at, like a car accident. I stand there a moment, gaping, and then see that Grandma's wheelchair is drawn up to the table and she's snoozing upright. I walk past Little Mary and sit down to wait for Grandma to surface, so I can at least say good-bye to my oldest living relative.

While she's sleeping, I watch her. I've never seen anybody old as her. I like the name Mary Virginia. Grandma Virginia. She has the softest skin, silkier than a baby's, and her hands are little delicate curled claws. Her eyes are covered with thin membranes of skin. I think perhaps she can see right through her lids, they're so transparent. I do know, from before, that she can stare a long time at you without blinking. She has not allowed anyone to cut her hair, I see, not for a very long time. Maybe an entire hundred years! It is braided into one thin white plait and wound into a bun. Her ears stick out a little as her hair is so thin. A pair of white shell earrings hang off her earlobes, which are fragile as flower petals. Most remarkably, I notice when she happens to yawn, she still seems to have most of her own teeth. Though they are darkened by time, her teeth are still strong.

Suddenly she's looking at me, those bright eyes tack sharp. Startled, I say, ridiculously, "Grandma, what sharp teeth you have!"

Mary Virginia laughs, soft and breathy, and says, "The better to eat you with!" She has a very sweet ancient type of laughter that comes out in panting gusts. We laugh together. She tells me that she had a full French grandfather who counseled her on the importance of scrubbing her teeth with a peeled willow twig. She takes a cracker from the table and shows me how she chews and bites with the vigor of a young person. The strength of her teeth, she says, is the key to her longevity.

"What's that?" I touch a long piece of weaving in her lap. She shows me that she is making a belt, finger-weaving it from strands of yarn, braiding a sash with such precision that it will look like it was created on a loom. She pulls the flat piece of weaving taut and frowns at it, picks at an invisible flaw. Here's how to do it, she says, and makes my fingers follow hers. We work in silence, until she nods in satisfaction. All of a sudden, her eyes spear me, sharp, and she puts the sash down and folds her hands on top of it. Clearly, she has thought of something. I imagine her mind as a pinball machine, one of the old-fashioned, nonelectronic kind. A thought ricochets off over a century of personal memory, lighting up and ringing associations that only connect because of the speed and arbitrary motion of the original thought.

She gazes at me so long and with such reptilian stillness that I think she might be having a stroke. It is odd to look at her and think perhaps she has lived through the final efflorescence of human culture and thought. She is perched on top of the pyramid, Grandma Virginia, a tiny, pinched gargoyle riffling a pack of cards.

"I am pregnant." I tell her quietly, so my sister will not hear. "Are there illnesses in the family? Anything my baby might inherit?"

Her expression does not change. Probably my identity, our place in time, the muddy river of reality, all of this is bundled in shadow. Yet the word "pregnant" may have registered, because that word triggers a story, and then another story, many of them. Listening, I

realize that her tales are so practiced that Grandma Virginia probably tells and retells them all the time. And here I am, new audience!
It doesn't matter who I am. Her memory shifts. The narrative is all
that matters. She seems to have lived out many versions of her own
history. Once she begins to speak, nothing can distract her. I hear
the Story of the Two-Faced Child, the Tooth-Spitting Grave, the
Talking Drum, When the Frogs Sang Like Birds, the Story of the
Dog That Shit a Diamond Ring, the Unholy Mirror, the Nun Who
Fed Her Baby to a Sow, the Nun Who Swallowed a White Ribbon
and It Came Out the Other End White Too, the Twenty Dead Who
Appeared at Mass, an Avalanche of Fish, the Much Confused Sister,
How One Twin Killed the Other, a Weightless Apple, Boiling Rain,
and others which I can't just now recall.

As soon as she finishes her stories, Grandma Virginia drops her
head and sinks into a motionless and rigid sleep. I wheel her into
her room and stand her up beside the little single bed, then lower
her slowly onto the mattress and lift her legs over and set them
gently down. Her little tan moccasins stick straight up. I cover her
with a bright quilt made of all different versions of yellow calico—a
golden cloud.

When I come back out, my little sister is still sitting in front of the
TV. She has on so much black eyeliner that her eyes smolder demon-
ically into the changing screen. I begin to count her piercings—her
ears have six or seven each. Her earrings look like twisted nails and
screws. She has sprayed her bangs straight up into a black woodpecker's crest. The rest of her long, thin hair—permanented and
bleached and colored with those purple highlights or bleached again
and again—hangs down her back in a dead and crinkled curtain.
She's made some changes to her outfit, added a pink bow to her
hair. She's wearing an incongruously sexy baby-doll nightie, ankle
socks, and white Mary Janes. The cuteness contrast has an effect
even creepier than when she dressed in full-on Goth. She's sort of a
nightmare kitten.

"Hey." I sit down next to her.

She maintains her stony pose.

"Hey," I say again, "what's up with you?"

"What's it look like?"

"I mean in general, what are you up to in a general way, and what do you think about what's happening?"

"What what's happening?"

"You know, the world changing, us going backward maybe, what they're finding out."

She looks at me with black contempt. Her lips part in a snarl and the pink bow in her hair bobs up and down like a sinister butterfly. She nods as she speaks, agreeing with herself.

"You're just a stinking slut. You suck, you impostor. You're not my sister, you're an STD. You're a piece of syphilis."

Her hatred is simple. Predictable. Her outfit keeps throwing me—cutie-pie vampire. But I tear my gaze away and try to hold my own.

"You're suffering from misplaced self-disgust," I tell her. "Your feelings have nothing to do with me. I've never hurt you."

"And I heard you tell Grandma you're pregnant, but I can see it anyway," she sneers. "You're such a whore."

"Oh, really. How do you think being pregnant makes me a whore?"

My heart is surging but I keep my voice calm. I've always found that the best way to deflect hostility is to ask questions. But Little Mary is like a politician, adept at not answering the question asked but sticking hard to her own agenda. She stays on the attack. There's a frilly white garter on her leg.

"You got adopted out and grew up rich and think you're smart as hell, but you're not even a good Catholic. You had premarital sex! Ooh!" She opens her painted eyes wide and screws up her mouth like a wooden doll's. I want to slap her. She sees how close she's come, smells blood.

"You probably fucked a priest and now your baby's gonna be a monkey. And it won't get born with a silver spoon in its mouth, it'll be wearing a little black and white collar like so—" Little Mary jumps up and begins to dance around making hooh-hooh monkey sounds and putting her fingers to her neck. She's talented. She's like the dark side, the devil version of her supersmart dad, Eddy.

"You're possessed," I tell her, and embarrassingly, my voice squeaks. "Your brain's all cooked on meth."

"Oh yeah!" She cocks her fists. "Oh yeah! Let's go!"

But then she slumps down and in a typical display of sick emotional lability begins to cry. Fat tears swell from her eyes.

"Don't tell Daddy, don't tell Mom, okay?"

"I think they know. They live around you. For godsakes, they smell your room. I can smell it from here."

"Will you help me clean it, huh?"

I look at her, my mouth drops open. She's just met the sister she didn't know existed and she wants me to help clean her room? It is so bizarre that I might be charmed, in a weird way, were it not for the room itself. That unnatural disaster. I stand up and follow her to the open door.

Little Mary's room has the odor of rank socks, dried blood, spoiled cheese, girl sweat, and Secret, a miasma that seeps out of the open door. The room is knee-deep in dirty clothes she's packed down and walked on—sort of a new conglomerate flooring. Within the stratified layers of clothing I can see potato and corn chip bags, cans of pop she hasn't even drunk dry. A tiny haze of baby flies circles an old can of orange Sunkist. Stuff is balled up, pasted together with sparkle glue, thrown on the wall, smearing the windows. Spray-can confetti hangs off the fancy fanlight fixture. Bras and thongs, those are every place I look. Pink glitter thongs, black ones, gold lamé, sequined, lace spiderweb and zipper thongs, thongs with little devils on them. Little Mary has undressed by kicking them up onto the blades of the fan. The curtains are balled up around the cockeyed rods and there's broken glass sifted over one entire corner of clothing-floor.

"It's your mom's job to make you clean this," I say, feebly.

"Yeah, maybe," says Little Mary. "She read in a parenting magazine that it is best to pick your battles with teenagers and that a teen's room is her own personal space. But I'm"—her chin trembles and her painted mouth sags—"just don't know how . . . too much."

"I can't face your room," I tell her now, but I try to be kind. Obviously, she's suffering from some heritable mental instability— Eddy's the source, most likely. And it's all come out in the state of this room—the den of a crazed ferret. Worse. I begin to think apocalyptic thoughts. Little Mary's room is like an opening to hell, like there's a crack in it that goes way down into the earth. While I'm thinking this, Little Mary takes a deep, sobbing breath, and edges past me, into that ninth circle. I step away as the door to her room gently closes and I reel backward, sit down on the couch. I move off the warm spot she's just vacated. After a while, watching the nothingness, I decide that I will leave a note for Sweetie. I get up, lift my bag, take out a pen, and find a scrap of paper on which to compose it. As I am writing the words *It was such a pleasure to finally meet you,* Sweetie arrives with Eddy, in his pickup. When I hear them drive into the yard, I look out the window. Behind the pickup, I see a Volvo just like Glen and Sera's drive up and stop. First Eddy and Sweetie emerge from the pickup. Then, I am way past astounded. Because my mom and dad get out of the Volvo. Sera approaches Sweetie like she already knows her. They all start talking. They must have worried about me. They must have always known Sweetie and Eddy. The explanation doesn't really matter, though, just the fact that Sera and Glen are *here.*

From the picture window of the house, I can see them in the driveway, all four together now, gesturing and talking, a phantasmagoria of parents—I don't understand it, but it's happening. Now they are actually walking toward the house together. I am at the center of some sort of vortex. I can hardly maintain consciousness. I hold the strap of my backpack in one hand, and lift my laptop in the other, and slowly retreat. I walk backward, navigating through the living room, somehow, by subterranean memory, not bumping into anything. I put my hand behind my back and there is a door-knob. I turn it, and I back into the room, Little Mary's room. I close the door, the reverse side of which is pasted over with hand-drawn green Magic Marker hearts, vintage stuff—a tragic-eyed Siouxsie and the Banshees poster, an Alien Sex Fiend T-shirt, a thong with actual little silver spikes in it, held up by a tack, many German beer coasters, and what-all else. Frills, those too. Bucketloads of frills—lots of candy-pink flounces and bows. I turn around. Little Mary is sitting on the gigantic pile of clothing that is probably her bed. We look at each other. Her eyeliner has run down her face in two tracks like the tears of a tragic clown. She looks operatic now and when she opens her mouth I think that she might scream, or belt out a high C, anything but use a normal voice and speak to me as a normal person for the first time.

"You changed your mind? Oh, wow! I know it's a lot to ask," she says. "But this is, like, a big statement. Really nice of you. Thanks."

I look down. At my feet there is a box of black Hefty Steel Saks, no doubt placed there by Sweetie as a subtle hint. I bend over, put my pack and computer where I hope I'll find them again, and pull the first plastic bag from the box.

"Let's put all of the colored dirty clothes in this one," I say, hold-ing up the bag. "And the ones we need to bleach, the white stuff, in this one." I hand Little Mary another black trash bag. Her pink bow bobs and sways again, sweet and strangely demure.

"Your look's kind of shocking, I like it," I tell her.

"Goth-Lolita," she says, almost shy.

She takes the bag and looks at me with something like grateful awe. I don't have to bend over yet. I can pick up one limp black piece of clothing, another, another, off piles at waist height, off hooks on the wall. I pray that as I do excavate ever deeper there are no used condoms or old puke or large insects in the pile I see that I will have to peel up from the floor, layer by layer.

I hear them out there, now, coming in the door, together, talking.

And now I see that my prayers about the contents of the floor piles are definitely not answered—Saint Jude, I think, who answers hopeless causes. Please send me a clean pair of rubber gloves. There are actually layers of Chinese lady beetles from last fall's infestation, but they are dead, and crumbled to dust. There are thongs like aggregate rock, glued into patterned bricks. I just heave those into the bag. But all in all, I think, even as I use a dirty sock to pick things up I can't believe I'm seeing, all in all, considering what things are like in the living room, I would definitely rather be in here.

Yes, the whole thing is awkward, more than that. Eventually I'm too hungry and tired to go on cleaning. As soon as I emerge from Little Mary's room, in order not to have to make conversation, I greet all of my parents with a bright smile.

"Oh, I see you've met one another!"

"Yeah!" They all answer at the same time, smiles pasted on their chops. My suggestion, that we all take a sunset tour of the reservation, is greeted with such relief that I know my desperation's mutual. So we all go out, leaving Little Mary absorbed (Whoa—forgot I bought this one!) in sorting thongs in her half-cleaned room. Riding without seat belts in Eddy's pickup, we see the old round house, the school, the racetrack, the lake, the turtle-shaped tribal office buildings and fiberglass eagle, and the confusingly circular clinic. We get out and play a few slots at the casino. It is dark by the time we drive over to the Superpumper.

We examine the pumps, then walk into the store, up the candy and condiments aisle, down the utilities and snack foods aisle, over to the fast-food cases and the pressurized latte machine. After the entire station is admired, I watch as without a word Sweetie picks up a pair of clean plastic tongs and uses them to pluck a wiener off the hot moving bars of the countertop grill. Carefully, she puts the dog into its bun, pumps a line of ketchup and a line of mustard along its oily flank, then nestles the finished thing in a fluted paper rectangle. Sweetie then presents this hot dog to my adoptive mom.

I freeze. I watch.

Sera has often held forth on the thirty-nine different deadly carcinogens contained in cheap hot dogs such as the one she is holding now. The nitrates are implicated in esophageal and stomach cancer, the red dyes in systemic foul-ups, the binding agents are bad as warfarin, and among the preservatives there is formaldehyde. And then there is the meat itself. Animal scourings. Neural and spinal material likely to contain the prions that transmit Creutzfeldt-Jakob disease. Hog lips, snout, anus, penile sheaths, jowls, inner ears. I don't know how to rescue her. For that hot dog is an innocent gesture of pride and conciliation. It says so much. *Thank you for raising my daughter. Thank you for sending her back to me. I am grateful for this chance and want to be friends.* That hot dog says all this, and more. Yet it is a chilling object, a powerful nexus of poisons representative of dumb, brutish animal suffering.

Sera raises the thing to her lips. I see her take a bite.

One bite, another.

She eats the whole thing, smiles, and says, "Thank you, that was good."

Child, if ever I poke fun at or even gently deride my adoptive mom's fierce virtues, if you ever see me roll my eyes at one of her tirades or groan *yeah, yeah* when she makes a point I've heard a thousand times before, just remind me of that gas-station hot dog. The day she ate it all. It was a magnificent thing she did. I saw her, at that moment, as a hero.

———————

Sera and Glen drive back to the casino hotel where they are going to stay, Sera tells me bravely, so that I can have some time with my birth family. As I hug her good-bye I know she wants to tell me more. But she holds back. She wants to make my first visit to my biological reservation family *good*. She wants goodness. That is who and what she and Glen are.

So I do stay with my new family and I even, surprise shock, sleep in Little Mary's room. On a blow-up mattress. On clean sheets. With three fans going. Before I go to bed, I have a moment with Sweetie, a kiss-good-night moment, in the living room. That's when I tell her about the baby. When I tell her, she just hugs me. She sits on the couch next to me with her arms around me, hugging me, for about ten minutes, and it does not seem awkward at all, though I become very conscious of her breathing, of the catch in her chest from the cigarettes, and the scent of her green apple shampoo. My Potts family doesn't seem to be the hugging sort, not like my Songmaker parents, who are always touching, always including me in a knot or a tangle of embraces, always enthusiastically twined. There is something showy about the Songmaker closeness, though it is perfectly genuine. The Potts do not seem to think of themselves as "warm." So far they haven't defined family characteristics and they certainly do not seem to manufacture them. But when Sweetie hugs me, it is with a gravity and composure that makes the hug into a serious blessing. While the hug is going on, our eyes are shut—that's right. My Potts mom and I sit on the couch in front of the TV hugging with our eyes shut for about five minutes, maybe even ten. I am comforted by the hug even though I gradually sense that Sweetie actually does know about the rumors of weirdness in the childbearing universe. I feel in her body, as she holds me, a wordless physical concern.

"A baby!" She pulls away from me and puts her hands on my shoulders and looks into my eyes. "A baby." I think she might dissolve into sobs and gulps, but she only hugs me again, this time with bursts of back pats. There is so much feeling in her and she suddenly seems so open and so revealing of her heart that I decide to ask about my biological father.

"Did my father, my biological father, have any features or genetic illnesses that my baby might inherit?" I ask her. "I should know, now, Sweetie. Please tell me."

"Oh, god." She draws away from me and jams her hand in her pocket and pulls out the shoelace, puts it in her mouth. "Makes me wanna smoke." She begins to chew the lace. "I only had one yet today. I don't wanna smoke around you neither." She waves her hand at me, pulls passionately at the shoelace between her teeth.

She wants to tell me, she says, but she still freezes when she attempts to talk about him. Their relationship was one of trauma and heartbreak, she says.

"He's a kinda medicine man."

That intrigues me, probably more than it should. Perhaps there is someone in my background with extraordinary powers, after all. The words "medicine man" give me hope. Maybe Sweetie went to him for healing and maybe something else happened, they fell in love perhaps. Maybe his family could not accept her. Things got so bad that she drank and drugged until I was removed from her. It is all suitably vague.

"It would mean a lot for me to know," I say, although I already see that my fake memories might be the ones to keep.

"Ey"—she looks at me with the shoelace dangling—"ey."

"Yes," I prod. "Was he tall, fat, skinny? How brown? What did he look like?"

"Kinda good-looking in a brutal way," she nods, her eyes wide. "Like his face, it was high-boned like them Lakota guys, and he was tall. From a knife fight scarred here, and here." She lightly touches her left cheekbone, her upper lip. "Not so good-looking when I met him. But he had a dark power."

I smile at her, eager for more.

"You're kidding! Oh my god, a dark power? Like an Indian Darth Vader!"

Sweetie shrugs and looks away and I know she will say nothing more now. I suddenly realize that what I said was way too close to sarcasm, or maybe it was the way I said it. I've embarrassed her and I am instantly ashamed of myself. Sweetie goes to get a drink, she says, of water. I think she might hook herself a beer from the fridge and I get even madder at my thoughtless remark. Maybe this attraction to a scary kind of energy in men is passed down from woman to woman, through time. There was Sweetie's mistake, and I have had my share of sociopaths. But no more. I have broken precedent, for your father is neither enraged nor depressed. He is not a twisted spiritual advisor. He is not a desperation junkie or a mental health survivor. He is, however, not my type.

The next morning, before I leave for the casino, to meet Sera, I turn on the television. Reports are coming in of experiments hastily conducted on fruit flies, DNA experts who say on the molecular level it is like skipping around in time, and that small-celled creatures and plants have been shuffling through random adaptations for months now. And hasn't anyone noticed that dogs, cats, horses, pigs, et cetera have stopped breeding true?

And yet . . . there is something about this wash of information that strikes me as *too much*, and what I mean by that is the information seems flimsier, with bouts of . . . cuteness. Why would I think this? Am I infected with Eddy's paranoia? I lean closer. The people who are reading the news are different, I think, and although I never watched the news much it seems that the people are all the same person. And they don't seem like trained television journalists. They stumble over their words. Fret. They make faces. The women are fewer, the ones who appear seem awkward, all in their twenties, white with white teeth, yellow or brown hair, sparkling eyes. The men are all white with white teeth, sharp jawlines, sparkling eyes. I switch through the few channels that come in, over and over, increasingly panicked. There are no brown people, anywhere, not in movies not on sitcoms not on shopping channels or on the dozens of evangelical channels up and down the remote.

Something is bursting through the way life was. Everything has changed while I wasn't looking, changed without warning or word.

I hit the power button and try to breathe. Adrenaline isn't good for a baby, right? Eventually, I go to the kitchen and sit down for tea and toast with Sweetie. Little Mary is already off at school, and Grandma Virginia is still dozing lightly underneath her golden quilt. We talk of little things, ignore the big. I call the casino to talk to

Sera and Glen and make plans, but they checked out early. Probably they decided to drive back down to Minneapolis, but Sera does not answer her cell phone. Out of range, I think, but it makes me uneasy. As I leave, Sweetie hands me a folded sheaf of paper through the car window and says, "Read this when you stop to pee."

The first is from Sera. It says, "Martial law. Remember what that means." I do remember.

Okay, I think. I can do that. Get prepared. Stock up. Get my money. Hide my passport.

The other papers are from Eddy.

PAGE 3028

An Announcement That Brought Incongruous Joy

By rights, knowing what we do know even now, the announcement made to me by my stepdaughter should have been a reason to kill myself today. I should have feared the inevitable pain that a pregnancy in times like these—uncertain to say the least—will bring to her and to our family. I should have wanted to opt out of my role. But instead, as she told me she would be having a baby, I found myself thinking in a very natural and even excited way about this child, who will be our first grandchild. It was an unexpected reaction, given that in this present world crisis we have no idea what this child might be like, and given that Mary a.k.a. Cedar is so recently rediscovered. But I am not about to argue with any positive emotion that breaks through the darkness of the veil. I felt as though for a moment the curtain was ripped aside and the light shone lovingly in.

Then, just as abruptly, the curtains were again pulled shut.

At present, although the counter of my convenience store is brightly lit, and I have just handled a large number of lucrative transactions, I once again exist in the blind monotony of my illness. The pen is too heavy to lift.

After shopping at the giant discount grocery halfway back down to the Cities, I go next door to the Wells Fargo bank branch. I've kept eight thousand dollars in an old-fashioned savings account, which I'm supposed to be able to access anytime. The teller, however, purses her lips when she sees my withdrawal slip. "I don't think so," she says, sliding back the slip.

"What do you mean?"

"I don't think we've got that much cash today."

She's a round, burly, fluffy-haired blond lady with apple rosy cheeks and bright lipstick. She's wearing lime green with dark red touches here and there. If she were in her twenties, she could definitely be one of the fake newscasters. Maybe I look more Native than usual today, darker and more raven-haired from being on the reservation. I hope that's it. I hope she's not telling the truth.

"I'd like to see the manager."

"He's off."

"Well then, I'll wait."

A wilting, heat-mad line is forming behind me. The teller— Marjorie, a name plate informs me—says, "I'm going to have to ask you to step aside, ma'am."

"But I can't do that." I use my most pleasant passive-aggressive manner. "I need my money because I'm pregnant."

With a deep, resentful, ominous stare, Marjorie picks up the telephone and pushes a button. Her cheeks purse, she pulls in air. Puts down the phone.

"Okay," she hisses at me, "walk back please and Hawaii will be waiting for you."

And this woman named Hawaii is waiting. I quickly fill out paperwork and close my account. Hawaii counts the money out in hundreds and fifties.

"You've got a nice name," I say. She was probably conceived in Hawaii, I think, on a happy and expensive honeymoon.

"What's happening?" I ask her.

She shrugs. Her face is pale. She looks up at the clock.

"I don't think we'll last til noon."

As I walk back down the hall, I see that the line I was in now stretches out the door. I cross the parking lot and enter the red doors of a Target, where I do something overly normal and self-indulgent. I shop for you. I buy tiny clothes and blankets and diapers, even a couple of toys recommended for newborn babies. I fill two huge white bags and pay with my emergency credit card. I ignore the lines around the bank, stretching on and on, into the parking lot. I pat you. I get into the car, but instead of starting it up, I freeze. The line to the bank is even longer. And the cash is probably, now, being parceled out to each person in small amounts. If things go way south, and we head into a barter economy, I need the new cash.

I see a drive-up liquor store at the end of the strip mall. So I drive up.

"I need some help," I tell the clerk, a droopy fellow with spiked gray hair.

"All right." He leans on the window.

"What do people like to drink when they're desperate?"

"Anything. But you don't look desperate."

"It's not for me, it's for the end of the world."

"Oh, that. Well, pull around and I'll load you up."

"And while you're at it, twenty, thirty cartons of Marlboros?"

"No problem at all."

It is as if the liquor store man deals with end-times hoarders on a regular basis. I load up. Put it all on my credit card, again, in a bet against the survival of credit card companies. On the way home I make another stop and fill the spaces between the cases with a thousand dollars worth of shotgun shells, bullets, and deer slugs. Back on the road, I drive with calm care. If I were stopped, the car searched, could I claim that I was stocking up for a drunken target-practice party? I'd be the first to arrest me. And what about a random spark of flame? I drive carefully and am exceedingly relieved when I pull into my driveway. I decided to unload the cases through the half-built garage, then treat myself. I can't wait to clean out a drawer for you, to snip off the tags and wash the newness from everything that will touch your skin. To gather up the little T-shirts and jumpers and flame-retardant sleepers and place them in perfectly folded piles.

AUGUST 11

My midwife, Gretchen, scheduled an appointment for me on a health plan left over from a job I had last year. My COBRA has lapsed, but all hail some computer glitch, because it worked. But even Gretchen isn't going to show up today. She doesn't want to risk getting caught on the insurance thing. I refused amniocentesis but persuaded her to order me a class 2 diagnostic ultrasound mainly because I knew the equipment was sophisticated and I wanted to see you as clearly as I possibly could. I've researched you, kiddo. You are between months 4 and 5. You have passed through the age of miracles. Gone from tadpole to vaguely humanoid and lost your embryonic tail. Absorbed the webs between your toes and fingers and developed eyelids, ears, a tiny skeleton. Grown a 250,000-neuron-per-minute brain. You can already squint, frown, smile, hiccup. In fact, you are hiccuping regularly as I walk down the long, sage green corridor.

The medical attendants in the ultrasound room are unusually perky, cheerful, and snoopy.

"Didn't anyone come with you?" one asks.

"The baby did."

"Just pull your shirt up," says another in a gratingly musical voice. I am on edge because who wouldn't be? And also, I am suddenly self-conscious about being so alone among these strangers. Apparently other women bring friends, maybe even a husband.

A brawny curly-headed blonde helps me onto the table and I tuck my shirt up underneath my breasts. The doctor, tall and business-like, unsmiling, enters and shakes my hand. He sits on a stool next to the swivel chair just at my right thigh, where a technician, another young blond woman, but sinewy, more serious and formal than the first one, touches a keyboard, adjusting a computer screen.

"Let's get going," says the doctor.

The technician puts a dollop of clear gel on my skin and holds the probe like a fat pencil. I know the probe contains traducers that produce and receive sound. The machine is already producing sound waves at frequencies of 1 to 20 million cycles per second. Impossible of course to hear. Propped on my elbows, I watch as the computer interprets the signals bouncing off you, a modest white mound in the dim air.

"This will be cold," says the technician, but it isn't very cold. I put the attendants out of my mind. My pulse jumps. I am thrilled to be exactly here. I decide that I have come alone on purpose, in order to meet you in the privacy of my heart.

The technician moves the wand carefully, stopping twice. "There you are," she says as she discovers you. She rotates the traducer to one side of my stomach and keeps moving it. At first there is only the gray uterine blur, and then suddenly the screen goes charcoal and out of the murk your hand wavers. It is detailed, three-dimensional, and I glimpse tiny wrinkles in your palm and wrinkle bracelets around your wrist before your hand disappears into the screen's fuzz. There is something about your hand, just a feeling, and I am upset for a moment. Just a hand—but a sense of clarity and power. I want to get off the table. I want to say *Enough, no more,* but at the same time I want to see you again. The way you waved, just that second, and disappeared—I am so overcome that I can hardly breathe.

"Can you tell the gender?" I ask. "Can you see?"

But nobody in the room is listening to me, nobody hears. I see the arch of your spine, a tiny white snake, and again your hand flips open, pressing at the darkness. The technician touches out knee bones, an elbow. Then she goes in through the thicket of your ribs. The heart, she says. I see the hollows of the chambers, gray mist, then the valves of your heart slapping up and down like a little man playing a drum. Your whole heart is on the screen and then the technician does something with the machine so that your blood is made of light moving in and out of your heart. The outflow is golden fire and the inflow is blue fire. I see the fire of life flickering all through your body.

I whisper, or sigh, and I want to cry out. The room yawns open. I have the sensation time has shifted, that we are in a directionless flow of time that goes back down infinite tunnels and corridors, as if this one room in the hospital has opened out onto the farthest stretches of the universe.

"Can you do that again?" I murmur, but the doctor is very intent now, pointing and nodding.

"There," he says, and the technician clicks something.

"Can you tell if I have a boy or a girl?" I ask, louder. But no one answers. The technician is intent, focused utterly on what she sees. They are inside of your head now, peering up from beneath your jaw and then over into the structure of your brain, which I see as an icy swirl of motion held in a perfect circle of white ash. It looks to me as though your thoughts are arranging and rearranging already, and as I imagine this I also know that there is something wrong, something off. The atmosphere has changed; the doctor is silent. The picture is fixed. They are looking at it, and looking. They will not stop looking.

"Boy or girl?" My throat is scratchy and dry. I see nothing on the screen, now, just white marks. Still, they can't seem to take their eyes away until I cry out, I actually yell.

"What the fuck do I have?"

They both turn and I see that they were trying to think of what to say to me.

"We've got one," says the doctor in a careful voice. I hear the rustle of the technician stepping closer. The doctor's eyes are wide and staring.

A crack opens deep inside, a dark place, and fear seeps into my heart. I am suddenly extremely calm.

"It's Down syndrome or some kind of virus or a throwback . . . something bad."

"No, absolutely not." He smiles now, reassuringly and even with some excitement. "It's all of the measurements. The skull, the verte-brae, the bones, the hands, all of the measurements."

I swear I see the glimmer of tears in his eyes.

"Measurements? What does that mean?" I ask.

The doctor takes the hand of the eager-looking technician and gently draws the wand away from my body. He is a kind man, I see now, a blurrily normal man about my Songmaker father's age, with a square, worn face and blue eyes lighted in the screen's glow.

"What that means is we need to keep you here," he says. The doctor casts his eyes down and sends the attendants away. Once they are out of the room, he thrusts a copy of the ultrasound into an en-velope, throws it at me. He jumps away feverishly and tells me to get dressed.

"Hurry," he says.

I pull on my clothes behind the screen, dash out. He slams a roll of white cloth tape into my hand and tells me to tape him into the chair.

His voice is filled with desperate authority, like in a movie, so I know that instead of voicing the movie confusion and needing to be convinced, I might as well bind him into the chair. It is clear he wants me to escape. Who cares from what. While I wind him into the chair, he asks if I have any special ethnicity. I mean, my hair and eyes are dark but my skin is medium to pale, so I don't stand out as Native unless people already know.

"Yeah, I'm Ojibwe," I tell him.

He asks me about the father, is he white?

"As milk," I said.

"Then get the hell out of here."

He points out the back way, the back stairs, and tells me to wave the envelope and pretend I'm a delivery person.

"When you get out, don't tell anybody that you're pregnant," he says, "and use that last strip between my teeth."

———

In addition to cassette players, a VHS player, the usual hipster record player, and old-fashioned speakers, Glen and Sera keep an old-school tube television in the hall closet. It only comes out for *Masterpiece Theatre* or big events. Now, we need it. Glen is rigging up a sort of antenna. He says that the government has seized the cable companies, but there is still some independent local programming and sometimes an unexpected glance at CNN. The curved green-gray screen spreads on from a central point. He uses a button on the actual TV set to change channels one by one until he finally gets a clear picture and some news. We settle back in the rough orange and mustard yellow couch pillows. The real newspeople have still not returned to the shows, but suddenly there is more content. The talking heads are not military experts or pundits or policy wonks but scientists of every background pulled from the laboratories and classrooms, emerging as though from a dream, their faces still flattened in shock. They rub their eyes, tap their chins, blink rapidly if they are women, and squint if they are men. We are mesmerized and can't stop watching them one after another and all with the same tics and all saying different things that end with the same advice. *We don't know. Be patient. Science doesn't have the answers right away. Truth takes time.* And meanwhile the station has invented a swirling set of graphics—humanoid figures growing hunched as they walked into the mists of time, while in the background Beethoven's Fifth Symphony dissolves into a haunting series of hoots and squawks.

On other channels, the cameras are shaky and the nervous reporters are reporting on how there is no reporting. How people are out in the streets, demonstrating against not knowing what they should be demonstrating about. The signs are question marks of every color and size. The churches are full, the sports bars stuffed. People are floating in bewilderment out of their houses onto the sidewalks, even in the punishing hot air. I have come home to watch the world end. Not that it ends! That is the weirdness of it. Here in Minnesota the people interviewed say, *I just wanna know. Is it a big deal to wanna know? We'll be okay, right? I just wanna know.*

Nobody knows. I curl deeper into the big sectional couch along-side Sera and Glen in the blessedly air-conditioned house where I grew up, a huge and comfortably renovated brick and stucco prairie-style place, in a pleasant part of Minneapolis near a wide green lake invaded by quagga mussels and purple loosestrife. Bubbles of public speculation float over us. During one of Sera's many self-invented ceremonies, which she put together from her eclectic readings on indigenous culture and Rudolf Steiner, we placed sacred tobacco all around our house and then smudged white candles with sage and stuck them in the ground and lighted them. We ate bread, walnut pâté. I drank ginger beer, and my parents drank wine. We curled up on blankets in the grass and sang peace-march songs until we fell asleep. It is one of the best memories of my life. I suppose that I was wishing for some kind of comforting ceremony now, but perhaps the search for information camped around the TV was it.

Today is the day I've promised myself to make the announce-ment. To tell Glen and Sera I'm pregnant. I tried just after the news broke, when I walked in the door, but I felt so sorry for them. They are devastated on such a fundamental level. Sera sits in the down-stairs den, in front of the TV's ancient bulk, her long, beautiful white-gray hair streaming down her back and her eyes full of tears. The ice blue yarn of a sweater she's knitting is heaped in her lap. Her fingers are frozen around the needles. It is so rare that she can't knit; I don't know when I've ever seen it. And there is dear Glen with his skinny little ponytail, his perfect chambray shirt wrinkling and un-wrinkling with each troubled breath, his eyebrows working up and down over his rimless eyeglasses. Glen takes my hand and holds it. I grip his hand, hard. We're solid. Ours is an uncomplicated love. He gives one of his soul-pressed sighs and says, "We don't need words."

"Yes, we do," cries Sera, gripping the fancy skein of silk/Italian wool blend yarn. "We need one word. We need the word 'love.' We need it worse than ever. What if the word 'love' is to vanish from the world?"

Glen's sigh catches in his chest, and then I blurt out what I've come to think may be true. I say it to comfort poor Sera, but I take heart myself.

"No," I say, "this is love. This is what's happening. This is creation's love of creation."

Glen smiles gently.

"Mother Earth has a clear sense of justice. You fuck me up, I fuck you up."

I look at him, skeptical.

"That's not what I meant," I protest. But he just nods. Of course, he doesn't know how personal this is for me.

Sera looks annoyed with both of us, but she addresses me. "Who said that about love, the pope?" She has despised every pope, even this one.

"No," I say, "me. There's no official reaction yet from the Vatican."

"Your pope will come through," says Glen. "He's such a mensch."

"Mensch? Forget it with the irony, Glen. That unmenschenable will deny it all or declare it's God's will."

"Maybe it's God's will," I say, just to get a rise.

"And maybe this is just humanity's biggest challenge," says Sera. "We should invest in one of those genetics companies. They'll try to turn this thing around with gene manipulation. It will be big."

We turn back to the screen, riveted by some paleontologist, whose book jacket with the title *Deep Time* flashed briefly on the screen as he spoke.

"We do not have a true fossil record of human evolution," he says, "or any other species' evolution for that matter. What we have are bits and pieces that have survived and surfaced over millions of years. Millions! That's like playing 52 pickup with one deck of cards flung over the entire planet and expecting to come up with a full and orderly deck. So if evolution has actually stopped, which is by no means fact, it is only speculation, and if evolution is going backward, which is still only an improbable idea, then we would not see the orderly backward progression of human types that evolutionary charts are so fond of presenting. Life might skip forward, sideways, in unforeseen directions. We wouldn't see the narrative we think we know. Why? Because there was never a story moving forward and there wouldn't be one moving backward. The monkeys gaining upright posture, for instance, losing body hair, the cranium enlarging. No. We might actually see chaos. We might roll back adaptation through adaptation, the way canines will revert to type left on their own until they reach a wild dog-slash-wolflike status. Or we might skip straight to a previous hominin. . . ."

"Which would be?" Sera turns to us wide-eyed as the station breaks for a car commercial.

"Homo erectus, perhaps." I have of course been paging through whatever I could find on the subject. "Or maybe Homo neanderthalensis."

I was really hoping for the latter, but it turns out their DNA is mostly different from ours, and we don't have much of it. They married in, got absorbed, but who they were is still mysterious.

"And then there's Australopithecus, anamensis, or afarensis. There's Paranthropus boisei, Homo habilis—"

"Dear god," Sera mourns, her voice breaking, "there goes poetry, there goes literary fiction, there goes science, there goes art."

"Cave art was exquisite," says Glen. There is silence, but he takes a deep breath and forges gently on. "We have no idea of the capacity of our ancestors to think and feel. Perhaps they'll be intelligent."

Sera turns on him with an agitated yelp and flings the yarn aside. The needles clatter across the floor.

"I can't believe you, Glen! You're PC even about the foraging apes our species may become in only a few generations."

She speaks sharply, but she is looking at Glen in a pleading way that slowly becomes alluring. They are already drawing close in this crisis, and I decide to leave them alone. I walk out to the kitchen, pour a glass of antibiotic-free milk, and drink it looking out at the bursts of zinnias, daisies, lythrum, and digitalis in the yard—they still look normal, no change in their colors yet. This is an unusually cool day for August, which means it is only ninety degrees. A hot breeze stirs the heavy weight of leaves in the sycamores that line our street. I try not to think of how my parents are contending with the crisis; they have always had a hot sex life, and as a child I knew more about it than I wanted to. Glen and Sera didn't believe in shutting up and although their bedroom is on the farthest end of the second floor, away from mine, our house is old and their warm kittenish cries, their weeping, and what sounded sometimes like hard work, even furniture moving or séance-table dancing, traveled through the ductwork. When they took matinee naps together, I ravaged the kitchen, just as I am doing now, knowing that Sera would emerge from their bedroom and waft downstairs looking blurred and peaceful. She wouldn't yell at me. She would clean up after me and cook something solid, maybe her usual Sunday vegetarian lasagna, which we would eat at the wide old antique table that had actually spent a previous life in a nineteenth-century Irish pub. They'd fallen in love with it in a Galway antique store and had it shipped over. My parents are both lawyers. Sera, who was a nurse-midwife before she went to law school, represents home birth, doula, midwifery practices, and other community-based health-care concerns, and Glen is an environmental lawyer. They rely on substantial trust funds, which they shifted to bonds way back before the technology stock bubble burst the second time, then shifted out again, into real estate, then flipped their houses just before the last housing crash. Which is to say, they are shrewd as only market-based-society suspicious trust-fund liberals can be.

I want to tell them about you so much, but I am having trouble, and it isn't that I don't think they'd understand. For instance, there is that letter Sera gave to me with an earnest right-mindedness. The Songmakers even said they would be willing to visit my reservation family—which of course they did. I haven't fully explored why, and now is not the time, but I haven't forgotten. Anyway, Sera and Glen have always supported my explorations of identity. I know they would embrace and support me now. But they're overeager about some aspects. They want a piece of Native pie and I don't really have any pie at all. I just have you.

I'm not angry with Sera for disparaging your kind, whatever that may be, and although I do feel pleased that Glen stuck up for cave paintings I refrained from telling him that they were created by people pretty much like us only 14,000 years ago. Not even an eye blink. I am beginning to see that what the paleontologist says is true—we do not understand how much time has passed on this planet and we have no concept of our limited place in the enormousness of that time. But numbers are haunting me, big numbers. Time is not like millions in things, or money, or people. In terms of time, a million years is almost ungraspable. My brain wobbles when I go past recorded history. I can't imagine 4.4 million years, which is thought to be the outside figure on the amount of time we've been roughed out as proto-human. Homo erectus just goes back just a mil. We've been ourselves, Homo sapiens, for something like 300,000 years. We got to be us somewhere in the Pleistocene. I positively can't go to billions—the 4.6 that is our planet's age, or imagine 100 million years, which is the amount of time that dinosaurs were the dominant life-form on earth. Dinosaurs lasted so much longer than we have, or probably will, yet their brains were so little. Meaning that stupidity is a good strategy for survival? Our level of intelligence could be a maladaptation, a wrong turn, an aberration. This should be a terrible thought to me, extremely disappointing, but somehow, perhaps because I am carrying you, little baby, I can't seem to feel the level of consternation that this news causes in everyone else.

Perhaps it is because I saw your brain in an icy whirl, your blood as fire, your tiny hand—which maybe was not a normal baby's hand? Still, you are wondrous, a being of light, and I am not afraid.

"Are you all right?"

Sera appears in the kitchen and lifts away my empty milk glass. Then she begins in an eager and precise way to remove bins of sugar and flour. She takes out her graduated measuring spoons and expertly scoops out and tosses salt and baking soda into a bowl. My mom often cooks when troubled, and before I decide whether to give her question an honest answer she has mixed up a batch of pancake batter.

"That's a strange thing to make on an August afternoon," I say. "We should be eating corn on the cob or watermelon, shouldn't we?"

But she is already ladling the batter onto a smoking black cast-iron pancake griddle—it has a gleaming pitch patina and belonged to her mom.

"Comfort food."

"Okay, Mom. But I still think it's odd."

Sera seems mesmerized by the pancake batter she spilled with such slow expertise that it made a perfect circle. She is watching for the little bubbles in the center that will tell her when to flip the pancake. Her hair is now twisted on top of her head with a beaded clip, and her ragged, sexy chignon shines with a metallic vigor. Early on, she went not gray, but silvery white; her eyes are deep blue and her skin very fine and clear. A winter fairy queen is what she always looks like to me—ethereal and wise. Not that I always agree with her occasionally whacked ideas.

"Mom."

"I'm sorry now." She puts her spatula down with a sudden flailing clatter and claps a hand to her mouth. Her eyes pop with tears.

"What?"

"Your vaccinations, darling. Is it too late?"

Throughout my childhood, again and again, filling out forms every school year, Sera refused to vaccinate me. It is her suspicion that additives in the shots or the vaccines themselves cause autism or mercury poisoning. I was one of several students at my alternative school unprotected, though, and I was fine with it until I read about Native susceptibility to European viruses. Nine of every ten of us died of measles, smallpox, what-have-you. As a descendant of that tough-gened tenth person I had some natural inherent immunity, but still. Now, Sera's sudden horror at the coming possibility of mayhem, rampant disease, whatever else, irritates me so intensely that for a moment I let her suffer.

"Yeah, it's way too late. I'll probably contract adult-onset polio, or a blazing case of the measles. Maybe I'll keel dead of whooping cough before we find how this all turns out. I'll be sorry to miss it."

"God, Cedar, please don't. We'll get a doctor."

"You don't have a doctor. Which I think is wrong."

"Glen has one. We'll get his doctor to vaccinate you."

"Mom, vaccinations take years to work. You need a whole cycle of them. Remember when you were vaccinated? You'll be safe, at least. You'll be the one holding my hand as I puke black blood and itch myself to death from smallpox."

The pancake starts burning and she scrapes it off and throws it in the garbage. She looks at me, stricken for a moment, then suspicious. It dawns on her that I wouldn't actually say these things if there was any possibility of them coming true.

"Cedar."

"Yes?"

"Did you get yourself vaccinated?"

"Of course. When I was eighteen. For you, not vaccinating me was a class thing. Upper-class delusionals can afford to indulge their paranoias only because the masses bear the so-called dangers of vaccinations."

She ignored what she would usually have called me being obnoxious, and just stood there, struck with relief.

"You never told me you did it!"

"Well, duh, I didn't want to get you mad."

"Oh honey, I'm so happy. I'm so relieved!"

She leaves a new pancake to burn while she comes over to the counter and buries me in a hug, a really satisfying hug. I am glad to get a hug like this, for my own reasons, not hers. I need that hug so much that I cling to her until those tears in her eyes fall.

"You're vicious." She stands back, wiping at her face with the palm of her hand.

"You should get your tetanus shot. They're good for ten years. It's an ugly way to die."

"I will, I will," she promises, "though I don't think that contracting tetanus is going to be the big problem."

"Cholera?"

"No," she says, "reproduction."

I form my lips around words but no sound emerges.

She succeeds in making two perfect pancakes, and passes them to me on a plate, whipped butter swirling in the center. And there's expensive real maple syrup from Canada because maples here no longer produce. Sera has always loved presenting Glen and me with artful snacks, with made-from-scratch chicken soup when we were sick, with bowls of garlic mashed potatoes when we were sad, and now, with cornmeal pancakes to stave off the apocalypse.

Glen enters and sits down with his plate of pancakes. He cuts his into buttery squares, pours half the syrup over the cut squares, then forks them rapidly into his mouth. I've always known him to eat quickly when emotionally disturbed.

"Slow down," says Sera. "You're upset. I mean, of course you are. But slow down anyway."

But his eyes are distant and black—people sometimes think that Glen is my real father. When I was little, his hair was totally dark. He shows the Norman Conquest in the appreciation of his food, too, and his love of rituals surrounding meals. When he cooks, all else stops. Sera and I used to sit at the counter drinking wine while he crushed basil, toasted pine nuts, happily struggled over complicated recipes. So it's a sign of his distress, just shoveling food in, and this afternoon he can't seem to stop. He doesn't hear Sera, and he finishes the pancakes hardly pausing for a breath. When they are gone, he looks at us, bewildered.

"I think of one thing, and then another, and I don't know what to do."

"Well, here's one thing you don't have to worry about," says Sera. "Cedar got herself vaccinated. She won't get anything major."

I open my mouth to speak, it is the perfect moment to announce that I have contracted, so to speak, the most major thing of all, given the situation. I put my lips around the words "I'm pregnant," but just can't blurt them out. Sera is so happy with my tiny bit of news; the odds of my survival are suddenly, irrationally, increased in her confused thoughts. I just can't ruin her sole moment of hope. So I begin to talk to my parents about the numbers, the millions and billions, even knowing that they aren't going to understand on a visceral level, the way timeless time got to me when I looked at you on an ultrasound screen. They aren't going to see into that measureless dimension. To add the shock of you to the crumbling of their foundations is too much.

We waft outside. The late summer light bleeds on and on. My parents share a bottle of wine and don't notice that I drink lemonade instead, or that I cannot finish my pancakes. We sit on the back porch. They wave at neighbors, trot to the fence to chat, wiping sweat off their foreheads. We make plans to stay, to run, to hide, to live normally. We decide to stay vigilant, then argue about whether vigilance is a strategy. And all the while as the light slants lower and lower, bathing us in a gorgeous, smoldering glow, my heart slowly cracks. The deep orange-gold of the sun is pure nostalgia. An antique radiance already sheds itself upon this beautiful life we share. I grow heavy, rooted in my lawn chair. Everything I say and everything my parents say, the drift of friends, the tang of lemonade, the wine on their tongues, the cries of sleepy birds and the squirrels launching themselves without fear in the high tops of the old maples and honey locusts, branch to branch, all of this is terminal. There will never be another August on earth, not like this one; there will never be this sort of ease or precision. The birds will change, the squirrels will fall, and who will remember how to make the wine?

We laugh at funny memories, we hold one another's hands. We agree that this whole development is a bitter triumph for secularism. Creationism bites the dust, big-time. But as my parents fall silent, and I look at the landscaped yard in the failing light, and wonder how the birds will turn out, I know that we've come to the end of science. Human beings might be saved by science. It might happen, but I am quite sure even then there will be no true explanation. If evolution has reversed, we'll never know why, any more than we know why it began. It is like consciousness. We can map the brain and parse out the origins of thoughts, even feelings. We can tell everything about the brain except why it exists. And why it thinks about itself. So the more I consider all of this, the more it seems that our predicament would be best addressed by an acknowledgment of the *Anima Mundi*, the Soul of the World.

I say good night and walk slowly up the stairs, carpeted the day after I hit my head at three, tumbling down those stairs when they were hardwood. I suffered a slight concussion. I still have a tiny scar at my hairline. The story is that Sera called a carpet store the next morning and bullied them into an emergency installation. So my footsteps are muffled creaks, and heavy, but my hand on the polished banister is light. I brush everything I pass, as if to touch it good-bye. That night, as I am falling asleep in my childhood room, which is used partly as a guest room but still has my soccer trophies and dolls in it, I lie on my back and fold my hands right over you. As I descend into welcome unknowingness, I bob up, once. *There is something I have to do*, I think. And the next morning I remember that I have decided to write this—your diary—a record and an inquiry into the strangeness of things.

I creep out while Sera and Glen are still shut in their bedroom, mumbling themselves awake into another day of realization. I will have to write from the familiarity of my own lair of thought in South Minneapolis, my house on a forgotten dead end running right up to an unused railroad embankment. I bought the tiny bungalow with money I inherited from my Songmaker grandmother. I'm lucky. The backyard pours into the tangle of forgotten railroad right-of-way, overgrown with scruffy trees. As I pull out of my parents' driveway, I look back through the rearview. Something is off. I stop the car. The porch lights, which usually burn through the night, into morning, are extinguished. The street is without electricity.

The whole neighborhood has lost power. Which is not unusual, and yet it seems that something much worse has happened, for my graceful childhood street has the stillness of an ancient dream, the muted perfection of a "before" disaster photograph. I try to shake off this disquiet. But all the way back along the calm, empty South Minneapolis streets, I feel that, instead of the past, it is the future that haunts us now.

AUGUST 15

I have already felt you move. Your bones are hardening, your brain is hooked up to stereo—your ears. So you can hear me, you can hear my voice. You can hear me praying in the car and as I enter the house. You can hear me as I read aloud the first words of my letter to you. I am going to tell you everything, bit by bit, day by day.

To begin with:

I lift the envelope that holds your ultrasound picture. I'm scared to look, still I slip out the picture and press down the edges. But the ultrasound doesn't tell me much. The markings make no sense to me. Carefully, I tape your first picture onto the cover of this bound journal. Then I use a roll of clear packing tape to cover the picture. But I'm disappointed, disoriented. I thought women loved their ultrasounds, saved them, so maybe I'll get a feeling for the gray and white blur of limbs and head that feel so alien yet ordinary.

Our house is a small two-bedroom rambler, backyard a blissful disorder, front yard tangled too. Entry set far back from the street. It is a place I could afford only for its lack of a garage, which remains half built. The outside is plain beige and the inside also similarly mute. I've only made my imprint on the kitchen—a friendly yellow—and the utility room—space-age white. The walls I've newly added insulation to are open—I have the Sheetrock but I haven't closed them up. A work in progress. Still, this is our haven and our den, the place I can be merely the nameless being I am, a two-decade-plus collection of quirks and curiosities, the biochemical machine that examines its own mind, the searcher who believes equally in the laws of physics and the Holy Ghost, in reading my favorite theologian, Hans Küng (the one chastised by Ratzinger but loved by our present pope), and trying to live by the seven Ojibwe teachings, Truth Respect Love Bravery Generosity Wisdom Humility, which I've only read about and do not know from, say, a real Ojibwe person.

I sit down on the edge of my bed and untie my tennis shoes, lifting each foot onto my knee. Then I kneel beside the bed, as I always do, grab my rosary from around the post and say a few Hail Marys, for comfort. I crawl into bed and sleep for two hours. You kick and somersault and I dream as one does in the light—fitfully, racingly, dreams of paranoia and those CNN graphics. The telephone wakes me, an old-fashioned analog landline. The ring sounds like it might be your father's ring and I don't answer it. You rock from side to side in the cradle of my hip bones. I sit up, and gulp down a glass of stale water. It is late morning now. I pick up the academic paper I was reading what seems a light-year ago, titled "The Madonna's Conception Through the Ear"; it is an examination of the belief that God's whispered breath caused the Incarnation. After twenty minutes, I put the pages down.

"What did he *say?*" The ceiling is cloudy, sandpapered, rubbed almost blue here and there like real sky. "What was the word that just *did* it for Mary?"

The word intrigues me, now more than ever, the idea of a word so uncanny, a word so powerful, a word actually so divine that its expression infuses a woman's body with a pregnancy of godly nature.

Of course, I know that for most theologians the Incarnation was not caused by some literal and actual word or utterance. The word is an idea, the idea of God. Küng has pointed out that the Incarnation itself could not be related only to the mathematical or mystical point of the birth or conception of Jesus, but must be related to Jesus's life and death as a whole. Still, the idea of this actual word continues to preoccupy me and to suggest that somewhere outside the actual human experience of words spoken, words thought, there exists a language or perhaps a pre-language made up of words so unthinkably holy they cannot be said, much less known.

Perhaps you will know how to speak this language. Perhaps it is a language that we have forgotten in our present form. Perhaps you are dreaming in this language right now. And perhaps there is a word that has changed the course of human existence. A word written in the depth of things, a word within the quantum and genetic and synaptic codes, a word that told all beings and all life—enough.

Sometimes my brain races so hard I can't keep up with it, which is why I'm glad I live alone. I don't know what I'll do when you are here. Write on your diapers? On you? Here and there, I scribble messages, notes, ideas for the next issue of *Zeal*. I have to somehow imbue the in-progress issue with the shattering development; I have to figure out a theme. I have several articles and a dozen academic papers to sort through and decide whether there is something I can use. As always, I will probably end up writing a contribution myself, too, under an assumed name.

For lunch, I cook and eat a whole bag of frozen peas with butter, drink two glasses of milk, fry two vegetarian burgers and place them between two pieces of bread with sliced pickles, mustard, ketchup, and why not, an onion. As I bite into the onion, all of a sudden I know, completely *know*: this issue's theme will be the name of my church and subject of the ear/fuck paper—Incarnation. My issue will examine the breadth of thought on how Christ's divinity was made flesh. What could resonate more with what is happening right now? Now that it appears we might be losing our own spark of divinity, our consciousness, our souls?

New energy of purpose claims me and I clean the kitchen, wash and dry every dish, and when everything is put away I go into my workroom.

My desk is a large, sturdy, portable banquet table set up on one side of the utility room. The other side holds my washer, dryer, and wall-to-floor steel shelves of white file boxes neatly marked with dates and titles of my projects and back issues of Zeal. The only windows are small rectangles set high into the west wall. But I have full-spectrum fluorescent bulbs in the overhead panel and two natural-light lamps at either end of my desk. When I turn on all of the lights, the room is a brilliant white, the blue screen of my computer the only major block of color. On Glen's advice, I've fixed electrical tape over the aperture that holds the computer's camera. It seems absurd, but he made me promise.

I am the utterance of my name. I sit back in the chair and stare at the white wall. This line of a fragment of the gnostic text *The Thunder, Perfect Mind*, is the last sentence I wrote before I drove north. It is unlike me to reference writing other than canonical references, and the tractate is troublesome. But I am drawn to the text and have read it so often that I have much of it by memory. *For I am the first and the last. I am the honored one and the scorned one. I am the whore and the holy one. I am the wife and the virgin.* Perhaps it is the voice, I think, so arrogant and so alive, using antithesis to cause in the reader's mind the romantic dissonance that occurs when one attempts to comprehend the unknowable. *I am the midwife and she who does not bear. I am the solace of my labor pains. I am the bride and the bridegroom. And it is my husband who begot me. I am the mother of my father. . . .*

I am comforted by the voice—it is so ferociously modern, so timeless that it is perfectly of this time. For here I am, maybe a walking contradiction, maybe two species in one body. Nobody knows. A woman, a dweeb, a geek, a pregnant degreeless dilettante straddling not just millennia but epochs. I am also an insecure Ojibwe, a fledgling Catholic, an overstriving brain cooking up conflicting dramas. I can't help myself, I overcollect trivial ideas and can't distinguish them from big ones—yet the Incarnation, that's *big*. That's *pertinent*, I think.

Perhaps we are experiencing a reverse incarnation. A process where the spirit of the divine becomes lost in human physical nature.

Perhaps the spark of divinity, which we experience as consciousness, is being reabsorbed into the boundless creativity of seething opportunistic life. A great wish courses through me. I am curious with desire. I want to see past my lifetime, past yours, into exactly what the paleontologist says will not exist: the narrative. I want to see the story. More than anything, I am frustrated by the fact that I'll never know how things turn out.

My old-fashioned phone rings and continues to ring. I've kept it because Glen and Sera insist. They don't trust cell phones. First the Stingray, now the translucent Jellyfish bobbing around in parks and yards. They capture cell phone information for big corps who bombard your phone with calls. The landline is unlisted and has a strong filter. Your father is punching a redial button. He's frustrated, of course. At some point, I am going to have to answer my phone. Or unplug it, I think, and reach toward the receiver but do not pick it up. You make a rolling swerve deep in my pelvis and tingling needles shoot down my thighs. I lean closer to the desk and to the keyboard, writing my introduction, "imagine what it was like for the young woman, Mary, to feel the extraordinary kicks and shocks of her unborn child and to know that she harbored a divine presence, the embodiment of God's Word. Yet, what she felt was probably little different from what all pregnant women have felt, throughout time, ever since we could both feel and be aware of our feelings. This bewildered awe for the mysterious being we harbor certainly borders on a mystical apprehension. . . . "

But the words on the screen are suddenly so paltry and finite and thin, impossibly futile. "Pregnancy is a wilderness of being," I type, then rest my hands on my belly, think for a while, then type again: "In this wild state the markers are so ordinary and mundane that the grandeur I feel as well seems delusional. Perhaps at all times and in all countries women with child are actually at risk. At some level we are quite insane. We go about the business of the day and find out that our baby, like every other baby on earth, will be a throwback of some kind. We can't imagine what yet. Our entire evolution up until now has apparently been coded into some part of the blood or tissue we haven't noticed or deciphered."

Now it's too late. Our bodies have always remembered who we were. And now they have decided to return. We're climbing back down the swimming-pool ladder into the primordial soup. We pregnant ladies find this out and make sure to take our folic acid supplements and get some sleep, all while growing within ourselves a unit of life so complex, regardless of its evolved state, that only the Koreans can make even one of its fingernails with all of their technology. And here I am, wiring a whole new brain in my sleep, some kind of brain. My body is accomplishing impossible things, and now there is something wrong, *most terribly wrong*. . . . As I write these last words my knees begin to shake and the shaking travels as a shudder up through my body and wrenches a cry. And the sound of my own cry, ugly and raw, startles me. I go silent for a moment and then began to weep, in low gut-wrenched sorrow, a baffled, fearful sobbing that leaves me beached after a while in my desk chair, still facing the calm, blue screen.

I am sitting there, thinking into the blue, when, without my touching the keys, a woman's face blooms onto the screen.

"Hello," she says, just to me, her eyes meeting mine. "I am Mother. How are you today?"

I do not answer. My computer camera is taped over, but the speakers must be on. There must be a problem with the power button. It's as if she knows I'm here.

"How are you feeling?" she asks. Her voice is drenched with warmth. "I care. I'd like to know."

Her face is round and white like pizza dough. Her cheeks sag. Her smile is tiny with thin stripes of red lip. Her brown hair, a Prince Valiant helmet, sits firmly on her skull. Her shrewd brown eyes twinkle. She is wearing an apricot-colored blouse with a draped neckline.

"How are you feeling?" she asks, again, and again. "How are you, dear?"

AUGUST 20

All the lights on, the blinds shut, the reading lamps glowing on my desk, white paper and white walls. I try to call your Songmaker grandparents but there is no answer on any of their numbers. I don't leave messages. They'll call me back when they can. I have avoided the computer after it conjured up the helmet-haired entity. I still have my cell phone but I am cautious and only check it once a day for news. I scroll through to try and shield myself. No cellular data. No location services. Anyway, the news. There is more consternation, greater piles of details that seem more misleading than useful, a specially convened emergency session of Congress, more findings. Men in dark suits staring at large-screen ultrasound images. Men in dark suits peering at freeze-framed ultrasound babies and speculating about just what the abnormalities in the neocortex could mean in terms of cognition. And also what it means that male sexual organs are not developing properly. Sometimes not developing at all. The number of females conceived has apparently risen. Still, I have a feeling you are a boy.

Stop thinking about the future.

Now is all we have, I tell myself. Work on the *now*, the hereness, the present, the moment of extreme hyperawareness which is also linked to Sera's most profound mental exercise, her meditation, and which is something I have trouble with. I am more comfortable with the before-ness or the after-ness of life. I am happier dissecting the past or dreading the future. I really have no proficiency at simply experiencing the present. But since the past is so different from the future that to think back at all is like looking down the wrong end of a telescope, and since the future is so disturbing that to give in at all to my imagination is enough to cause a full-blown panic attack, it is really best for our mutual health if I stay focused on what is most immediate. I have to treat myself like a skittish horse. An animal ready to bolt at the sight of the big picture. Stick to the periphery. Pull on a comforting set of blinders.

Hide the liquor.

All I have to do is fit the bottles and the ammunition into the walls of the house, wherever I've added the insulation. For the rest of the day, fitting bottles into the walls, boxes of ammunition here and there, screwing the Sheetrock back on with my handy electric drill, I keep thinking about Blessed Mary. I think about her while I tape the seams. Later, I'll skim-coat the seams. Then repaint. I enjoy doing monotonous home repairs. It's satisfying. While I seal off the booze I can meditate. I put the cigarettes in plastic tubbies and ease the tubbies into the crawl space behind the boiler. Once I've got walls on, I break down the liquor boxes and put them out in the garage, into the recycling, which may never be picked up.

After all of this is done I drive to my usual grocery and am surprised to find it well stocked. I load up on salt, rice, beans, whole wheat flour, pancake mix, lots of canned vegetables, and peanut butter. I also buy luxuries. A bottle of juice, a crisp New Zealand apple, a stack of stoned-wheat crackers, and a ball of mild white mozzarella. At home, I set my treats out on my desk. How long, I wonder, will there be a snack like this to eat—cheese from a cow milked in Italy, crackers packaged in New Jersey, fruit squeezed in Florida, an apple from the other side of the world?

Today's job is editing the church newsletter. I take a deep breath, and turn on my computer, just for word processing. I feel it is my duty to write for the parish. As I've said, I joined the church to make friends, and to bug my parents. But I love my church. It is a humble place—no limestone cathedral, no basilica. It doesn't even have the name of a saint. It has the name of my present obsession. Holy Incarnation was founded to care for the most destitute people in the city, the cast-asides, the no-goods, the impossible, the toxic and contaminated. It is a small glass and brick and cinder-block place with no convenient parking. It is very different from the exurb Protestant churches that I have also attended, with their vast asphalted lots, their vaults of stone and cement, their jumbotrons up front to show close-ups of the minister. Mine is not a church of the saved, but a church of the lost.

As I am putting together the Thoughts page, my screen goes dark and swirly. This time she floats slowly into focus from the depths.

"Hello, dear. How are you?"

Her full cheeks are cement gray this time, set hard around her smile.

"Mother is thinking all about you. Would you like to tell me about your day?"

I shut down my computer.

My hands are trembling. I push myself away from the dark screen. But I can't get up. Can't move. The phone starts ringing, and it won't quit. It rings continually for ten minutes, then falls silent for a moment, starts again. Twenty-five minutes after the last ring, there is a knock at the door. That is the length of time it takes for your father to get from his apartment to my house, so I know he's standing on the front steps right now. It is too late to douse the lights. He knows that I am home, and still I sit paralyzed before the dead computer. The door begins to shake. He is rattling the curved metal handle and pounding on the wood. Soon he begins shouting my name. My street is quiet and ends at an old railroad embankment. As I said, it is a forgotten cul-de-sac, a street untouched either by gentrification or destitution. It is not a through street. I am sure my neighbors are peeping from between their blinds or glancing around the sides of their curtains, curious. I leave my office and walk down my dark hall to the door. I stand behind the shaking frame and take about six deep breaths before I can trust myself to talk without my voice shaking or my throat shutting.

"Go away."

He hears me, and quits. We are standing silent on either side of the shut door. I put the palm of my hand against the doorknob and then lower my forehead to the wood. I can hear him breathing on the other side and I am sure he can hear me as well. The door is constructed of three panels, the top a large rectangle and the other two below, neatly margined. The wood is stained a dark reddish brown and the grain underneath the varnish is umber, streaked and tangled.

"Open up, Cedar, I have to tell you something."

I cannot let him in, but I can't leave the door, either.

"I'll call the police," I say at last.

"I'm here because of the police," he says. "Have you heard? Have you seen the news?"

"No."

"Please, let me in right now so I don't attract more attention. I don't want anyone to see me out here and get suspicious. Please, it's true, I swear."

"What's true?"

"They're coming for you."

———————

They are rounding us up. Here is what your father told me, once I'd let him into the house and doused the lights. By a narrow majority the House and Senate have voted to strengthen and give new powers to what began so long ago as the Patriot Act. There were articles I, II, III, IV, and now we are up to V, section 215 of which still allows our government to seize entire library and medical databases in order to protect national security. This newly expanded decision, now only hours old, empowers the government to determine who is pregnant throughout the country. Your father says that the surgeon general they had was fired and the new one has announced that pregnant women will be sequestered in hospitals in order to give birth under controlled circumstances. It is for our own safety and we are required to go voluntarily. Those who do go in right now will receive the best rooms. The best rooms! Heart in my throat, I think of the doctor who probably put himself at risk. He gave me the ultrasound picture. He knew. Best rooms. Hysterical. Will women turn themselves in thinking that a bit more privacy, a better view, an extra chair, is worth it? We're not going. And I am lucky, we are lucky. Because I used that old insurance card from the job I had working on the alumni magazine at the University of Minnesota, we will be hard to find. The card has an old box number, no street address. But in the middle of the night, I sit up, eyes wide. I used my credit card to buy baby clothes at Target. I paid my credit card bill online. I slip back down into the tangle of blankets. I am being pregnancy-purchase-tracked by Mother. Your father sleeps beside our bed on a pile of couch pillows. He has folded his wings. We are all three together for the first time. But we are already half-way found.

———————

Now it is done. Days pass. We cannot leave each other. Ever.

———————

I keep sending the same telepathic messages: *Call me, Mom, call me, Dad, call me, call me.* I touch in their number, but they are not home. Then one day someone picks up the telephone on the first ring and a woman says, "Songmaker residence, can I help you?"

The overly pleasant voice is not my mom's, but it is familiar. Fulsome, full of inquiry, too avid. I put down the telephone. It is an old-fashioned black touch-tone with translucent buttons and black numbers. I don't know what sort of information it holds or whether my messages on my parents' voice mail can be accessed and traced back to me, here. Although my telephone bills come to my box number, my street address must be in the company's records.

All day, I keep hearing that voice, the lilt increasingly sinister, *Can I help you?* A parodic melody. *Can I help you?*

AUGUST 25

I saw my first gravid female detention this morning in a mall parking lot where your father had driven to get Subway sandwiches for the two of us. It was stupid to go out, but we were disoriented by our long seclusion and I persuaded your father to take me after I looked critically at my reflection and decided that I didn't show. When you give something a name like *female gravid detention*, it becomes official. I was careful. I wore an overcoat, though it was warm, and of course I didn't intend to get out of the car. Once we'd parked, I squeezed down and opened the car window. That's when I saw her. She was a petite woman wearing a red and white flowered smock. She had warm brown skin and wore a buttercup yellow scarf that pulled her hair back in a perky bun. She was wearing flip-flops and I was close enough to see that her toenails were painted the same clear scarlet as the red in her dress. She was perhaps in her early thirties and looked about seven months along—not terribly obvious, but observably pregnant enough, I guess, for the two police officers, one male and one female, to approach and question. While in the sandwich shop your father watched his sandwich artisans construct my sub and answered questions like Wheat? Cheddar? Jalapeño peppers? The police officers apparently asked to see the woman's driver's license. She looked confused, annoyed, as she reached into her purse and pulled out her wallet. Perhaps she hadn't watched the news. And of course she had done nothing. She decided that this was a mistake. Her pregnancy did not occur to her. The female police officer tipped up a pad, peering at and typing in the name on the license. The pregnant woman at first questioned the police aggressively. Then her mouth shut in a straight line and she began to look nervously at the entrance to a large discount shoe store where, perhaps, a friend or family member might appear. When her name apparently showed up in the files, the male officer grasped her elbow. She went rigid. She twisted toward the shoe store and a look of distress came over her face. A man appeared in the doorway, a white man holding the hand of a little girl a paler brown than her mom, about five years old.

Perhaps his wife had gone back to the car for her purse, or perhaps she was coming from another store. He looked both ways along the sidewalk, impatient. Perhaps they were buying shoes for their daughter and he needed help deciding, or perhaps the child hadn't liked any of the shoes that were displayed in the store. The little girl was a small version of the mom, pretty and alert. She wore a pink sundress with white daisies printed all over it.

Suddenly, the little girl spotted her mom and pointed at her; the officers were attempting to coax her along to the squad car. The mom wouldn't go. The male officer began to pull the pregnant woman's arm and the female officer, poker faced and wooden, had now positioned herself on the other side of the woman and was trying to lift her. The man in front of the shoe store bolted forward and the pregnant woman cried out and flung herself toward him. People on the sidewalks and in the parking lot now stopped still to watch, frowning. They must have noticed that the pregnant woman was strikingly pretty, and her smooth rounded belly made her even more sweetly vulnerable. Her husband approached swiftly looking as though he had a reasonable query on his lips. The police ignored him and started dragging at his wife. She planted her feet in refusal. Her husband was a medium-sized man, but suffused with anger and protective belligerence he seemed to grow larger. His neck swelled and his eyes narrowed, the veins in his throat pumped. He grabbed the male officer and tried to wrestle the man down, but the police officer, more agile and trained, quickly flipped the man onto the ground and drew his gun. He pointed the gun at the man's face. The little girl, who had followed her father, stopped short and began to cry, her face a crumpled flower. A bystander pulled the girl into the crowd. The female police officer succeeded in pulling and pushing the pregnant woman all the way up to the car, but the crowd had now grown. Several people had begun to shout. A terrible sound came from the mom—a wail, a shriek, a roar—as she was stuffed, kicking, into the car. The male officer handcuffed the husband, sitting on the small of his back and twisting his arm. He was pointing his gun at the bystanders, who shied back, though some were still yelling. The officer was young. His lips disappeared into the white rock of his face until he was all teeth. He jumped into the car and drove off, not quickly, no sirens wailing, so there was then an unreal and frozen quality about the whole scene in which the only sound to hear was the high-pitched, broken sobbing of the child.

I'd hunkered way down in my seat by then. I had pulled up my knees and wrapped my arms around my thighs so that I was balled protectively around you when your father returned with my wrapped sandwich and a large soda in a waxed cup, the straw pushed inside the cross cut into the leak-resistant top.

"Did you see it?" I said. "They took away a pregnant woman."

Your father looked at me, his brown eyes round and still. "I was in there debating mustards. I missed it."

"What should we do?"

"Did anybody see you?"

"No."

We drove quietly and carefully out of the parking lot. The little girl was still sobbing. People were bent over the handcuffed man. I rolled up my window. As our car moved away I experienced a sinking sensation, a crawling panic, nausea. I closed my eyes and let it overcome me and swamp me. The feeling boiled up like an inner stink. By the time we reached home, I understood that I couldn't bear that I had done nothing. Little sweetheart, I had to protect you. But still, I was ashamed.

We walked in the back door so at first I didn't see the note that had been slipped underneath the front door, a note in Sera's handwriting.

Don't call us, honey, and don't leave any messages. We're all right. Stay safe. We took all of the records.

The Names of Angels

Zaphkiel, Zadkiel, Camiel, Raphael, Haniel, Michael, Gabriel, Malchideal, Asmodel, Ambriel, Muriel, Verchiel, Hamaliel, Zuriel, Barbiel, Advachiel, Hanael, Gambiel, Barchiel, Geniel, Enediel, Amnixiel, Azariel, Cabiel, Dirachiel, Scheliel, Amnediel, Ardesiel, Nociel, Abduxuel, Jazeriel, Ergodiel, Ataliel, Azeruel, Adriel, Egibiel, Amutiel, Kiriel, Bethnael, Geliel, Requiel, Abrinael, Aziel, Tagriel, Alhoniel, Cherub, Tharsus, Ariel, Seraph, Uricus, Amaymon, Paymon, Egyn,

and then there is also Phil.

The Angel Phil is the seventh Olympic spirit of the moon. According to a book and manuscripts long banned in my church, the Angel Phil can change all metals into silver. He governs all lunary things and heals dropsy. He can show us the spirits of water and make us live three hundred years. He has a great, full body, soft of color like a black, obscure cloud. A swelling countenance with bloodshot and watery eyes. A bald head. Teeth like a wild boar. His sign is rain. Sometimes he appears as a king riding on a deer. A little boy. A woman hunter with bow and arrows. A cow. A goose. A garment of green or silver. An arrow. A creature having many feet.

And sometimes he is just Phil.

Except for the part about the bloodshot eyes, the bald head, and teeth like a wild boar, the description of your father, my angel Phil, is metaphorically accurate. It is taken from the Treatises of Dr. Rudd, which reside in the Harley Collection of manuscripts in the British Library. But I am sure that other sources, primarily myself, would describe Phil in more intimate depth as sweet, hot, big, funny, good-natured, a liberation-theology Catholic who cannot operate in any other church.

We fell in love last year. Or, more accurately, Phil fell in love with me. Working on a Christmas play we gradually got to know each other—coffee, drinks—but we carefully kept ourselves in the company of others. It was not until months later, as we stored props and riffled through equipment one evening in the basement of the church, that we found ourselves suddenly alone together. Phil put the wings on. I helped strap them over his T-shirt. He turned around. His beard and thick hair looked absurd with the wings. We both went silent.

"Did you always want to be an angel?" I asked.

"They always make me a shepherd," he said.

"Or a wise man?"

"Baby powder on my beard and a velvet robe. All it takes."

I looked too long into his sweet eyes. His stare was calm and kind. Before I knew it, we were on the floor.

They had closed the church. Turned the lights off from the top of the stairs. Didn't see the bulb burning far back in the storage closets where I was looking first at the honey-colored slats of the old wooden ceiling, then at Phil very close-up and personal, then at the marble chips embedded in the polished terrazzo floor. The prop closet was too much for us. We stayed hours, all night. I tried a gown on, a mantle, a veil, the helmet of a Roman centurion. He wore sandals. I suppose it was sacrilegious, but it was also hilarious. We made love dressed as Jesus, Mary, Joseph, the Angel Gabriel, and Santa Claus. We were the Three Wise Men. Herod, Pilate, and two gay shepherds. And at last we made love as ourselves. We slept in a pile of clothes, woke at dawn, hung the costumes back up, and walked away, exhausted lovers plodding through a new world.

We kept seeing each other, but I tried to space things out. To stay away from him, if I could. Most of the time, I couldn't. I decided that if he didn't ask about birth control I would keep not using it. But then he did ask, in a way that let me know he wanted me to use it. Not a dad, then, I decided. In late spring I bought a test and when I knew for sure that I was going to have you I sat down outside in my tiny backyard. I leaned against the trunk of the beautiful old sugar maple that grows there; it was just putting out the festive red tassels that precede its new leaves.

All I knew for certain was that I wanted a child.

I wasn't sure I loved your father right then. Oh, I loved to be with him, there was no doubt of that. I was even compelled, infatuated? And he let me know that he was wild about me. But durable love is more complex and comes from deep knowing. I think you need both the instant and the deep to classify as love—we definitely had the first. The thing was, except for Glen, men had messed me up. And lately, in general, they had become militantly insecure. Within many churches, men were forming supersecret clubs with even se-creter subchapters. There was no telling whether Phil was part of one or not. If he belonged to one of those clubs he wouldn't tell me even if I asked. On the day I took the dipstick test, the phone rang while I was sitting underneath the maple. I bolted inside to answer it. As soon as I heard his voice I said *I'm pregnant* and then I slammed down the phone and locked myself in the bathroom, where I ran a hot bath and got into it and lay there until it got cold, whereupon I ran more hot in and so on even though eventually I heard your fa-ther pounding at the door and yelling. I didn't answer the door. I had decided that although I maybe loved him, I didn't trust him. Was I crazy? I don't think so. The question is whether I am crazy now.

"I am not going back, you know." Phil looks at me as he starts eating his sausage sub. "I belong here with you and our baby."

Phil's a vegetarian most of the time but he loves meat and becomes carnivorous in times of stress. His family is Italian and Spanish, but from way back a century ago at least when they came out to set-tle Pig's Eye, as St. Paul was called then. Phil's ancestors worked the building trades, put up the basilica and the cathedral. Stonemasons, carpenters, tile setters, bricklayers, artisans of plaster and paint. And Phil ends up a parishioner in an unattractive modernist-style church with no details other than geometric stained-glass windows—a rhomboid and a parallelogram. Our church has an austere cockeyed bell tower. A props trove inherited from two Catholic schools bull-dozed long ago. Plain wood pews. Abstract hangings. And that terrazzo floor polished to a high gloss, it turns out, by reformed drunks.

So do I love him at last? Child, I need him. It is hard to tell the two apart.

Yet Phil is the rarest of animals, a genuinely good person who doesn't make a big deal about his unusual niceness, and who, in spite of this niceness, has a sense of irony.

"I'm going back to my place just long enough to pack my stuff," he says, "and I'm taking a key so you can't lock me out."

Phil's happiness radiates across the table. He reaches out his big square hand and cups my balled fist. I haven't ever had to depend on anyone like this since I was a child—for food, shelter, safety. I don't want to depend on anyone now in this way.

"Have you told any friends about the baby? Have you told your parents?" he asks.

I've talked constantly to Phil about Sera and Glen, perhaps because I am so worried about them, but I haven't told him about the strange, sweet voice answering their telephone. I haven't told him how many messages I left, or about the one I found slipped under the door. Now, when I do tell him all about these things, he looks so serious that I'm immediately struck through with tremors of anxiety. My chest hurts suddenly; I can't seem to take a deep breath. His voice catches when he tries to speak. He clears his throat in distress.

"I don't know how to say this—"

"Oh my god I hate when people say that!"

"Okay. Cedar. It is now a crime to harbor or help a pregnant woman. So if Glen and Sera know maybe they decided to disappear."

Hearing that you are suddenly a danger to others, besides wanted and hunted, gives a peculiar jolt. I'm thrown into myself, and can hardly answer.

"Glen and Sera don't know I'm pregnant, or they'd be here. But I told my Potts family." And then, because I need to change the subject, I hit the table with my fist. "Phil, we need some food."

"Right. I'll hit a grocery store on the way back."

"Here."

I hand him a list of high-protein and long-shelf-life items. I'm glad I shopped when I did, but I'm nervous. I tell him we need a water filter, and he raises his eyebrows and says, "Where am I going to get this?"

"Camping supply store." I also give him some of the money I got from the bank.

"It's a good thing I don't show yet," I say. "Nobody in the neighborhood knows."

Phil's expression shifts; he leans across the table and cradles my face between his workman's palms. Love builds in his face and eyes and takes away my breath.

"You show now, Cedar," he says. "You do show. I want you to remember that. Don't even stand in front of a window."

Phil does not return and of course I can't reach him, or my parents, or my Potts family. Cell phones locaters can't be turned off now so Phil has buried our phones, swathed in layers of plastic, in the Pioneers and Soldiers Cemetery. Sometimes the internet works, but I've told Phil how this Mother apparition appears and he agrees we can't use it. My fear of leaving the house causes me to do what I do when I panic. I read and write to divert myself.

You kick, you remind me of your existence. An update. Last week you began to absorb sugar from the amniotic fluid you've been swallowing. Your little digestive system now can handle the sweetness. Your bone marrow's making blood cells and taste buds are forming on your tongue. Your brain and nerve endings are mature enough to feel touches. You graze your face with a finger, suck your thumb. You're over seven inches long and you weigh as much as four sticks of butter. If you're a girl, you've just made all of the eggs you'll need the rest of your life. If you're a boy, you got your balls this week.

Trouble Not Loving Phil

Some men smell right and others don't. You know what I mean if you are a woman who breathes in the fragrance of the stem end of a melon to choose it or if the odor of mock orange or lilac transfixes you or if you pass a piece of woody earth and know from a gulp of air that the soft, wet, fleshy foot of a mushroom has thrust from the earth somewhere close. Men smell good in all different ways. Salty vanilla. Hot dirt. New grass. Bitter leaf. Some are disturbingly odorless. Others dope themselves up with cologne. You can smell fear, vanity, secret meanness, a lonely heart, envy, and cruel thinking. Likewise, easy confidence. Even goodness. You can smell if a man likes you.

Phil smells as if he's been in the sun even if he hasn't, and he's warmer than most people. His skin is very smooth on the tops of his arms and shoulders and chest, but his hands are callused because he likes to make things out of wood. Sometimes he smells like that clean and honest moment when a saw cuts into a board. There is a brownish gold Mediterranean undertone to all of Phil. Even his voice has that feel to it—a sunny depth. Phil is five years older than me. The first time I ever smelled Phil we were sitting in a booth in a coffee shop. Someone told me to squeeze over, and I tipped toward Phil. There was the slightly scorched odor of ironed cotton. Then the tiniest hint of sweat. I had the urge to lick his neck.

———

Phil's not back yet.

———

Like so many Minnesota boys, Phil was raised on dairy products bearing the image of the Land O'Lakes Butter Maiden. She is the logo on the waxed cardboard one-pound butter box, a lovely, voluptuous Native girl kneeling in a lakey landscape, holding out a dish of butter. Like so many Minnesota boys, Phil folded her knees up to make breasts. He gazed at her $^1/_{16}$" shadow of cleavage while eating his toast. She was a constant in his life. That night in the props room, dressed as Joseph, he confessed that after he met me, the Butter Maiden had started to haunt his dreams. She walked off the blue and yellow box in a short dress of fringed buckskin. He said she wore high-heeled leather moccasins. She looked like me. How flattering, I said, meaning the opposite. Instead of butter, she offered, in his dreams, whipped cream, sour cream, whole milk, and fresh mozzarella. That is not a Land O'Lakes product, I said to Phil. I know, but fresh mozzarella is one of my favorite foods. It's round and slippery, he said. He told me that in his early twenties at the University of Minnesota, he majored in wildlife biology and thought he might become an ornithologist, but he had realized that in a few years there would be few birds for him to study. He would be studying the history of birds on this earth.

Phil told me that around the same time he understood this fact, his one serious relationship ended badly. He took a vow. Do no harm, to anything or anyone. Save nature. He decided to dedicate himself to preserving bird habitat, and got an advanced degree in ecology. Since then, he has tried to protect the natural world wherever possible. Without being specific, he told me that he's gone beyond the law. He has also infiltrated some groups that he doesn't agree with. He did this on his own, he said, because he could. I wondered, now, what that meant? Because he could? Because he was a white man with white male standing in a world where in some places that got him into those groups? When he'd taken his vow he'd struggled so hard, he said, that he thought he'd forgotten about human love.

"Guess not," I said, back then, staring into his eyes.

"Guess not," he answered, staring into mine.

AUGUST 29

I am typing late into the night, trying to keep myself from logging on to the internet, when Phil taps at my window. I run to open the door and in stumbles Phil with two Cub shopping bags and a loaded, beat-up black backpack. He's unshaven and weary, his eyes are bloodshot with exhaustion, and his hair is stiff with dirt. I sit him at the table and pour him a glass of water. He tells me that there's no food in the stores. Everybody figured out all at once that there would be a food shortage, so people are hoarding food, stocking up. The supermarkets are open at weird hours, whenever some shipment comes in.

"Where did you get this?" I rummage in the bags. "Peanut butter! Mixed cocktail nuts. Granola, peas, corn, crackers, more peanut butter. Baked beans."

"Church basement," Phil says. "Left over from funeral and wedding meals. There's more in the car."

"Potted cheese."

"Nothing fresh, but they are selling fresh stuff in the streets here and there, I mean it's August. The farmers' market is going, I've heard. It's not that there's no food right now, but there's panic about the long term."

"We should get fresh stuff. I'll dry it, can it, freeze it. Do you think there will be electricity?"

"I don't know. Nobody knows."

Phil is quiet, drinking his water, gulping it, nervous.

"And why were you gone such a long time?"

Phil draws me onto his lap and I lean against him. Then he tells me there's a complete news blackout now—no newspapers, no television, radio extremely sketchy. Nobody knows exactly what is happening. There are news kiosks all through the city where people congregate to share rumors. He was gone a long time because he bought a lot of guns. There is nothing to say after the phrase *a lot of guns*.

"I've got them locked in the trunk. I backed up onto the lawn. I thought I should tell you about them before I brought them in."

I slide off Phil's knees and walk around the kitchen, straightening and arranging my yellow and white checkered curtains, which slide together on fake brass rods. The thing about the guns is just incomprehensible. It's as if Phil told me he had a rhinoceros on a leash out there. My family has never owned a gun or had one in the house; we support several campaigns to end gun violence. We are not the kind of liberals who make big noises about how we aren't the namby-pamby knee-jerk types and how much we like our weapons. We are firm. I had assumed that Phil thought like me.

"We can't have guns in here," I say to him.

"I don't want to either," Phil says. "But sooner or later it's going to come to that. They're offering rewards now for anyone who turns in a pregnant neighbor, acquaintance, family member, whatever. There's billboards. Ads up on lampposts. It's true."

My brain is buzzing. My voice is tiny.

"What are they doing with all of the women?"

"I don't know." Phil stands up and holds me against him.

"What are they doing, Phil? You know something. . . ."

"Word is . . ." He doesn't want to say.

"Tell me."

So he does tell me. All of the prisoners in the country have disappeared. Most people say they have been euthanized. Or freed, which Phil doesn't believe. The prisons are for women.

"I thought the hospitals . . ."

"Those too."

"What about the babies?"

He keeps holding me, won't look at me. I can feel his heart pound. After a while he whispers.

"They keep some of them."

"Some?"

I keep standing in his arms, but my knees are turning weak and beginning to shake. Pretty soon he is holding me up. His face is in my hair and I can feel how tired he is from the sag of his shoulders. But when he speaks he seems angry—not exactly with me but he is looking at me when he talks, voice shaking.

"It's like they said it would be, Cedar. Don't you remember?"

"No!"

"They have a registry, Cedar. Remember?"

"No."

"How can you have missed it? You went to the doctor."

"My doctor let me go. I told you. And stop glaring at me."

"Yeah." He looks down at his feet. Speaks to the floor like a sullen teenager. He smells like sullen teen too—rancid sweat, old clothes, gasoline.

I turn away and focus on what I remember about the ultrasound doctor and his questions. Did he mutter something? There was more, I was sure of it, there was more. *We've got one*, he said. The sudden meaning of the words stops me from repeating them. He said the measurements were right, I think. But *We've got one* seems to mean the opposite.

You kick and roll. You are agitated. I decide that I have to calm down because I don't have the fortitude right now. I can't take another shock. It is hurting you.

"That's okay. I've had enough." I concentrate on the gasoline smell on his clothing.

"You got gas, too," I say.

"What there was of it. I pumped it into some plastic jugs because I think it'll get siphoned from the cars. Neither of us has a locking gas cap. We should park the cars around the back of the house."

"I've got to talk to my mom and dad."

"That's another thing."

"What?"

"I think they're okay. Sit down."

"Tell me!"

"Yeah, of course. I went over to your parents' house because you couldn't get them on the phone. I just didn't know how soon we'd get out, if ever, or maybe we'd have to run. I thought I'd better tell your parents you're okay. So I went up to the door, knocked, and people who didn't fit how you described your parents answered."

"Who were they?"

"They were evasive when I asked their names. They asked me in."

"Did you go?"

"Sure. They were extremely polite. I asked them if they were relatives, what they were doing in the house, and so on. They said that they were taking good care of the house for Sera and Glen until they got back. I asked from where and they got all concerned. Gooey sweet. They were very worried, they said, about the whereabouts of the Songmakers. They had just been going to ask if *I* knew where the Songmakers were. They were hoping that I had some information on them. I said no and they made a show of being very disappointed. Then they brought in a cake."

"A cake?"

"A fresh lemon cake. It was very good."

"You ate the cake?"

"I wanted to know what was happening. It was really like some kind of dream. They kept talking about your parents and how careful they were being with all of their things, how well they were taking care of the 'beautiful Songmaker residence,' and how if I should run into them by chance would I let them know that I had seen Glen and Sera and by the way, who was I? What was my relationship to the Songmaker family? How had I met them?"

"What did you say?"

"I used to work for them, a landscaper. I was concerned about their landscaping going to weeds."

We stood together for a long while, quiet, just breathing. After a while I asked who was in charge. Phil said God. I said that was the most terrifying thing I'd ever heard and he said, "Yeah, me too. That's why I bought the Bushmaster."

AUGUST 30

Phil is hiding our little arsenal in the basement crawl space and late in the day I go down with him to look at what he has rounded up for our protection. He has laid them neatly on towels, the new ones with their owner's manuals; he is learning to use each one, cleaning and loading them. There are five weapons. A Rossi handgun, a .38 special with a laser grip that beams a light on the person you're going to kill so you won't miss and they'll have a red second's warning they're about to die. He's got a beat-up 12-gauge pump-action shotgun with six boxes of bird shot and six boxes of deer slugs. Another black, evil-looking 12-gauge that's the same as the other, only scarier. A high-tech-looking rifle that Phil taps and calls Bushmaster. There's ammo for it, and last, weirdly, there is an ornamental Custer's Last Stand Tribute Rifle. It's in a case with a label on its side.

"Is this for real?"

"Open it."

I lift the hinges on the case and there it is, cradled in green pseudo-suede.

"Where'd you get this?"

"Where I got 'em all. One of our fellow parishioners is a gun dealer. I bought it off him."

I take out the rifle and hold it under the light. Both sides are heavily decorated—one has a thick-of-the-action-type engraving of the battle, plus portraits of George Armstrong Custer and his two brothers, Thomas and Boston. On the other side chiefs Gall, Low Dog, Sitting Bull, the Crow scout Curly, plus the only survivor of the Custer command, a gelding named Comanche, are carefully engraved and finished in what looks like real gold.

"I got it cheap because it's a reproduction, a lever-action '73 model Winchester. I mean, it works but it's not that useful."

"But wow."

"But wow?"

"I'm having that kind of Old West–type feeling—I think I'm channeling my unknown maybe Lakota father—I could be related to the guys on the Indian-stock side of this gun, you know?"

No answer.

"So you got it for me?"

Phil shrugs. "I don't know. It was there. He wanted me to have it."

I put the rifle back in its special display case. Then I touch the barrel of the Bushmaster semiautomatic. Smooth as glass, and warm. It makes me want to puke all of a sudden. I'm in a knot, confused. I actually think I like the Custer's Last Stand Tribute Rifle.

"Put them away, Phil," I say. "Get rid of them. You took a vow to do no harm." But it's actually me I'm scared about.

He sits back. The guns are scattered between us. He draws a huge breath, holds it, and looks at me. His face twists and I can't tell—tears? Sweat? A few drops leak down the sides of his cheeks. He blows his breath out fiercely, shakes his head, and keeps working.

AUGUST 31

We have decided that we need information as much as anything else, and that Phil will work at the church and return here secretly. If he cannot obtain gasoline to operate the car, it is a four-mile walk. But he finds right away that the city is adapting, the way all cities do. Although there are endless lines when anything from gas to butter appears, people have quickly organized. There are dates and times for everything to sell and trade, and neighborhood centers for information dispersal. There are already clandestine radio broadcasts and wildcat cable and some sketchy wireless internet connections, even a shadowy television signal. Phil brings an old TV and a radio over from the church basement and we check at odd hours—four and five a.m.

One pre-dawn, we see the image of Mother fading in and out. She looks haggard, much older, tinged with green like the head of the Wizard of Oz.

"I am back," she says, glaring exhaustedly up from under her eyebrows. "They failed to destroy Mother. I will always be here for you."

She licks her dry lips and whispers.

"I wonder if you have the courage to save the country we love. We need you to be a Patriot. We need you to volunteer. If you are a woman, if you are pregnant, go to any of our Future Home Reception Centers. WV. Our chefs are waiting for you!"

I slap the controls and turn to Phil.

"What was that? Volunteer for what?"

"You don't want to hear," he warns, as usual.

"Tell me."

"It's about frozen eggs and sperm. There are special centers."

"With chefs?"

"And even better, actual food."

"What's this WV?"

"Womb Volunteers. Listen."

On the radio someone describes a raid on an in-vitro clinic by members of some militant organization we've never heard of. They plan to use one thousand Womb Volunteers to gestate the embryos they've liberated from that clinic's deep freeze. There is crackling. A sudden interruption and a young woman's voice.

"We took the leftovers. The embryos not labeled Caucasian. We're going to have them all and keep them all. We're not killing any. All are sacred."

The news report goes on, ducks are not ducks and chickens are not chickens, insects are nutritious, and there are ladybugs the size of cats.

SEPTEMBER 1

Further description: My backyard's unused rail spur has not yet been converted to bicycle trail. That in turn merges with an overgrown and half-abandoned shipping yard and several acres of city park that lead to a corridor of wildness, ravine, tangled groves of grapevine-throttled trees, and an abrupt drop down a steep bank to the soggy headlands of a serene, almost hidden lake. Because of the luck of this convergence, I have always seen an unusual number of birds and animals for a person who lives in the city. Now that I cannot go out of my house, I spend my time near the window most private, the lavish rectangle of glass that looks out into my backyard. I set up a desk underneath the window where I can write to you every day, and because I'm there so much, I see the birds that come to feed on the purple fruit of two large mulberry trees. I've often thought of cutting down these trees. They drop buckets of berries in the grass and all August the yard smells like wine. Now I'm glad I didn't. Maybe next year, if there is one, I can dry the berries out. Maybe I can gather them at night. I see squirrels flow up and down the oak tree that might provide, come to think of it, an emergency source of food in the fall if I can figure out what to do with the acorns. The friendly squirrels. I'll plug them with the Custer's Last Stand Tribute Rifle. Occasionally, a deer wanders in. I see rabbits, chipmunks, several varieties of woodpecker, neighborhood cats, finches, robins, nuthatches, sparrow, ravens, crows, and my favorite bird, the chickadee. There's a garter snake living under some rocks piled in the corner of the yard. I've seen a fox, rats, ducks, and a wild turkey. I suppose that I see more animals than my neighbors to either side because they've got strict, tight chain-link fences at the borders to the railroad land.

Today I see something I have never seen before. A bird about the size of a hawk swoops off the oak, down into the mulberry branches, and then hops about among the leaves. Its tail is very long, and it seems to clutch at the bark and twigs with claws poking from the hinge of its wings, like a large bat. I glimpse its head—beakless, featherless, lizardlike, rosy red. The feathers are a slate blue with black tips. The bird, or whatever it is, seems to be eating both fruit and the insects that would be hovering around the tree and crawling on its bark. A graceful thing with fluid, darting movements, it behaves exactly like a lizard-bird. It is captivating. I find the folding binoculars and watch it for as long as I can. In spite of what this tells me about the fate of living creatures and the world in general, I am lost in contemplation. I have that sense of time folding in on itself, the same tranced awareness I experienced in the ultrasound room. I realize this: I am not at the end of things, but the beginning.

I spend the rest of the day oddly jubilant. I do my exercises, read my books. The day goes quickly, and I use some hot sauce Phil brought to spice up a Thai noodle and peanut butter dish for our dinner. We shut the curtains and eat by candlelight, not only because it's romantic, but in case anybody tries to look in the window. I show Phil the drawing I've made in your notebook/letter.

"Archaeopteryx or something like it, probably not the actual transitional organism, but some species very close. Maybe Confuciusornis. Did you see its mouth clearly? Did it have teeth?"

Phil is helplessly excited, the way I am, and after we eat and even though it's dusk, he sits in the backyard waiting for the bird to appear. He says that other people have heard of sightings, here and there, of unusual animals. He says, haltingly, that some scientists have been tinkering with genetic repairs.

"What's that mean?"

"I don't know if it's with plants? Animals? People? Or maybe it's with the babies. Why they're keeping some of the pregnant women cloistered."

"Cloistered sounds bad."

My heart strikes hard, alarm bells, and immediately I try to forget what he said. Phil goes on talking.

"Every service system seems controlled by a separate group. Every city service negotiates with other services. People are forming their own civilian militias, their own rescue posses, hiding pregnant women. Nobody knows anything for sure though. The first thing that happens at the end of the world is that we don't know what is happening."

Later, from my window, I watch Phil sitting at the edge of the yard with my binoculars in his lap. From time to time he lifts them and eagerly searches the tops of the oak and mulberry trees. His shoulders are rounded and powerful, his bluntly cropped head of black hair is all ruffled up. He has a passionate mouth, a long, straight nose. His entire being is presented to me unself-consciously, and I find him irresistible to watch. Looking at your father floods me with tenderness. Little being; here we are. It is week 23 and your lungs are getting their surfactant. You're making breathing movements for practice, and you could just barely survive in a NICU, but the blood vessels in your brain are so delicate that you could have a hemorrhage, especially deep in the middle of your brain, the germinal matrix, so you're much better off with me. Next week you'll get your inner ear for balance. As for me, I'm getting milk. I'm getting ready for you. And I must tell you, since we'll be in hiding once you're here, I suppose, that I haven't done badly today with being stuck indoors. Sometimes I'm good at living within limitations. Besides, after all is dark and silent in the street, we go out, all three of us.

Our street never was brightly lighted, and now a few lamps have sputtered out. The light doesn't penetrate at all into the woods, which is where we go. A small path I know winds through the trees, and once the moon is up we can see just faintly enough to make our way.

As we walk along the inky path, taking small steps, shuffling, we hear noises to every side. Small rustlings, scurrying sounds, odd hoots, now, and bitter coughs of night animals. Phil has one of the guns, and even so, we're nervous. But to be outside and freely walking together is a pleasure so intense I feel everything too much—the slight movement of air on my face, the softness of duff, the terrain of bark under my hands, the touch of leaves against my clothing, my skin. It all fills me with a charmed awareness. I slide a black leaf between my fingers, tracing the rigid vein up the middle. I gulp the darkness in, the rich turmoil of earth.

SEPTEMBER 3

The United States Postal Service has apparently conducted secret negotiations with the National Guard and they've formed a joint entity within some states. Each state, that is, which has decided not to answer to the central government, which may not exist, which may be one of the supercorporate entities who have hired the contract mercenary armies that have no country but green money. The entire mail operation is funded by the cash exchange between the customer and the mail carrier. The postal worker takes the cash and pays the National Guard outright for protection, keeping a salary, too. It costs a dollar to mail each letter. Mail service has become the only reliable form of long-distance communication, and everyone uses it now. There are two deliveries a day. It is a quiet morning. I have been awake through dawn, listening to the low and secret calls of the doves in the trees behind the house. There is no wind and the leaves are perfectly still. Phil is gone. I used to know most of the bird cries, but now there are new sounds in the leaves. Some are menacing and dry, others are ravishingly sweet, both familiar and alien.

There is the sudden growl of a motor—a very loud truck. I lift the side of a curtain to see that the mail is being delivered.

An armored personnel carrier prowls the street. A soldier perches behind a mounted swivel machine gun and two others beside him carry assault weapons. Wearing the same dull blue uniform that he always did, plus a helmet and bulletproof vest, our neighborhood postal carrier steps from the passenger's side of the vehicle. He is a wiry, pleasant Korean-American man whose smile puts soft crinkles into his face. His name is Hiro. He begins to walk his usual route, absorbed in what he has sorted, making certain that names match with addresses, flipping the envelopes along his arm. On the street beside him, the soldiers are alert, scanning the rooftops, swiveling their gun side to side, addressing large handheld telephones that might be old-fashioned walkie-talkies.

I retreat into the living room, sit down in the old green armchair in the corner, and wait. The mail fits through a brass slot in the panel next to the front door. From my chair, I can just see the basket into which it will fall. As I am waiting for Hiro to turn down my side-walk, walk up my front steps, and drop the mail in the slot, I can hear the tiny gears edge the kitchen clock's big hand forward. In the tree out back, the mourning dove calls again. The truck's motor turns over, rumbles forward, pitches. You kick. Hiro's footsteps approach. He drops the mail into my house and turns away. I used to chat with Hiro when he'd bring the mail, and I suddenly feel the silence. I get out of my chair and walk over to the door, pick up the mail. There are two envelopes of appeals, one from Holy Seal and one from Children's Way, another three are bills, which I suppose I still have to pay. There are two papers that may or may not fit the theme of the current *Zeal*. And there is a letter from Eddy.

Dear Cedar,

Things up here are interestingly chaotic. We've had to barricade the store, as there has been looting. Our tribe has formed a militia quartered at the casino. Quite a number of us see the governmental collapse as a way to make our move and take back the land. Right now, nobody gives a rat's ass what we do. Still, I hate to say this, but in a generation it won't matter. That's the truth of the situation. The wealthiest will get ahold of the technology to reproduce and those few Homo sapiens—at most a couple hundred thousand as there are half a million frozen U.S. embryos and not all of them will take—those few people will own the rest of us, the monkeys.

Except for you. And your baby. I never dream, but I did dream. I dreamed that your baby was fine. Started running as soon as it was born.

So come up here as soon as you can.

I am still doing really well, Cedar, in spite of my worry over you. Please come up here, and stay. Your mom is gone a great deal of the time, as she participates in a round-the-clock camp-out vigil on grass near the shrine. Your saint has recently been sighted, and boy, is she pissed. More on that later. The mail truck comes through the main road once every three days and I've got to run to get this on it. Don't worry, we're all eating. We've moved everything out of the store into our basement and the foodstuffs have a long shelf life (Twinkies approx. forty years). Supersize us! Grandma's fine and your sister, with no TV to watch, has finished Thus Spake Zarathustra and is immersed in Simone Weil's biography A Life. Ha, ha. I enclose carbon (!) copies of some recent pages.

PAGE 3032

Negative Sleep

In the sleep that I do not sleep every night, I find the comfort of mind that enables me not to kill myself throughout the next sleep-tortured day. I call this state of mind, in which I think of sleep but do not actually sleep, negative sleep, for want of a better word. For it is only negative the way a piece of dark film is the shadow image of a photograph—I don't mean for there to be within the term a value judgment. Especially so because within this dusk of thought, positive sensations bloom. Awake in darkness, I feel the joy of my breath entering and leaving my body without effort. When I match my breath to Sweetie's slightly clogged exhalations, I become aware of time's sweet generosity. This is eternity, right here, for eternity is nothing other than awareness of time going by. To lie beside my woman for three hours and fully experience each breath we take together. Bliss. It is the fourth hour that completely sucks. Anxiety worms in. Thoughts of duties tomorrow that will be enlarged by the desperation to rest. Resentment. She sleeps good, why not me? And worse. She rolls over or snorts as I am finally dropping off, causing tears of frustration. The brain starts raving. The brain moves out of its skull and prowls the home looking for a better resting spot.

The floor? The couch?

Only with the greatest of efforts am I able to return to a state of negative sleep, that or a drug. I've tried many and some work temporarily but all that are effective are also addictive, and I wish to have but one addiction. Thought. The pleasures of the mind. Thought saves me in the end. I find that if I try to solve some knotty ethical issue or plan the next few pages of my manuscript, the abstract focus triggers a quick avalanche. Slumber hits. As the room brightens I am lulled into a gentler state and by the time Sweetie rises I am nodding off for real. I'm out. If no one wakes me, I can remain comatose for hours. But usually there's an emergency for me to tend to by nine o'clock. I do often rise in a state of bitterness. But memories of my negative sleep tide me over and I do not kill myself.

PS: Must scrawl this in: Surprise visit from the Nagamojig. Bimibatoog.

I am so excited at receiving a letter from Eddy and by the last line, which I look up in my Ojibwe dictionary and find refers to song— i.e., People who sing; i.e., Songmaker—that I made the mistake of opening it next to the slim rectangle of windows that flank my door on either side. So when the doorbell rings, I automatically look out of the window straight into Hiro's face. He smiles gravely at me and waves a letter with a green slip stuck to it—apparently I need to sign.

I open the door before thinking, then try to shut it, too late. Hiro instantly registers my pregnancy and steps in front of me, anxious that I not be visible from the street. He blocks the door, makes no comment, gives me the letter. It is hand-addressed in writing I do not recognize, and there is no return address.

"Do you know who it is from?" he asks.

When I say that I have no idea, Hiro gently lifts the envelope from my fingers and removes the green slip, then hands back my piece of mail.

"Given your condition, I would advise you not to sign this," he says. "I'd advise you not to link your name with a physical address. And don't open your door to anybody else."

I step back into a safer, shadowy spot in the hallway, and Hiro scans the street.

"I'll have a letter to mail tomorrow," I say.

"Put it underneath the mat with nothing sticking out, nothing visible. Tape your dollar onto it. Don't let anybody see you."

Hiro lifts his finger up and shakes it.

"Nobody!" he says.

Then Hiro leaves.

I walk back to the kitchen and gaze out into the backyard mindlessly, through the binoculars, then without them, for about an hour. At last I feel a bit less anxious about everything—my parents appearing at Eddy and Sweetie's *on the run*, Eddy said in Ojibwemowin. And me stupidly showing myself to Hiro. I am able to make myself a lunch of fresh corn with butter—yes, both are available. I thought this might be the last we'd see of corn—a technology-dependent crop, but as it is genetically enhanced, its whole physical backslide might be very much off. There is no telling. Things aren't going backward at a uniform or predictable rate at all. Phil has told me that broccoli and cauliflower don't turn out anymore—he's talked to someone who says it all comes out a weedy, wild, cabbagey kind of plant. Yet there is corn, and even better, popcorn. Phil found bags of it stuffed under the church kitchen sink, left over from a Good Friday showing of *The Passion of the Christ*.

I eat alone, stuffing popcorn into my mouth, watching the fuzz on the television screen falter and clear, words burbling through, nothing intelligible. I'm just eager for any sort of information, I suppose, even unintelligible scrawls. I desperately miss my parents, both sets. And now I am terribly worried about Sera and Glen, for Eddy and Sweetie will no doubt have told them about my pregnancy, which will cause them to return to the city where I gather they are being hunted by the same sort of people of harrowing goodwill who are presently living in my childhood house. I can't think what Glen or Sera might have done besides live the life they've always lived, but maybe that's enough.

> *Dear Eddy and Big Mary and family,*
>
> *I am doing very well and do not need for you or anyone to visit me, as I have got support and am feeling just fine. It was wonderful to hear from you, and I'll write again soon. Just be sure you take good care of yourselves. Please tell me what my special saint is pissed about.*
>
> *Love, Cedar*

SEPTEMBER 5

I work away at my desk before the screened window overlooking the back of the house. The leaves are a dense green and the hum and clicking chatter of bird sounds merges with my flow of thought. Then suddenly I look up. A young man. He is peering in the side window, fingers cupped around his head to block the glare from the glass. I can see the outline of his face, eager and flushed. His eyes roll, taking in the room. I can't tell whether I've been seen or not. I slip from my chair and crouch underneath my desk, from which I can just see the kitchen and the back door. The knob of my yellow kitchen door slowly turns as this balloon-headed boy tries to enter. But the door is locked. It always is. Now a scrabble of voices rounds the side of the house and I catch sight of two young men. They are fair, fresh, neatly dressed in pale orange and coral-pink button-down-collar shirts. Their torsos are soft and round, the shirts are tugged hard to peg smoothly into belted and pressed blue jeans. There is a tap on my front door. I hold my breath. Silence. I creep along the bottom of the wall underneath the window, into the living room, where I can see my side of the front door.

"We know you're in there," one of the young men calls out in a light, cheerful voice. "My name is Clark! No need to hide. And this is Emeric! We're friendly! Just out doing a little neighborhood survey. Didn't you get our newsletter? The invitation?"

I suddenly think of the return-receipt letter, which in the agitation that accompanied receiving the letter from Eddy, I left on the table in the front hallway. I never looked at it. This must be what they are talking about—the letter, the invitation. Now a piece of paper slips gently under the door and slides onto the linoleum of the vestibule. I think that I hear them walk away, but I can't be sure. I let the paper sit there. I watch it until the sun goes down.

Dear Neighbor,

Please come to a picnic! Housing records indicate that you have not yet registered with your new residential authority regarding change of address, and we are concerned about the title to your house—a possible extinguishment of title is distinctly possible. This is a chance to clear up any problems with your residence permit and to meet new friends. Food will be provided by Uniters. Please bring your driver's license or other former United-States-government-issued enhanced form of identification, as well as proof of home ownership. September 8, 5:00–10:00. Under the tent in True Manna Park.

We'll see you there!

Clark and Emeric
Uniters

When Phil comes home, rolling quietly up the lawn and around the back of the house, I show him the invitation and ask him where True Manna Park is located.

"I would guess it's the park on the corner," he says, giving me that under-the-eyebrows look I've come to know as the one he uses before he tells me some new piece of disturbing information.

"That's Manito Park."

"There's new names," he says. Then he informs me that two or three mornings ago everything had new names. All the street signs were changed overnight. It was a massive project, impressive. Even the streets with numbers got switched.

"They are now . . ." He stumbles. "Well, they're Bible verses."

"I don't live on Boutwell Street anymore?"

"Well, you do according to the U.S. Postal Service. They're still operating under a secular postmaster general. Otherwise, you live on Proverbs 10:7."

Wait, I think I know that verse.

"The memory of the righteous is a blessing, but the name of the wicked will rot?"

"Yeah, pretty much."

Phil and I sit down together on the couch, contemplating the fact that someone wants our names, which are probably classed as wicked, to rot. The blinds are closed. We are lost in confounded silence. He reaches out and puts my hand in his and folds his fingers around my fist. We have a few days to decide what to do and my mind is riffling through options. Go to the picnic disguised somehow? How? I'm really poking out now. Even I can't deny that I'm obviously pregnant. Hiro knew immediately. Not go at all and wait to see what happens next? Run? Run where? But Phil has thought way ahead of me and come up with something different. The light is very low—just flickers of one of the candles from the two dozen boxes of votive lights that Phil swiped from the church. My couch is deep and wide, a hand-me-down from the Songmaker recreation room, soft with heavy down-stuffed cushions. Phil pushes me gently back into the cushions and then gazes at me, his face all shadows.

"Cedar."

His face changes and he slides down my body until he's kneeling on the floor with his face pressed against my belly. He looks up at me, the light warm on his bones. His eyes are full of darkness.

"Will you marry me?"

SEPTEMBER 6

So that's how your father and I decide to get married. Phil is going back to the church today in order to forge papers and signatures, seals and credentials. Our priest is helping lots of people, he says. He'll create a marriage certificate for the two of us and Phil will bring it to the picnic along with the title to my house and whatever papers we can concoct to make the two of us seem as one. I'll be gone, of course, on a church retreat of some kind. Phil's got a social smoothness that he's developed in his work—that will help a lot. I think he'll some-how convince the neighborhood association that he's legit, or that we are. As for getting married, I know it sounds cut-and-dried, as though we decided out of expediency, but that's not how it felt.

Looking into the dense and noisy green out in back of the house, during the day, I think of how physically happy Phil and I can be. And when that happens I close my eyes and listen to the roar and clatter of the world as it rushes by. We are rushing too. The wind is whipping past us. We are so brief. A one-day dandelion. A seedpod skittering across the ice. We are a feather falling from the wing of a bird. I don't know why it is given to us to be so mortal and to feel so much. It is a cruel trick, and glorious.

———

Dear Cedar,

Writing by return mail. The Nagamojig are gone now. Ingiiwiindamowaananig. According to your mom, Kateri

Tekakwitha appeared in a cloud of mist exactly two weeks ago today. It is true that she appeared to Jeff "Skeeters" Monroe, in his cups and after an unusually grievous monetary loss. But as he is reliable otherwise, on the tribal council (hysterical laughter), she contends that his version of the event is credible.

Skeeters says that a beautiful Native girl, traditionally dressed, gradually emerged from a cloudy ball and stood balanced on the point of her boulder. She jumped down in a swirl of buckskin and stood on the grass. On her face there was no beatific smile but a steely frown. She stared at him, for a long time he says. Her hair was brown, her eyes were brown, her skin a light gold. She said, "All of you are nothing but a bunch of idiots."

Jeff was the first one to sober up and quit gambling, and since him there has been a wave of sobriety vows. Where she stood on the grass, just under her feet, two crosses were scorched into the sod.

Of course, there were those who visited the site and then bet big the next day, believing she'd improved their luck. I don't know where all this gambling money is going anymore. We're losing track of things. I'm trying to persuade the council to keep closer tabs on the casino revenue and take back our land but there is sort of a runaway what-the-hell feeling here. Yet even with the utterly lost, to whom life and death are equally jests, there are matters of which no jest can be made (Poe). The world out-Herods Herod. The gigantic clock of ebony with brazen lungs, whose music made the giddiest grow pale, has struck.

So that's the big excitement. There have been round-the-clock vigils.

Sweetie's vigiling right now. People often hallucinate during times of stress. Still, I think your saint is right.

SEPTEMBER 7

I have spent the day meticulously constructing a secret food cache in the basement. I have my tool bucket and my drill. The basement wall/foundation is cinder block, two thick, except for one unexpected place that an electrician showed to me way back when he displayed the old grounded wires for the former owner's computer room. There is another little crawl space beneath the foundation of the back porch. If I pry two blocks loose, I can slide in sealed plastic containers and cans, then replace the blocks. I have already put the cigarettes in there, but I need to enlarge the opening. I spend the afternoon chipping at the mortar and slowly I succeed in removing the blocks. A normal-sized person might actually fit inside this truly hideous and claustrophobic little space. Not me though. I'm the size of what in medieval times they used to call a hogshead barrel. I'm so heavy and round, now, that I find myself wishing that I could be moved around on casters.

You have eyebrows, eyelashes, even a little hair. Your footprints and fingerprints are legible now and the complex components of your eyes have formed even though you will not open your lids for a couple of weeks. Sight is the last sense to develop. The nerve connections in your hands are still perfecting themselves. Your brain, the big question mark, has been making 5000 neurons every minute ever since you were four weeks old. Every nerve cell can make 10,000 connections. All along, the neurons have been steadily migrating to their destinations. I guess they just know where to go from the moment they are formed. They travel in waves, millions every day, moving along glial pathways. You've got all of your neurons now, billions and billions, and with every second two million new connections are made between them, more connections than stars in the sky.

While I am down in the cellar, thinking these things, working on the stash, fitting the blocks back into the wall, I hear a woman scream. Then maddened rough barking from a deep-chested dog. The ripsaw shriek seems to come from the trees and yard out back. The barking too. I rush upstairs and I see, out the back window, not a woman but an enormous, powerful sand-colored blur. The animal bounds through the air toward a shocked-looking chocolate Lab, which disappears in its embrace. The thing—some kind of great cat, all muscle and powerful guile—tears long front fangs into and chokes down the bleeding haunches of the dog right there, and then drags the dog's head and torso up into the big oak tree. It secures the carcass in the crotch of a couple of branches and then stretches itself along another branch.

When Phil comes in the door, I call him into the kitchen and tell him that a giant cat is sitting out back in an oak tree munching on a chocolate Lab.

"I didn't know cougars liked chocolate," he says.

I stare at him thoughtfully until he looks away, then he turns and glares back at me.

"You've lost your sense of humor."

"That's not funny."

Phil looks down at his shoes and I can tell that his feelings are actually hurt.

"You are not registering this," I say in my most intense voice, "there is a *saber-toothy cat thing* in the oak tree *eating* a chocolate Lab."

We lock gazes and then, all of a sudden, with no warning, we are both collapsed in laughter, spinning out of control, crazy, weak, until we're gasping on the floor.

We go out on the roof instead that night, and Phil hauls along the Bushmaster. We sit on the low peak in the shadow of the small brick chimney. From there, as we are on the side of a hill, we can see down over the half-grown trees that replaced giant elms, into the miles of neighborhoods that spread south from downtown. They are lower-working-class and working-poor neighborhoods with rickety old Victorians or small ramblers like mine packed together neatly, just a strip of lawn between, or maybe a chain-link fence. Everything is dark now. Just flickers of light. Sometimes, rarely, a bonfire or a larger fire illuminates some corner of the city. Tonight, a house spouts huge orange flames. The cries and shouts are too small and far away to hear. Even the crackle of gunfire, far off, inconsequential as a string of firecrackers. And the sky has bloomed, it is verdant with stars. I've never seen stars like this before. Deep, brilliant, soft. I am comforted because nothing we have done to this earth affects them. I think of the neurons in your brain connecting, branching, forming the capacity I hope you will have for wonder. They are connecting, like galaxies. Perhaps we function as neurons ourselves, interconnecting thoughts in the giant mud of God.

"What really happened," I say to Phil. "Do you know, do they know?"

"Your explanation, God got tired of us, makes about as much sense as anything I've heard," says Phil.

Again, it seems to me that he wants to elaborate, to say something else that is dangling in his thoughts. But he holds my hand with both of his hands. His hands are always warm and I let myself be enveloped.

After a while he starts talking again, and we both pull out everything we ever learned or read about in biology classes, about duplications in the human genome. How the duplicated genes and chromosome segments suggest that our genome has doubled, maybe even more than once. When's unclear, but roughly around the time we diverged from one of our vertebrate ancestors—500 million years ago, give or take a mil? Anyway, this doubling means that our genome is full of rearrangements and repeats. Riddled with redundancy. On one hand, this gives us a certain evolutionary advantage because we've got some built-in flexibility. A copy of a DNA sequence can mutate, can even find out whether its new function works, and there's often a spare to carry on. More often, though, there is this weird thing that happens.

We stop talking. Phil shifts the heavy rifle, pulls me against him. I'm still looking up into the sky.

"The weird thing?"

We talk about how the redundant gene, or twin, becomes a kind of ghost gene, a silent pseudogene. An untranslated DNA sequence.

"So imagine, metaphorically and physically, what this says about us," I say.

"We carry the history of our genetic mishaps."

"And we live with, and our bodies are aware of, the successful history of our own mutations."

Exactly right—folded quietly and knitted in right along with the working DNA there is a shadow self. This won't surprise poets. We carry our own genetic doubles, at least in part. What if some of those silenced genes were activated? I don't know how, but what if they were? And they decided to restore us to some former physical equilibrium?

"What if?" I say, and you kick, hard. "Here, feel."

I put Phil's hand on the place I felt you, but you've shifted away. I understand why so many people did not believe in evolution before last month, and still don't, and never will. It means that perfect physical harmony, grace, and in Darwin's phrase, endless forms most beautiful, resulted slowly as the result of agonizing failures. In their eyes, evolution makes life on earth a scenario of bloody, ham-handed, ruthless, tooth-and-nail struggle. So they point to some miraculous structure, like the eye, each part dependent on the next, and say *There*, how could that be done piecemeal? How could anything but perfection produce perfection? Impossible! But there it is, I think now, the evidence coded and encrypted within each drop of blood, each hair and fingernail paring. For every intelligent piece of design, for every perfection, ghosts of failures exist, too. Mistakes. Whales have vestigial leg bones, pelvises, from their land origins. We survive with certain of those imperfect flaws in our design, the most immediate for me being that the size of the human upright and walking female pelvis is often incompatible with the size of a human baby's head.

"I'm not afraid," I say to Phil, only out of bravado. "I am really not afraid to have our baby."

"Right this moment? Or all the time?"

"Usually, I'm scared."

He buries his face in my hair.

"There's midwives, underground midwives, already. We're going to get you one."

"There are?"

"I just heard about them."

"Yeah," I say, after a while. "That explains things."

"What things?"

"It explains what Sera's doing and why there are fake people living in my family's house."

SEPTEMBER 8

Phil comes back from the neighborhood picnic with a paper plate of cold cuts and a schedule of Uniter church services that the two of us are strongly urged to attend. He says that all the churches are going to be required for federal use.

"Federal? Like there's a government?"

"A church government. The Church of the New Constitution."

SEPTEMBER 15

I haven't written to you. It is getting harder to keep track of things. I sleep as though drugged, half the day, all night. I'm groggy. Phil says that you must be having a growth spurt. I have never been so sleepy. I have had to discipline myself. I said that I was good at living within limitations, and it is true, but that is only because I adhere to a rigid schedule. I have constructed a minute order in my day that I follow to the letter—not just as best I can, but *no matter what*. I do not allow myself to crumple or stay in bed, because I know that if I give in, I will curl up in a fetal ball around you for the next three months. I might sink into an undifferentiated state of dread or go catatonic. That is my secret. I keep it from myself and from Phil—how close I am to unraveling. How crucial it is that I adhere to my routine.

I get up each morning at seven a.m. That is the first act of will, the supreme one. But Phil helps. He holds me. I wake up and turn to him, and he just holds me. I do not tell him what I feel because sometimes, now, he gets impatient with us. He usually helps me out of the bed, though at times he doesn't understand how exhausted I am and pushes a little. He even seems a bit rough, though he's under such stress, he probably doesn't even notice. My favorite are the moments when he admires you, us, strokes me, and says you've grown. That's the temporary lift I need to rise. I go into the bathroom and wash my face with a washcloth. I bury my face in the wet weave and it is often here that fear overcomes me. I wring the washcloth out and look at myself. I see the influence of Sweetie in my face, and I wonder about my mysterious father. There is no chance that I will find him, now, but I do not think that I'll ever get over not seeing him. Dark, she said he was a full-blood. Very brown. I didn't get his skin tone, but I will always wonder if my hands, my eyes, my elbows, are just like his. I will always wonder if I speak like him, laugh like him, walk his walk, alive or dead in this world. And I have other things to wonder about:

Will this be the day that I am discovered and taken away? And what then? What would they do to you? I use a cleansing cream to wash my face. I use it sparingly. I don't know if it can ever be replaced. I have a pretty good supply of toothbrushes, though. And I floss carefully because I've heard that pregnant women are at risk for cavities and I don't have a dental plan—who knows whether that will matter? Then I brush out my hair, which is growing fast, it seems. Is it from pregnancy hormones or just fear? Probably hormones. Stress makes your hair fall out. I put my hair up in a towel while I take a shower. I wash my hair every other day. That is also important. Having clean hair helps my outlook. There is water, note. And on most days electricity. But we use it sparingly, no air-conditioning, and I can hardly move for the heat. I dress as best I can—it's not as though I kept a stash of maternity clothes on hand in case I got pregnant— Phil has let me wear some of his old shirts and I can still fit into my jeans, unzipped. I wear moccasins and cushy socks. We're well into

September and soon I hope will come a slight edge of coolness in the morning air, just a hint of the fall I remember from childhood. This used to be my favorite time. As for winter, that is gone, a ghost season.

Breakfast is important. I am careful about breakfast. We don't see eggs anymore, but there is still bread and there is also jelly. In fact, we've got a lot of jelly. It's left over from the church breakfasts: tubs of it, cans, little jelly packets, jars. We have jelly with toast and oatmeal and I stir jelly into my tea. After breakfast, I brush my teeth again to get rid of all that jelly. Then it is time for Phil to leave, which is the second hardest part of the day, partly because I sense how much he needs to leave.

It is not that things change all of a sudden after the rush of our first, heady, giddy, sweet, falling-in-love weeks. It is just that we've got big worries. Distractions and fears.

Once Phil is gone—that is the very hardest. Still, I don't cling to him as he's leaving, I just exist. I do not think ahead or think behind, even two minutes. I taste him and touch him and feel the life of him. I register as much of him as I possibly can absorb. I sponge him in. Then the door shuts and I take a deep breath. Let it out slowly. I want to stand rooted to the spot and let Phil find me exactly where I was when he left. I want to crumple to the floor like an empty suit of clothes. I want to cry, and sometimes I do cry, why not? *Who will hear me, among the angelic orders?* But mostly I say to myself that it is time for my daily routine of pregnancy exercises. One hour of stretches, weights, resistance bands, yoga from a book. If I do the hour the good endorphins will be released in my brain and I will be able to stick to the day's redemptive routine. If I don't do it, I don't know. I don't want to know.

Finally, when my exercises are finished, I clean one room of the house besides the kitchen, which I always clean. I just clean one room because I need to rotate them, I need them to actually get dirty. When that's done, I go to my desk. Ever since I was nearly discovered, I am very cautious about working at my desk by the window. I check the yard through the blinds, I wait, I am patient. I consider moving back into my laundry room, but there is my limit. I can't do it. If I could not look out on the trees I am sure I would succumb to the fear that's dogging me. With the window to look out of, I can calm myself enough to work on *Zeal*, and write to you.

SEPTEMBER 16

I have been staring at the back of a square-backed kitchen chair, an old wooden chair painted white, and I have been thinking for some time now thoughts that I cannot believe I am thinking. These are not thoughts I can confide. I cannot talk about them to you. I can't tell these thoughts to anyone. They return with such persistence that I fear I am losing control over my mind. No, I cannot say them or even describe them, but I wonder, Do you feel them? Do you somehow absorb and sense the content? I hope you don't, I pray not. I am dangerously imperfect and I would not have these thoughts if I was a better person. I guess that is true enough. But then again, how could I not? Have these thoughts? When I am trapped by the content of my body? By you?

Later on, I decide that maybe I'm not so terrible to want to get rid of you. It is really not you, or me, it is the situation. I forgot. If everything else was predictable, I could accept you, completely. I could. I am sure.

SEPTEMBER 17

The borders were sealed off years ago—the border crossings between the United States, or whatever we are now, and Mexico and Canada. Neither of them want us. But illegal as we are, Canada still functions as the escape hatch in the roof of this country, though the fence is well guarded and people are constantly hunted down and returned. There are still many ways to cross, on foot or by boat. I think that is what Sera and Glen have done. Knowing I'm in hiding and worried about being followed, they probably decided not to visit me but instead to go north. I hope they were able to transfer their assets before selective banking started. I hope that I was not alone in thinking to clean out my accounts.

"How much money do we have?" Phil asks.

"People are still using cash?"

"Not always, but it works half the time."

He's made the bulk of our cash off selling little jelly packets in the vigorous city street markets.

"A thousand. Plus I bought some cartons of cigarettes."

Phil's eyes warm with admiration.

"Cigarettes! I can buy anything with those. People smoke like crazy now."

I've got a thousand counted up, wrapped in the empty freezer, in newspaper. The rest of the money is buried under a flagstone by the back door. Why I don't tell Phil about all of the money, about the liquor and ammo at that moment, I don't know. But once I haven't told him, it is impossible to suddenly tell him. I say nothing.

"We've got to keep alert now," he says.

"I am alert! I'm so alert I can't stand it!"

Phil puts his arms around me, and says that he's going to take the money and some cigarettes to buy false identity papers, so we can follow my parents. He repeats, again and again, that I must not go out and I must not for any reason show myself in the doorway. He has come home to find me excited and agitated and walking around an inexcusably messy house—there are things out of place all over—!—

"I won't. Why would I?"

"You're having trouble."

I'm not though. He doesn't see me all day, how hardworking and down-to-earth I've been all day. And it isn't easy with the wind high, with the trees crashing their limbs together out there, with the dry leaves changing color and the sky that hot autumn blue. It is very hard. I want to go out. Couldn't I just be very fat, or stooped, in a wig of white hair? Couldn't I just be a potbellied man or a nun? A nun? Of course I could be, and Phil could obtain an old-time habit, couldn't he? Why couldn't I go out, then, anywhere, and walk in safety?

"Because," says Phil, "nuns don't wear habits very much, or at all, as you know. It would be so obvious, Cedar."

"I don't think so, Phil, I really don't. I've seen nuns in habits."

"Where? I mean besides in a nuns' nursing home or convent?"

Phil sounds exasperated and I am sorry to cause him any additional anxiety, but I really don't think that I can bear to live inside for another day.

"Where?" Phil demands.

"Airports."

"Exactly."

"What do you mean?"

"If you saw a nun in a habit, she was from somewhere else: Italy or Latin America or, I don't know, Poland."

"Is that true?"

"When is the last time you saw a nun in a habit somewhere in the streets, in a normal place?"

I think hard. "Gay pride parade?"

Phil starts to laugh, then he stops with his mouth open and his eyes lose focus, like maybe he's just remembered those days.

"All right." I try to stay calm. "I'll think of something else to wear outside."

"What, an elephant suit?"

I turn away, stunned, and cannot answer. I rise before him in my beautiful bulk. I tear up, but can't speak. I begin to straighten things. I've found it difficult to get through my day unless the things in the house are put away in their places and perfectly aligned—somehow they never stay quite right. Oh, I don't use a ruler or tape measure. I can do it all by eye, but it has become important to me that the little world in which I carry you is nicely maintained.

"How messy I've let things get," I say calmly. "Me in my elephant suit."

"Everything looks perfect," he says. "Cedar, I'm so sorry. I don't know what made me say that."

"Maybe it's the real you. Maybe you aren't who I think you are."

Phil comes over to me and tries to hold me in his arms. I hate him. I feel a sting of disgust because the jacket he wore falls to the floor and he bumps the chair into misalignment with the table, but then his arms are holding me and I'm enveloped in his human presence. My heart pumps faster and I grab him and hold on. I try to absorb his reality, his normalness, his non-pregnantness. I try to forgive his short temper and his maddening mobility. Besides, I know something's wrong with my thinking. I just can't tell exactly what it is since I am, of course, inside of my thinking.

"We're going to get out of here," he says.

I bury my face against his chest, run my hand along the collar of his shirt. His thick black hair is growing so long it is starting to flop over his forehead.

"Here." He holds my hand and takes something from his pocket and before I know it he has slipped a golden ring onto my finger. "And I've got one, too." He puts his ring on and then grins at me with that big, sweet, wide Phil smile. "There. Married. Hi, honey, whadja cook?"

My head clears suddenly. I know he's kidding and I cling to that.

"I forgot to cook."

"That's my baby, and it's okay. I scored crackers and cheese."

"Crackers and cheese?"

I'm looking straight at Phil. My eyes brim over, I'm crying all of a sudden, my face is streaming, my nose is running, the tears that have been pressing up behind my face all day let go in a burst that seems to crack my chest open. My heart hurts like it was punched. I can't bear it—crackers and cheese! It reminds me of all the wonderful, normal times that I have eaten crackers and cheese with my parents or friends. So many times in my past life and I've never appreciated how comforting and convivial those times were. Phil takes my hand and leads me to the bedroom and shuts the door. He pulls back the covers and helps me get comfortable against the pillows. I'm still crying, hiccuping, choking on my gallons and gallons of tears. I'm ashamed of my overflow, but helpless to stop. I keep apologizing and Phil says it's all right, it's all right, but after a while he becomes very solemn and says would I please consider that he was an asshole. I am not an elephant. And we now have conjugal duties to perform and with my permission he'll commence what is after all a very import-ant part of all marriages.

"Plus, voilà! The rings! We've got the rings!"

He waves the tiny box. We put our hands together. Mine is like a paw, chubby from my baby weight and dimpled at the knuckles. But the ring still fits.

"It's a very beautiful ring," I finally say, "and I think that we'll be all right."

Phil climbs into bed beside me. As we begin to touch I feel the rightness between us return. It happens slowly, look by look, ques-tion marks and kisses. I don't think you're ever going to read this. Honest to god. I doubt you'll even want to. But if it turns out that you do, I can always tear out this page where I talk about making crazy passionate love while pregnant, can't I, because I suppose it might traumatize you in the event that things turn out in some way where psychic trauma still has meaning.

SEPTEMBER 18

You now weigh as much as eight or even twelve sticks of butter, and you open your eyes from time to time. You must know when I face the window; perhaps a soft radiance envelops you. I wonder if you feel the way I do on some mornings, waking, stretching to the light in warm physical joy, before I remember. Yesterday I actually felt you hiccuping. If you are a baby boy, watch out for migrating testicles; they are now on their way from their place near the kidneys, moving through your lower body to their perfect scrotal placement. If you're a girl, your clitoris is right out there, obvious, although your labia are very small yet, tiny flower. And you've got better lungs. You're losing that bizarre lanugo hair. I know that all this keeping track of your development is a big assumption, maybe wishful thinking, on my part. I know all bets are off and I should form no expectation. But I am your mom and keeping track is what moms do.

SEPTEMBER 21

In the middle of the night, we are awakened by someone tapping on our window. The wind is scraping the branches together and a low voice burbles behind the glass. I roll out of bed and crouch on the floor, my dreams still heavy, some sort of endless chase, dramatic and confused. We don't dare look outside. Phil puts his hand on my back and whispers, "Stay down." I hear him take the loaded Rossi out of the bedside table drawer. He sneaks into the kitchen. The wind shuts off. Someone's talking. Then I recognize Eddy calling out, "It's me, Eddy," and "Me and Sweetie are looking for Cedar." Phil crawls back to me—I am hiding in the closet. "It might be Eddy," he whispers. And I say, "Of course it's Eddy," because I knew somehow that he and Sweetie would come.

"Let him in."

So Phil eases the door open and Eddy slides into the kitchen. I light a candle and there is Eddy's fox face. He's grinning, shy, glad to see me like he's just paying a normal family visit.

"Hey!" He shakes Phil's hand and nods, awkward and pleased with himself.

"You hungry?" I ask.

"Does the pope shit in the woods?"

As Phil turns away, I see that Eddy is sizing him up, deciding whether he's going to be cool with Phil being the father of my baby. He's watching everything that Phil does, eyes narrow, folding his arms and stroking the side of his face. This seems like an instinctively fatherly thing to do, but even though Eddy hasn't earned the right, I'm not upset.

I make sure the blinds are all pulled, then sit Eddy down at the kitchen table.

Yesterday, Phil got hold of a case of Cup Noodles, and now I heat up six containers, two for each of us. The gas went out on the gas stove and we don't know how to get more, but with the electricity still going, our microwave works. Soon we have hot noodles, and we sit around the candle, slowly spooning them into our mouths.

"Salty," says Eddy. "And good."

He goes on, "I had to ditch my car. Just one or two cars on the road. Didn't want to stick out, draw attention to your house, so I left my car at an old buddy's. Inside of his garage. I walked over here, about six miles."

"Just to visit?"

"Plus other reasons. Hello from your mom and so on, and Little Mary, too."

"She probably sent me a double-index-finger greeting, right?"

Eddy opens his eyes, nods a little, like *You know her well.* But only says, "On the contrary, she's hoping you'll clean her room again. Grandma sent this."

It looks like the red finger-woven sash she had been working on, only I see she's made it much wider and longer.

"It's a baby carrier," says Eddy. "She's working on your cradle board, too. But this is for starters, I guess. And me, I'm here because I've been thinking of a plan to get you out, the way I helped Glen and Sera."

"I'm assuming that you got them across the border."

"Yeah, it worked out. I got hold of some buddies I know up there. We take a canoe out on the south side of Rainy, in the dark, not using a light, and we paddle it up across the border. Major workout. It's pretty hard to patrol that whole area, and we've got some slick ways of disappearing behind those islands. Take lots of camping gear and you could last a month, still heading north. Sera and Glen will know where to pick you up. They're getting to be old hands."

"So they're up there, safe, you're positive."

"Oh yeah."

My whole body feels lighter, with relief, and you tumble to one side, jut an elbow out, kick me gently in the ribs. I put my hand over you and smile.

Eddy puts down his first cup with a little sigh, starts spooning up the second. "The water's open year-round now, still it gets below freezing once in a while. We have to plan this pretty quick. I mean, you've got to get up there in the next couple of weeks. You're due late December, I know that. We've got to get you settled in."

"We should go tonight," I say.

Eddy strokes his face, thinking again. "Maybe."

"There's lots more stuff we need to get together," says Phil. "What about the cold-weather camping gear? I don't want to find ourselves out there unprepared. I've got a place I can go for subzero sleeping bags."

"It won't really be that cold," says Eddy.

Phil keeps arguing. "But I need more ammo for the guns. We've got to have some powdered food for emergencies, and a lot of stuff, my God, a *lot* of stuff."

"We've got a good tent," I tell him.

"You can pack that around with leaves, make a warm little house," says Eddy.

"Hatchet, rope, fishing tackle." Phil can't stop.

"Well, you've got a good start," says Eddy, "so get the stuff together by next week. I just came to see you, really, to get you going. I don't have a date nailed down with my friends and the boat, but now I'll get hold of them. Then I'll come back down and get you. But it's got to happen quick."

"Now," I say. "I think it would be better to just go now."

Desperation chokes me. I want to walk from this house. I want to disappear. The edges of my dream are still with me, the endless running, the chase, the certainty of capture.

"Please, I *know* we'll get caught here."

"Take it easy," says Phil, stroking my back.

"I won't take it easy!"

But Phil convinces me that we just aren't ready, and after a while I know it is no use arguing. They will not take me up north, out of here. *Out of here.* And I have this dark sense, then, a weight coming down. That feeling should have told me.

Plus this: While we are saying good-bye to Eddy, my computer switches on. All by itself. I haven't touched it. Nobody has touched it. We whirl to it in surprise. It isn't plugged in and I have let the battery die.

"Hello dear, this is Mother. How are you tonight? I am worried. We don't seem to be communicating very well."

Phil steps behind the computer, jerks it up, and smashes it on the tile counter. But it won't disintegrate.

"Please get in touch with Mother. Please get in touch," it says, in pieces on the floor.

PART

II

They have us. We are alone together now and I have only the barest idea what their plans are for us—though I assume not good, I know not good, and a trembling, low-down, crazy, stark anxiety pulls my every nerve. Here is what happened. We were raided, I suppose you'd say. Though there was no physical violence. Phil was gone and there wasn't any use I could see in putting up resistance. Even now, that I went willingly almost confuses me. The guns were loaded. I could have run to the bedroom as the woman entered the kitchen door. I could have locked myself in and sat on the bed with the Rossi in one hand and the Bushmaster balanced on my arm. I could have made a stand, gone down fighting, at least kicked and clawed. But number one, you would have died with me or at the very least been hurt. I've never actually fired either one of those guns, and probably would have screwed up the action. Number two, there would have been no point. And number three, I have this weakness. Nice people paralyze me. Dark-skinned people who are nice, especially. The woman who tapped lightly on the door after she had picked the lock, then opened the door and poked her head around it with a cheery halloo! was round and honey-brown, all sorts of pretty, a mixture of several races. Her face was delicately freckled and her straightened auburn hair was curled softly and sprayed away from her forehead and cheeks in a Betty Crocker halo. She wore jeans, Keds, and a raspberry cotton tunic sweater. She wore a few pieces of clean, contemporary, tasteful gold jewelry, and she carried a covered basket.

That the basket held a handgun beneath the red and white checkered napkin was something I didn't learn until I had compared notes with my roommate. Bernice had come for her, too. Only my roommate had put up a struggle and her boyfriend had charged Bernice, who slipped the gun from underneath the checkered napkin and fired, twice. She said Bernice had stepped aside and let the boyfriend crash into the stove, turning over hot soup, which he hadn't reacted to, falling, so she thought he was dead. "She killed one of her own," my roommate mourned. "She murdered my beautiful black boyfriend. So I know they won't fucking let me keep my baby." Bernice handcuffed and led my roommate out while she was in shock, so she didn't know for sure. She keeps repeating the story.

"She had me out the door before I could go to him. You know, she's a trained police officer, former U.S. Marine, or some shit."

I'm so glad your father wasn't home.

Who turned me in? Who tipped off Bernice? I keep wondering if it could have been Hiro. Or maybe the coral-shirted boys, Clark and Emeric, who dropped the invitation off. Little Mary. I suppose it could have been Little Mary. So anxious to get rid of me. Yet, I cleaned her room! In fact, the more I think about it, the easier it is to convince myself that it was definitely my sister, jealous, lying, high or enraged, my sister who called the tip-line, the UPS line, Unborn Protection Society, and offered the following information about me. Cedar Hawk Songmaker. Pregnant. 119 Boutwell Street (Proverbs 10:7), Minneapolis, Minnesota. And had them dispatch Bernice.

After Bernice radioed her backup help—a UPS truck—that I was cooperating nicely, she sat down with me and talked to me. She listened to my arguments, waited while I told her all of the reasons I was afraid to go along with her in . . . not a squad car. She drives a very clean silver Camry fixed in just one way. The seat belts lock automatically and only unlock when hers is released. This is another fact I would not have known had not my roommate ridden in the Camry, too, and tried to leap out at an intersection.

My roommate's name, by the way, is Agnes Starr. She insists that her great-great-grandmother was Belle Starr, the famous outlaw, and that she's going to break out of the hospital. I'm going with her, even though I'm surprised to find that this place, the maternity ward, is so orderly and shiny, so pleasant. The food is not standard hospital fare but much better. I feel at home here. On some level I don't want to leave. We're on the sixth floor and as we're on a hill, our window has a gorgeous view of the eastern side of the city and the Mississippi River. We can see people crossing the University of Minnesota bridge, little people's heads bobbing to and fro. I guess maybe they are even still going to school. Or they could be soldiers. There is another rooftop, three, four floors beneath us, and another and another roof, all various heights. Beyond us, trees and more bunches of trees glowing in fall colors all along the river. Russet, hot yellow, pink, orange, and deep bloody red. The thing is, I don't think the leaves had changed yet when I was captured. They were green, a few were yellow. I am paranoid that I've been asleep for weeks, but I'm no bigger. A nurse told me the date. I try to think of another explanation, but soon lose the thread of my thoughts. I watch the sun rise each morning, lighting the steel beams of the bridge, touching the brick walls with hands of fire, passing bars of radiance along the gravel and the asphalt toppings on the roofs below. As the warmth advances, mist lazily floats from the still, green leaves of far-off bushes and giant trees, and swirls in the scarlet and green maples, dogwood, viburnum. The elms are turning gold and come to think of it they must be giving me drugs.

My experiences are enchantingly visual and spookily intense.

I have this notebook, your letter, because Bernice helped me get together a bag of special things that I would need in the hospital. I added this, of course. I opened your drawer, the one where I have been keeping your layette, and I took out the newborn one-piece stretch terry jumpers, the package of flowered receiving blankets, the plastic mirror toy/rattle, the tiny fist-sized striped hats, the little bitty newborn diapers and booties. I put them in the bag with my nightgowns and sweater and T-shirts and stretchy bras and tie-waist pants. I slipped my nail file and nail scissors into the lining of the bag—they haven't found those, yet. I grabbed the *Zeal* files and the books that happened to be shelved together near my suitcase, and dropped them in: *Is That in the Bible?* by Dr. Charles Francis Potter; *Hildegard of Bingen*, by Sabina Flanagan; *Raids on the Unspeakable*, by Thomas Merton; Saint John of the Cross's *Dark Night of the Soul*; *The Life of Kateri Tekakwitha* by Evelyn M. Brown; and *Utterly Mad*, a Ballantine paperback that says it is "dangerous as a three-week-old liverwurst sandwich," edited or authored by William Gaines and bearing on its cover a portrait of Alfred E. Neuman dressed as Napoleon. I also grabbed my favorite rosary, the one made from olive wood from Israel, and stuck it in the pocket of Phil's jeans. I was wearing one of his flannel shirts, a soft red and gold plaid. Bernice held my hand as we walked out to her car and she said, "Don't be afraid. Your baby will be beautiful."

And I looked at her and thought, Either she is a very good person and incredibly deluded, or else she is completely evil.

Because they don't intend to give you to me, I'm sure.

I have found a slot just inside the heating register where this book just fits. Maybe the nurses know where your book is hidden and maybe they don't. Maybe they remove it and read it while I am sleeping. I do not care, really, and they probably don't either. Little one, I think we're both going to live.

SEPTEMBER 28 MORNING

"Ooh!" says the nurse. "A Christmas baby!"

She's got a little notebook computer with my chart inside and she holds the info on her hip. She beams at me, weirdly beneficent. She has noticed your due date and coos again at the idea of December 25, oblivious to the outrage of my roommate. Agnes Starr, black-rooted blond, droopy-lidded, with heavy, snarling hot-red lips, loudly gags.

"You fucking hypocrite, you murdering little bitch, don't pretend everything's okay." She speaks in even and calculating tones, with a thrilling dramatic control. Sort of like Little Mary, who turned me in, I remember now.

"Don't fucking do this, Fatty! We're women, too, you slime. I haven't seen one woman yet take her baby out of the delivery room. What do you do with them?"

The nurse glances indulgently at Agnes, smiles, then beams harder at the two of us and trills. "Almost lunchtime!"

"Answer me!" yells Agnes.

The nurse snaps the lid shut on the computer and hustles out the door.

"What the fuck do you do with them!" Agnes screams after her. She falls back against the pillows as the doors shut. Agnes is almost thirty-six weeks. She says they schedule the C-section as soon as the baby is viable and that she thinks she is nearly there. They've done two ultrasounds this week. She thinks it could be any day. She says I've got about six weeks to plan how I'm going to get out of the hospital.

"I'm busting out tonight," she says, "and by the way, don't take the vitamins."

I've already taken mine this morning.

"Hide it in your cheek, not under your tongue. Sometimes they make you stick your tongue out. Once the nurse leaves, go take a pee and flush it. You're feeling good right now, huh?"

"Yeah."

I have the most intensely comfortable feeling of peace and order. I am in the center of a glowing configuration, a perfectly safe and clean little habitat. This room has evenly painted golden walls, three photographs of dewy flowers. The sheets are heavy, white, starched cotton. Brilliant white waffle-weave cotton blankets cover both of us, me and Agnes, who is softly radiant.

"Oh, Agnes! It's like a five-star hotel!"

She squints at me, grinning. "You dumb bitch." There is a black space between her front teeth, a sexy gap. "I felt like that too for about three days. I wasn't even pissed off about Bernice shooting Mark. You have a guy?"

"Yes, yes, I do!"

Guilty start. I haven't given Phil much thought, she's right. I try to imagine, now, the scenario of Phil returning to our house and me not being there. He'd be frantic, he'd go nuts, he'd bolt to each room and shout my name into the dissonance of empty but familiar space. I try to keep picturing Phil's reactions, but it exhausts me to imagine anything abstract. It seems impossible to feel anything but a calm and pleasurable acceptance of my comforting little hospital world.

"Does he know where I am?" I ask Agnes. "I mean, do they tell the dads?"

"Oh, right." Agnes laughs at me. She gets out of bed and toddles over to the window. She is carrying her baby low and her hips are skinny, so her stomach sticks straight out in a perfect ball. Her thin gown is made of the odd institutional material they use. The old boxer-short stuff, complex blue-figured checks, drapes down her front in a dignified flow.

"You're right. I just feel great," I say. "Nothing's wrong even though I know on some level that everything is wrong."

"Just wait until you flush your happy pill," says Agnes. "Reality's a bitch. A heavy bitch. Fuck. I'll be outta here though."

And she is, though not the way she hopes.

The drug knocks me out around eight p.m. so I don't know it when she tries to leave that night. She doesn't make it. When I wake this morning she is tied into the bed next to me, her wrists and ankles bound in hospital restraints. Her face is swollen and pasty pale. Her eyes are shut. She's deeply asleep, snoring lightly. Breakfast comes, but she doesn't stir. I only pretend to swallow the vitamin I'm given in a tiny paper cup, and by the time the nurse leaves the room it has begun to dissolve against my back tooth—bitter, metallic, sickening. I spit it out into the toilet and flush it away, then wait.

Around noon, Agnes starts coughing.

"Pillow!"

I bring my pillow over and prop up her head.

"Thanks." Her voice is hoarse, her eyes loll backward. Trying to stay awake, she frowns, screws up her face, shakes her head to shed the drug.

"What happened?"

"Water, washcloth."

I bring her a glass of water, she gulps it down, then I sponge off her face with a cold, wet cloth.

"Yeah, that's better."

"How did you get out?"

"Down the hall . . . the other outlaw." Her eyes droop shut. I shake her.

"Tell me! How?"

She tries to keep her eyes open, blinking furiously, staring. She gasps out a few words.

"Had it worked out . . . she got the guard back over to the nurse's station for coffee. Those guys talk while I take the stairs down to the lobby. On my own, then."

"How come they didn't see you?"

Agnes's eyes shut, her mouth drops open, and she's out again, snoring. I go into the bathroom, get the washcloth wet, bring it out, and wipe her face, her throat, wrists, arms. I shake her.

"Uh-oh." She grins slightly, rousing herself. "I had on this paira extra-large blue scrubs, lab coat. Actually, actually . . . oh, uh, I made it out the side doors to a Dumpster. Alla way down there. I was sposed to pretend to have a smoke, then this frienda mine, watching, she'd get me."

"How? Who?"

I shake Agnes harder, desperately, but she's gone again.

"How did you contact your friend?" I ask her sleeping face, over and over, but I can't rouse her this time. I sit on my bed watching her sleep. It's funny, watching someone sleep—how it tells you things about them you'd never know when they were awake. Agnes looks so sad in her sleep, for instance, not angry at all. Her sorrow is so naked. It is like the sorrow of the Virgin Mary, her knowingness, her foresight. And I'm helpless to change things. All I can do is untie her restraints. I do that, and then I watch over her, knowing I'm no protection.

One hour later, two nurses enter the room and draw the curtains around Agnes.

"Wake up," I cry. I swing my legs over the sides of my bed and struggle through the curtains. "What are you doing with her!"

"Just prepping her," says one of the rosy, chubby nurses, a woman Agnes calls the Cheesehead. Her voice is sweet, cheerful, even kindly. "Don't worry. It's a happy day, Cedar, it's time for Agnes to have her baby!"

"You'll see your friend in a couple, three hours," says the other, a skinny black-eyed brunette with long yellow teeth, as they pull aside the curtains. But just as they are getting ready to wheel her out, Agnes comes to. She wakes in absolute silence, no warning, and flips out of the bed. One minute she's totally limp, faking, and the next she's got a fist and a foot out and she's ripped the IV out of her hand. She springs up, uses the light aluminum IV stand like a kung fu fighting pole. She slams rosy Cheesehead on the side of the skull and cracks the skinny nurse across the throat so that suddenly they are both bent over, gagging.

"Help me!"

A thin Somali orderly in blue scrubs darts in and seizes Agnes from behind. He crashes down, his nose spouting blood, when she cracks him with a back head-butt of her skull. I run over and sit down on him—oddly, he stays still. He could throw me off, but he doesn't—He whispers, "Keep sitting on me." Either he's a pervert, I think, or he's on our side and wants to stay out of the way, giving Agnes a chance. So I keep sitting on the Somali man, who struggles beneath me in a halfhearted way. Agnes whirls, grinning at me, her white ass glowing through the wings of the hospital gown. Then she flies out the door, down the hall. I jump up and get to the door in time to see her bowl right over a chubby, short male doctor, who sprawls, groping for his glasses. I run out after her, into the hall, and see that with incredible quickness she's got to the emergency stairway. I take two steps. The last I see of Agnes is the black vigor of her bleached hair roots and the abrupt yellow of the ends as her hair flags out, flying through the staircase door.

The OB doctor bumbles to his feet and yells for help, but it's too late.

After that, I ask every nurse who comes in where Agnes went, if she got out, if she's all right. Every one of them gives me a pleasant smile, a little laugh, a cheery wink.

"Oh, Agnes? She's fine. She went home."

OCTOBER 5

They replace her with a young Asian woman who radiates intensity. She's both demure and severe. Intimidating. She has either stopped speaking or speaks no English, and she might be insane. She stares into space, humming off-key monotonous tunes. She plucks at the weave of her blanket, removing long strings which she begins to wind into a ball, tiny the first day, much bigger the next. She has apparently unraveled her blanket all night. She hides the ball when the nurse comes in. The blanket is halfway gone. The woman reminds me of a perfect industrious spider, so quiet, fingers moving, moving, moving. She gets on my nerves and the food tastes horrible now. Lunch is a tan piece of seared flesh-substance, with canned beans and a quarter of a rotted tomato, a plastic bowl of cold, white pudding. I can't believe I ate this food and liked it—that drug was awesome. The room is drab, the paint stained and peeling, and the photographs are tattered and saccharine. One is a big daisy with nineteen petals and three out-of-focus leaves. Another is a picture of a cozy Cape Cod with light flooding out the windows onto a bank of ratty snow. I hear the other women's voices, whining or furious, and smell rank smells—shit, fear, chemical exhalations, isopropyl alcohol, and the food, always the spoiling food. Oh, the drugs have worn off, for sure, with a vengeance. It is very difficult to flush the next morning's vitamin. I want my happy hospital back again. I want to sit here and contemplate how big you're getting, how healthy, your little lungs continuing to strengthen. Your brain building config- urations in rapid waves. Thoughts occurring, perhaps. I want to marvel at even the sharpest of your kicks and punches. So active! But I'm sick knowing what happened to Agnes. I think they killed her during her C-section. I think they have cremated her. I think there are full-time full-capacity crematoriums going night and day in the exurbs. And I also cannot stop my mind from weaving scenarios of dread and terror about my parents, both sets, about Little Mary, and especially about Phil.

My heart squeezes and pumps with an uncontainable energy, a useless urge to rush to him and comfort him and have him save us, too, by the way.

My roommate's blanket is completely unraveled and she has a couple of huge balls of yarn hidden in the undercarriage of her bed. The nurse brings her another blanket, then leaves two more when—with a delicate sneeze and a sweet smile, a mimed shiver —my roommate indicates that she is cold. For a moment, I think she's in her right mind, but then as soon as we are alone again she works obsessively to pick apart a beginning point on one of the new blankets. Soon she begins unraveling it exactly like the first.

I'm going to have to plot my way out. I wish Agnes had left the name of what must have been a helpful nurse, *the other outlaw,* she said. I don't know how to find the nurse except to talk to all of the nurses. Get to know them. Engage them personally, make friends with them if I can. So on the fourth day after Agnes either escapes or dies, I rouse myself and begin to walk the corridors; it's exercise any- way, and rocks you to sleep. You're very active now, twisting, bump- ing me hard. I need to walk in order to calm these frequent attacks of fear and adrenaline that overwhelm me when I think of what will happen to you, or think of what has already happened to Phil.

I keep imagining him walking into the house and not finding me there. I imagine his rough cries. I know exactly how his face would look, registering disbelief, then growing knowledge, then a kind of unsettled anger, at first frantic and then resolute. He's going to find me, I think that he already knows where I am. There will be a sign. I must stay ready for the sign, remain alert, prepare myself, stay strong. So I drink the powdered OJ and eat the rancid eggs, the strange bread, the curdled milk, and the coffee-type beverage so acidic it brings tears to my eyes. I eat the bean paste and slimy orange slices, the wads of wet Kleenex that are supposed to be mashed potatoes, and I walk up and down the one corridor, observing the routine, looking for a hole in the day.

OCTOBER 8

I continue to make light chat with the nurses—and I ask the one nurse who has stayed clear of me, stayed behind the desk, in fact, if she knows where Agnes Starr went. I have already nicknamed this nurse the Dweeb. She's a pale, skinny, chinless, thick-eyeglass-wearing nerdy type of woman. She is unnoticeable, really, as manila as her stacks of folders. But when I ask her my question, "Where did Agnes Starr go?" she blinks at me, draws closer, looks at me carefully, waits for another nurse to leave the desk, then tells me the truth.

"They cornered her in the lobby, took her down. Knocked her out, solid. Agnes never made it off the delivery table."

I stand there looking at the nerd-nurse, the Dweeb, who calmly regards me, her washed-out eyes now steady behind her thick, round, Coke-bottle-bottom eyeglasses.

"You're the one who tried to help her."

"I'm Jessica, they call me Jessie."

"The other outlaw."

"Whatever. You can't talk to me again, you'll blow things."

"But I need your help, please. I've got to get out."

"Yes," says the mousy, bland, limp-haired, and cave-chested woman, her voice brightening to a false luster as another nurse approaches, "I'm working on that. Believe me, I really am."

I turn away.

"You're all alike," I say to the other nurse. "She wouldn't let me use the phone."

"You know there's no phone service," says the nurse in a melting, soothing, frightful voice. "Let's go back to your room, shall we, and see if we can put a movie in for you."

I follow her back to my room and don't watch one of the movies from the little library—*The Bells of St. Mary's*. The nurse puts it in, but I keep my eyes on my hands. The movie is cover, allowing me to think. For the next few hours I sit picking apart my waffle-weave blanket, reducing it the way my roommate is doing, to an angry ball of yarn. As I wind the string, I begin to talk and then just keep talking, why not? I'm sure my roommate doesn't understand me, but I've got to hear somebody talking, a voice, some form of understanding, even if it's only myself.

"You and me could be related," I say to her. "Have you ever heard of the Bering Strait? The land bridge theory?"

My roommate just keeps picking at her blanket and smiles gently at me. She feigns listening politely, and I somehow appreciate that. I notice that she uses a square knot when she pieces together stretches of yarn. On my walks, I take dirty blankets from the hampers in the hallway, bundle them under my robe, next to you. If she's up to something, I want to be working with her. So now I'm picking my own blanket apart just the way she does. Talking to her.

"We possibly share the major DNA haplotype B marker found in most American Indians as well as people in Ulaanbaatar," I tell my roommate. She gives a tiny, polite, oh-you-don't-say smile. "Not that all Native views coincide here, mind you, there are plenty of people who believe that their particular tribal origin spot—hill, lake, cave, mountain—is the real place they emerged from. As much as I'd like to believe the same, I was raised with a reductionist worldview and think at least some of our people came across the land bridge in a steady migration, a trickle really, for tens of thousands of years. Then there were the people who navigated the sea to South

America. And the ones who dropped from the stars. Over a hundred million of us until de Soto's pigs got loose, Pizarro coughed, Captain John Smith sneezed. All that. Diseases killed ninety-nine percent of us. Of course, your and my families lost touch over time."

She makes a pleasant humming sound of assent.

"But I feel comforted to renew the acquaintance now," I say, and nod at her. We smile a bit idiotically at each other until we hear a nurse approaching. We quickly hide our handiwork. My roommate pretends to sleep and I paste a dreamy drug-addled smile on my face. The nurse who is working with former Dweeb nurse, now Jessie, brings us a couple of peanut butter sandwiches for lunch, with a side of army-green boiled peas. My roommate pretends to wake up. She nods and twinkles her eyes at the nurse, who says to me, "Isn't she adorable?"

"Of course," I say.

"Has she said a word?"

"Not yet."

"Well, I'll leave you two to enjoy your lunch."

"Thanks. This looks soooo good!"

"Bye-bye," she says to my roommate. "You little China doll."

As the nurse turns away my roommate watches her, unblinking, from under her eyebrows. She tips her head to the side, smiles. Deadly.

"Wow, I hope you never look at me that way," I say, impressed.

She opens her mouth, as if she might speak. But shakes her head and goes all demure again.

"Oh all right! You're so fucking mysterious! What the hell? Why don't you say something?"

Her hands come out. She begins making signs. I took American Sign in high school, at Southwest. So I just laugh.

"You fake," I say, furious. "I don't know what the fuck your game is."

But she won't say a word, so I eat my lunch. I really am grateful for the peanut butter sandwich. It's less disgusting than most of our lunches, although the bread is stale and dry. I choke down the spoiled peas for your sake. There's a glass of powdered milk. I stir the lumps out with a fork and drink it in a gulp. Then the two of us go back to work. Now, just to bug her, I keep talking to my room-mate about various pre-Columbian civilizations, touch on crackpot theories, mull over the Kennewick Man, mention skull size and race and anthropology. She nods and hums and keeps winding her ball of yarn. We've now taken apart four blankets and have a substantial number of rolled balls hidden in the bottoms of our beds and the ledges underneath and beside the heating duct covers, which I've un-screwed with a piece of Bic pen and pried away from the walls. Most important, I still keep this notebook, your letter, securely hidden. I don't know what I would do if I couldn't write to you. I don't think I could stay mentally alive. This is my only drug. The books in my bag were confiscated, and my envelope with the pages of *Zeal's* next issue. They have not been given back although I've asked for them every day. When I can't write, or wind yarn any longer, I say the rosary. At least I've got that. It's soothing, the mindless repetition, the smooth beads, the Mom of Infinite Mercy whose cool hands and blue robe I imagine while I am saying the prayers. Only I have to wonder: Is her mouth duct-taped shut? Is she going to answer? Will Kateri? Is anyone listening?

OCTOBER 9

Maybe they *were* listening. An astounding thing happens. It is really more than I can stand and the strangeness of it electrifies me. I get mail. I am making my usual corridor stroll up the one thousand and six alternating blue and tan linoleum tiles set in one hundred and sixty-seven rows of six with leftover spaces filled by strips that come out to, I figure, about four tiles in all as they are very thin strips. I am walking down my side of the twenty-two-bedroom ward, past the ten rooms, on each side, then the central nursing station and ele-vator/lobby/door-to-stairs, and then on past the other rooms, which are always closed and so just numbers to me. Midway back in my walk, the twenty-ninth pass of my morning, I pause at the desk to chat up one of the younger nurses. The elevator opens behind me. Someone brushes my flimsy robe. I look to my left and there stands Hiro, holding the mail out at arm's length. He puts a rubber-banded stack of envelopes into the hands of the nurse and then turns away without looking at or acknowledging me.

I wait until I am back in my room before I put my hand into the pocket of my robe and in amazement draw forth a letter. A letter. My roommate sees the tip of the envelope. She looks down at her yarn ball quickly, but I catch the glint of one eye. I walk into the bathroom and run water while I open the letter, which at first I am positive is from Phil, and I read.

The letter does not say: *I love you more than life—my life or any life— and I am coming to get you. Stay strong.*

It does not say: *Go to the stairs at 4 a.m. and I will be waiting with a group of people I trust to break you out of that place and take you with me.*

What it does say is this: *Phil turned you in. Be careful and watch for me. I love you, my darling girl.*

The note is written in my Songmaker mom's handwriting.

Later on, I tear the note into a thousand bits and flush the pieces down the toilet, all except for the line *I love you, my darling girl.* I crawl into bed, breathing hard, my heart dead, my breath skipping, burning my lungs. Phil was the one who betrayed us. Angel Phil. I press the little piece of paper to my cheek and shut my eyes. I don't cry. Crying's for the little things, I guess. For all the night and the next day I stay catatonic, then on the second day I sit up, weak and dizzy, and eat my rotting breakfast and swallow my vitamin. That day, I blur out, winding yarn. On the third day, with a vast effort of will, and with deep regret, I flush my happy pill. And I think to myself that maybe Sera's wrong. Maybe she doesn't know as much as she thinks she knows. Without the first part of the note to look at, I begin to wonder if I even read those words at all. Phil's fake ring stays on my finger, and I try to forget.

OCTOBER 12

It happens today, same as before. I stand at the counter, making agonizingly pleasant bullshit small talk with the roundest, most obnoxiously cheerful nurse of them all, Orielee, when behind me the elevator swishes to our floor and stops. The doors open. I know Hiro's tread and I feel him brush by me. This time I clap an arm down on the pocket of my robe and turn away, shuffle the opposite direction from my room. I make two more corridor walks before going into the bathroom and huddling over my message.

PAGE 1019

Cured by the Apocalypse?

It is apparent to everyone around me that I am taking perverse pleasure in the contemplation of this massive biological reversal. During the first week that this great symmetricism was revealed, I laughed my head off every night in front of the television. It was not just derision or amusement or outright glee at the reactions of the Know Nothingism nothing Knower creationists, Methodological Naturalists, Anti-Common Descentists, Wedge Strategists, and Macroevolution naysayers who persisted in denying the fundamental elegance and truth of evolution. True, that was very satisfying. It was more. It was awe. In spite of the hardship that a rending of the social fabric might cause for my beloved family, not to mention great unknowns in the area of reverse evolution that will probably result in mass starvation, I was and remain exhilarated. I have started reading Exodus in order to witness the working of the design: 1:18, 2:4, 3:8, 3:18, 3:32, 4:1, 7:18, 7:28, 9:9, 10:6, 13:7, 13:14,

14:11, and 14:19. The opportunity to witness the working of the design unraveling. The sheer thrill of the plan coming to light in each detail. Who says any complexity is irreducible? IT IS BEING REDUCED ALL AROUND US RIGHT NOW. I have the chance each day to marvel at the vast dismantling, and do not want to kill myself so that I can see more of the world's inner workings.

It should not take a biological apocalypse to cure an Indian man's depression, but hell, sometimes here is paradise on earth and there are times I just feel great.

Love, Eddy

I read this piece of writing over and over. At first I'm disappointed, then I shiver with anger. Depressives are so selfish, I think, so full of himself he can't even imagine the danger that I am in. Oh well, if it comes to that, I just met him. What do I expect? But I can't let go. I keep thinking of that feeling that I had, that true connection. And his visit. I keep trying to figure, trying to understand why Eddy would send me such a self-absorbed message, until eventually, somehow, I know that there must be something else hidden within it. I start looking for words, trying to figure out a code. If only I spoke Ojibwe, this would be easy. Like the old code-talkers. But I'm so deculturated, I think, swamped in a wave of self-pity. I put the letter down. Pick it up again. It takes way too many readings—my brain must be mush. Duh, Exodus! Typical Eddy joke. He never reads the Bible so this must refer to an actual exodus. An escape. And the numbers must be the working of a design.

It isn't hard to get a Bible in this place. Even the Slider approves of my request and smiles thinly as she hands over The Zondervan Compact Reference Bible.

Exodus 1:18 is about the refusal of midwives to do the bidding of the king of Egypt and kill all male Hebrew babies. I have a panic attack right there. What is Eddy trying to tell me?

And then I realize the numbers don't line up. He can't be referencing Exodus. The message isn't in the words but the numbers.

I take a closer look at every number in Eddy's letter. For instance, page 1019.

But there are over 3000 pages in Eddy's book.

It could be a date. It could be the date they are coming to get me. 10/19.

Cured by the Apocalypse?

At last, after the thousandth reading, I see it—the verse numbers refer to the sentence and a specific word in that sentence: 1:18 means the first sentence, eighteenth word. I use the code to mark the right words.

It is apparent to everyone around me that I am taking perverse pleasure in the contemplation of **this** massive biological reversal. During the first **week** that this great symmetricism was revealed, I laughed my head off every night in front of the television. It was not just derision or amusement **or** outright glee at the reactions of the Know Nothingism **nothing** Knower creationists, Methodological Naturalists, Anti-Common Descentists, Wedge Strategists, and Macroevolution naysayers who persisted **in** denying the fundamental elegance and truth of evolution. **True**, that was very satisfying. It was more. It was awe. In spite of the hardship that a rending of the social fabric might cause for my beloved **family**, not to mention great unknowns in the area of **reverse** evolution that will probably result in mass starvation, I was and remain exhilarated. I have started reading Exodus in order to witness the working of the design: 1:18, 2:4, 3:8, 3:18, 3:32, 4:1, 7:18, 7:28, 9:9, 10:6, 13:7, 13:14, 14:11, and 14:19. The opportunity to witness the working of the **design** unraveling. The sheer thrill of the **plan** coming to light in each detail. Who says any complexity is irreducible? IT IS BEING REDUCED ALL AROUND US RIGHT NOW. I have the chance each day **to** marvel at the vast dismantling, and **escape** killing myself so that I can see more of the world's inner workings.

It should not take a biological apocalypse to cure an **Indian** man's depression, but hell, sometimes here is **paradise** on earth and there are times I just feel great.

Love, Eddy

This week or nothing in true family (reverse) design plan to escape Indian Paradise.

So whatever is going to happen, this week I will be in my true family. And wherever I'm going, I believe, it's Indian Paradise.

———

And that night, awake, there is a radiance.

Full, soft, startling, the moon hovers right outside the window.

I turn to see whether my roommate is sleeping and find instead that she is sitting up, and moreover, that she is engaged in a very interesting task. She has knotted the ends of thirty or forty strands of yarn together and she holds the knot that they spring from between her slender, bent toes. She keeps the yarn taut with her feet as she leans over the loom of strands that move through her fingers with a mechanical swiftness. She is finger-braiding. Old-time finger-weaving. Grandma Mary Virginia's trick. An Ojibwe method of creating fancy sashes, wall hangings, belts, tumplines, and ropes.

I get out of bed and walk over to her. Her face tilts up to me, her eyes wide and fathomless. She freezes, waiting. I reach across the covers and touch the sash, then point from her to me, her to me, then I clasp my hands. She nods. When she tires, I start working on the sash and from then on it is the two of us. The two of us against them all.

———

She won't tell me her name and so after that night I think of her as Spider Nun. Yes, she's pregnant, but still nunlike to me because she's so severe. But also potentially a superhero. I do not see exactly how Spider Nun and I will make it out the window, as it doesn't open but six inches, to let in air. And the only way down is straight down. We are six stories up, but there is another roof three floors beneath us. If we could get out the window, we could tie one end of our sash to the bed and rappel down the side of the building. I can imagine us, I can see us, the moon new as it will be soon, letting ourselves over the lip of the window ledge, slowly walking down the side of the building. I can see it, but I know it will take upper body strength—a problem for pregnant ladies. I look around the room and decide that I will work on my arms, lifting and setting down the chair in the corner, trying to develop enough muscle to enable me to carry, legs against the wall, my 159-plus pounds of self and baby down three stories of brick wall. That is, assuming we can get out the window. Highly doubtful, but then, no other choice presents itself.

So I keep braiding the strands, knotting with careful pressure knots, making the rope as strong as I can. As Spider Nun and I work together, one of us weaves or unravels, just beneath our bedsheets and blanket. The other is at the door, listening closely to every movement in the hallway. By now, I know each one of the nurses and can tell who is coming onto which shift. I know their names and I know as much, from friendly conversations, as they will tell me about their families, lives, origins, daily trials, and moods.

This morning, Orielee's on. I can tell by the scratching swish of her pressed uniform. She is the only one who actually starches and irons the patterned scrubs that all of the nurses wear. The fabric between her legs rubs noisily as she pads from room to room. The hospital is of course an Internet Use Zone, which means that every nurse who carries a computer has been thoroughly cleared, checked by rigorous security, found by a committee to have done nothing, ever, that could possibly be construed a threat. Orielee has let on that she consented to be investigated. She told me with an almost shy pride that anyone trusted with a computer now and access to the internet has never, ever, expressed what she calls a "new unconstitutional" idea. Has never purchased anything unusual or given any sign of owning an interior life or living by any other set of rules but the given rules. Not that the rules are posted anywhere, or listed, or described. I keep asking her. It seems they are an unspoken set of rules that some people have been living by for years, and others haven't. And those of us who didn't are now outsiders. Those who did live by those rules have power, though in many cases it is only a little power—for instance, only the privilege of typing a patient's vitals twice daily and once nightly into a computer that may or may not have a connection to the world outside of the hospital. I don't think Orielee is all that high clearance, because she talks a little too much. Today, she tells me about her own daughter's second pregnancy, about how the family brought her in right away and how her husband got to be with her throughout, how he was even there when she miscarried, "as a lot of these gals do." Since the baby was born dead, there is no point in asking what happened to the child. Orielee wouldn't go so far as to tell me what happens to any of the babies. I ask if she has a picture of her daughter's first baby, and she says, "Not on me." But then she relents, or is tempted out of sentimental pride, to show me a photograph of her daughter's first child, her two-and-a-half-year-old granddaughter.

"My only," she says, "I guess."

And I jump on that to say, "Wouldn't they let your daughter keep the baby next time, if she didn't miscarry? Since she turned herself in right away, I mean? And since the baby's, you know, so cute?"

Orielee shakes her head, sighs, does not answer.

"Let's get your blood pressure, hon. Sit still."

An automatic cuff squeezes my upper arm, holds on for a moment, threatful and impersonal, and then lets go.

"Your pressure's good, hon."

"Could you see if I can get my books returned?"

"Sure."

"Really, could you? I need them. They're religious."

"Oh, that's right. You told me yesterday. I'll look."

That's as much as I dare push. I don't have much hope. But Orie-lee surprises me just before she leaves her shift by bringing in my books and setting them down on my bedside table. I am so happy to see my books and even my envelope of the unfinished issue of *Zeal* that I feel my whole face breaking into a big, fat, beatific smile.

"Oh gosh, somebody's happy," says Orielee.

"Where were they?"

"They were just mislaid, you know. They always were okay, I mean, one's by a monk and the rest are about saints. Except for the *Mad.*"

Orielee's face never moves but her laugh is a burbling little chuckle, like the noise water makes under ice. She spooks me—simultaneously way too friendly, then her eyes so calculating and her laugh so odd. Her laugh is what I do not trust. It's cold, the real her. She might be trying to win my trust so that she can rat me out.

Like Phil.

"Thanks!"

I don't dare thank her too much, either. I don't dare let her know how much these books mean to me—sanity, other intimate voices, other perilous survivals. I immediately open St. John of the Cross's *Dark Night of the Soul*, and read hungrily. The first lines quiet me. *On a dark night, kindled in love with yearning—oh, happy chance—I went forth without being observed, my house being now at rest. In darkness and secure, by the secret ladder, disguised—oh, happy chance. In darkness and concealment, my house being now at rest. In the happy night, in secret, where none saw me, nor I beheld naught. Without light or guide, save that which burned in my breast.*

Over and over, as I pick apart and wind, unknot, unravel, wind, by the inch, by the hour, by the piece, by the skein, my freedom and your life, I repeat these lines that seem so perfect to me. I'm working on *the secret ladder*. St. John's words bring me peace. For it shall be as it was, I think. The meek shall inherit the earth, the undone shall take it over, the backward shall take it back, the unformed and ancient shall form it new.

OCTOBER 13

I find out that Spider Nun flushes her vitamin too; actually, she holds it somewhere in her throat and then coughs it into a Kleenex when the nurse leaves. She wads up the Kleenex, puts it under her pillow, and then smiles at me with an alert, even-tempered sweetness. Later, she flushes the pill. She's a *dear*, say the nurses. Spider Nun keeps the balls of yarn in the mechanism of the bed, underneath her mattress. I quickly see why she has begun to weave the balls of yarn so quickly into sash or rope. The yarn balls are difficult to hide, awkward, unruly, ready to roll out unexpectedly and reveal us, while the rope itself need only be thrust between the pillow and pillowcase, or even, in an emergency, rolled up and stuffed inside of our nightgowns. So just as soon as we can, we turn the blankets to yarn, then to rope. She has done about six feet already, and I've finished two on the rope, taking turns. We've worked most of the night weaving what yarn we had, then picking apart our respective blankets, winding again, weaving, so that by morning we're in need and cannot ask for blankets again since the same nurse, Geri, on today, gave us the blankets the day before yesterday.

Geri is a little slow—one of those soft, brown-haired women with melting eyes who registers things a beat behind normal, and gets things wrong, and is forever being told what to do by the other nurses. She often seems to exasperate them and might, in fact, be the one nurse we could actually get away with asking for more blankets as she could easily forget she gave us two already. But I think that we should save her for an emergency, and I indicate that I'll go out into the hall and try to take the blankets on my two or three times daily walk.

First, though, we hide our rope in the safest place we can find, inside the heating duct along with your notebook. I use the nail file I'd tucked into the seam of my backpack to screw and unscrew the duct plate. Then I press the nail file into a crack where the bathroom mirror meets the wall. Sometimes Spider Nun puts the rope into her pillowcase—if it isn't the day that they change the bed linens on our side of the hall. Spider Nun has nothing to do until I return with the blankets, and I can see this bothers her. Her expression's worried, jumpy. She pulls at her hair, sniffles, stares out the window, nods anxiously at me.

"She's up and about," says Geri, popping into the room. Geri has an annoying habit of referring to everyone around her in the third person. Perhaps it serves to distance her from her patients.

"Yup." I'm pleasant, chipper.

"Is she wearing her slippers? Oh, what a good preggerpot she is!"

I want to deck Geri for calling me a preggerpot, that or fall down laughing. Preggerpot! Behind Geri's back, Spider Nun's cute look turns poisonous. Could she be outraged on my behalf? Gives me the warm fuzzies.

We are supposed to wear our sticky green foam hospital booties everywhere, to prevent falls and the spread of foot diseases. And yes, like a good preggerpot, I've got mine on. Like elf shoes, they come to a little point in the front. The elastic cuts my instep. I wish I had a pair of polar fleece socks, some really nice booties, lamb's wool, maybe real moccasins like Grandma Virginia. I shuffle off in my flimsy nightgown and voluminous, lightweight hospital robe. The hall is bright. Sunlight enters either end from tall banks of shatterproof windows. I know they are impossible to break, because I've stood near, looking out. I noticed that the windows are actually double thick with a sandwich of extremely fine wire running diamond-patterned in between. This may have been the Psych Ward before—which would also explain our window's re-stricted openings, though I think that is standard in hospitals and maybe in hotels now, too.

The handsome Somali man, who seems to have forgiven me for sitting on him, smiles as I pass. I greet him and ask after his wife, who is apparently responsible for preparing our awful food on some days.

"Oh, she's good," he says. I've asked his name, but he won't tell me. Still, I continue to believe that he is sympathetic to us and that we might test his sympathies even further somehow—without endangering our plan. He works nights next week and might look the other way. He might, at least, go along with a diversion when we break the glass of our window. I do not have a plan for how we're going to do that, exactly. I'm not sure that anything that my roommate and I can actually lift together is heavy enough to shatter that window. It is not, however, a part of the plan that we can try out beforehand.

Our friend pushes the canvas-bag-hung laundry cart just outside the door to the room, and brings out an armload of dirty sheets, pillowcases, and blankets. With a polite gesture to me, he leaves the blankets on top, then goes back into the room. Geri is on her way down the hall, though. She pauses, her brown eyes lowered conscientiously to her computer. She goes into a patient's room, but the hall is still not safe. Farther down, a couple of nurses are immersed in a conversation. One nurse I do not know, and the other I call the Slider. She is the most dangerous of all of them, the sneakiest; I never hear her footsteps, only a sliding hiss as she enters the room.

I must keep walking. I can't appear to hover near the laundry cart. I step toward the two nurses, holding a hand to the small of my back, as though I've got the usual pregnant-lady backache, though I'm lucky and do not. The Slider notices me and turns to her fellow nurse—obviously they've been discussing a patient, a procedure, something I am not meant to hear. They watch me pass. The Slider's eyes are deep-set and shiny as black ants. The nurses resume their conversation, then halt abruptly when I turn and walk by them again. I smile, moan a little, holding my back, take another turn, walk away. Impatient, they let themselves into the nurse's pantry, where they keep a refrigerator full of snacks, a machine that sometimes produces ice, and a warming oven that keeps blankets heated up for those who are soon to deliver their babies.

The corridor is now empty and I make my move. I control my walk and approach the cart at a normal pace, recheck the hallway quickly, snatch two blankets, and ball them under my arms and against you. My heart rate goes up and I feel a buzz. You kick, hard. I waddle back to my room, enter, pull the privacy curtain, and stuff one of the blankets beneath my roommate's sheet. Spider Nun smiles in excitement, her teeth even and white as a little girl's milk teeth. At once, she begins her work of undoing. I settle into my bed and beneath the screen of the other blanket I start unraveling.

Winding yarn reminds me of my knitting days at Waldorf school, and how we learned to neatly ball up the yarn and undo the skeins, how it felt to knit all together in a room, singing, in our classroom with the fairy-pink walls and rosette ceiling. I made a scarf. I think Sera's still got it—she was thrilled that I'd made it of her favorite color at the time. Black. They let a child knit with black! It looks so pretty with her pale hair. Now it is surely put away somewhere, in our house which is inhabited by the people who did things properly in the world as it was before, and who have inherited it now. While we are working, we keep the television off so that we can listen for people approaching in the hall. Spider Nun has a watch and soon indicates that lunchtime has arrived. We put away our work and pretend to be absorbed in a show I've clicked on—a continuous tape of a documentary movie about the reproductive lives of penguins—which we've seen already dozens of times. When lunch comes, we eat it all, swiftly, trying to absorb nutrition before we actually taste the food. I take the trays back out to the lunch cart and we return to our room. The bustle of lunch subsides. We wait for a vitals check. The Slider enters, her feet sighing along the floor. Her flossy brown hair is set in Victorian doll ringlets around a wrathful, pinched face. When she speaks I am so frightened I'll betray something that I fix my eyes on her hard lipsticked orange mouth. Her thin shoulders hunch and her glittery black eyes drill me. Even her voice sounds clenched. She takes our pulse, blood pressure, temperature, all in silence, now, frowning. Blood samples. Urine samples. All collected. She decides for some reason to check the pupils of our eyes with a little flashlight, and to take bits of nail clippings. She snips a strand of hair from each of our heads and seals it into an envelope, fills out a label on the envelope.

"So what are you taking all of these little bits for?" I can't help asking. "Are you making voodoo dolls?"

The Slider's eyes go harder, trying to squash me, but I fade away, intentionally lose focus.

"Or maybe you're putting together a Frankenwoman. Is it a cloning thing? C'mon, these are my bits. I want to know!"

She ignores me, which is good, I shouldn't speak at all. Try to stay inconspicuous. Draw no attention. Don't laugh. She asks the usual questions about fetal movement, and carefully records my answers. Spider Nun doesn't say a word, but the Slider jots things down anyway. All of a sudden, the Slider jerks back Spider Nun's bedcovers, as if she'd find a baby hidden there! I hold my breath, sure she'll find the half-picked-apart blanket. But my roomie has cleverly positioned the blanket underneath the top, intact, waffle-weave blanket, and the blankets stick together. There is nothing out of the ordinary. Panicked anyway, I pretend I'm sleepy and yawn, then cry out to distract the Slider.

"Is it normal to sleep all of the time like this?" I ask her. As she turns to answer me, the ball of yarn Spider Nun was just working on slowly rolls from under her pillow and bounces off the bed, then begins to roll across the floor toward the Slider's feet. I yell up at the ceiling.

"Ow!"

"Ow, what?"

"The baby just kicked me real hard. Ow! Again! Feel!"

The Slider comes to me and bends over my bed. She moves her stiff, hard little hand across my belly. Pauses. I feel you shrink away from her hand—so dry, white, and cold. Meanwhile, Spider Nun creeps from the bed, following the unrolling ball of cotton yarn. It meanders between our two beds and then stops just behind the Slider's feet.

"I don't feel anything," the Slider says.

"Wait! Here!"

Obligingly, you shift and turn. I yell again.

"That's normal." She sneers. "You're full of juice today, aren't you, dear. If you can't calm down, I'll be glad to order you a sedative. Would you like me to put a request in to your doctor?"

"Who *is* my doctor?" I ask.

Spider Nun has crept behind her, and now snatches up the yarn. I grab the Slider's hand.

"Don't worry," I cry out, passionately. "Really, I'm fine."

She wrests her hand away. Whirls around. Spider Nun's back in bed, covered up, looking indeterminately sad. She has this profound, tragic, silent stare that she sometimes directs into space and from which she will not be distracted. The Slider doesn't even try. She just gathers up all of our body samples and departs. We turn off the penguin channel and drowse, waiting to see if she returns. We sleep an hour, two. We need to sleep during the day so that we can stay up weaving all night.

OCTOBER 14

We are at twenty feet now, and you're getting so big that I've got to get out of here. You're pushing on my lungs, and I'm breathing hard and quick. If I don't move around enough, one side of my butt goes numb. Got to leave! We measured our rope last night by laying out the rope on the floor—I have size-ten feet and can pretty well work out the length by walking the rope. I figure that we want twelve feet for each story, and an extra eight for the piece we tie to the bed legs. There can't be much of a drop at the end. We can't afford too much of a jolt, we are afraid of hurting our babies. At least, I assume that Spider Nun feels the same as me.

Orielee comes in and wakes me for another ultrasound but first she takes my blood. I get my blood drawn every day, but Spider Nun gets hers taken twice a day, which alarms me. She's so small that it seems to me that she must need every drop she's got.

"I don't mind having my blood drawn," I say to Orielee as she ties an amber rubber tourniquet around my upper arm and snaps at my veins, to make them rise, "but can't you say something about my roommate? She's getting her blood drawn twice a day. It's too much! And anyway, what are they doing with all of this blood? Drinking it?"

"Well, I guess they're checking it," says Orielee. "And yeah, it says here I'm supposed to do her. Poor little thing, says here she's not gaining a bit of weight. It does seem like a lot."

Orielee bites her lip and shakes her head as she looks at Spider Nun, but her sympathy is so exaggerated it seems false.

"Why don't you just take a little extra from me," I say, "and leave her alone? Can't you see how weak she's getting?"

Orielee sighs and presses the needle in. She's very good, and does it so lightly that it hardly hurts.

"That's sure nice of you, but I can't do that."

"But she's getting weak!"

"And between you and me," says Orielee, "I've seen where some of this blood we take they never even look at."

"You mean it goes to waste? Nobody even drinks it?"

"I shouldn't say, but yeah, I mean no. It goes to waste. Still, I could lose my job substituting blood, and sometimes they do check."

"Who's they?"

"Researchers." She gestures vaguely out the window, toward the bridge over the Mississippi where all day people are still passing between the campuses.

"The U's still going?"

"Most things are still going," says Orielee. "But they're making lots of different rules. New rules all of the time. A person has to be so careful."

"Not to break the rules?"

"Yes."

I rush into a set of lies.

"And sometimes you don't even know what they are! Like me, I didn't know I was supposed to turn myself in, I had no idea."

"How couldn't you?" Orielee seems astonished. "It was all over the place, still is. Ads, even billboards and stuff. You couldn't miss it!"

"Yes, you could," I lie some more. "I don't read the papers and don't watch the news. I was happy, but I was sick a lot, too, so I stayed indoors or sat out on the porch. People saw me all of the time and nobody said anything. Nobody turned me in."

"Well . . ." She looks at me doubtfully.

"Well, what? I mean, they just came and got me. But nobody actually turned me in, I don't think."

"They . . ."

Orielee's eyes are very round and maybe even a bit teary at the corners. She wants to tell me something.

"Maybe . . . ," she softly says. I wait. She takes a deep breath and looks quickly at the door, then at Spider Nun, who is sitting straight up in her bed with her eyes closed, apparently meditating.

"There was this man," says Orielee, "who was helping lots of women hide, I guess, and they got him. I think I heard they followed him to where you live. So he was helping you, too, right? It's okay, understandable really, it was just his belief, you know, to hide the women. But they got lots of names from this guy." Her eyes are round, very round, and her mouth makes a little *o* before she says, "Because they can do that, you know, with their persuading methodologies. Everybody talks."

OCTOBER 15

Last night, I picked apart an entire blanket and saved it carefully and stayed up weaving through the long hours until dawn. Tears leaked out of my eyes as I worked. My fingers started to chafe and bleed. Spider Nun finally took the rope from my hand. The adrenaline wore off and I collapsed. I slept all of this morning and tried to continue sleeping on into the silence of my heart. But I am awake. There is nothing but Phil's face and my face and Phil's hand and my hand and Phil's heart and my heart and the old, old, words *What have they done to you?* I open Thomas Merton's *Raids on the Unspeakable.*

Into this world, this demented inn, in which there is absolutely no room for Him at all, Christ has come uninvited. But because He cannot be at home in it, because He is out of place in it, and yet He must be in it, His place is with those who do not belong, who are rejected by power because they are regarded as weak, those who are discredited, who are denied the status of persons, tortured, exterminated. With those for whom there is no room, Christ is present in this world. He is mysteriously present in those for whom there seems to be nothing but the world at its worst.

In this thought, at last, I find a scrap of comfort. I have always believed in a tortured god from reading Catholic history because I know this: there is nothing that one human being will not do to another. We need a god who sides with the wretched. One willing to share misery. I keep on winding, and weaving; my rope twists in my hands. It is near lunchtime and I put my ball of yarn beneath the covers. I compose myself and wait. Spider Nun waits, too, consulting her watch. Soon enough, we hear the rattle of the lunch cart, the tiers of plastic trays bearing sludge, and we pretend to be asleep. The door opens. I look up. When I see who holds the lunch tray my brain skips. Sera sets the tray on my bedside table and cautions me with a look, but she can't help it, either. Can't help being suddenly overcome.

I put my hands over my mouth, but tears start up in my eyes and I cry out, muffled, "Mom." Sera looks at Spider Nun.

"She's okay."

"I don't have much time." Sera wipes at her face, fiercely whispers. "Look, I'll be here tomorrow. I'm with Jessie. Don't try and talk to her though."

"Where's Dad? Where's Phil?"

"Your dad's okay. . . ." She hesitates.

"Phil?"

"We don't know."

"Get us blankets, Mom." I pull back the covers and show her a glimpse of the woven rope. "Have Jessie get us blankets. Our rope is nearly long enough. We need help getting out though. Somebody's got to help us break a window."

The other food delivery woman sticks her head in the room. "C'mon!"

"Okay," says Sera, loudly, grinning at us. "This is going to make it easier," she whispers. She's amazed at our work and I am as proud as a preschooler. She turns away, and I'm swept through with such a sense of desperate love I can hardly help from crying out, begging her to stay with me. Her silver fairy hair is caught up in a net. She has lost weight, she is angular. She turns to glance at me over her shoulder and I see that she has her capable face on, the face she wore on my two emergency-room visits, the face of packing the car for a vacation, the face I saw during Glen's idiotic affair, the face of Thanksgiving dinner preparations for thirty people and the face of teacher's conferences. It is the face that got me into college and the face that got Glen out of jail after many an arrest during protests. The face of *I'll take care of it*. The face of *failure is not an option*. The face of the household general. I breathe a long, deep sigh and eat every bit of my lunch.

OCTOBER 16

Two orderlies walk me down to ultrasound again. The same attendants are always there. They treat me with great kindness, impersonal serenity, but no matter how hard I beg they will not let me see you. They will not turn my pallet, or bed, to the screen.

"No, darling, no, hush now." They stroke my hair and fuss with my threadbare bare-ass hospital gown. They are used to women pleading with them, I suppose.

"How far along?" I say. "Healthy? Boy or girl?"

"Healthy, oh, very," says the brown-haired woman. But she will not let me know how far along your body has progressed, how big or small you are, how close to what they call viable. Afterward, I try to question Orielee.

"Tell me. Please. I know it's on the chart," I say, but on this she is adamant. She won't even give me a hint.

"I'd lose my job and probably my clearance," she says. "Give me a break." She also says that she is sorry and that she'd want to know, too, but at least she doesn't take Spider Nun's blood.

"I'll make up some excuse."

Spider Nun nods at me in relief as she rolls the sleeve of her hospital robe back down. Her eyes are deep with meaning. She keeps staring at me. I know that she wants to speak—but maybe she really is voiceless and hasn't the power. We now have nearly thirty-two feet of rope, and it is very difficult to hide. It is so chancy, now, that we won't dare work on it except in the darkest and quietest hours of the night. So we'll get less done. Today we pick apart as much as we can, and wind the yarn. Our hands are a problem, cracked and raw, dry from the hospital air and we use up all the hand lotion they give us. We don't want to raise suspicion by asking for more. But even worse than lotion I miss lip balm. I remember the days when I had three or four tubes going at a time. On my desk, in my pocket, in my purse. My lips are so parched I can't take it anymore. I go out on my usual walk and loiter near the front desk until Jessie sweeps out from the interior back office with a pile of charts. I shouldn't bother her, it's dangerous, but I can't help myself.

"Could I please have some lip balm?"

"I don't have any. Ask your nurse," she snaps. Her eyes are telling me to back off. "She's right behind you."

"You need something?"

It's the Slider, whose approach was so quiet and unnerving that I jump a little in my skin.

I use my meekest voice. "I'm sorry. I just wanted some lip balm. Or maybe Vaseline."

The Slider's mouth twists. "We're not a spa. We're trying to keep you alive so you can have your baby safely. Here, not out there." She tips her head savagely toward the window at the end of the hall, the shatterproof glass.

"There are lots of women dying out there, who don't turn themselves in. Your babies aren't easy to deliver." She opens a cabinet, reaches behind some files, pulls a small plastic tub from what must be a secret stash.

"Thanks." I put it in the pocket of my robe and keep my fist jammed around it. The Slider has her own obscure reasons for trying to scare us. There is no reason you'll be any more difficult to deliver than a regular baby, that I know of anyway. Still, her comment nags at me. She gets to me. Even if we escape, I have no idea where we'll go, how we will elude recapture once we're out. I've always heard that convicts who plan long-term and elaborate escapes from prison are, on the whole, easy to recapture and rarely stay free more than a couple of weeks. It's the afterward, the impossibility of hiding anywhere you haven't already been—that's the hard thing.

The little tub turns out to be menthol rub. It's useless, but we take turns smelling it. Sera doesn't bring the lunch tray, but maybe she's on duty for dinner. We fall asleep for the afternoon in our dim, serene, horribly ugly but deceptively safe little room. My sleep during the day is always deep and dramatic. I have vivid dreams that seem so real they could be visions or events. Today, Grandma Virginia visits me again, and in the dream she helps measure my rope. "Take a rest," she says. "Anweb. I'll do some." Her crooked little fingers jump and fly along the cords. "Watch out for the husky one," she says. "She's worse than the Slider." She means Orielee, the one I was beginning to trust. And sure enough, when we wake up, Orielee's come to change the linen on an unscheduled day and at a very odd time. So it is just luck that we decided to hide the rope in the heat duct before we went to sleep.

Cheerful, bustling, Orielee tears off the sheets and shakes the pillows out of their cases. She pretends to clean under the mattresses, examining them minutely, making sure the seams are sewn, the undersides intact. She checks our little closet, patting it all over inside, and she opens and shuts the window curtains as if some sort of contraband might fall out. She goes into the bathroom, and I hear the clank of ceramic as she opens the toilet tank. The only place she doesn't check is the heating vent. I screwed it back on, as usual, with the nail file, then hid the nail file. She finds it wedged behind the bathroom mirror—not actually a glass mirror, but a polished piece of stainless steel.

"I'm going to have to take this," she says, emerging from the bathroom. Her voice is sweetly regretful, but contains a partly hidden glee, and I'm relieved that I never did entirely trust her. Orielee twists the nail file in the air.

"How come you were hiding this?"

"Where'd you get that?" I say. "I could use a nail file."

Orielee pockets the file. But she steps near and tries, casually, to spot the condition of my fingernails. My hands are spread on the blanket and my fingernails show—ragged, torn. The file was never worth using to shape them.

"Maybe it belonged to Agnes," I tell her. "Please, can't I have it? I need something for these!" I wiggle my fingers at her. I feel a twinge of betrayal at blaming Agnes, but then I think how much she'd have wanted to help us escape. I think of her blood-red, chipped, sexy nails. Without the file, what will I use to screw and unscrew the heating vent plate? I try not to think about this until Orielee's left the room, and once she does, I look at Spider Nun, miming dismay. She looks back at me, her mouth a delicate bow. She holds out her hand, fingers splayed as though to show off a brand-new manicure. She's let the nails of both of her pointer fingers grow long, saving them somehow even during the weaving, or maybe using them to knot or cut bits of yarn. I am skeptical, but later that night, when all is quiet, she adeptly uses her finger to screw and then unscrew the vent plate.

I laugh. "What I wouldn't give to have your nails!"

She just smiles again. Sera didn't come at dinner, either, and I'm just hoping she's on in the morning and can make it to our room. We work all night, me and my friend Spider Nun. I like watching her, like just being around her. I wonder if I will ever know her name.

OCTOBER 17

Morning, and Sera still doesn't come. I am worried that the routine here is disorienting me, even though I've become adept at getting rid of my vitamins. We have only eight feet left to do on the rope. But I'm so terrified that we will be discovered and our rope confiscated that I decide this must be the last night we work. I now convince myself that a slight drop at the end is less hazardous than losing our chance to escape altogether. And Spider Nun is looking so terribly worn out, so weak and so skinny, that I am afraid if we wait much longer she won't have the strength to lower herself down the side of the building. Before noon, the Slider comes in and jabs us, takes our blood, pee, more nail clippings, swabs from our mouths and noses. She weighs us and listens to our babies, jotting long notes into her computer. The Slider hardly speaks to us while she is performing these tasks, but I'm happy because I'm hoping that if she is on today and Geri is on tonight, then Jessie will be on tomorrow after midnight. The nineteenth. The date in Eddy's letter.

Noon. Sera brings our lunch trays. Two of them. One tray contains our food. The other tray is covered. She says, "Hide all of this and look at it later." She gives me a piece of paper, which I slip into my bra. Then she swiftly kisses me, holding my face a moment in her cool, winter-mom hands. As she leaves, I feel her fade from me. Under the green towel on one of the trays, there is a hammer, a sort of folding cane, and a tiny old-fashioned tape recorder with an actual tape in it. So Sera and Glen, to go vintage. There are also four Power Bars. What these things have to do with our escape, I can't tell. But Spider Nun quickly unscrews the heat vent, I put them in, and we divide the food onto two trays. We eat every bite—a mushy spaghetti with indeterminate meat in the sauce. Powdered milk. Congealed cornstarch pudding, butterscotch or maybe just scorched. After our check, I go into the bathroom and read the note from Sera. *You can eat this*, says the last line, *it's sweet rice paper and the ink is nontoxic!* I want to laugh, but I do eat the escape instructions, and they're pretty tasty.

Spider Nun and I sleep away the afternoon. I wake once and look over at her face, so pure in repose. Her forehead is like a river stone, moon warm, shining with light. I am so anxious that I cannot sleep and so I watch the sky deepen. The sun goes down, fiercely, casting radiance from the west into the eastern sky, where it edges the clouds with a blaze of gold lace.

Dear baby, I want you to see this world, supernal, lovely. I want this world to fill your eyes.

We take turns, one sitting by the door and listening to the noise in the hallway, the other weaving the rope. The one by the door stands up when someone's coming, and the weaver hides the rope. If it looks as though someone might come in the door, the lookout jumps into bed and the weaver pretends to sleep, too. This happens about a dozen times tonight and helps to keep us awake. The night is long, though, and writing this also helps me to stay alert. Also, if I'm falling asleep I panic trying to think of what we will do once we are really out of here.

I have a pretty good idea what would happen to us if we stayed. They would take you. They would study you. And as for me, I would first have to survive your delivery, and plenty of women do not. They die during anesthesia, I think, especially if, like Agnes Starr, they make trouble. But even if I did survive your delivery, I might not be set free. There are rumors. Early on, we heard about Womb Volunteers, but maybe there were not enough of them and so there is talk of a female draft now. I've overheard snippets of conversation. Women are being forced to try and carry to term a frozen embryo from the old in-vitro clinics. That or be inseminated with sperm from the old sperm banks. I don't know whether to believe these things, but here I am.

Thinking.

Evolution starts: a miracle. Evolution stops: a miracle. Life follows the pattern of the vastness all around us. The universe is expanding and contracting in timeless time. The earth 4.5 billion years old, the sun due to supernova and swallow us. And then contract again. Well, that's what I think, and I am obviously only a lay observer of the great mystery, the simple *why*, which no scientist can answer any better than me.

We get our rope to what seems long enough, almost. We fork the end so there are two long, tough ribbons of rope to fasten to the leg of the bed. Then we practice the knot, over and over, with variations, until we can do it with our eyes closed and are sure it won't slip.

OCTOBER 19

Our last day in the hospital. In the morning, we sleep as long as we can, preparing for the night. Later, Spider Nun rips four or five long, thick strips from a stolen hospital gown. She is going to use the gown to make a bundle, the contents of her suitcase. I will use my backpack for my own few things—the books, your blankets and newborn clothes. My jeans and Phil's shirt I'll wear underneath the robe. I'll wear the jacket I brought, but carry the shoes in the pack. My sticky green elf booties will be perfect for walking down the wall. We manage to choke down our lunch. Everything goes well, no hitches. We even take a nap. Yes, everything goes perfectly until the nurses are about to change shifts. Then Orielee comes in.

Even though I tell her that the Slider did all of this today, she writes down everything, our vitals, the works. She extracts blood, does cheek swabs, cuts our hair again and tucks the strands into little envelopes. She tidies everything up on the tray and she is about to leave when she glances down at the heating vent, focuses, and frowns at it thoughtfully.

"Orielee, can I ask you something?" I want to distract her, but she refuses to hear me.

"Hey!"

She stares still more intently at the heating vent, then gets up, walks over, and creakingly kneels down to peer inside. Spider Nun and I get out of bed. Orielee pants to her feet and turns to us. Just the fact that we are standing there, stupidly panicked, confirms everything. Her face is neutral, she isn't letting on what she will do, but as Orielee walks away from us to the door she gives that mirthless little gurgle, her laugh. As soon as she does, Spider Nun springs behind her and lightly swings that strap of cloth torn from her hospital gown over Orielee's head. She jerks it tight, from behind, so quickly that Orielee's feet go out from under her and she is down, sitting on the floor, her center of gravity tipping her back as Spider Nun twists the material. Tighter. Tighter. Orielee's face flushes to a deep red. She throws up her hands, flailing them around to grab Spider Nun, who is on her knees behind Orielee, still twisting.

"Fucksake! Little help?" says my roommate through gritted teeth. She flashes her eyes at me. Her thin arms are straining to contain the big woman's energetic bucking.

That's when I do the thing that will send me to hell. I jump down off the bed and grab Orielee's hands and twist them behind her, fast in my grip. She rolls over, kicking and drumming her feet. I throw myself over her, sideways, to hold her down. Spider Nun keeps twisting with both fists, more, tighter, until Orielee's eyes and tongue pop out and her face goes purple. Our faces are almost as rigid and horrible as hers. I'm on top, now, so I see her eyes. The wild, penetrating look, her irises pinpointing me, blood seeping into the corners of her lids and bloody tears running down alongside her nose. At last her legs relax and splay open and she is dead.

Spider Nun falls over gasping and gagging for air. I shake a pillow out of its case and pull the case down over Orielee's head, so there is just her body to contend with. That's bad enough. I am riveted by Orielee's Garfield-print scrubs jacket with cartoon panels of Garfield looking at a volcano, Garfield in a jungle, Garfield bored, with a book in his paws, Garfield critical of a houseplant.

The only thing for me to do is treat the fact that Spider Nun spoke as normal, along with the fact that we have killed Orielee. Normal.

"Let's try and fit her into the closet," says Spider Nun.

We take all of our things out of the closet, then we try to hoist Orielee in through the double door. We prop her up inside and tie her onto the clothes hooks using another strip of hospital gown. We latch the door tightly. Orielee hadn't picked up the tray of our samples and put it back on the cart yet. So we do that. We put the cart in the hall outside of the room. We're both dizzy, so we stagger back to our beds and throw ourselves under the blankets. Half an hour passes. We are numb, buzzing. There is a sick thump, a straining creak, as Orielee's body settles inside the closet. We hear a nurse come by and say, "Oh, *here's* her tray. She must have checked out early. It's her birthday." We hear them wheel away the cart. There is silence.

Spider Nun and I turn slowly to look at each other.

"So what's your name?" I ask her. "I'm tired of calling you Spider Nun."

"You called me that?" She doesn't smile, but her voice goes from dazed to amused. "My name's Tia Jackson."

"Tia? Jackson?"

"My family has been here for six generations," she says with hardened indignation, "probably longer than . . . oh, forget it. Ha. I forgot you're an Indian."

"Right."

"Do you feel awful?" she says after a while.

"Not yet. I'm probably still in shock or something."

"Yeah."

"How come you never spoke?"

"First law of capture. Never let them know you know their language."

That seems like very good thinking, and I ask if Tia's learned anything.

"Well, besides the land bridge theory, which oh my god you went on about forever? I do hear stuff. They don't kill them, anyway." She touches her stomach, gently. "The ones born alive so far are more physically adept. They grab things earlier, walk sooner. They are bigger. Nobody knows about speech. Not that many have, you know, spoken so far."

"I assumed that they studied them," I said.

"Let's not go there," says Tia.

"Did they really kill all of the prisoners?"

"It depended on what they were charged with. Some of them were trained as bounty hunters and sent to find us. One of them found me. Was that your mom who gave us lunch?"

"Yes. Why didn't you at least talk to me?"

"You could have inadvertently given me away."

"So are you ready?"

"I am so very ready," says Tia Jackson. "And you, are you going to tell me what was on that piece of paper you ate?"

I tell her. After a while they bring dinner and we try to choke down everything. They take away the dinner trays. Again we are alone in the room, in the silence. I can't help looking at the closet, and neither can Tia.

"It was her birthday," she says.

We spend some time sitting very still, trying not to throw up the food we've eaten, food we need to sustain us during our escape.

"We shouldn't talk about her," I say at last. "We should talk about other things. What were you before?"

"Designer," says Tia. "Textile patterns. I get ideas all of the time. I work fast."

"Married?"

"Yes, but I took my ring off, threw it under a bush. I know exactly where. I'm going back for it. I didn't want them to have anything."

"Where did they catch you?"

"Outside my studio."

"Does your husband know where you are?"

"I don't know," says Tia. She shakes her head and turns away from me, more emotional than I've ever seen her. "I just don't know." Her voice is thin.

"If you go home, it's the first place they'll look."

She just nods, resting her forehead on her clasped hands, on her knees.

"It's hard now that I can talk to you," she says. "Before, it wasn't so real."

"Pretend like it still isn't real," I say.

But the hours drag on, so slow. I read out loud to her from *Is That in the Bible? Where did Hebrews wear kilts? What man wore a hat trimmed with blue lace? Who gave soup to an angel? Who went fishing naked? Who ate a mouse behind a tree? Who thought his conscience was in his kidneys?* There is a Bible verse to answer each question. First Chronicles 19:4. Hanun does this to David's servants. Exodus 28:37–38. Aaron wears one. Gideon, Judges 6:19. Peter, John 20:7. Sacred mice are mentioned several places in the Bible. The Psalmist: "Thus my heart was grieved and I was pricked in my reins" (kidneys).

We become hysterical, breathless with fear of what we are about to do and what we have done. We eat one Power Bar each, holding each little pinch on our tongues—a taste out of the world of before. Then at last we hear it, the scream from the other end of the hall, the patter and slam of panic, running, the diversion that our friend has devised to shield the sound of breaking glass.

We shut the door, set the odd, canelike gadget under the door handle. I start the little tape recorder with the volume turned all the way up. There will be eight minutes of silence and then voices will start responding to anybody trying to open the door, so that nobody thinks we're gone yet. Tia gets our clothes and packs and I take the hammer out from under my pillow and begin to smash the window. It doesn't break into jagged pieces, but with about the sixth blow it turns into a web of glass pebbles and just comes apart, tumbling out of the frame and down the side of the building. There's a wild rush of air. The lights on the towers glitter in the clear night. The two of us tie the rope to the leg of Tia's bed, pushed tight against the wall, and we throw the rope out the window. It slithers down, nearly touching the roof of the floor below, I think. It's long enough.

The air rushing in is excitingly cool, delicious. We are used to the stable indoor air of the hospital. We've got the clothes we came in underneath our hospital gowns—my jeans slide dangerously down my hips, completely unzipped now. I need suspenders. Tia's got her possessions bound onto her back—the tiny layette, her few extra clothes. I am not being all that altruistic. Letting her go first is the only thing to do. She's much lighter. If I break the rope somehow or the knot won't hold, that's two of us who won't escape. There is no moonlight, and except for the lights on top of the radio towers, just a few places illuminated below us. The city is dark now, mostly, and the bridge across the river ghostly black. The Mississippi glistens like an oiled muscle. Tia says, "Here I go." She carries her baby gracefully, a compact slope of belly, and as she climbs up and balances on the sill she looks nimble as a dancer, and eager.

"Wait!" I say. "All the glass!"

I put a pillow under the place where the rope will pull taut going over the edge, so it won't fray. Smiling at me, Tia sets her legs on either side of the rope and then edges out and over the ledge of the window. I secure my pack, kneel on the sill and radiator, looking over. I watch her teeter down the wall, carefully, but quickly as she can, too. When she's about halfway down there is a knock on the door. Then a crunch as someone tries to open it. I tap the rope to let her know, and she scrambles down more quickly. I hear a thunk and the rope bounces up—I am afraid she fell hard at the end. I am over the edge quick as I can get there, braced at the side of the brick building. As I take the first steps down, I hear pounding and the tape recorder switches on. Sera's voice, very loud, on the edge of panic. "Wait a sec, something's jammed! Okay, I'm trying, too." And so on. The stick jammed against the door is one of those instant security locks that you can take to a cheap motel. Intruder safe. I can only hope that it will hold.

The Power Bar and the adrenaline make it easy for me, at first, and I glide down scarcely thinking of the height, which is good. About halfway down, I get dizzy and have to pause, cling to the rope, and brace myself against the wall. I look down inadvertently, or not exactly down, but over my shoulder across the river, which is worse. Because I'm just a big-bellied spider on a string and my arms are shaking. The sky's so big, so dark, and there is nothing between me and the roof below, except this braided rope. I think of Grandma Virginia, her dry little claws, still braiding, and the scratchy breathless fever of her laugh. "I'll help you!" she says, and at the thought of her, so frail and endless, I keep going. Tia's at the bottom, holding her belly, breathing hard, silent, waiting, and when I touch down I am suddenly so drained with relief that I don't think I can move.

"C'mon!" Tia's frantic, tugging my arm. "Your mom's blocked the door open. I can see the light. Get your ass up, quick."

And so we creep along the wall until we get to the door that Sera's kept open with nothing more than a salad fork. We melt inside and start running down the stairwell. Then all of a sudden, Sera's charging up the stairs—there's something wrong. We're supposed to meet her at the bottom. She grabs us. "Move, move." And we hurtle down the last of the stairs and out to where a recycling truck idles alongside six huge green Dumpsters. We vault into the passenger's side door as the truck pulls out of the service lot. We're on the wonderful slimy floor of the cab, which smells more of feet and burnt rubber than garbage. Mom grabs us and helps us into a well behind the seat, full of clothes and tools. We feel the truck moving. The motor rumbles powerfully under and all around us. I am holding on to you, and on to Sera's shoulders, just trying to get my breath back. She strokes my hair, tells me to put on the padded coveralls, the reflective-signal-taped jacket, the helmet. Tia, curled in the seat between Sera and the driver, is rolling into the huge clothes. The helmet balances on her head, her neck a frail stalk. She grins at me.

"Shawn." The driver, a skinny, rickety man, tall with cavernously beautiful brown eyes, in his thirties, puts a hand out. He's a heron man with a big pale beak. And those eyes. You could fall into his eyes. Hands on the wheel in tattered fingerless gloves. "We're going to our new MRF, Material Recycle Facility. First stop on the underground."

As soon as he says this, fatigue hits me like a drug. I'm falling asleep, with my head against my mom's back. As I drift off, I have this feeling of sweetness and security, an ease so intense that I know it must go back to my earliest days with Sera, before I could talk or even knew whether I existed, before an I had formed into a me. There was this goodness, this care, this presence, this dozing sleep. She is still stroking my hair as I come to and the sky is a pre-dawn gray, pink lifting at the edges. We enter what Shawn calls the Merf through its gated checkpoints. There are two fairly new trailers at the entrance, at the edge of the truck parking lot. A huge garage door at the other end opens automatically, and Shawn drives us in. The outsize door closes behind us with an echoing boom and Shawn says, "It's okay now. We can get out." So we step down from the truck, dazzled. At the end of the garage, there is a partially enclosed area with a woodstove.

"Go ahead." Shawn motions past a mountain of recycled stuff toward the bathroom. "I'm gonna beef up this fire, to take the chill off. Just jump back in the shitter if the big door opens again, okay?"

Shawn stalks over to the stove, uses a can opener to neatly remove the top from a can of baked beans. He puts the can on top of the woodstove with a pair of tongs, and looks at us with his calm, melting brown eyes. I can smell the rich sauce and little white globs of pork before the stuff is even warm. We go to the bathroom, a big locker room filled with greasy coveralls and bins of stinking boots. We use the toilets and wash, just with water, not the scratchy slabs of Lava soap streaked black. Our hands are now rope-burned as well as blistered and chapped. Sera stays out with Shawn, keeping watch. Before leaving the bathroom we poke our heads out. All seems quiet.

The beans heating in their tin bean can exude a summery hot-dog fragrance. Shawn spoons out half a can each of bubbling and hissing beans, into steel bowls.

"We're safe here," says Mom. "For now."

Tia and I sit against the wall on overturned plastic tubs. We sip at each spicy brown spoonful, suck down each soft bean. You stir and roll as if you feel how good I am feeling right now. Sera brings us mugs of hot raspberry tea, and we find out the rest of the plan. Which Sera and Shawn are making up as they go along.

"Okay," says Shawn, "I'll get you back down to the post office later on today, or early tomorrow. Depending. Then we're putting you three on a mail truck running up north. Your people"—he nods at Sera—"will be up there, somewhere, you know where. I don't want to know."

I am assuming that Sera is in touch with Eddy and that he has his own plan in place for getting us farther north, deeper into the bush, maybe out to the islands in the boundary waters.

"I'm not going," says Tia.

Her pointed chin juts out, her expression is fixed. "I'm going to find my husband."

Sera nods carefully, sighs. Her eyes go a sweet, faded denim blue. Her white hair tousles from under her cap. She's such a pretty winter-spirit mom, with her pink cheeks and delicately curved, berry-sweet red lips.

"Oh, sweetheart." She takes Tia's hand. "I know how you must feel, but it's so dangerous. They'll be watching your family so closely."

"I know that he's figured something out. Even if he hasn't, I'm not going. Leave me in the post office. I'll hide out in the basement and send a message to him. He'll come and get me."

"And then what?"

"I don't know. They can't watch everybody. I just know it's going to be all right. I feel safer in the city than out in the sticks. We won't be obvious, especially once my baby's born." She strokes her lovely down slope. Smiles. She only smiled once in the hospital that I remember—the first time I stole her a blanket. I hope her child will be a girl. She wants a girl.

"Anyway, I just won't go. And you know that if I'm not committed to your plan, I'll be a drag and a danger. So let me off at the post office."

"Think it over," Sera begs. But I am quite sure that Tia, who had the idea first of braiding a rope and descending down the side of the hospital building, has made up her mind.

Shawn puts out his big, rangy, skeletal hands. "Let's just all think about it. Talk it over. We've got some time. Cookie?" He opens a battered package of macaroons—stale and utterly delicious.

Shawn brings us back to an equipment storage area and shows us a walled-off secret room, just behind two giant sorting machines. One conveyor pulls off soup cans with magnets. Another shoots aluminum cans down a chute using what Shawn calls an eddy current. The secret room is filled with drums of food, he says, scavenged stuff. You'd be surprised what people still toss into the recycle bins. Behind the drums, there's a little nest of patched mattresses and couch pillows covered with heavy subzero sleeping bags.

"Okay, you two," says Shawn, "cuddle in. Your mom's got some heavy-duty paperwork to attend to. You'll be safe here. This whole compound's guarded." He puts his hands in his pockets and pulls out two platinum-colored automatic pistols—the kind you see in movies. "Yep," he says, grinning, "you'd be surprised at what people get rid of. Sleep tight now, little mice. No fear."

"I don't know why," I say to Tia, as we pull ourselves into the sleeping bags, "but I think Shawn's Irish and I have always trusted the Irish."

"How about the Chinese? Have you trusted us?"

"Hey, we're related, and you know it. I taught you all about the land bridge and you just smiled enigmatically. So mysterious. I didn't know what the fuck you were."

She laughs at me. "B-movie inscrutable's my thing, right? I wanted to talk to you so bad. It was the hardest thing I ever did. Climbing down the wall was easier. Braiding that rope was easier. I really wanted to be friends with you."

"Well, now you're deserting me for your husband."

"Dicks before chicks."

"It's the other way around."

"I know. I do want to stay with you. We never talked about your guy, either, and I wanted to ask you so bad."

"Okay. I'll tell, but you first. You tell me about your guy. Is he Chinese too?"

"Nah. We went to high school together, never dated then. But I feel like I've known him, well, always. I went to kindergarten with him."

"Private school?"

"Mmm."

"I was Waldorf, then public school. My parents are that kind of liberal."

"Mine moved to Arizona, and Clay's died. His dad was a cereal company CEO—big house on Lake Minnetonka. Second house in Costa Rica, the Pacific side. If we can get down there."

"With a baby?"

"I know. Maybe California."

We're quiet. "But you really love him."

"I do. Maybe he's a waspy Wayzata guy, but he's smart, kind, sexy, makes me laugh. All that."

Her voice drifts off. I try to reel her back. "I'm surprised they caught you. I mean, you seem so protected, right? Out-there suburbs in a big fort couldn't you have just disappeared?"

"I took a chance, went to my studio. I just didn't get . . . I really couldn't believe that it was happening. That's the problem with privilege, money, in this sort of situation. False sense of security. But they got me in the street, no ID, and I pretended to have no English. I know Clay is waiting for a sign from me. I'll have him come and get me. Clay and I always planned that if one of us disappeared or there was a third world war or something went wrong in a big way, we'd stay home, guard the house, wait for the other person as long as possible. So I'm sure Clay's there."

"Tending the home fires."

"Sort of, yeah."

We sleep like the dead, a raw, black, hallucinatory sleep. We sleep away the afternoon and when we wake up it's dusk—around five or six o'clock. Sera has sandwiches—real bread, real sliced turkey, even mayo. And canned milk heated up with cinnamon and chocolate. She leaves us alone with the food and we eat in little bites, sip the hot chocolate.

"So tasty, I could cry," says Tia.

"It feels sort of sacramental, eating real food again."

"You haven't told me about your husband," Tia says.

I look at her and don't know how to start, but my expression must tell her quite a bit.

"That's all right," she says, after a moment. "We'll catch up some other time."

OCTOBER 20

This notebook has become my life, or perhaps better to say that this notebook has become the way I remain connected with my life, and with you. The black hardbound cover has peeled in places, or scratched down to the gray pulp. But your tape-protected ultrasound looks perfect. The back, with its blank for your name or picture, surrounded by sticker garlands of roses, doves, and pointing cherubs, is smudged. These foolish little signs of romance are showing the wear of much handling. As is the photograph I took of the sign in the empty field. I have picked up bits of paper from the now and from the before, as mementos of the curious world you will be entering soon. Many tiny pieces of paper, blown from bags, fluttering off the giant pile, lie in drifts here and there in the Merf. I smooth them out and add them to the envelopes of scraps that I taped to the inner cover of your book. They have made their way here from all corners of the earth. Lemon candy wrappers from Spain and many tags—marked Made in China, Taiwan, USA, Sri Lanka, Berlin. There are cards printed in Korea and little decorative bits of gilt and lavender wrappers from France, Australia, Indonesia. Torn and smudged photos. Wine labels from New Zealand. Erection instructions to some long-lost tent manufactured in Taiwan. There are scraps of iconic American soup, mac & cheese, scouring pad, and laundry soap packaging. Envelopes with beautifully printed stamps juxtaposed for merely utilitarian purposes—yet bearing along some mysterious effect. In the facility's medicine cabinet I find a bottle of glue, and a pair of tiny nail scissors. Fitting and gluing my little tag-bag of treasures together occupies me. Tia's sleeping. Sera, I've barely seen.

Among the many items stored or jettisoned in the back room there is a small oil painting on masonite. The little painting is well done, though one corner is smeared with what might be congealed egg. Perhaps it was thrown out by mistake, the victim of a household purge. On the other hand, it may have been rescued from a flood or fire, for the background is dark. But looking closely, I see that is the result of careful work, not mud or flames. The painting is simple. A pomegranate and a water glass (either empty or full to the brim) are set upon a spotlighted piece of vast and perhaps even endless tabletop. When I first looked at the pomegranate and the water glass, I thought of two people. The water glass, one of those large bistro glasses good for iced tea, looks perfect from a distance and chaotic up close. The pomegranate is a swirl of tiny strokes—rose and mandarin pink and a smoky scarlet. It does not touch the glass, but casts a shadow into its interior. There seems to be a tense but loving relationship between the pomegranate and the water glass. Perhaps, I think now, like the relationship between you and me.

You decided to exist. I don't really figure into your decision. Life is all for life. All for selfish continuance. And the two objects sit, one ripening, upon a tabletop that stretches into the shadows.

———————

Tia wakes up and rubs her hands across her face. She is, of course, accustomed to watching me write in this book, and so she doesn't ask what I am doing, she snuggles back down and dozes as I scratch on. The ceiling is high and the air is very cold. I've cut the fingers from a pair of mismatched, cheaply knitted, scavenged gloves, like Shawn, so that I can hold this pen. I'm afraid we won't get out. Afraid that the night is not deep enough to hide us. We may run endlessly, even after you are born. And I am afraid that my mom's absence means that something out there is going wrong.

All of a sudden, Tia says, "Hey, I'm bleeding."

But it's not blood, or there's not much blood. It's clear—maybe amniotic fluid, I think.

"I'm going out, to get my mom," I tell Tia. "Don't worry. She knows what to do."

I give Tia a stack of paper towels, settle her into my sleeping bag, and hang hers off a hook in the wall. Tia's face is a bloodless white, a gray color, and between her eyebrows a crease suddenly forms. Her forehead is scored with a knifelike shadow. She seems smaller, and I see with chilling clarity that the huge baby will not make it out of her. It's trapped, a sailing ship in a bottle. She will have to break. This stuns me—I can't catch my breath as in equal fear you jam yourself high in my rib cage, just under my heart, shouldering my lungs aside.

"Go, go, then," cries Tia, her face crumpling.

I move, fast as I dare. The floor is slippery with torn wet newspaper. I edge through the door into the gray and green industrial hallway. From there, I slip along the rubber treads set in the painted cement, to the windowed door that leads into the big garage. Through the smeared yellow pane I see my mom. She is dressed in coveralls, and she's talking to someone I haven't seen yet. He could be dangerous. She could be heading him off, feeding him a story, explaining us away. I should wait, and I do try. Her focused stillness as she listens to the man tells me that she's playing a part, acting out the role of a listener. She is never this nonparticipatory, this quiet, in a real human interaction. But I need to get her attention. So I walk down the hall a bit farther, try one door, which is locked, and then the next, which opens into an office. An office that juts into the garage, with a window, which is how I succeed finally in attracting Sera's attention. I wave my arms like semaphores through the window until I'm pretty sure she sees me. I point. I leave. Surely she will get the message and she'll follow me back to the storage room, to find out why I'm panicked.

Back in our hiding place, Tia is a little better, breathing carefully and curled up with an old fake fur pillow—gray shearling, matted and gnarled.

"That's really dirty," I say, upset because she's usually so fastidious.

"Don't take it away," says Tia.

Uh-oh, I think.

"I'm feeling something. I think I am feeling a twinge. A squeezing sort of feeling." She puts the pillow aside and her baby juts between us. "Here." Tia takes my hands and puts them on the base of her stomach where the bands of muscle tighten as she speaks, and she says, "See?"

"Yeah, but maybe," I say, "they are those Braxton Hicks contractions that don't mean you're going into labor yet."

Still, if she doesn't, I know that there's a risk of infection after the baby's waters break. I hold her wrist and take a look at her watch, timing her next contraction, and the interval between that one and the next, and so on. They're quite mild, she says, no pain. But they are only five minutes apart. And as four of them go by they seem too unmistakably regular and synchronized to be anything but labor. Still, she is in no pain. And now I hope that Tia is one of those phenomenons, women you hear about, even before getting pregnant, women who barely have time to lie down on the kitchen floor, the women who have their babies in the backs of taxicabs, the women who don't feel any pain, either, or just a little, the women whose babies practically fall out of their bodies. We all long to be these women.

"There's another one," says Tia, and she looks even better, now, like she's amazed, happy, pleased with herself. "Is that good?"

I'm pretty sure that the onset of contractions has also released some sort of natural opiate in her brain, the chemical that mercifully dulls fear, inflates courage, and makes us eager above all else to see our babies.

Only Tia isn't all that much farther along than I am, and we have no way of knowing, since they wouldn't tell us what they saw on the ultrasound, if her baby is ready to survive yet all on its own. So I don't know which to hope for—that she have the baby, or not go into labor—not that my hoping makes a difference, after all. I'm also hearing that noise as she fell to the roof, off the rope. I wonder how hard she landed, but don't want to remind her. The only thing I can do is sit with her and time her contractions, which stay at exactly five minutes apart for half an hour of awful mental strain— I'm desperate for Sera to come and tell me what to do. Finally, she knocks. I jump up, run to the door, and push the dead bolt back. Sera puts her arms around me.

"For godsakes, don't *ever* go out again," she says. "That was a regional manager who may or may not be ready to spill the whole thing. We don't know how much he knows or what his opinions are, politically speaking. He could be ready to report us all. Or he could be . . . What's going on?"

"Hi," says Tia faintly. "I'm having my baby."

"Her contractions are five minutes apart, regular."

"My water broke," says Tia, her hands about her stomach, eyes deep. She's lost in sensation.

Sera kneels beside her and asks questions, professional-sounding questions. It's a relief. She smoothes Tia's hair back, off her forehead, and smiles. She holds Tia's wrist reassuringly between her fingers, and says that her pulse is excellent.

"Do you know how many weeks you are?"

"Thirty . . . maybe thirty-one?"

Mom nods comfortably, but I see her smile tighten.

"Have you practiced Lamaze breathing?"

"I used to practice with Clay, before they got me."

"We're going to review a few things. Cedar, you can practice too."

We huff and puff, do cleansing breaths, panting breaths, together, in a welter of pillows and sleeping bags and blankets. I get dizzy and I think that Tia hyperventilates, too, because all of a sudden we're acting like a couple of six-year-olds. Tia sticks out her tongue and rolls back her eyes. I bare my teeth and cackle. Mom gets into it with this exaggerated "Hee, whoo" type breathing that you see in birth movies. She twists her head around, shuts her eyes. "Oh yeah, the natural high." She gets Tia loosened up, even laughing, and it touches me to see my mom acting like this, so unlike herself, in order to take Tia's mind off where we are.

"Should we be making this much noise?" I ask.

"Probably not," says Sera. She mimes a big exaggerated hushy face, and Tia keeps on breathing noisily, laughing, snorting. Suddenly she quits and goes silent. Her eyes widen.

"Ow!"

She makes a ragged sound of surprise, but Sera coaxes her into a breathing pattern. For an hour, that's how it goes. The contractions are becoming uncomfortable now, maybe painful. I can tell they're absorbing Tia's focus. She still talks between them, but her forehead squeezes up and her eyes swim with inwardness, stark and bewildered. Her face is so stripped and pure when she's immersed in a contraction that I want to kiss her. I do kiss her on the crown of her head. I hold her against me and Mom crouches next to her.

"Am I going to have my baby?" she asks in a normal voice, after one particularly hard contraction. Light beads of sweat have popped out on her forehead. "Is it coming now?"

"No," says Sera. "Not for a while. But it's time for me to check you, see how far along you are."

Sera takes me aside while Tia is between contractions, limp and lost. She nearly goes unconscious when her contractions let up. "I have to see about sterilizing things, and make sure we're safe here. I have to leave for a moment, find Shawn. Are you okay with her?"

"I think so."

"Nothing's out of the ordinary—just she's not to term."

Then Sera leaves to get her bag. While she's gone, I hold Tia's hand. I spread her tapered fingers out and knead them, massage my energy into her palms.

"That feels good."

Then a contraction starts and she wades into it with a hopeless bravery, deeper and deeper, until at its peak she's all the way under. I take off her watch, strap it onto my wrist, and tell her when she's halfway through. The stretch is tightest, the pain most intense, at thirty seconds, but after that she slowly surfaces.

"That helps."

Four minutes apart, now, and less time for her to rest between contractions. Mom comes back with Shawn—his face is solemn with alarm. With his skinny body and flapping lambskin helmet he looks like a Minnesota Frankenstein, and I almost laugh. He's got black industrial poured-plastic moon boots on, huge things, buckled to the knee. When he kneels next to Tia, he is incongruously gentle.

"I'm going to carry you out of here," he says. "We're going out back between the container stacks, to the caves. We think there's gonna be a raid in a few hours."

Out in back of the station, the ancient banks of the Mississippi, dry cliffs now, are riddled with empty caves left when the cliffs were mined for sand. The great banks are warrened with places that over the years have been used to store everything from Prohibition liquor to explosives to drugs. These were gangster hideouts, speakeasies, homeless people's squats. The man who started St. Paul, Pig's Eye Parrant, kept a tavern in one of the caves. Hermits and crazy people have made the caves their home. Children have been lost in the caves, died in the caves, and a coffee shop or two are still set into the grottolike foundation of the caves. One is a ballroom where high school proms are held. Some are wired up for heat and rented to stores—livable.

"Won't they look there?"

"Well, maybe," says Shawn. "But we've got caves behind the caves, you know? Those lead into a labyrinth of tunnels. St. Paul sits on top of a whole other world. This place, you're sitting ducks. In the caves you've got little back doors, weird ways of getting in and out, belly-crawl passageways. Like the way we're going," he says, gathering Tia in his arms. "We're going through the basement of a house set right against the base of the cliff."

He tenderly adjusts her in his arms and stands. I jam your notebook in the backpack and we go. Tia's having a contraction, breathing hard, her eyes shut, leaning against Shawn's oil-stained blue jacket. Sera and I carry all of the bedding, plus she's got a black roller bag that she totes behind us. It is dark now, so if we skirt the big yard spotlight we are going to be okay. It's hard keeping my balance with the sleeping bags, the blankets, my backpack, not to mention you. I take stiff little pregnant-lady steps, anxiety-laden steps, as we move down a dim trail past the hulking bales of cans, plastic, metal containers, boxcars, vast chewing and smashing equipment, all silent and dead still. The cool is lovely. Almost really cold. We go through several openings in four layers of link fencing—you can't see these openings until you're right at them—and when we squeeze through and close them they are again invisible. We wind around the base of the cliff, the massive old riverbed wall, until we come to some houses and broken-down businesses and little boarded-over shops. One of them, which looks abandoned like all of the others, has a side door. Sera pulls away a padlock and opens it. Shawn looks carefully all around us before he steps into the gloom. We stand for a moment in lightless, cold quiet. Then Sera lets us through another door, handing me a little pencil of an LED flashlight. Shawn carries Tia down a set of creaky stairs. In the basement, Mom sweeps her light at a wall of shelves and cabinets. She opens one of the doors and gently pries loose the wooden backing, which reveals a whitewashed wall. It takes a while to realize that it is actually a door set into the wall, one with a latch string left out down about a foot off the floor. Sera pulls the string, which lifts a bar on the other side, and Shawn ducks in with Tia.

"I better get back," he says. "She can walk from here?"

"It's common practice during labor," says Mom. "It helps the baby come faster."

"I'll be okay," says Tia. "The contractions stopped. Maybe out of fear? I haven't had one since we left the garage. Let's get where we're going."

Shawn retreats. We're in here now with Tia until her baby comes. If anything goes wrong, there is no Plan B. No crash C-section.

"We're going to be all right, you'll see," says Sera. Her voice is almost blithe, but her assurance can't be real. I follow her in. We slowly toddle single file down a skinny, rough-walled passageway. The way gets narrower, the ceiling buckles. We hunch lower and lower until we are crawling on our hands and knees—the gravel cuts into my kneecaps and palms. I try to drag our stuff with me and sometimes have to inch along on my side like a worm. I break out in a terror sweat. I am underneath tons and tons of rock—massive and senseless amounts of rock. I try to make my mind a blank, try to meditate, follow Mom without thinking. But then we come to a heavy wall with a black mouthlike aperture beneath. It looks like a medieval dungeon wall. We are supposed to slide underneath. Tears stream down my face.

Mom edges under on her stomach, and pulls her stuff behind. Astonishingly, Tia rolls through quick as a cat.

"Come on," says Tia, panting, "push your stuff through."

"I can't do it," I whisper.

"Do you need help?" says Mom.

"I can't do it. I'll get stuck." And I do get stuck. Mom gently torques me this way and that, rocks me along under the stone, pulls me through inch by inch. My heart is beating so fast I almost pass out. By the time I am on the other side I'm sick. The two have to wait while

I go to a corner, walking upright anyway, to puke. There is a shrine where I stop, a niche carved in the rock. In it, there's a little plastic statue of Mary. Her blue cloak and peach-pale face are grimed with sooty dust. I say two Hail Marys and feel a little better. In her presence, I will be all right. Maybe she's looking after me—she *should* be looking after me. It's her job. I put a little pebble at her feet, an offering, among many other little stones. People like me put them there, grateful for her protection as they squeezed under that nightmare stone.

"Let's go," I say.

The air is bad, stale and oxygen thin, mineral smelling, dank. It makes us sleepy. Mom says to breathe deeply, concentrate on breathing. I break into a clammy sweat and try to control my racing heartbeat.

"Stop," says Tia.

We hold her as she gasps. Her breathing surges and she cries out. "It's a bad one."

"A good one, a good one," says Sera, and in the thin flashlight's beam I see that Tia wants to belt her for saying that. I don't blame her. But unless Sera is relentlessly cheerful about our situation, at some point we'll probably just sit down and get hysterical and die. When Tia's done I pat her back and help her stumble along. The passageways widen precipitously, then narrow alarmingly. We climb a tiny set of steps cut into the rock, a winding set of stairs. Then we pass through a dark esophageal tunnel.

"There's a domed room, warm, just ahead," says Mom. "It's wired for electricity and there's even a tiny stove, vented to the outside. And Shawn put a drum of dried soups and stuff in there, too."

"Ramen?" I say.

"Maybe." Sera's trying to cheer us along. "That's how come I've got the roller bag. It's filled with gallon jugs of water."

The news of water and hot soup seems to galvanize Tia and she tries to stride through the passageway. "I just want to be lying down when the next one comes," she says. But she isn't. It is the next one after that.

Our little room, a real cave, has got limestone walls and lumpy stone jutting out all over. There are some ancient handwoven rag rugs on the floor, and a futon, chewed by rats. I stuff back handfuls of batting until the mattress is intact enough for Tia to lie down.

"Put these down on top of the sleeping bags," says Sera.

She's got a bunch of hospital pads in her roller bag. Plus antibacterial wipes, a surgical sewing kit, alcohol swabs, sterile latex gloves, and those eyedrops mandated by state law even though the last thing this baby's got to worry about is an STD-induced eye infection. Still, I'm so relieved and impressed with my mom that I put my arms around her—you in between us. She holds my face and speaks, looking into my eyes.

"We're all going to be all right, especially Tia. Don't you worry."

This sort of against-the-odds cheer used to drive me crazy. Now I suck it right up. I bury my face in her soft black scarf I knit for her. After everything, she's somehow kept that, run away with it. I stroke it and want to cry. Then Tia yells and we're back in her labor. I sit down with her and train my flashlight on the watch. She's down to three minutes apart now. Sera passes her flashlight up and down the walls until she locates an industrial extension cord dangling against the stone. She plugs the stove in, finds a small lamp, and plugs that in too. She turns up the oven and opens it wide—in a few minutes the room seems a little warmer. There's a heavy tarp rolled up over the doorway and Sera lets it down, now, to keep in the heat. There is a saucepan and a teakettle in the drawer beneath the oven. She fills the kettle with water and puts it on the top back burner. I hold Tia in my arms as she goes through five more contractions. Then five more. I think she must be ready to have the baby. Sera puts on a pair of the sterile gloves. Her hands look ghostly.

"Right after the next contraction, I'm going to check you," she says to Tia, and she does. Her face is remote and far away.

"Pretty soon now, huh?" says Tia in a tough, scared little voice.

"Well," says Sera, "you're dilated."

"How much?"

Tia and I are prepared to hear that she's ten centimeters, that she's ready to have her baby.

"Two," says Sera.

"Two? Two? Oh god! Oh shit!"

Tia throws herself back against the rolled end of the futon, into the sleeping bags. I can feel the despair swirl out of her, the flailing fear. "No! Here comes another!" And Tia reaches out and grabs my hair so hard that she's pulling it out and we both scream. She tears at my face with her screwdriver fingernails and manages at the same time to lash out with one leg and catch Mom's jaw with her heel. Sera goes down, stunned, kneels on the floor and then tries to crawl forward to help me pin Tia. But Tia's slim, strong legs kick too fast. She rakes out again with her talons, scoring down the other side of my face, drawing blood. I think maybe what the Slider said was true, or maybe it's a curse for murdering Orielee—these babies can't be born without medical intervention. Something terrible, unnatural, is taking place and we are doomed to die in a welter of bloody, ago- nized hysteria.

Tia goes unconscious when the contraction stops. Her hands go limp. She shuts her eyes and begins to snore.

"Is she going to die, Mom?" I whisper. "Is she trying to kill us? What's the matter?"

Sera rights herself. She's already got Neosporin out for my scratches and is touching my face with the grease.

"Oh, Tia just now? Honey, that's normal."

———

I feel funky, sour, and Sera gives me a couple of her antibacterial wipes, cautioning she'll need the rest for the delivery. Tia is now making progress. I don't know what else to call it. Progress, of course. Going through increased pain in order to get into even worse pain that will mean the end of pain. Clearly, once you're in labor, you're in. The only way out is through. By some handy miracle of utter denial, I don't take Tia's labor personally. Don't feel the clutch of terror that I probably should, watching her struggle to climb out of each contraction. Her hands and legs move rhythmically. Like she is crawling up and down vast cliffs. She does not complain. She seems to have decided to obey the pain, not fight it. Her face is burnished with sweat. I offer sips of water. Sera touches her lips with her fingers, smears on beeswax lip balm. Tia doesn't talk to us anymore, she just crawls into the pain, up and over the lip of the incline, and then crawls down into a little nest of sleep.

Hours pass. I can't believe I write this. *Hours pass*. I do not understand how her body doesn't break. She stays whole, as far as I can see, but her eyes roll back to the whites. And she greets each oncoming contraction with a powerful sound, a growl that starts low in her ribs and rises in pitch until, at the ceiling of her contraction, it is a cougar's scream. I heard that sound twice, once in my backyard and once out camping with my parents in Glacier Park. They closed around me in their sleeping bags and none of us slept again that whole night. Now the same sound from Tia rises in the little cave, until Sera says, checking her once again, "It's time to push. Push!"

Instantly, with the first push, Tia turns into a human being. Although her face swells, grotesque with blood, and her eyes bulge when she bears down, between the pushes she is weirdly animated. She's herself somehow. She talks.

"Am I going to see my baby soon?"

"Soon," says Sera, "soon. Ready? Now . . ."

But this baby is stuck. There is no budging it. *Hours pass*. I really cannot believe that I have to write that again. Tia is still pushing, her lips drawn back. Her eyes bloody and a tiny vein broken on the crest of her cheekbone. Mom takes the old chair in the corner and knocks the seat out. Tia sits in the chair and pushes down, into gravity, into the rock, into the earth, straining her hips to break. In this way she begins to move her baby. I've got my hands ready, sterile-gloved, underneath. No baby. I don't recognize Tia. Her face is twice the size it should be and her hair is needles. She's pulsing electricity. She is magnificent. But scary. Her eyes are sunken and her mouth drags at air. At one point, I think that she is dead. No motion. I freeze with her. She takes a huge groaning breath in and pushes again and there is the crown, the top of the head.

"Easy now, easy. Let's just let your baby slip out," says Sera.

Tia's sound comes from the stone itself, the cave talking. With the next push the baby's head is out, eyes shut, unmoving. I am cradling its face. And then another push and here is the rest of the baby and I'm on my stomach on the floor of the cave wrapping the baby as Sera, next to me, clamps off the cord and cuts it. Sera takes the baby. Tells me to catch Tia before she falls and to put her down on the bed. And then there is the first hint of fear in her voice, the first sign that Sera's scared.

Tia reels off the chair and I nearly drop her, but we manage to tumble down onto the bed. Mom is working on the baby. She's hunched over and she sucks something from the baby's mouth, spits, then puts her lips to its tiny face and puffs. Tia's bleeding. She delivers the placenta, but keeps on bleeding. I squeeze her hands. Raise her hips.

"Stop bleeding. Stop it right now. Stop bleeding." I say this in a commanding voice, and I glare at Tia fiercely, as if it is her fault. And her eyes open. She looks at me very sweetly.

"Okay," she says, dutifully. "I will try. I will."

And she does it. The sudden flow quits.

"That's good, you're doing well," I hear myself say. That is all I've been saying for hours. But now there is a new thing to say. Only I'm not going to be the one to say it. I refuse. I have been through too much with Tia to be the one who has to tell her. Sera will have to do it, when Sera herself understands. When she stops the useless little puffing sounds over there by the chair. When she stops hunching over the little bundle in her arms. When she sits up. When she just fucking quits. Which doesn't happen for a long, long time. So long that I think, *Sera, say it. Say it, now.* But she does not. That baby's dead, but Sera doesn't say that. Eventually, she crawls over to us and says something like *Your baby didn't make it*, or *Your baby is in the spirit world*, or just *Gone. I'm sorry. Gone.*

"I want to hold it," says Tia.

Sera gives the baby to her all wrapped up in a swaddling blanket.

"A girl," Sera says.

Tia uncovers its face and it looks like any baby, a crumpled little stone-idol face, only a blue-gray color. The silence and the stillness of this baby is godly. I get up. I fall down. I am on my knees. I worship. Tia croons, holds her baby, and begins to sing. Not a song composed of words, but a song made up of sounds that I will hear later, in a different place. Sounds that were made a hundred thousand years ago, I am sure, and sounds that will be heard a hundred thousand from now, I hope. As she sings, I fall asleep beside her—her songs do soothe a baby, the one in me. I can feel you stretching your limbs, turning, settling, and you're alive. You're so very alive.

OCTOBER 21

When I wake up, there is no baby in Tia's arms. She is sleeping, not dead. I check her breath with my hand. Her face is warm. And Sera is in the corner on a little camp mattress, sleeping too. Everything's been cleaned up. The blood. The bloody placenta. The bloody blue pads. Everything's balled up in a white plastic bag in the corner. I can see the bag glowing in the dim lamplight. Sera's thought of everything. I see movement, though, now, and for a while I think it is part of some dream. There's an unreality to it. But then very slowly I understand what I am seeing—an undulating brown fur mat or rug is actually rats carefully rooting out and removing what is in the white bag through a precisely chewed hole. And more rats are piled on something placed upon the little table. They have shredded its covering. They are moving in a bizarre way, on the table, back and forth, swarming, swimming, over one another, diving into a pile of themselves and diving out again. I jump up but I am silent. I do not want Tia or Sera to see this. I do not. The rats aren't scared of me. They just swarm thicker, faster, in a soundless, squirming excitement. I take the broom and sweep at them, but they are a tide and just keep lapping back. I see my mom's boots, there in the corner. Frye boots. My mom's hippie boots. She started buying them in the seventies and never quit. I put them on. I stand there for a moment in the boots, and sort of work out what I'm going to do. Then I stoop over and grab a rat by the tail. Quickly, I swing it around underneath my mom's boot and crush its head. The cracking sound pleases me. I do another, and another. Soon, they notice. There is no sound in the cave but the crack and crack of my mom's boots. I am really full of admiration for these boots. They are made of leather so thick that a rat can't get a tooth through, and the heels are heavy enough to crush a rat's skull with one crack. I crack again, maybe twenty or thirty times now, I don't know. I crack until they understand, maybe from the rat shrieks somewhere beyond the decibel level that I can hear, what is happening. That's too much for them. They are gone. Suddenly, they just disappear.

They've ripped apart the baby's blanket, so I wrap the tiny idol up again, tightly. I do not want Tia to realize. Then I take your striped cotton flannel blanket from my pack. It's a blue and yellow plaid, very pretty. I secure it around Tia's baby. There's a couple of tin boxes where the food is stashed. I retie the garbage bag and stuff all of the bloody pads in there. I arrange the bodies of the rats in a circle around us. My mind is not right. How could it be? I know my thoughts are bizarre, extreme. I take the baby, then, and curl up next to Tia. We sleep a long, long time. Maybe days. I don't know. The next time I wake up, the baby is gone from my arms. The crushed bodies of the rats are off the floor. In the lamplight, I see Sera at the stove and I smell something good, something with broth, maybe onions. There is a buttery type of smell. I am overpoweringly hungry and the horror is reduced to a bitter aura, more like a dream. Tia's sitting up. She is even at the table. The same table.

"How can you be sitting there?" I ask her.

"I feel better," she says.

She is wearing a snowmobile suit, too small, maybe child-sized, because is it bubble-gum pink with lavender trim and it has the three Disney princesses embroidered over her heart. Her boots are good, Sorels, a grimy white with yellow fur. She's eating noodles, eyes downcast, in a satisfied and even excited way. Her lank black hair falls forward with each bite. It occurs to me that losing her baby is not all bad. Obviously not. Without a baby, Tia can move in the world like a normal person. She is free. She can leave this cave as soon as she recovers, and go anywhere she wants. Tia can stroll on sidewalks in broad daylight. She can step into a coffee shop and have a coffee, if there still is coffee. She can sit down and read a book, right there, in the public eye, and she will not be arrested. Her tummy's going to flatten out and she will not have to run away to hide her baby. There is no baby anymore. No one to drag her down. She will have to register for the womb draft, but there are surely ways out of it. She will not be subject to this freakish sense of continual paranoia. She will not have to live in a cave. Or with rats. As I watch her eat the soup my hunger fades. She has passed through the valley of the shadow, and even if she feels grief, which surely must come, she is on the other side. My valley lies before me still.

I have a moment of resentment before I remember. We have murdered. We will never be free.

"Come on. Get up and have some soup," says Sera.

"Are you really okay?" I ask Tia. I sit beside her on one of the big metal drums. My movement sets you into motion, too, and I put my hands upon you as you turn and twist, upend yourself, shoulder me. Then I feel the goodness of you again, the rightness. I'm back. I'm not sure that the sight of me won't trigger Tia's feelings. She does look at me a little sadly, but also I can tell that she feels very sorry for me, and worried for me. She is gentle with me—definitely on the other side.

"Don't you hurt? Aren't you bleeding?"

"It's not so bad," she says. Of course, she didn't see herself from

my perspective, but it seems to me incredible that someone so desperately at the very physical extreme edge of herself should now be
sitting at a little table slurping soup. Someone whose baby's died
and . . . but she doesn't know the rest. While I was sleeping Sera
probably took the baby and she buried it or got Shawn to do it. Something. I do not want to know. I know enough. Her baby's gone and
you are here. And I am all around you. I am your home, a land of
blood and comfort.

I have never eaten anything as good as that soup. My hunger
comes back with the first lovely swallow. Tia and I eat three cans of
it before we stop. Sera brews some tea for us—hot raspberry, good
for the uterus. My womb is the size of a great big cookie jar, while
across from me, Tia's womb is swiftly shrinking back to the size of
a fist. She'll be able to walk out of here tonight, or rather, tomorrow morning. Three a.m. That's when we're leaving. I'll walk out,
too, only trundling you, waddling beneath the cover of darkness.
Sera's telling Tia that they've gotten in touch with her husband. Clay
apparently kept the faith just like they had planned—stayed home,
waiting. He will be parked at the Perkins in St. Louis Park, just off
394. When the recycling truck stops at the Dumpsters, he'll drive up
and get Tia. But she won't go back to her big house in Minnetonka
with the slate steps and entryway floor, the cathedral windows looking out over the water. She won't sauté onions on her stainless steel
range and sleep in her pillow-top-mattressed king-size bed, curled
up, a lump in the plush goose-down comforter. She and Clay are
going to make a run for California.

The thought of her going fills me like a cry. A confused strangeness chokes me. I can't look at her now. I'm jealous not only of her
freedom, but that she will return to her husband, who has a right
to her, while I have no right, being just a friend. I'm just someone
who loves her the way you fall in love with someone who has been
through life and death with you. I want her to stay with me and look
into my eyes when my time comes, like I did with her. I want her to
help me have my baby.

Rich thoughts, longing thoughts, stupid thoughts. I can only write them here. After we are finished with the soup and we bring more tea to our sleeping bags, Sera sits with us plotting the outline of our escape. The lamp glows. I know this is a bit foolish, but it seems to me it casts a light that is magical and sweet. For it will be over soon. There is enough heat from the oven to warm our aperture inside the cliff. This is a cozy little spot, a perfect shelter. I could almost believe we were the lost children and the wise queen of a fairy tale were it not for the scrabbling, the constant stream of rat noise, the scritch of tiny claws behind the stone and outside in the corridor and under and all around us. Once in a while, a fight will break out and the rats will screech, high squeals, battling over something. Waves of them across the ceiling, invisible, loud with some excitement. I try not to listen, and do not flinch when Sera glances at me. I asked her to trade her boots for my shoes and she has. She knows the reason.

"I hate rats," says Tia, hunkering over. But her face has color, energy has restored itself to her skin, her arms. I'm shocked at the resilience of her.

"I don't mind them," I say.

I work away on this chronicle that I am writing for you, in spite of you, and for myself, to calm myself. It takes my mind off the rats, off losing Tia, and off our own complicated, harrowing future. Sometimes I wish I was more blunted, that these thoughts and anxieties that bump and twirl around and around in my brain, exhausting me, would quit. I work away on *Zeal*, again correcting another of my fake priest's doctrinal examinations of Catholicism and evolution.

Evolution has never been a very controversial part of Catholic discourse, even though the archbishop of Vienna has made some retro noises on the subject. In his 1950 encyclical Humani Generis, *Pope Pius XII declared that Catholics would not betray their religion by believing what science has determined about the evolution of the human body just as long as they accepted that God was responsible for infusing that body with a soul. Thinkers like Pierre Teilhard de Chardin, a Jesuit and paleontologist, have*

*embraced the concept of evolution as a way to describe the ongoing growth
and perfectibility of humanity within the evolving perfection of the cosmos.
But we have seemingly reached the end of what Teilhard de Chardin hoped
would be our apotheosis. Maybe T. S. Eliot had it right. Our world is ending
not with a bang but a puzzled whimper.*

I put the work down. All is momentarily quiet. As there has not
yet been a chance, I tell Sera that it is time, now, for her to go into
detail about what's happened to Phil.

He knew what was happening, she tells me, he knew when it would
come. He knew that Bernice would raid my house with her cheery
halloo! He knew that she would take me to the hospital in her
Camry, and there was nothing he could do about any of it.

Three women were living in the basement of our church. He was
sheltering them; other parishioners were helping. Three women I
knew from church, two of them with husbands and one with a boyfriend who deserted her. Phil was running back and forth between
the church and me. The women in the basement were caught when
a neighbor noticed number 10 cans of beans delivered to the back
door of the kitchen entryway and nobody brought them in. So she
did. Then heard voices. Then heard nothing. Before they even knew
she'd found them out, a retrofitted UPS van was pulling up beside
the church. The church was raided, and Phil was taken into custody
by very friendly people. The women were taken to the hospital—a
different one than mine. Nobody knows what became of the women.

Phil was housed in the Fifth Precinct police station, where he
was nicely treated, fed, warm, interviewed for two days. He was
asked many times about the whereabouts of other women and he
always said that the only ones he was helping were the women in
the church basement. On the third day he was taken downtown, to
the basement of City Hall, an ornate old brownstone building with
a clock tower and a couple of blocks all to itself. City Hall is now the
headquarters of the Unborn Protection Society. The old UPS trucks

haul people there for questioning. They still have the phone number to call on the back of the truck, the 800 number, which is what the neighbor used. Phil was interviewed at the old City Hall and then sent out to the UPS offices in Burnsville, where he was scheduled for a truth seminar.

These truth seminars can only be administered by ordained ministers and overseen by the military. They are conducted according to certain laws—precedents set by the church a few centuries back have come in handy.

Sera becomes agitated. She can't speak. She begins to weep as she talks.

The only people who really know the definition of torture are the ones being tortured, she says. It is useless, hideous, to ask the torturers to define the act. Unless, of course, they agree to undergo what they define, they have no authority in the matter. No academic degree means anything. No doctorate. No lawyer's shingle. No education. No citing of precedents or principle. The only thing meaningful in the definition is the word made flesh. The body has the last and only word. So when Phil told Sera very simply that he was tortured he was saying that he was sorry. Sorry that his body had reacted and given up my name and address.

"Don't blame him," says Sera.

"Well, duh," I say, looking at her. "He's a human being."

She is silent, looks down at her hands, so I know that she knows. She will tell me everything that happened to Phil if I ask, but I am not going to ask.

OCTOBER 23

Sera and I hook Tia's jolly, pink, padded, chubby arms in our arms. Tia's much better but we don't want her to bleed again. We proceed very slowly. I'm feeling fine—the soup brought me back. I'm short of breath but have recovered most of my energy. I feel strong, and although I'm shielding my heart from the thought of Phil, he's there.

He's drawing us toward him, I can feel it. Once we're out of the
tunnel, through the abandoned house, we make our way back along
the chain link to Shawn's truck. Once again, we're stuffed behind
the seat with old boots, clipboards, oil cans and wrenches and sandwich wrappers. We're taking 494, then we'll run up 100 to 394 and
over to Louisiana Avenue. There, we'll drop Tia at the Perkins. Once
she's safe, we'll head back to the city and drive to the post office
building. Sera and I will be dropped off there to stay in a safe room
until we hitch north on the postal truck. As we jolt along I hold
Tia against me. She's weakened from the walk and maybe bleeding slightly again. It seems to me that the brash energy she felt at
first has gone out of her. She sinks against me with a gray grief that
she knows her husband will not understand. I am the only one who
does, or can, the only one marked in the same way by what happened to us. To say good-bye we have to cut our minds apart. The
experience has bent us. For the thirty minutes or so that it takes to
reach the Perkins parking lot, I just hold her. The engine is so loud
we couldn't talk together if we tried.

We turn onto 100 and haven't been driving two minutes when
there is a sudden whirl of lights, a siren, the lights intensifying until
they're right behind us. Shawn keeps driving.

"Get down!" Sera covers us with tarps, piles junk over us. Tia's a
lot easier to hide than I am now.

"I'll get out and talk to him," says Sera.

Shawn slowly pulls onto the shoulder, but keeps the truck
idling—not that making a break for it in a recycling truck would
make the slightest sense—but it helps us to imagine he could do it.
Sera says again that she'll get out, but Shawn says she looks super-
fakey swimming in her Carhartts, skinny swan neck barely holding
up her helmet, and he'd better do it. So we sit alone in the truck after
his door slams and under that tarp I am hit by such a powerful wave
of fear that I begin to shudder, can't quit, can't control myself, really.
I just shake. Tia puts her arms around me and hugs herself to me so
tightly that it's like she's trying to weld us together. But I'm falling

FUTURE HOME OF THE LIVING GOD

to pieces. I am positive now that I'll be discovered. I'll die, we'll die, back in the hospital. I'll be killed real slow for killing Orielee. And they will kill you, too. My mind races like crazy and I get terrible pictures under the garbage-juice tarp, under the discarded coffee cups and greasy jackets. I'm in labor in a white, white, room. The Slider is there to keep me company. She smiles whenever I'm in pain. I faint. Maybe pee myself. But when Shawn comes back he puts the truck in gear and we move off.

"That was interesting," he says to Sera. We poke our heads out. "We've got another pickup to make. Route J. 4778 Knox," he says. "The guy's daughter is six months pregnant and she will be waiting in the garage on our regular pickup."

Shawn mumbles the route and address until he won't forget it. He never writes anything down. Holding each other, Tia and I bump along until we feel the truck make a swooping turn and another turn. It halts and idles in the lot of a Jiffy Lube right behind the Perkins, next to the trash enclosure, shielded from the frontage road.

"Stay down," says Shawn. Then he says, "Easy, Tia, poke your head up a tad and look out the left-hand window, over my shoulder. Tell me if the car and the guy behind the wheel belong to you."

Tia eases her body past mine, carefully, until she's looking out the window.

"Yeah, that's him."

Her voice is thick and teary, but what is there to say? We lock hands a moment.

"Get out, now," says Sera.

"Walk, don't run," says Shawn.

She's out the door. I peek up over Shawn's shoulder to see her approach the gray car, the shadowy man inside. She ducks in the passenger-side door. The car calmly reverses, turns, and rolls out of the parking lot. And that's that. She's gone, my Tia, that's all there is.

"Let's fire it up," says Shawn, pressing on the gas.

The Minneapolis Post Office, perhaps the only major Minnesota building built to withstand an earthquake, was made in 1934 out of Kasota stone, a golden pink rock quarried in Mankato, Minnesota. A number of other buildings in the city, new and old, are made from this unusually pleasant stone. I have noticed the rock. I think it gives buildings a warm feel in the harsh winter, a kind of glow, and I've always liked going to the post office for that reason. Also, it is stalwart looking for an art deco building. No decadent elegance. The post office has a broad-shouldered look. It was designed to be seen from a distance, approached slowly and with serious postal errands in mind, but it has been surrounded by the city, so now it looms beside you without warning.

We enter through a roll-up door on the loading dock, which we reach only through several National Guard checkpoints. We do it in early daylight. Everybody needs their recyclables hauled, right? Shawn and Sera don't think that this connection will last longer than a couple of weeks more, but it works for us. Sera and I are out of the truck and whisked in so quickly that I hardly get more than a backward glance at Shawn. He's wide-eyed, nodding, nervous. Once we're in, a small pink-cheeked woman with a cockatoo crest of white hair takes us to a room in the vast lower level where the mail is sorted among a gray-toned warren of offices, staff meeting rooms, and utility closets.

She puts us in a closet containing a big soapstone sink for cleaning mops. The closet has a small window carefully trimmed out. On the corners of the window there are small square tiles of lilies, brown, with green tile background. We are facing north, and silvery-gray river light floods through the old-fashioned frosted glass. Although there is hardly room to lie down, I am not in the least claustrophobic. The room is cold, and clean. Even though the white-haired woman clicks the door shut as she leaves and locks us in, I am suddenly filled with the sense that we're going to be all right, that we're going to make it out. The comfort that the details on the window give me is perhaps extreme—but the fact that human beings thought to invest a mop and broom utility closet with a touch of charm gives me hope. Mom and I sit down on the floor, cozy up on a couple of couch cushions.

"Come here," she says, and I creep near, lean against her. She pulls me to her with a sigh and strokes my hair. I look at the lilies on the window, the calm light through the panels, the careful way the tile was inset, countersunk into the wood. How the flowers were fired and colored into the design. Perhaps this sort of gesture will be lost, perhaps it is a function of consciousness that we don't need in order to survive. Perhaps this piece of evolution makes no sense—our hunger for everyday sorts of visual pleasure—but I don't think so. I think we have survived because we love beauty and because we find each other beautiful. I think it may be our strongest quality.

"Here." Sera adjusts me, reaches into her pack. She unwraps a granola bar and hands it to me. A real foil-wrapped oats-and-honey bar—the kind we bought all the time in gas-station markets just a couple of months ago. They're rare now. I eat it slowly, dissolving one oat at a time, melting myself into her once again. Her back's against the wall and I think I may be too heavy for her.

"You're okay, you're fine," she says.

I am flooded with exhaustion. It rolls over me and shuts my eyes midbite. I wake probably a couple of hours later, shocked to consciousness by dreams, seeing Orielee's eyes lose life, her feet drumming on the dirty pink hospital linoleum. At first I don't even remember where I am, but when I realize I'm still in Sera's arms I sink back, and let myself cry, luxuriantly, tears popping from my eyes and cooling my face. Weeping feels sweet and profound, but maybe it's not a safe thing to do, so I stop. Sera has not moved, not put me down, in all that time. Now I move away from her, sure she's aching. She rolls her shoulders, stretches out her arms. Her hair shimmers in the light. I stretch too, then curl up on the floor. She gives me a drink of water from the bottle she carries.

"Would they have killed us, I mean, in the hospital?"

"Lots of women don't make it out," she says carefully.

"I see so much," I tell her, "I feel so much. Too much has happened already, and it's unbearable."

She puts her hand on my back. I know she's searching for what to say, but what she comes up with sounds pretty thin. "We've all had to toughen up, even your dad."

This makes me laugh.

"Yeah, Glen the softie. Do you know exactly where he is?"

She says nothing for a few moments, then whispers, "No."

"Are you not telling me because . . ."

I look at her and point all around the little room. Cup my hand to my ears. Are we being listened to?

She gives a "maybe" shrug, so I lie back down next to her. No use unloading the big weights around my heart yet. I want to ask her if I'll be okay, but I should not mention Tia out loud. I'm also haunted by what that sneaky nurse, the Slider, said about these babies being extra difficult to deliver. Will I survive and will you? Was Tia's labor really normal, and the baby's death an anomaly? I want to tell Sera what we did to Orielee. I want to share the burden of my horror, my dreams of the moment of the killing. How I watched, that moment, before I joined in and helped Tia. Held Orielee down. Her neck was heavy, I remember that now. I couldn't feel her bones anywhere. Her shoulders, her arms, even her elbows seemed padded by fat. And yet the colors in her eyes were so delicate, the blue irises, cornflower bright. She stared at me, then through me, to the other side I guess. And her feet would not stop pounding on the hospital linoleum.

"Are you still hungry?"

Of course I am. I'm always hungry. Ravenous, like a dog. Mom has a lovely bag of mixed nuts, unsalted, and I try to eat each one slowly, carefully, extracting the max in flavor and nutrition. I ask her if Tia's labor was normal, and Mom assures me that it was. She thinks that the baby probably suffered from the fall back at the hospital, because when she examined the placenta she found a place where it had ruptured. The baby itself did not make things difficult, she tells me again. She is positive that I am not going to have complications.

"How come you're positive?"

"I asked your birth mom and grandma about their deliveries—all completely normal."

"Those things run in families?"

"For sure."

I think she's exaggerating, but this does make me feel better, and I'm even more encouraged when Sera takes her stethoscope and blood pressure cuff out and listens to my heart, and then finds your heart. I listen too—a little whuffing sound. She puts the cuff around my arm, pumps it up, times my pulse.

"Your blood pressure's fine," she says. "Baby's active?"

"Real active," I say, proud, but she just nods. I have this moment of longing to share my happy moment of pride in you, and I miss Phil so much I have to shut my eyes and breathe slowly, rhythmically, so that I don't start to cry.

"Can you talk about Phil?" I mouth his name.

Sera nods, but looks uncomfortable and spooked, so I let up.

"Do you have anything else to eat?"

She rummages around in her pack again and takes out a Lunchable, one of those cheese and pressed-meat snack boxes, mostly packaging.

"Sorry."

"What do you mean? I longed for these. You wouldn't let me eat them!"

"Enjoy."

I take the little package apart and eat every bite of cheesy cracker and baloney, but I'm still hungry, and parched, too. I drink most of the bottle of water, then I try the tap on the mop sink.

"Safe?"

"I think so." I gulp down the rest of the water and fill the bottle again.

"He's probably growing. I think I'm having a boy."

Sera doesn't react like a grandma's supposed to. Her face stays neutral. An abrupt stubbornness comes over me.

"You could at least *act* like you're happy," I say.

The light is dim, her eyes are clouded. She won't smile because she never acts. This is the part of Sera I can't stand, her inability to prevaricate, to tell the nice lie, whitewash, even to make someone feel better.

"C'mon, just pretend like you're happy," I say, my voice miserable.

"Well, I can't. I'm hoping . . . Well, it was very sad, but at least your friend's free now."

"Don't say it, don't say it!" It's like she's darted me, put an arrow into me, the sudden hurt is that intense. "Don't you dare say it!" She wants me to lose the baby. And I'm suddenly furious at my mom and wish that I could get out of this mop closet just so I didn't have to sit so close to her. I don't want you to be affected by her lack of instinctive love. I move as far away as the couch cushion allows. I think of curling up on the hard concrete floor—but she's the one who should get off! And the thing is, she's not sorry. She won't apologize for what she considers honesty. Why should she, even when it hurts somebody else, somebody desperate, somebody who needs a lie?

"I just hate it when you will not *compromise*," I hiss.

"It's my truth," she says, sadly, moving her shoulders in a defensive shrug.

Her truth. It's like she's bent two electric wires in my brain together. I feel sparks.

"I'm so *tired*! You and your fucking truth!"

She glares at me and I know what she's thinking. I'm not grateful that she came back to the city, that she found out where I was, that she somehow got a job at the hospital using impossible-to-obtain fake papers, got a job in food service, handled all that meat and meat-based substance. All for me.

"I know you want me to lie," she says bitterly. "Well, tough. I can't. I wish the baby had never happened."

I jump to my feet, now, sizzling with anger.

"Oh, do you? Never *happened*? How easy, I *wish*. I wish, I wish. I *wish* I'd never been adopted. How's that? How absurd is it to wish something never had happened?"

"Ah, well . . ."

Now she's quiet and gets all reflective. In a moment I know that I will be ashamed, for as usual I have gone too far. It will be me who apologizes, me who says how sorry I am, because the next thing she'll let me know is how hurt she is. Stricken to the core. *Wish you'd never been adopted? How much truth is there in what you just said?* She'll say that, or maybe she'll just maintain that little-girlish studied silence that even infuriates Glen.

But to her credit, Sera only says, "Enough." She lifts her strong, thin hand, so pale in the almost dark that it shines like porcelain.

"Your hand, it looks so saintly, like a statue," I say, my voice all sour and harmed.

She doesn't take that bait, either. We don't go toward the old Catholic business, although there's an attraction to go there, a pull. Maybe we need a fight, to warm us up, because we can't seem to take the right turn out of the tangle of our irritations. Though I must admit she's trying harder than I am, for she manages not to go much further than "We haven't heard much from your pope."

And I can't really parry that, so I just sit back down and feel the letdown, the emptiness, the resentment over the fact that nobody but me appreciates your presence here on earth. I'll just have to appreciate you twice as hard. I'll appreciate you for everyone. I think of Eddy's letter of happiness, and the hug that Sweetie gave me. Before I know it I say to Sera, "Maybe it's a cliché, you know, about warmth and *acceptance*, Mom, but my birth family was real glad for me up there."

I feel her stiffen, and I know that I've hit the bulls-eye, which doesn't make me feel in the least bit better, but now it's too late.

"Oh," she says very quietly, "well, they would. I mean, Cedar, it's easy to say how marvelous your being pregnant is, but when it comes right down to it, you know, the hard thing is to look clearly at the situation. The tough thing is to see the problems it presents." She nods to herself, clearly steaming inside. Now that we're equally hurt, I go in for the last word.

"There's nothing wrong with showing a little positive emotion, Mom; it won't kill you to be loving."

But now I've taken it right over the edge, I guess, because Sera's head slowly bends and her shoulders curve and her face is in her hands. As soon as she sobs, I'm a fountain of tears, and after a while we are both moaning and hiccuping. And that's it—a not untypical Cedar/Sera fight, no lasting hurt done, as long as we end up crying in each other's arms.

Once most of the employees go home, the white-haired lady unlocks the door and lets us out so we can go to the bathroom. We take some rags from the mop closet to wash ourselves with, and scuttle down the hall behind her. She brings us to a special, private bathroom that must have been constructed for the use of the postmaster or one of the higher-up postal officials, and here again, she locks us in. She says she'll be back later and she walks away, jangling the keys on her belt. I'm not sure what all the locking and unlocking means, but I assume that there must be postal workers who do not know that we are hiding in the building.

The bathroom's made out of that gold-pink stone, polished, plus a brown marble trim. The mirrors are framed in brass but the faucets have been replaced with new aluminum spigots. The water's cold of course, but it feels good to wash. We even have a bar of strawberry soap from Mom's pack. The hospital mirrors were made of reflective steel, and my face was a blur. So as I wash and dry my body, I am overcome with the sin and embarrassment of pride. While Mom is in the toilet stall, I look at myself in a real mirror for the first time since I was at home, and I marvel at my breasts. They are like big fake breasts, magazine breasts, completely drop-dead gorgeous. They stick straight out and when I put them back into their old worn bra they swell—great cleavage. I turn back and forth, catching the light, dazzled with myself—my skin is so clear, my hair so thick. And you're this giant ball, hard and resilient, sticking straight out over my skinny legs. It is a shame to cover up such glory with long underwear, overalls, boots, a jacket. I'd love to wash my hair but Mom says that we should ask how long we've got. We don't know what's going to happen to us. So I jam a dark blue postal-worker stocking cap on over my hair and when the white-haired lady lets us out, into a darkened hall this time, I follow her.

"We're loading now," she says to Mom, and we slip through the dim night out to the dock where the back of a semitrailer truck stands, its back door rolled up and open. It is a shimmery, prickling, peaceful night. A slim man wearing an earflap hat gestures us forward, onto the truck. We step into the shadow of the trailer and hunch through a narrow opening past stacks of mail crates. I only see that the slim man is Hiro when we reach the front of the trailer, just behind the cab, where there is a sort of cage—protection against the mail crates in case they topple. He helps us into the thin space and shows us hammocks, bottles of water, quilted blankets— the kind movers use to protect tabletops. There are two black down jackets and two sets of heavy-duty snow boots. A bag of food and a covered bucket.

I thank Hiro and I try to hug him, but he ducks his head, shy or restrained, and only says, "I don't know how long you'll be in here."

"Who's this mail for?"

"Towns north."

"Any junk mail?"

"No junk mail anymore." Hiro grins. "One of the few positives. How are you feeling?" He looks at me, his head inclines, he waits for me to answer, his face beaming as though I am just any lucky pregnant woman.

"Good," I say. Hiro nods, satisfied. He is wearing a quilted postal employee jacket, but his scarf is a knitted orange and black Halloween scarf.

"Only a week to go," I say, pointing at the scarf.

"No tricks, just treats, this year," he says, making friendly, nonsense small talk. "I am not driving, but don't worry. Chris will get you there before the candy is gone."

"Who's Chris?"

"Me," says a man stepping through the stacks. He's short, shrewd and boxy, powerful; he's got a dark goatee and underneath his CAT cap the start of a scroungy mullet.

"Chris will take good care of you," says Hiro.

"How come you've looked after me?" I ask Hiro just as he's about to go. "How come you found me at the hospital? Brought me the messages?"

Hiro looks surprised at my question, taken aback, as though I should know. "You were on my route," he says.

We're settled in our cage, wearing the heavy boots and jackets. Mom folds the movers' quilts so that they fit inside the hammocks. There are metal hand- and footholds in the walls of the truck so we can climb, catch, roll into the hammocks, and swing free. Mom takes the higher one, and that night, as we swing lightly in the knitted hammocks, the truck moves slowly along. I think how surprising some people are. Hiro has casually risked his life for me because I am on his mail route. Recycling-truck Shawn, with the tragic brown eyes, is devoting himself to the rescue and hiding of pregnant women. Tia's husband did exactly what they'd agreed, and now they are together.

Slowly, in the dark truck, not a crack of light coming through in any part of the walls, I am lulled to a sleep that goes straight into Orielee's murder. I resist, choke out a warning to myself. But it seems I have to pass through her death, through her kicking and grunting, through the pupils of her eyes, every time I begin to fall asleep. Once I pass through the murder and Orielee's legs splay open and Tia falls

backward, gasping, onto the floor, I relax into a black unconscious-
ness. I dive in, submerse, and breathe oblivion, my favorite element.

OCTOBER 24

Stuck at a weigh station.

Peeing in the covered bucket. Reading by flashlight until Mom
stops me, telling me we'll need the batteries. They are LED batteries and should last for a real long time, but I suppose she's right.
Luckily, a thin gap in the truck's siding admits a slash of radiance
that I can move across the page. It is only about a half inch wide,
so I move the notebook forward as I write, then return it to the left
edge of my knees, then move it forward again. I'm probably this
hungry because you're adding baby weight—you are supposed to
gain about half a pound every week from now on. Seems like a lot,
to me, and I wonder if your hiccups have anything to do with how
fast you're growing. I use you as a kind of shelf, resting a cup of tea
on you or this book. Your lungs are still fragile, little bits of tissue
paper, but your brain is zipping with electric energy and all parts of
your brain are lots more mature. To create all these new cells and
keep you alive, I've made a lot more blood, and my heart's beating
about 20 percent faster than normal. Women often get hemorrhoids
around this time, and sad to say, the crummy and erratic food has
affected me in just this way. I need green things—roughage, as Sera
calls it. Next stop, she's going to find some, even if she's got to stew
up fallen leaves. It's so ignoble, really brings me down, humbles me
a lot. I just want to cry when I know I have to take a shit—it hurts so
much, sweat pops out on my forehead. Mom's emergency supplies
do not include hemorrhoid cream but she thinks that she can score
Metamucil. That, dear baby, is what the future's come down to. My
butt's both numb and painful, and I really don't want to think about
my butt this much, so it's really good that I am beautiful.

I am going to complete the pages of *Zeal* before we get off, because I can send them back with Chris. I'll address them to my printer, and maybe even ask them to retrieve my mailing list from the last issue. I can picture those last issues neatly stacked on the shelf just beside my plastic box of stamp rolls and scissors. I wish that I could occupy myself, now, writing the addresses of my three hundred subscribers out on stacks of manila envelopes—if I just had manila envelopes!

Dear subscribers! You mean so much to me!

That is *not* how I'm going to begin my editor's note, or introduction to this issue, but that is how I feel. Grateful for their constancy and support. I owe this issue to them and it occurs to me that perhaps—would it make sense? Should I add something personal about my own pregnancy, and tell them how profound the physical experience has been in shaping my views on the Incarnation? It is surely not necessary to include many details about the father—a cursory note will be enough. The more I think of it, the more convinced I am. This pregnancy is nothing short of momentous, and instructive, and I should share whatever truths I've gleaned from living through it. If the printers think that there will be trouble, perhaps they can distribute it underground. I don't know. But I do think it is important that I share with my subscribers the truth.

Dear Subscribers,

This may be your last issue of Zeal *magazine, and so I want to take this opportunity to thank each and every one of you for showing your support by sending in your checks and keeping up my subscription list. I have news that may upset some of you, but I think it only right to come forward and say that I am pregnant, and that so far the pregnancy has gone well in spite of the relentless persecution that I have suffered along with every other pregnant woman in this time. I am writing now from a secret location, and am indebted to people whose names are unknown to me. By the time you open this issue of the magazine, I may very well be holding my baby in my arms. I hope so. I have learned a great deal about the subject of this issue—the Incarnation. That my body is capable of building a container for the human spirit has inspired in me the will to survive. It has also shown me truths.*

Someone has been tortured on my behalf. Someone has been tortured on your behalf. Someone in this world will always be suffering on your behalf. If it comes your time to suffer, just remember. Someone suffered for you. That is what taking on a cloak of human flesh is all about, the willingness to hurt for another human being.

I have seen a young woman in labor endure more pain than Christ did in his three-hour ordeal on the cross. She suffered continuously for twenty-four hours. And I have heard of labors lasting much longer. To bear this child, I will go through whatever pain I must. I can't help wishing for an epidural, but this is why I'm writing. This is the Incarnation. The spirit gives flesh meaning. We're only meat bundles, otherwise.

I believe in this issue that my colleague Father Mirin Thwaite sheds light, just as Bartolomé de Las Casas did in arguing for the existence of the souls of indigenous tribal people of colonial South America, that the children born during this present time will be possessed of souls whether or not they are capable of speech, and should be considered fully human no matter what scientists may conclude about their capacity to think and learn. I mean, I still don't know what's going on—but had to throw that in.

Also in this issue, another paper on the Incarnation concerns the actual moment of Immaculate Conception, and examines textual and artistic evidence that the orifice of impregnation for the Blessed Virgin Mary was her ear. Taking into account recent left brain/right brain studies, the author concludes that a word whispered in the left ear would have affected Mary's right hemisphere and caused the deep flood of emotion so crucial to mom-child bonding. This emotional "baptism" may have allowed

*Mary to go forward, even knowing that great suffering was to
result from her baby's birth. I can only say, from my point of
view . . .*

Sera is awake—it is as though I can feel her thinking above me in her
hammock. I've been jolted out of the knife blade of radiance that was
enabling me to write, and I've scrambled back into my swinging bed,
the most comfortable place to ride. The movement is lulling, the air
is greeny black. Yet I fight sleep. Fear comes over me and I struggle
to stay awake—I do not want to lose control of my thoughts and
go back to Orielee's murder. Instead of lessening, growing dulled
with time, muted, the memory or dream is growing more and more
powerful. Each time it's worse. I am experiencing it as a drama that
unfolds with such swift violence it shakes my bones.

This can't be good for you, the stress.

We jolt on and on. Miles. Eventually, it occurs to me that maybe
I really do need to confess what happened, get it out of the interior
of my mind. And since there is no priest I have only one person who
can hear my confession.

"Mom?"

But now she's fallen asleep. I call her, louder; she wakes and answers, a little grumpy, "What is it?"

"I need to talk to you."

"Uhhh."

"Really bad, Mom."

She sounds extremely tired, moody, and groggy, but I'm overcome with the urge to clear my conscience. Maybe I can confess to
her in her sleep and that way I'll feel better, having spoken aloud,
and she won't know what I've said and what I've done.

"So Mom, I have to tell you something. It's been eating away at
me and I can't sleep very well, can't sleep at all, really. So anyway,
Mom? Here goes. I killed, I *had* to kill someone, Mom, back at the

hospital. See, we were just about ready to leave when this nurse named Orielee, she was okay though she wasn't trustworthy and she definitely was a snoop, the nurse discovered that we were hiding our rope in the heating vent. Mom?"

"Yeah . . . I'm listening . . . ," she mumbles.

"Good, okay, so then Tia and I thought maybe she had not seen it or she wasn't going to give us away. And we had jumped up and were walking behind her, I mean, we couldn't have looked guiltier! Maybe we wouldn't be here, maybe we would have let her go, but then as she was going out the door, she *laughed*. That laugh, it just said everything, you know? You know, Mom? Mom?"

"'Course, honey."

"Okay. So Tia had ripped off a strip of her hospital gown—she was taking that apart to make a bag to carry down her stuff. She threw this strip around Orielee's neck and started strangling her with it. Of course, there was no getting out of it once she started killing the nurse—we couldn't exactly stop and say *excuse us*, could we? I didn't know up until that time that Tia even could speak, but she glares at me and says, *Little help?* That strikes me as funny now, sorry! Little help! And she's killing this poor nurse with a pretty name who is going to betray us. I thought it would be the Slider who found out, but no, it had to be Orielee. I'm sorry, but I wish that it had been the Slider, because she was so easy to despise. I keep thinking, now, of how somebody had to discover Orielee stuffed in the closet, hanging off the clothes hook. That would be a sickening shock, huh, seeing her? I tried to turn her face away from the door, and we'd covered her head with a pillowcase, but still. So anyway, what I'm telling you, Mom, is that I committed a murder. I have to go to hell now, I think. I don't know if I can be absolved or not—I'm saying lots of prayers, of course. I've got my rosary in my hand this very minute. But if I do have to go to hell, I'd like to know what it will be like. What do you think it will be like, Mom?"

"Huh?"

"Mom?"

"Uh-huh?"

"What will hell be like?"

She's silent, but she stirs around a little and soon I can tell, even in the dark, I don't know how, that she has finally risen to consciousness and opened her eyes.

"Did you ask what will hell be like?"

"Yeah, what's your version of hell?"

"I think, honey, well I sort of think it's right now. I mean, things always could get worse, knock wood, if they should catch us, but Cedar"—her voice gets very gentle, as if she's really shocked that I haven't figured this out—"hell is what's happening right now, here on earth."

"I never thought of that, really." I let the notion settle in. Then I wonder. "Politically or otherwise?"

"By otherwise, you mean everything going backward?"

"Turning around to the beginning. Maybe that's not the same as going backward."

"Well, it is for me." And her voice is so sad, when she says this, beyond tears. Pure loss. The Catholic definition of hell is just that— pure loss. Loss of God. There's fire too, but I think it is more the metaphysical torment of unknowing. The flames of eternal confusion. So perhaps according to this definition she really is in hell. I am stricken with this, and want more than anything to make my mom feel better. Nothing I can say will really cheer her up. I also realize that she most definitely did not get the gist of my confession, and I do not feel at all that I've lightened my shame and guilt. But I can tell her something else.

"Here's something strange, Mom, please—just hear me out. I have this feeling, as I carry this baby into life, that things aren't really going backward. Things aren't really falling apart. All that is happening, even the purest chaos, physical and personal, even political, is basically all right. I know it seems naïve. You might even say it's hormones. But the feeling is so powerful that I have to tell you.

I am happy. Awful things are happening all around us, true, and I have done the most terrible thing of all, but I am happy at the very pit of myself. I feel this stupid joy. A sense of existence. A pleasure in the senseless truth—we happen to be alive. We didn't ask for it. We just are."

She's quiet, but it is a listening and considering silence.

"That's all I've got to go on, right now, Mom," I add. "So maybe if you're thinking of a way to talk me out of it, you shouldn't."

"No," she answers, "I wouldn't do that."

Later on, she says, "I really wish that I could feel it too."

And I say to her, "Mom, when you see this baby, I think you will."

"I hope so," she says in a very small, doubtful voice, in the dark.

We don't talk for a long time after that. But in my mind I answer her, swinging in the blackness, my heart pumping fast with a love that is burning richer and hotter with every fresh new cell of blood, every icy flash of neuron, a love of you, a love of everything. Fierce, merciless, sticking to the world like blazing tar, this love expands. And I'm thinking—of course you will be happy when you see my baby, yes, you will be overjoyed. He is the light of the world!

PART

III

Full of dandelion greens and gas-station ramen, I lounge in a cushy fake-leather desk chair. An attention to my comfort is the only notice I am shown here—no hiding me, no concern about gravid female detention. Eddy sits at the head of the tribal council meeting table. He has won another election in which he did not mean to participate, but opportunities within the chaos were too good to pass up, he said. He is still working on his endless memoir, only there is, he says, a bit more redemption. The meeting table is expanded by the addition of several heavy-duty plastic banquet tables, because there is a crowd here. It is standing room only although we are not in the usual meeting room but on the community college basketball court. Behind him, a hand-drawn reservation real estate map is unrolled across the wall. The land parcels on the map are carefully platted out and colored—green, yellow, purple. Eddy explains that like almost every other reservation, ours was lost through incremental treaties and then sold off in large part when the Dawes Act of 1862 removed land from communal ownership. Some land was parceled out to the Ojibwe, the other land was "excess" and homesteaded out to white people. If the land included lakefront property, it was declared excess with an eye to the growing number of city people who wanted to escape to a cool rustic home during the heat of summer. On Eddy's map the land owned by non-Indians is yellow. The green is State Forest. The purple is tribal. Most of the map is yellow, some green, a bit less purple. The room is full of tribal members, more are clustered in the doorway, and the halls are stuffed with people too. Nobody says a word. They are waiting for Eddy.

He stands up, and when he speaks his voice is light but resonant. "Hello, my relatives," he says. "Every week from now on, we meet, same time and same place. Over the next month you will see this map change. The green parcels can already be colored in— changed directly from green to purple. We have secured state land. The yellow is what we are working on now, and I think we are being reasonable. We're not taking back the whole top half of the state, or Pembina, Ontario, Manitoba, or Michigan, all our ancient stomping grounds. We're just taking back the land within the original boundaries of our original treaty. We *were* all set to conduct a compassionate removal of non-tribal people living on our land at present, but I am relieved to tell you that we haven't needed to put removal into action. They've all removed themselves. The lake-home people have gone back to the Cities. Let us bow our heads and pray for their plight."

Heads bow, words are muttered. Behind Eddy, my little sister, who has gone from Goth-Lolita to Overheated Preppie, is wearing a tight oxford shirt the color of Pepto-Bismol, shiny brown penny loafers, a ponytail, and tight little-boy khakis. She is looking at another map on a flip chart and using a purple marker to shade in the land parcels. Her marker squeaks on the glossy paper. A woman in an elaborately beaded hair clip makes a motion to speak. Eddy recognizes her.

"There's been trouble."

Eddy nods. "Most of the yellow parcels that you see are clustered around the lake, and these are ninety-nine percent lake homes. Uninhabited at present. We have used a lottery system to reclaim the property for our homeless, or tribal members living in substandard housing. We have also begun to house our returning urban relatives. As half our population lives off res, we're set to double in this crisis. We will gain back many of our urban brothers and sisters, and enjoy the benefits of more teachers, professors, doctors, lawyers, artists, poets, and gang members. Yes, there has been trouble. We have had to take some unusual means to solve problems. We have mobilized our police force, our Ogitchidaag. We tried to conduct compassionate traditional police work."

Eddy sighs and looks around the room.

"But some people just keep fighting our compassion, you know?"

Little Mary finishes the last bit of coloring and stands back from the map. Everyone looks at the map, quietly, the people behind me craning to see. The map is substantially purpler now and there are little gasps, murmurs. A few of the old people looking on are weeping silently with their chins thrust out. I see an older man wearing a cap that says Iraq Veteran. Tears are streaming down the lines of his face, down his neck, into the collar of his shirt.

OCTOBER 28

I have pumped up the cushy blow-up mattress and made my nest on one side of Little Mary's room. I am lying on my hip with a pillow between my legs because my back hurts. She is curled in about two acres of yellow and green crocheted afghan. I have one too. The result of Grandma's knitting. Mary's room is tipping back into derangement again, but she seems to have made heroic efforts to control the understory. No strata of mashed insects, soda cans, and chip bags. Just clothing. At the moment there is no place I would rather be. Though I am supposed to be moving somewhere else, probably farther north and safer. This feels like a burrow. The hills of her balled-up clothing almost feel protective.

"So." Mary leans over the edge of her bed, looks down at me. Her eyes are completely outlined in swoops of purple eyeliner and she's done lavender eye shadow up to her brows. The purple, she says, is a political reference to tribal clawback of treaty land. She's still wearing the Pepto-Bismol blouse and has added a huge green bow to her ponytail.

"The baby? Are you scared?"

"I'd be crazy if I wasn't scared."

She nods, flops down on her stomach, folds her arms, and rests her chin on her wrists. She tells me that she's been talking a lot to Grandma. She tells me that Grandma has hinted that we have "supernatural" blood.

"What does that even mean?"

"Maybe we're, like, Rugaroo people. The ones who change to wolves?"

I can believe it of Little Mary with her fangy smile and blazing witch eyes. She has changed her lipstick to magenta pink—it glows in the dull light.

"Do you know if you have a boy or girl? Or twins?"

"I had an ultrasound, then more ultrasounds while I was in the hospital. They didn't let me see the last ones, but the first one I saw. I still don't know the gender, but I have this feeling it's a boy. There was only one baby. Nowhere to hide another."

Little Mary turns over in her bed, stares up at the ceiling, her hands on her little caved-in belly.

"This sucks so bad," she said. "I wanted to have some babies, maybe, like someday."

She turns back over and looks down the edge of her bed. The dusk is deepening and the room is quickly transformed and obscured by shadows. She bites her shiny hot pink lip and frowns at me.

"Who's the dad?"

When she says this, a wave of feeling hits. Forgiveness. Remembering. This excruciating mixture of pain and joy seems, in retrospect, happiness. I'm so eager to talk about your father. Although she hasn't asked for details, I describe his deep soft voice, his good-natured face, warm eyes, thick black hair. I tell Mary about his capable square hands, his favorite plaid flannel shirts, about his scratched-up work boots. How much he loves real Neapolitan pizza. I show her my fake golden wedding ring. They didn't take that from me. Little Mary listens with complete attention and doesn't interrupt except to ask hushed grown-up questions like where he's from and what his family is like. I stop talking at some point. The fact I don't know whether Phil is alive or dead now catches up with me. And whether I can, truly, forgive him. My chest is so tight I can hardly breathe. The room swims around me, darker, carrying me away on a raft of exhaustion and loss.

As I am floating on that tide, something happens that may be supernatural. A presence sits on the edge of the blow-up mattress, weightless, formless, protective. It is a kind shadow. Maybe an angel. Magnetic and gentle, its love settles over me like a buoyant cape. Together, we sleep.

NOVEMBER I—ALL SOULS

Sweetie wakes me by tickling my feet with the tips of her fingers. The sun is late morning high. I've slept so long that most of the air has leaked from my mattress and my hip is touching through onto Mary's floor pads of lumpy clothes. I open my eyes a crack, see Sweetie, drift sleepward. It almost hurts to feel this good. Sweetie watches me. Her joyous pixie eyes are fixed on me. She's hardly smiling, yet her face is always on the verge of hilarity. We regard each other without speaking, an agreeable silence.

"How you feeling?" she says at last.

"Like I want to have this baby tomorrow."

I stretch hard and then cradle you, sitting up. Sweetie doesn't say anything, just helps me to my feet. I'm wearing a huge black T-shirt that says Anishinaabe Warrior, and a pair of shrunken sweatpants that tie underneath my vast belly. I look like crap, but I feel wonderful.

"I'm so big there's nowhere to really hide me. But are they looking? Does the tribal militia protect pregnant women? I want to stay right here. I don't want to go farther north. Right here is where I want to have my baby. Except . . . maybe not in this room."

Sweetie just says, "We'll talk to Eddy."

In the kitchen, the all-purpose connecting room of the house, Mom mixes brown sugar into the raisin-dotted oatmeal and gets ready to spoon oatmeal into Grandma's mouth. Grandma watches, her eyes sharp sparrow eyes, ready to peck. As Mom raises the spoon to feed a bite to her, Grandma snatches the spoon from her hand and begins to shovel in the oatmeal by herself.

"Okay!" says Mom.

She turns as I come in and her smile is subdued. She is worried about us being here, I can tell. Sweetie pulls up behind her.

"I'm gonna make you brown oatmeal cakes," she says.

Sweetie opens the little firebox and adds another piece of wood to the old cookstove with green enamel trim. Last August it was a homey decorative piece of nostalgia set in a corner and covered with knickknacks. Now it is the center of the house. Sweetie spoons a clump of congealed oatmeal onto a cast-iron skillet. Then drips bacon grease into the skillet, runs it under the oatmeal cake, presses it with a spatula. A delicious smell comes off the pan and she delicately lifts the edge of the oatmeal cake, flips it. More brown oil slides underneath. She tips the cake onto my plate. It prickles with delicate crust and is so good that I ask for another before I've finished the first.

Sera looks at me ironically, and the look I give her back says, "Yeah, bacon grease." I pat my belly. The black T-shirt is stretched tight.

"Only forty-two shopping days until Christmas," I say, my mouth half full of crispy oatmeal. "I should wear a bow around my belly."

It is like I've dropped a stone into a well. Mom's silence in the kitchen magnifies the words so they seem to echo. I look up from my plate because the sensation in the room is so peculiar—I can tell Mom is trying to control her hyperalertness and fear. They all know my due date, but only Mom is frozen.

"Hey, it was a joke!" I try to lighten the atmosphere. But nobody says a word. I sense that each hopes the other will speak first, but none of them can think of what to say, I guess, because one by one they shut their mouths. At last, Grandma croaks, "My first baby ran me ragged. Get me the album, Sweetie."

Sweetie goes into the other room to find it. I'm bewildered by my mom's stricken face, her stiff back.

"Don't worry, Mom."

"Of course," she says swiftly. "You'll be fine."

"I couldn't find your book, Grandma," says Sweetie, returning.

"Now come on, Cedar. We're gonna sit on the back porch before the air gets too cold. The sun's out nice today. We'll get some fresh air."

Sweetie's got a cigarette half hidden in her palm. She sees me notice it.

"My stash," she says. "When things blew up, we quick threw the inventory in the basement. Mainly, we use 'em for—"

"Trade," I say. "And nobody delivers on their due date. Don't stress yourself."

"Babies don't stress me," says Sweetie. She swivels her hips and strikes a match, poses to accept a light from herself. "I needed an excuse, though, to come out here and smoke. And talk to you."

"Me?"

"Yeah, you . . . wanna talk?"

"What about?"

She looks down at her feet, in cute moosehide moccasins trimmed with rabbit fur. Sweetie makes them. She's making a pair for me, and for you, baby. But she won't show them to me until you are born. Old-time Ojibwe superstition. She shrugs, blows smoke, and mutters.

"What do moms and daughters talk about?"

"Beats me. I'm not doing so hot with Sera."

I am stalling because this is so unexpected. Sweetie momming me when in truth I've almost begun to think of her like an older sister. Someone more like me than Sera, which makes me feel happy and disloyal all at the same time. But there is something that I want to ask Sweetie. And I want to ask her without getting hostile, or upset, because maybe I am starting to understand that her decision may have been more difficult than I could understand, before you.

"Did you actually see me, as a baby I mean, before you gave me away?"

I try to say this in a neutral voice but my throat quavers. And I can immediately tell that Sweetie was hoping to talk about something less fraught and emotional. But I don't feel like letting up. So I wait. She lights another cigarette.

"Shit," she says. "This is my last one. Okay. I had you, didn't I? So yes, I did see you. And Glen was there."

"Wait, not Sera? Just Glen?"

Sweetie eyes me carefully, then gives a little shake. "Glen was there first, I mean. It was, you know, this open adoption kind of thing. So we had a couple of days where I was in the hospital and I was . . . see, I was around Little Mary's age and pretty much the apple didn't fall far from the tree. She's just like I was. Only I was punk."

"Punk?"

"Yeah. Imagine. Me at nine months and neon-yellow mohawk. Rings and studs everywhere possible. I was still decked out when you were born. The delivery nurses kept coming in to take our picture."

"Do you have a picture?"

"Yeah. It wasn't in the album, it was in a little envelope I tucked in the back. Wait a sec."

She slips back in the house and is back before I can panic about the picture—a new possibly upsetting piece of story. She holds it out, carefully. The edges are soft and frayed. I realize that she's looked at it many times. This wrenches me, but in a sweet way. The photograph makes me laugh. Weirdly, it also makes me happy. Young Sweetie sits in a hospital bed against a backdrop of white pillows, pink carnations, rosebuds, and baby's breath. Lots of flowers! There are a couple of pink Mylar balloons almost out of the frame. I am a nondescript newborn, a doll bundle in her arms, and Sweetie in a hospital gown is smiling shyly, her face glinting with silver jewelry. Septum, nose bridge, medusa, labret, eyebrow piercing, even angel bites. Her bright yellow-green hair has flopped over and her eye makeup's smeared.

"You're so pretty," I say.

"Yeah, pretty weird I guess."

"No, pretty. And I do look like you. I see that now. Did you ever have doubts, I mean, about having me?"

"Nah. It was meant. At the time, I loved your father a lot. I wanted to have you, but I didn't live with Grandma then. I had my own path to follow. I couldn't bring you with."

"Your path led to Eddy and to Little Mary."

"Eventually. And it led to Saint Kateri. And because of her, I'm sure of it, my prayers were answered and my path led back to you."

Sweetie gives me a big funny eyebrow-raised grin that tells me the path was crooked and wild.

NOVEMBER 6

Mom's working on the dishes, cleaning the kitchen in that absorbed and militant way she has—working left to right she methodically wipes down each item and either puts it away or cleans beneath it and sets it back into place on the counter, properly aligned. She has taught me to clean the way she cleans and I have recognized it as one thing given to me through nurture, a tool I can use to stave off despair. I've soothed anguish and fought madness by minutely scraping at a stain on the counter or a burnt-in bit of soot on the side of a pot. I go inside, and for a while work alongside my mom, without speaking. At last, I get up the nerve.

"We've got to talk about this, Mom."

She puts down her rag and leans against the counter, frowning at the floor.

"What *this* do you mean? There's a lot of *this*."

I decide that I am going to use Sera on Sera. I'll pretend to be her. "Maybe we should assess the situation," I say. "Glen hasn't gotten in touch. We don't know if he has a place for us. There doesn't seem to be an actual plan other than getting this far. So I'd like to stay here."

"There is a plan," she says.

"What is it?"

She looks at her softened, soaked hands. Presses on her ragged nails. Sometimes I wish I could see my hands in her long thin fingers. My hands are more like Glen's hands, strong with big knuckles.

We sit down at the kitchen table and she reaches for my hands, holds my fingers.

"Look, Cedar. You're right. We haven't heard from Glen. But if he were in trouble, I'd feel a vibe. So I am sure he's okay, working on a safe place for you. Things change constantly. I think we'll stay put for now, but don't get too comfortable. You've got seven weeks left. So much could happen, right? The Church of the New Constitution has split the military. They're calling in drone strikes on the basis of voice and facial recognition, so people are holed up anywhere there is a tunnel system. There is a whole city underneath St. Paul now, in hospitals, universities, old convents, the state capitol, all connected underground. And the drones are so artful, so small, that we have to be careful."

"What do they look like?"

"Bugs. And there are Listeners out there."

"What do they look like?"

"Dust. Leaf mold. Seeds. And some are transparent floaters, people call them Ears."

"What do they look like?"

"Ears."

"For real? They had to be literal?"

"Maybe the snoops have a sense of humor. Some are soft, almost invisible. You catch one you can squish it like a slug."

"Were these things around before?"

"I guess they were being developed? Some corporation could be trying them out. They like to hang around the tribal offices. Eddy nets them. Puts them in this box with the recordings of the tribal council meetings going back thirty years."

"Ha. I hope somebody really bad is on the listening end. Someone who deserves thirty years of tribal council meetings."

Mom doesn't actually laugh, but she does smile.

"Weird, isn't it," she says at last. "How people just dumped the phones, the screens."

"As far from where we lived as possible."

"There are piles of them in the landfills and reclamation centers, all smashed and waterlogged."

"I miss the phones."

"I miss them too. Anyway, Sweetie's fired up the vintage radio."

"Vintage is the new *au courant*. And we're back to the moccasin telegraph," says Sweetie, coming up behind us. "Eddy has tasked our fastest kids and rehabbed gang members as runners. We get the news twice a day."

"They're like the old town criers," says Mom. "They have posts at eight places on the reservation. They run there, recite the news to whoever shows up, then run back."

"As for food and stuff," says Sweetie, "it's all barter. We have big town markets where nobody fights because we need to exchange stuff."

"People go to the markets under truce," says Mom. "You just can't be pregnant, that's all."

Her voice is sharp. Sweetie sighs, throws up her plump hands, and leaves the room. I look down at my black cotton beach ball, and my eyes fill with tears, like again she is accusing me.

"I'm sorry, on edge," says Sera. "Maybe I'm more worried about Glen than I'll admit."

Sera links her arms around me and we stand in Sweetie's kitchen, you between us. The wood range exudes a gentle heat and inside of it there are muted pops and sifting noises as the flames consume the wood. For the first time, last night, I did not dream of killing Orie-lee. The couple of times I woke, Little Mary's breathy purring put me back to sleep. I felt safe as an animal surrounded by hills of its own shed skins. Near morning, I dreamed of Phil. I saw him walking toward me on the highway.

"You know, Mom, my baby has a father." Resentment and pain clog my chest. She doesn't answer.

"I love him."

Sometimes I fantasize he didn't turn me in. I don't have a choice about loving Phil. I just do.

"I know you care very deeply for Phil."

Sera pats my back as she delivers these overly formal words, but there are tears in her voice, too, so I suppose that we both feel desperate for different reasons.

"You make me feel like there is something wrong with loving him."

She stares at me without seeing me, like she's making up her mind to tell me something. Then she tells me.

"Cedar, I've kept something from you. The survival rates for babies are dropping lower every month."

"That's not news," I say. But the words are awful to hear. I'm very still, don't want to pull away from her too quickly. Finally I take hold of myself. I stand up. But my head feels funny and I have to sit. I've entered a mental passageway and am walking down a set of lightless stairs. There is no railing. I can't see where I'm going. I just keep placing one foot before the other until finally I reach the bottom. It is black there and I am utterly alone.

Except that what Sera says has no basis in fact. How could she know? There is no reliable source of news. Why would she tell this to me anyway, if she was thinking straight? Maybe her tension over Glen has snapped a few strings and made her fixate on doomy predictions. She's depressed. I turn to Sera, give her a forgiving smile, and gently guide her to a chair.

"Things have been so tense, Mom. Why don't you rest for a while? There's no need to keep cleaning—it looks good in here. I'll make tea."

I pat her shoulder and fill the kettle with water. "It's okay, my baby's a fighter and so am I."

My voice is fake. She starts to cry although she doesn't really cry, just gives a little sputter. I smooth her hair back around her ear. She shakes her head, as if to shake me off. I'm still patronizing her, talking lightly, rummaging around for tea. She answers me with one of her lectures, like the amateur pedant she's always been. She actually tries to backtrack.

"We begin our lives at a cellular level as female—all of us—and we develop male or female characteristics in utero. And we don't know how many human species there actually were. How can we think we've found everything? Your baby may be just . . . normal."

"Right, Mom. Like you believe that! You just told me we're gonna die."

"You don't seem to see the risk, Cedar."

"Yes I do, but what's the point of believing it? I choose to believe we'll make it."

I pick up her professor voice, sit down across from her, and keep on lecturing.

"And not only that, but humanity is going forward. Maybe on some evolutionary forked road we used some form of parthenogenesis, like sharks, like the Komodo dragon. They are capable of fertilizing their own eggs. But maybe we aren't just copying ourselves. Somehow we have begun to absorb new and genetically appropriate material. Our bodies can use it to self-engineer our pregnancies. How about a million years ago, we began outsourcing fertilization. At any time our bodies could change their minds."

I'm trying to make Sera laugh or at least smile again because she's terrifying me. But getting her out of a bleak mind-set is never easy. She continues. Her voice starts again and lulls on, tender and gentle, somehow managing to still be condescending. I get it. She assumes what happened to Tia is going to happen to me. She doesn't think you will survive. But her words remind me of a teacher soothing a preschooler heartbroken over losing a stuffed animal. With a sudden rush of gall that almost chokes me, I hate her.

Wait. I love her. But I hate her. And I love her.

NOVEMBER 10

Eddy. Secretive and subtle, with a ferret's long-waisted whip of a body. He's growing out his hair and he doesn't slouch anymore. He smiles, a lot, and brings his hand drum home at night. He plays hand drum songs and sings warrior songs out on the porch. Says his songs confuse the surveillers. His voice is reedy and penetrating. He's singing the old songs that he learned from the old men, but also a few he's made up to taunt the Listeners in the air. He tunes the drum by heating it gently near the woodstove.

"Humans have always been superfluous troublemakers," he says. "But at least we've got good songs."

"Not everybody had good songs," I say.

Eddy looks thoughtful and then nods.

"You're right. Custer had no song."

"Mother—you know *that* Mother—has no song."

"People sick for power have no song. But your baby is going to have a song."

"Really?" I'm so pleased that I give a little jump, and my baby jumps too. "You're thinking it up?"

"I had a dream about a little baby," says Eddy. "He said, 'Where's my song?'"

"You're a good grandpa," I say.

I'm incredibly happy, and sit by the stove stroking my belly, wondering what the song will be like. In public now, Eddy gives speeches and makes pronouncements like he's always been an extrovert. At home, he hums and sings. When he finishes singing, he sits at the kitchen table with stacks of papers, old land deeds. He plots strategies. Thinks of survival measures, ways to draft our young people into working for a higher purpose. Where to get seeds. Pigs. Cows. Flocks of chickens. He wants to make the reservation one huge, intensively worked, highly productive farm. He's got gangsters growing seedlings in the grow-lighted aisles of casinos. He's got them raising free pot for everyone ever since a friendly Kiowa came north via Colorado and picked up the entire spectrum of medicinal varietals. Weed's our friend, Eddy says. Given to us by the Creator not only for trading to the chimookomaanag, but for medicating all sorts of pain and for soothing the freaked-out brain.

The chimookomaanag are the Big Knives, the white people, and so far they really haven't bothered us because we seized the National Guard arsenal up at Camp Ripley, which is on our original treaty grounds. Ours. They had an amazing array of snooping equipment, slightly out-of-date U.S. military stuff, which Eddy says we use to spy on the people who are spying on us.

"We're gonna be self-sufficient, like the old days," he says.

The gas pumps at the Superpumper are still being resupplied. The oil company could care less who's in charge. The casino was, of course, rich in cash. They still have reserves they have not touched, as does the tribal bank. Some places still run on cash, old U.S. government currency, because nobody has been organized enough yet to replace it. Eddy is also war chief, with a pack of elite soldiers at his command. As with every tribe, our nation has veterans—lots of veterans—and they are friends with lots of non-Indian veterans, and together they have organized and trained our people.

Our people. My people. Your people. I could never say that before. Eddy has decolonized the uniforms of the militia.

"We've got almost two full regiments. One of them is into the flowing hair, Last of the Mohicans. They tan hides, sew their own buckskins, drill with bows and arrows and M16s and . . . you don't want to know. I never knew I had it in me, Cedar. I'm surprised. I think about seventy percent of my depression was my seventeenth-century warrior trying to get out."

Eddy's been working out—he looks tougher. He looks straight on at people now. Sometimes, Eddy eyes me over the cup he puts to his lips, then lowers it without drinking. His stare, when it focuses on a person, is long-seeing. Unnerving. He sets his cup down.

"Just so you know. We are not giving up our pregnant tribal members. Our women are sacred to us. I'm afraid we will eventually get raided, though," Eddy says. "Whichever military entity comes out on top will probably remember about us. We don't know what direction it will come from, who will lead it, what they'll have for power.

But you could get picked up anywhere. So you are as safe here as anywhere. I guess. Only—" He whirls around, kills the lights, pulls me through the back door onto the deck. Out there, he relaxes.

Together on the porch we gaze into the bare gray trunks of the thick woods just behind the house. A man and a woman in camouflage and buckskins, holding automatic weapons, lean against Eddy's car in the driveway to the left of the house. I can smell the rich tobacco smoke of their rolled cigarettes. There's woodsmoke in the air, too, and a welcome sharp bright cold. Wolves? Coyotes? Dog? They begin howling just beyond the riffle of woods.

"I've never heard wolves before." I breathe, enchanted.

"Not wolves. That's us," says Eddy. "Our new unbreakable code."

He heard them while we were in the kitchen, and dragged me out because he needed to decipher their language.

"What are they saying?"

"Drones earlier, at the casino. We should go inside."

Once we're in the house, Eddy opens a padlocked army trunk that is pushed up against the wall. He takes a rifle from the trunk and hands it to me, with a box of bullets.

"I don't want this."

"It's yours," he says.

I look down at the thing in my hands—the Custer rifle.

"Phil give you this?"

"Yes."

"So he's been here."

My throat shuts. My chest clenches up. I try to give the rifle back to Eddy.

"Where is he?"

"Gone again. I'm sorry."

Eddy brings me into the garage and shows me how to load the rifle. I'm not an enthusiastic learner, but he says that he will teach me how to shoot.

"At what? Trees? Because I'm not going to shoot a tree."

"Okay," says Eddy. "Maybe we should go to the shooting range."

I carefully set the rifle down on the cement floor.

"Look at me, Eddy. I am filled with new life. I'm not shooting anything or killing anyone. I've already done that."

"Done that? What do you mean?"

Eddy puts his arms around my shoulders. I tell him about the escape, about Tia Jackson, about Orielee, about her death. To tell what happened makes it all so vivid that I hear myself crack, then sob as though I'm broken, which I think is true. Only a broken human could do what I did. Eddy holds me to his chest.

"Don't cry, my girl," he says. "It was you and your baby or that nurse, no choice. You did what you had to do."

"I tell myself that, but it still feels like murder."

Eddy coughs delicately. "In their eyes, it will be seen as a crime. They might come after you, so we'll have to make you a new identity. Luckily, I know someone in tribal governance."

I throw myself at him, hug him, and he hugs me back.

"How would you like to be Mary Potts again?"

"It sounds wonderful."

"We'll get right on it," he says.

I hesitate, but ask anyway.

"Were you ever in a situation like I was in? Where you had to kill someone?"

"No. I'm not a soldier. What you did was combat and most people train for that. I'm out of my league too. I'm trying to be a leader and it doesn't come naturally. I'm trying to act normal. Is it working?"

"Sometimes."

"Good enough."

"So Eddy. How are the sacred women doing? And the babies?"

"Good . . . they're all fine."

"Really?"

"Of course."

"No *of course* about this, Eddy. Mom says that babies aren't surviving. Probably mothers too. And from what I saw my friend go through, I believe her."

"Sweetie will tell you it's all due to her saint. She says Saint Kateri is watching over women in a special way."

"You're lying," I say.

"I'm keeping hope alive," says Eddy.

"I am looking for a miracle, so I'm going to find Sweetie. I want a ride to the pilgrimage rock tomorrow, please? That's where I need to pray."

Eddy says he'll drive us there, early in the morning, but I've got to cover myself up thoroughly.

"Drones never stay long, but you can't be careful enough. Bring a blanket."

Eddy says that he'll even pray, in his own fashion.

"In your own fashion? Prayer is just prayer, Eddy. You make it sound fancy."

"No, I do have a fashion. When I pray, I really get right down there with Mother Earth," says Eddy. "I prostrate myself."

Sure enough, the next morning, when we get to the stone and the statue, surrounded by well-watered sod, right out of the truck Eddy throws himself on the ground. Sweetie and I step over him and kneel on the trampled grass before the statue. I keep my blanket around me.

"He says he's praying, but he just wants to take a nap," she whispers.

We cross ourselves and raise our eyes to the saint. Kateri is a nicely made statue, expensive bronze, not some cast-resin piece. Her face is mobile, gentle, but not sweet or anemic like most Virgin Marys. Kateri is grounded and shrewd. She fixes us with a critical, assessing look as if she is deciding whether we are worth her intercession. I bow my head and pray. I throw myself into the prayer. As I pray, I feel something lift out of me, as though atoms of dread have an actual weight, as though fear was fine sand in my blood. I don't get an answer from Kateri, not in so many words. When Eddy helps me up my knees are numb, my heart is drained. For the first time in weeks, I am not afraid.

Then something flickers around me, a tiny bird, clicking and whirring. And a transparent oval floats past my clasped fingers.

"Keep your head down."

Eddy is behind me, folding my blanket around me, leading me back to the car.

"Stay hunched over," he whispers, "like you're really old."

I do as he says and keep the blanket around me as I fall stiffly into the car. I already know what's happened. I've been seen.

NOVEMBER 18

You haven't dropped into birth position yet. But you are heavy as a little brick, a strong little baby. I could have you now and you could probably make it outside in the world even without a NICU. I prepare for you to tell me you are on your way, but I don't know exactly what to wait for—which twinge, kick, premonition. Sera says that I will know when I feel labor start. Isn't that always the way women are supposed to know things, by "knowing" things? She's always close by, always in the house, so that I feel her presence way too much. We were already on each other's nerves. It gets worse. The cleaning is almost constant. You'd think after Mom saved me and helped Tia have her baby, she'd get a pass. I try, but one day irritation spills over. Mom is only doing her normal superthorough kitchen job. But I just can't stand the grating sound she makes scraping bits of charred food off the inside of a pot.

"Could you stop that for a minute?"

"Sure, if you want to eat off dirty plates."

"You're scraping a pan, not a plate."

"Be my guest."

I get up and start scrubbing away. She stands beside me, guilty.

"That's okay. You don't have to."

"You're always cleaning. It's so annoying."

"What else is there to do?"

"You can go outside, Mom."

My voice is angrier than I mean it to be.

"As for me, I have to stay inside listening to you scrape your stupid bean pans."

"I'd love to go outside, but don't you get it?"

"Get what?"

She takes her pencil and paper out of her back pocket. She maintains that it is the safest way to communicate. I think she uses notes when she wants to halt actual communication. She writes: If they see me here they'll know you're here.

After I read the paper, I crush it. The paper crushing infuriates her and she hisses.

"You just take for granted, don't you, that Glen is putting himself in danger, not to mention me. All for you. But that's nothing. If Eddy or Sweetie snap their fingers, you're nice as pie. God, we spoiled you. You're obnoxious!"

Obnoxious is the word she always used when I was a bad teenager, and she knows I can't stand it. Ditto spoiled. I always react venomously, but today I go over the top. I force her to answer the question she has avoided all my life.

"Mom, how did you adopt me? Don't wiggle out of this. Tell me straight. I need to know. This time I don't want your eye rolls. I want the truth."

We are standing by the sink. Outside, the November ground is slightly frosted over. The cool of winter. I face my blue-eyed Cinderella-godmother mom, who is biting her lip. Even wringing her hands, like in a bad stage play. But slowly she is cracking. Yes, I can see it—she will tell me. I nod, holding her gaze.

"You're not adopted," she blurts out.

What a weird reversal. Impossible to take that in. My mouth

doesn't work. I shake my head to dislodge my tongue. My hair flies out of its loose ponytail.

"You're not adopted," she says again. She is still furious and maybe, I don't know, wants to hurt me. Because she says an unbelievable thing.

"Glen is your biological father."

My brain does not believe her, but my heart does. My chest hurts. I reel to a chair. Plunk down. There is just no way to absorb this. But I get it—her anxiety over Glen and her anger at me have combined to the point where she's told the truth. Again, I try for words, but there are no words or even feelings yet. It takes a long time before I start to breathe, and then sadness overwhelms me.

"If that's true, if you kept that from me, I could have had my real father all my life."

"But," says Sera, as if she was waiting for this, "even though I'm not your biological mother, aren't I your real mom?"

I stare at her. The fact that I'm hesitating throws us both. She now looks horrified at what she has revealed and where this is going. I guess, as the saying goes, the truth will make you miserable and then it will set you free. Am I now free? Is Mom? Remember, I think, she ate a gas-station hot dog for you! I am in that calm stage of shock.

"So what happened? Why isn't Glen here? Is Sweetie my real birth mom?"

"Yes."

"So . . . she and Glen had a relationship. Like the Retro Vinyl clerk. That's why he's not here?"

"Yes."

"Quit making me tell the story!"

"Okay."

"Oh my god. Mom! How did he meet her? What was he doing?"

"He was representing the tribe. A land case."

I am suddenly overcome with hurt, with fury.

"I never want to see him again. Or talk about him."

But of course that isn't true. I always loved my father. I love him now. It all fits—the times people thought he was my real father. Our similar hands, hair, even our walk. I need to tell him how this affects me, because he'll care. Won't he? But if he really cared, he would have told me. I want to try and understand what happened, even though it blows my mind. I want the stabilizing effect his presence always had on us. Without him, Sera and I can't stop fighting. His light nudges, simple jokes, his ability to pry my mother out of her obsessive head-space, all that helped. I'm afraid she's going to clean herself to death. Oh let her! I hate my mom for keeping this from me, and then I hate her even worse for telling me. At the same time, she is the bravest person I have ever known. I will never forget her showing up at that hospital with a lunch tray. But Glen!

How could Glen have agreed to lie? Was he going to lie to me all of my life?

Suddenly it hits me. Sera's insecurity. It was Sera. He was protecting Sera so that they would both be equal as parents, so he wouldn't be the "real" parent and she the possibly lesser "adoptive" parent. He gave up his "realness" for her, but when he did that, he kept his "realness" from me. He kept me wondering all my life. And even Sweetie was in on the deception.

That's the worst thing—the unnecessary deception. How I always seized on our physical likeness, but pushed it out of my mind. And the weird loneliness I now feel about being tricked all my life. I leave the room, walk down the little hallway to sit by Grandma's bed. I am just too spent with the force of all that I must absorb to do anything but stare at the shape of Grandma Virginia, hardly a ripple in the golden covers. Her severe little face is upturned, catching the light. She senses my presence immediately and says, in her thin, breathy voice, "What is it, child?"

"I found out who my real dad is. He's my real dad!"

What an absurd thing to blurt out.

Grandma's thin lips part, a tooth glistens.

"Men are tricky. I should know."

Then she tells me a story.

The Fat Man's Race

I was in love with a man named Cuthbert who could really eat. He would sit down to the table with a haunch of venison, a whole chicken, two or three gullet breads or a bucket of bangs, half a dozen ears of corn or a bag of raw carrots. He'd eat the whole lot, then go out and work in the field. He was very big, but he was also stone solid, muscle not fat. He would grab me up and set me on his lap and hug me. He would call me his little bird. I was going to marry Cuthbert and had the date of the wedding all picked out, but then his sisters turned him against me. They told him that I was after his money, I wanted his land, and also that I was having sex with the Devil.

Only that last part was true.

Our priest had warned that each one of us has two angels, a guardian angel and an angel of perversion. An angel of right and an angel of wrong. That second angel will attempt to persuade you it is the first, and I suppose I fell for it. I was visited at night in my dreams by a man in blue—a blue suit, a blue shirt, a blue tie, blue shoes, but no hat. He had black hair and black eyes, skin the color of a pale brown egg, very smooth and markless. He would take off all of his blue clothes and lay them at my feet. His instrument of pleasure, don't laugh at me, was blue also, as though dipped in beautiful ink, midnight at the tip. I would admire him, then I would lie with him all night—you know what I'm telling you. In the morning I'd wake up sick over what I'd done. But next night it would be the same again. I could not resist him. He said the sweetest things to me, like a good angel, but the things he did were darkly inspired.

Now I ask you, how was it that Cuthbert's sisters knew

the shape of my dreams? When he told me that his sisters were telling this story around, all about me and the Devil, he laughed. They were worried about how I might have my eyes on his eighty acres cleared and planted, or the money that the bank kept locked up. He laughed until he shook about the blue suit his sisters spoke of, and did not notice how, when I heard that, I nearly went faint off my feet. I recovered. I thought about it. It did not take me long to realize that the only way that Cuthbert's sisters possibly could know about my devil was if he visited them too.

I grew furious and plotted out of jealousy to throw over my devil. I would have my revenge. I decided to kill him, though I wasn't sure just how to destroy a man who existed only as a phantom, without physical substance. Then it came to me that I must dream his death. I must conceive of a knife honed and sharp.

Each night, I dreamed a knife beneath my pillow. I dreamed about its shape and weight. I dreamed its black wooden handle. I dreamed its sharpness. I dreamed the gleam of white light off its point. I dreamed the way it would feel in my hands. I dreamed how it would fit between the dream ribs of my angel of perversion. I dreamed all of this so well that on the night I reached beneath the pillow and found the perfectly dreamed weapon, it was a memory of a dream I dreamed, a dream within a dream. His death was undreamable, however, and horrible. I woke soaked with terror and tears. The nightmare haunted me all morning as I prepared for the feast day of the Assumption. A celebration was supposed to take place at the church, and at Holy Mass the priest was to read the banns preceding my marriage to Cuthbert.

I was shaky that day and my mother said I was pale. But I made six pies. Three for Cuthbert. He was running in the fat man's race. Every year only the biggest of the big men lined up. Their race, comical and thunderous, was always the feast day's high point. At the end of it, the winner would have his choice of pies and a Holy Medal for a ribbon—Saint Jude or Saint Christopher or Theresa of the Little Flower. As we drove our wagon to the church grounds, I was almost giddy with happiness—I'd killed off the Devil and would soon marry Cuthbert. His sisters would wonder at the loss of their own blue demon, but they never would know the one who killed him was me.

Then came shock. As the big men lined up at the far end of the field, as we watched, pointing and making little bets of money on this one or the other, there staggered into the group a man in a blue suit and blue shirt, blue tie, blue shoes and with black hair and pale brown skin. Only he was much, much bigger than in my dream. He lined up with the rest of them. I don't know if it was me or Cuthbert's sisters whose eyes went wider, and whose jaws dropped farther, but it was only I who knew that having killed him in a dream, I had brought the Devil to life. And here he was, racing Cuthbert for the fat man's prize.

He didn't look well at all. I saw as they began to run. He was bloated and gray as a gorged tick, his skin almost dead green. He ran holding a hand against his ribs and I nearly shrieked as he passed and turned on me the flash of his red, robbed eyes. His mouth was open and I saw that it was filled with black blood. He and Cuthbert were neck and neck, out ahead of the others, and I saw that the Devil was taunting and mocking my husband-to-be, who flew into a rage of running and leaped forward like a stag to surge ahead.

When it was over, two men lay still at the finish line. One was Cuthbert, who died of a burst heart. The other man was dead all along, people said. When they opened the blue jacket they found a knife with a black handle buried to the hilt between his ribs.

So, said Grandma, I married instead a man who hadn't

an ounce of spare flesh, a man who hated the color blue and never wore it, a man whose sisters liked me. I lived with him for fifty-seven years now, didn't I, and the two of us had eight children. Adopted twenty. Raised every kind of animal that you can think of, didn't we, and grew our corn and oats and every fall dug our hills of potatoes. We picked wild rice. Now and then we shot a deer from off the back porch, and yes we fed our children good, didn't we.

Grandma's eyes slowly open after she's finished her story, and she goes on talking in her cracked-bark voice. She tells me that she didn't know when she made those six pies for the Fat Man's Race that she was pregnant. The father of her baby was the blue man in her dream, and her son was born with strange marks. *He came out with bruises on his back and bottom. So dark they looked indigo. Didn't seem to hurt. The Devil must have kicked this one out, said the medicine lady. But I said, hugging my baby close to me, no. No. Angels must have beat him to find out how much he could endure.*

Whatever else, Grandma's story completely diverts me from the sudden reversals in my own narrative. It also feels like a warning. My father and mother, both loving and lying to me. And Phil, my angel of deception. I need a real angel. A good spirit. At night, again, as I am falling asleep I feel the presence approach again to sit at the end of my mattress. Whether or not it is an illusion, this visitor is so calming, so powerful, that I float easily into a dreamless pure sleep.

Eddy hides me in the truck and brings me to the tribal offices. His secretary takes my picture and laminates my new tribal ID. I look happy in my picture. My cheeks are round and full. I am wearing a pair of eyeglasses not my own. My hair is shiny and long. I am a mixture of Sweetie and Glen. That's me. Mary Potts.

And what sort of being am I, really? First I find that I am my father's actual child, descended of a line that goes back to Richard the Lion-Hearted. Then I find that my heritage is also bound up in a sinister blue man who impregnated my grandmother in a dream. And you, with Phil as your father, a man who did harm when he tried to do no harm, carry within you the patience of ancestors who worked with stone. Sometimes I think of the grab bag of labels and photos that I rescued from the recycling center, the fascinating collection of printed words and images. Without act or will on my part, I am creating a collage of DNA and dreams, all those words made flesh, and I am doing it even in my sleep.

NOVEMBER 19

A piece of plywood slides out of place behind the boiler, and if a raid starts I can crawl in there, I guess, and disappear. Sweetie has made the entrance undetectable. It is an actual room, newly finished inside. There are no windows, of course, but the walls are clean and freshly painted. Mom and I make peace long enough to agree that we'll go inside when we're ready. So that is where you will be born. Underground. Safe in a dug burrow. Or at least that's what I expect. After you're born we'll probably still have to hide you. But things will change. They'll leave me alone. Sweetie says I've got a girl. She overheard Sera and me arguing and heard me talking about parthenogenesis. She thinks it's hilarious that we imagine we can make our own babies now.

"Immaculate Conception. According to Cedar! That's the new thing," she says, "but I still prefer Eddy."

I shouldn't have promised Eddy to keep this stupid rifle with me, but I can't put it back in the trunk because he's locked that. I tuck it down the side of my blow-up mattress, against the wall, loaded but with the safety on. Tired, so tired, I swoon into sleep as often as I can.

NOVEMBER 20

They make their way past the dogs, through the kitchen, the living room, to the bedroom where I am sleeping in piles of Mary's dead clothes. Some tiny sound, a squeak or cough, wakes me. I hear their stealth. One of the dogs starts barking, but far away, in the field. Maybe they lured the dogs away. I pull more clothing over me and I reach down the wall for the Custer rifle. I draw it up next to me, removing the safety. I whisper to Little Mary, who shifts in her sleep but doesn't wake. The door opens, light from the hallway spills in. Under the spaghetti of stockings, scarves, shirts, jackets, leggings, my eyes are shaded. I peer out from under the wreckage. She looks straight at me.

It is Mother. Her thick hair is fiercely sprayed, the bangs immobilized. Her dark eyes are sunken in her dough face. Her lipless mouth puckers in sympathetic consternation.

"Are you in there, dear?"

She is wearing a maroon quilted down coat that reaches past her knees. Brown mittens. Rabbit-fur earmuffs. Her eyes dart around the room and she whispers, "Can you believe this shit?"

With a thrill of pride in Mary, I realize that Mother can't even see me beneath all of these wads of clothing. Now is the time to shoot, if I could shoot, but of course I can't shoot. Anyway, Mother looks like she's already been shot. As she takes in the overpowering chaos and layers of developed filth, her mouth opens and shuts. Her face crushes in, distorted, like a softened take-out box.

With an air of sacred awe, Mother backs out of the room. I feel soundless footsteps glide down the hall. I slide the rifle back down along the wall. I'm so disoriented that I immediately decide that I did not see what I did see. I can only think of nestling farther down into my sister's pile of musty tights and limp dresses. Crawling underneath the chaos. Curling up in the endless yellow afghan. All I want is oblivion. Right after I hear the tiny click of the front door and the dog outside, barking good-bye, I thank my little sister and fall into a dead black sleep.

. . .

I am pulled down, down, sucked into this sleep. I wake with a hand clapped over my mouth, Phil's hand. He drags me up, out of my mattress cave and bundled clothing, keeps his hand over my mouth as he picks up the go bag I always keep beside my bed. He whispers in my ear as he drags me outside—"They're coming back." As he puts me in a smoke-smelling car—"Don't make a sound." As he coasts down the driveway and starts the motor at the mailbox—"If they found you there, they'd take out everyone. We're going to the gas station. It's empty. We'll sneak in and you can hole up. There's a van going north this week."

I've turned to pudding. I'm so groggy and astonished that a couple of miles go by before I speak. I am pretty sure I'm in a dream, and I don't want to wake from riding in this (very nice, where'd he get this?) car with a cushy interior. I don't want to wake from the comfort of the heated leather seat, the purring engine, the world rushing by. Only the fact that Phil is driving without headlights forces me to say something.

"Uh, Phil. Headlights?"

"I know, honey. But if I was using my headlights they'd know where I was right away and could track us from the air."

There is a half-moon, enough vague radiance to make out the road. Driving without lights we seem to float. The world to either side of the highway is black space, gray foam, the trees loom, then a building with shining black windows, then the reflective pillars of gas pumps. We turn in. Phil bumps over the curb, into the woods behind the Superpumper, pulling as far as possible into the brush. We sit in the car as the engine ticks down and cools. We are together in the night. I wake up.

"You turned me in."

In answer, he takes off his flannel shirt, pulls his T-shirt over his head.

"Feel."

I put my hands on his shoulders, down his back, catch my fingertips on the lumps and skin knots and terrain of scabs and scars. He puts my hand to the side of his cheek. I touch his face and hair—it is like a ball of twine has been glued in random lengths onto his scalp, underneath his hair. His voice rasps out.

"I'm like that all over, and it's worse inside. I don't even remember giving them your name. I thought I was a hero, but I'm not."

He put his shirts back on, gets out, and piles brush over the back of the car. Covers the reflective taillights. I pull a blanket from the backseat and huddle underneath. When he gets back in, closing the door gently, he says he thinks we should wait in the car and make sure they don't try breaking into the Superpumper.

"How do you know they're coming?" I ask.

"I was with them," he says briefly.

I mull that over. So, I'm sitting with one of Mother's helpers. And it is my angel, Phil, who still smells the way he used to, like inevitability and ironed shirts. Though where would he get the chance to iron a shirt? Maybe he just smells slightly scorched. I can't think clearly. It is powerful magic to be sitting next to Phil, who has survived, though he is covered with welts and scars. He is the father of my baby and I start to cry, silently, my face in my hands, the tears popping out and rolling down my fingers.

No I don't. I sit in the heated car seat, dry-eyed, outraged. Because I was right about the reason Grandma told me her story. It was indeed a warning.

Phil. Another angel of deception. Phil. Fucking angel of wrong.

"So, Phil, are we just waiting so you can get credit for turning me in? Are you going to drag me out when they get here? Maybe you got scratched up by a flock of chickens. How do I know you're for real?"

There's no answer for an uncomfortable piece of time. I can feel that Phil is struggling either with my grasp of the truth or my lack of gratitude.

"I guess we wait," he says at last.

"I guess I don't have a choice."

So we wait, and after a while I fall asleep. And after still more while, it is nearly morning. Phil says Eddy has opened the front door.

He helps me climb stiffly out of the car and we make our way to the back of the gas station, where Eddy lets us into the storage room.

"I'm going to start things going like usual," he says. "I got a buzzer on the door, extra loud, so you'll hear when somebody comes in. It's usually pretty quiet this time of day."

He goes away and we lock the steel door from the inside.

"So can we talk?" says Phil.

"Talk your head off."

I pull together another of my makeshift nests, this time out of a pile of tarps, back-stock sweatshirts, and Eddy's jackets. I curl up, still swimming with exhaustion and tension, and my thoughts drift while I listen to Phil explain how he was caught, where he was taken, what they did, what he said or didn't say. I tune in when he tells me that after he was released, he went back to my house, our house. The first time, he went back, got the guns, and brought them to Eddy. The second time, he went back because he remembered my stash of food and, to some small extent, what I'd hidden. In the cupboards, he thought. If there was liquor he could use it for trade. But this time the house wasn't empty.

"There was a woman sleeping on the couch," says Phil. "I knew her. Her name was Bernice and she was good at taking women into custody."

"She's the one who picked me up," I say. "She's the one who shot my roommate's boyfriend."

Phil peers at me.

"She was dead drunk," he says.

I sneak a look at him. Bernice must have found a few bottles from the stash. Phil goes on talking.

"A bottle of Jameson was on the end table, drained, with one of your Songmaker grandmother's fancy highball glasses, tipped over. Another empty bottle was at the foot of that overstuffed chaise. A carton of Marlboros was torn open beside and she'd piled her butts in your grandmother's favorite ashtray, that heavy one you told me was made of her wedding crystal."

"The nerve," I say. "But you have a good memory."

"Poor Bernice," said Phil. "She was getting drunk alone. She couldn't stand herself. I decided to immobilize her while she was drunk. Tie her up, gag her, I guess. Find out where she got the booze."

Then Phil grins at me. I can see his face in the gloom cast by a tiny vent near the ceiling line—I've never seen that sick smile before. His teeth are knocked out of one side of his jaw. I look away.

"I know the things she did, more than you can imagine," he says after a few moments. "Actually, I decided to kill her."

I can just see the fuzzy gray outline of his ruined features, the pits and scars and burns all over his face and neck. He turns to me, suddenly, grips my chin hard in his hands and crushes his mouth to mine. I know he has suffered, even suffered for me, but his grin was a caffeine jolt, reality. His kiss numbs me. My heart turns over.

"What did you do?"

"I started a fire."

"Not the most inconspicuous way to kill someone."

"It was kind of an accident."

"Nobody starts a house fire by accident."

"Unless you've got a gas can. I went in there. While she was groggy I poured the gas on her. Then I lit her up with my Bic."

"You did not."

"No, of course I didn't. She'd left something on the stove. You could smell it. She got up and staggered into the kitchen, grabbed the pan, which was smoking hot. She burns her hands. Staggers to the sink. Then she throws water on the fire."

"Grease fire?"

"I guess. Next she flaps dish towels on the fire and the towels flare up. It's almost comical. She throws them at the curtains. Massive flames. It's crazy. She was throwing fire around the room, laughing. She was high, too, maybe. So I just tiptoed away."

"So she did it to herself," I say.

"I was halfway down the street when I hear this big *whump*. I look back and suddenly fire's coming out of the roof."

"Probably the Finnish vodka."

"Oh. What a waste. Then as I was turning the corner there were explosions, rat-a-tats, like a firefight."

"The wall was filled with ammo."

A small voice inside me starts hissing *mortal sin mortal sin mortal oh my god I am heartily sorry*. Bernice was a terrible person, a killer herself, but there is no equivalence that absolves someone . . . me? Not me. I put my hands over my face, as if to hide from my wasted guilt.

"I didn't know where else to go," Phil says eventually. "I'm wanted. And they have searched the house here twice by now. They are probably everywhere, still looking."

"Wait," I say. "You said you were with Mother. Now you say you're wanted. Which is it?"

He stutters, filling me with fear.

"It's both," he says. "They picked me up. I stole a car from them and got away."

"Aren't they arresting enough women? What do they want me for?"

Phil looks at me in surprise.

"You don't know?" he asks.

"Know what?"

He stops talking, and now I don't want to hear it. But eventually I tell him, *Say it.*

"You might be carrying one of the originals," he says. "There aren't very many so they put you in special security hospitals. You already escaped from one."

"Originals? What are you talking about?"

"Just a regular baby," says Phil. "Like the ones before."

"So my baby's okay."

He doesn't answer for a while, then says, "Our baby. I'm the dad. Remember?"

My voice is scratchy, my mouth has gone dry. My blood starts buzzing and I am sick, faint. Then you kick and roll as if to tell me that you're healthy, you're ready to be born. And that's the moment I know, right there in the back of the Superpumper, that you're somebody. Before, to be honest, no matter how I tried to talk to you, the truth is I felt that you were not altogether *you*. You were a fragment of me. That's why I kept writing, to convince myself, to prepare myself for you to be a person, apart from who I am.

Now I feel you listening.

Phil is talking, musing, and his talking makes me ill.

"After all, it's a global crisis, it's the future of humanity, so you can see why they need to keep an eye on women. Every living thing is changing, Cedar, it's biological chaos, things going backward at an awkward rate."

Your kicks and rolls make me giddy. I am having trouble taking a deep breath. I am panting, quietly. The air is cold and sharp. Again, I think of Glen's words so long ago, in the old world, over pancakes, when life was still golden. How Mother Earth had a perfect sense of justice.

And you are still listening, under my hand, a peculiar new sensation. You seem to have tuned in to your father's voice, but like me you seem suspended, alert to something bad beneath his words.

"Don't get me wrong," says Phil. "I'm not with them, honey, I don't believe in capital punishment for abortion, but I understand. They're fucked up and scared. I'm with you like lots of decent guys! We're on your side, we're armed. But I sure could have used what you're telling me was ammo in those walls."

His voice is wistful, childish, and I can't even look at his damaged hands.

"The thing is," he says, very softly, "you have a treasure, Cedar, if our baby is normal. We would be in charge of things. Rich. Super rich! We'd be safe. If we somehow worked out genetically, I mean, to have a normal child the sky's the limit for us."

"We could seize power and found a dynasty," I say, meaning it sarcastically.

"That's right," says Phil softly, reaching for me. I bat away his hand and call Eddy.

THANKSGIVING

There never was a raid. Mother did not come back. Perhaps I hallucinated her. And maybe, let's hope, in the throes of eighth month's hormones I hallucinated Phil. But no, Phil was out the door once I called Eddy. The silver car backed out of the brush and Phil pulled out onto the highway. I wish he hadn't come here and hadn't disappeared. I'm hoping that when I wouldn't agree to his plan, he went off to figure out another way to found his dynasty. I'm trying not to think about him. We are sitting in the garage, guards posted just outside the door. The cement floor is covered with wild turkey feathers.

"Honey, I hunted," calls Eddy for the hundredth time, to Sweetie.

"You should have shot their damn feathers off," she complains.

I am wearing rubber gloves, so I'm happy with my raw smelly job. Dead bird, blood, feathers, a rich gamey odor. There are six turkeys to clean. I'm way too big and heavy to do much more than sit and pull feathers. I have to shift my weight constantly—one butt cheek is pins and needles, the other aches.

"Eddy's always got a plan with his turkeys," says Sweetie. "Some years he brines them. Some years he uses this green egg-shaped cooker. Some years he deep-fries the whole damn bird."

"Do we have to have the pilgrims?" says Mary.

Sweetie groans. Transcendence seekers have been passing through the reservation in tattered campers bearing Tibetan prayer flags. They are often looking for protection, or fleeing, and have put a burden on the militia. It is difficult to sort the mere yearning from the darkness that some of them bring. And then there are the Catholic pilgrims—neatly dressed, devout, setting up their Target tents, hibachi grills, and collapsible aluminum chairs near the statue of Kateri.

"They are on their own," says Eddy. "We'll feed our elders, our children, and our warriors. Maybe not strictly traditional, but hey, learn from experience. First Thanksgiving, we ended up with our heads on pikes."

But of course we end up making all of the food on the reservation, and feeding absolutely everyone.

NOVEMBER 30

In the dead of night, the only time we feel invisible, Sweetie brings me to pray at the statue of Kateri. I wear a blanket, a huge sleeping bag, and pads on my knees. Other people around me are praying too, keeping vigil, and the peace of it all, the stillness, the great pointed stars overhead in the blackest night, are of such comfort to us. As I pray along with the others, rosaries, Hail Marys, I keep my hand on my belly. Again, I know you are listening. I can feel you listening, breathing, puzzling out the sounds. I can feel you thinking.

In the middle of a prayer, I am hoisted onto my feet. I am wearing my backpack, which makes me awkward, and I can't see who's behind me. I put my arms up to try and pull hair, but it is a big guy with no hair. A squeaky-breathed woman quickly zip-ties my wrists together. Yelling, I'm dragged straight into a van. The doors shut. After everything we've gone through, after all we've avoided, it seems like I am being hijacked by some random pilgrims. Sweetie's running after the van, screaming. The other pilgrims are chasing after her. The statue dwindles. We turn onto the big highway. Home falls behind us.

The woman in the seat next to me is nervous like her husband, with lopsided pale hair, soft hands. She reaches over and straps me in. I try to head-butt her. Anxiously, she folds a blanket over me.

"I'm sorry," she says. "We're broke, so dead broke, and we have kids. We need the money."

"For turning me in?"

She doesn't answer, just sniffles and groans.

"Will you pray with me?" she asks in a hopeful voice.

"You are a monster with no soul," I answer.

"Now don't get all testy on us," says the man in the driver's seat.

Saint Kateri really let me down.

DECEMBER 1

I'm sure we all feel like this, every woman with a baby, because of the brain-bending hormones, but, dear child, I still have this stubborn notion we'll be all right. Even here. A sign above the entrance says Stillwater Birthing Center, but it is only a painted piece of canvas that covers Minnesota Correctional Facility Stillwater.

DECEMBER 2

Even though I have a thick piece of foam for a mattress and soft blue flannel sheets and a fuzzy pink blanket, I am still in a cinder-block cell. A disinfected cell, a nicely painted cell with an extra pillow, an extra-plush blanket, but a cell. There is a sink, a toilet, a fold-down cot, a wall shelf, a small plastic chair, and a bulletin board with pictures of babies taped on it. Which strikes me as sadistic, considering. The pregnant women roaming up and down the central walkway wear blazing neon-pink or peacock-blue jumpsuits. I have one of each. My blue suit has a dark round stain on the pants. It looks like old blood. You can never get it out once the stain sets. This time I got to keep everything inside of my backpack, and because I am now Mary Potts with a tribal ID I've evaded detection. It won't be long. Once they find out who I am, we're shit outta luck. So I'm writing to you before all that happens.

Although, I have to say, everything here looks poorly organized. The faucets work, but the water is rusty. The lights work, but lots of the bulbs are dead. The floors are clean, but that's because we clean them ourselves. The screens they use to watch us keep blinking out. Still, the doors upon doors to the outside are carefully locked. I can see people in the guard towers when I get to use the hallways.

DECEMBER 3

Every morning at ten a.m. we're seated in a room to practice for labor. The light goes down in the room. We sit on yoga mats. It is peaceful enough. We keep our eyes closed. We travel. This morning, while I am doing my counting and breathing, Orielee and Bernice come flying toward me. They are naked, moving fast, leaking coils of darkness from their mouths and ears. Smoke bleeds from their nipples, from their navels. Hot black steam flows out between their legs. A roaring noise beats from their bodies, like the sound of a vast crowd. I open my arms. They are alive! I am not afraid.

DECEMBER 4

Today two male guards collect me from my cell. They are wearing brown uniforms, but there is something sloppy and tired about how they are dressed. You can see a ripped, dirty collar of a T-shirt between the missing buttons of one guy's shirt. They bring me to a room that might have once been an office—there is a wall of bookshelves, a window, and a couple of fake plants—but now it is tricked out as a photography studio. Miguel, a slender man, curly headed, dressed in yellow, with melting eyes, reminds me of Prince.

He greets me as though I'm the loveliest woman in the world. "Hello, my hummingbird! I'm your personal makeup artist. Wow. Hmmm. You could be anything. What you want to look like? Whitebread? Brownbread? House Mom? Street Babe?"

He tousles my hair, pulls it up, lets it flop down. I ask him if I can be the Blessed Virgin. His eyes flicker with interest, his face goes solemn. He puts his hands on my shoulders and bends over so we stare at ourselves together in the mirror. The sadness in his face chills me.

"I see blue. We can't use headgear, so no veil, but I add some blue extensions. We get the sensation of blue. Your face is sweet. I'll make it sweeter. Your hair is . . . I won't do much . . . fabulous."

He parts my hair in the middle and strokes it down around my shoulders.

"It spreads out nice, like a cape."

"A veil."

"Like a veil."

He opens a fishing tackle box covered with stickers, filled with bottles of foundation, eyeliner, fake lashes, lipstick. It is soothing to have him study my face, touch my cheeks with his fingertips, dab here, dab there. He combs my hair out so gently that it feels like I am being touched by butterflies. I close my eyes and let him brush shadow across my lids. He then has me look up and flicks mascara onto my lashes.

"We'll go with a very light natural color," he says as he tenderly outlines my mouth with matte lipstick. He thriftily tears a Kleenex in half, uses the end. "Now blot."

He makes drama of pulling off my makeup gown, puffing it like a cloud, flinging it away and replacing it with a blue scarf draped around my shoulders. He leads me to a chair with a backdrop that is painted with a sunny circle of radiance. The glow surrounds my head once I am eased onto the chair.

"I'm the photographer, too, right? You're divine. You're special. You're a giver of life. That's right. Let all the beauty inside of you rush to the surface. Let your beauty into your eyes, your face."

Lunch is fried sweet potatoes and chicken soup, although apparently chickens are not chickens anymore—they look like pale iguanas.

"What's that?"

"A piece of skin."

The woman next to me dislodges the scaly skin from her finger and goes on eating her soup. There is a salad with odd thick leaves and gnarled tomatolike vegetables. Halfway through the meal, I notice the dining room wall. It is filled with portraits of women. They all have the same glow around their heads. As I walk up to the wall to see if my portrait is there, a burly redheaded woman stops me. Her face and arms are covered with tiny cinnamon dots of freckles. Her kinky red Botticelli hair is twisted up in a bun. She's about eight months.

"Don't go up to the wall," she says. "Don't look."

"How come?"

She purses her lips, like she has a lot to say, but she only gives a terse growl. "It's bad luck." Which is enough to keep me away from the wall, for now. I sleep away the afternoon under my fuzzy pink blanket. Dinner is a mushy glop of brown paste, plus a cup of sour berries.

"I miss food," I say to the women on either side of me. One is a thin Mexican American woman with a medium-sized seven-month belly.

"I miss food, too."

The other is a brown-haired woman in her forties with pink cheeks and purple eyeglasses. She says that she is carrying baby number three.

"Third time's the charm," I say. It is involuntary. She stares at me. Her eyes fill. She looks down at her plate.

"I hope so," she mumbles.

"Me too," says the thin girl. Her eyes are huge, haunting. Her name is Estrella. "I used to love roasted chicken. I made it with lemon. Won't catch me roasting a lizard."

"Maybe cows will stay the same, just tougher," I say. "What . . . what happens in here?"

"Where did you use to live?" the brown-haired woman asks me, loudly, looking around us. Then she leans close and whispers, "They used to just take pregnant woman. Now any woman who's child-bearing age. You can get picked up for running a stoplight or jay-walking. I'm here for shoplifting, which was stupid, but I needed food. Any mistake and you end up here."

"A nice little house in South Minneapolis?" she says brightly. "I lived in Northeast. The art district. I worked in clay." She flexes her hands. "But my work was sculptural. I didn't throw pots."

"I was a teller at Wells Fargo," says Estrella. Then she whispers. "At least you're already inseminated. When I came here I had to go through it, over and over. They leave you alone afterward with your hips up. See if you take."

There is a rustle of whispers all through the dining room, a swirl of motion in one corner. The burly redheaded woman is standing up in front of the wall of women. She is holding her belly. Her silence commands everyone's attention. Tears shining in her eyes, she nods and all at once, all together, the women start to hum. It is a beautiful, powerful, all-knowing sound. They open their mouths to sing a song that I already know. The song must be in me. Is it the song I sang to Tia? Maybe we all learned it in former lives, deep places, gathering grounds, caves and huts of sticks, skin houses, prisons, and graves. It is a wordless melody that only women sing. Slow, beautiful, sad, ecstatic, we sing a hymn of war and a march of peace. Over and over, many times, we continue singing as the guards take away the redheaded woman.

Mother moon and sister night, I think.

Saint Kateri. You owe me. So get busy and pray for us.

After we sing we file out in rows.

"What just happened?" I ask Estrella.

"Ask somebody else," she says, her face strained and desperate. "Please? Just ask somebody else."

But I don't have to ask.

After all of the other women leave, I slip back and stand before the wall. The women in the photographs are alert, smiling, hopeful, perfectly made up. Thanks to Miguel. There are women of every coloring and age, many younger than me, others older, some wear hats, head scarves, or a hijab, some wear a glittery barrette, even an old-school scrunchie. I step closer to read their names. Lily-Ann. Idris. Janella. Senchal. Megan. Vendra. Beneath each name are two dates. Birth. Death. And below that a line that says: *She served the future.*

I step back from the wall of martyrs.

DECEMBER 6

During mandatory Watching Hour, we sit on wobbly plastic chairs crammed together in the viewing room. Mother is the only channel. Sometimes she brings on Papa, a sunken-eyed man with stiff white side-parted hair and the same lipless hatch of angry whitened teeth. Mother surges into view, round cake-pan face, busy calm.

"Hello, my dears. Today I want to talk about the divinely infused eternal soul that you carry within you, and I want to say that I understand how difficult it can be to nurture this soul in your body. Maybe you didn't feel it was your time. However, you are blessed. Because God felt it was your time!"

"Here's the part where she's going to ask us to hold hands," says Estrella.

"Please reach out to your sister, and pray, pray along with me. Please reach out and hold hands."

On one side, Estrella's hand is dry and thin. A fuming black teenager on the other side of me grabs my hand. Her hand is restless and strong. As Mother talks, we hold on harder.

"Jesus, please get me the fuck out of here," the teenager whispers.

"Amen," we say together.

The huge fingers of a baby's hand splay behind Mother like a plump star. She gives a busybody nose twitch before she starts. Mother lifts her arms mechanically, up and down, working out her words like water from an old-fashioned iron pump. Her bangs are pasted in a smooth curve today. Her bright brown eyes peep out from underneath the fringe. When she gets excited her hair flops hound-eared to each side of her rough large-pored cheeks.

"You are here because you did something wrong," she says, "but this is a place of forgiveness. Open your heart! Your mind! Your body and your soul! Accept life. You can be absolved of anything you did, you can completely win back God's love, by contributing to the future of humanity. Your happy sentence is only nine months."

Her chins wobble and her thin lips blow her words out like bubbles as she enters her prayer.

"Always know that I care about each and every one of you. Women are powerful. You are empowered to the max. Women are heroes. Superheroes, in fact. You can talk to me anytime. You can bring me your worries, your concerns. I am all about communication, my dears. I care about each and every one of you one hundred percent forever."

We are not allowed to look away.

"These nine months will pass like a few weeks," she says in her thick voice. And to think, I could have killed her. My finger squeezes an imaginary trigger as she begins another endless prayer. A waterfall of burning syrup. I try to sleep with my eyes open. Nobody gets out of here in nine months. I'm positive. Nobody gets out of here at all.

DECEMBER 8

"You're due for your ultrasound," says the round dark woman at my door. Her eyebrows are thick and bushy. Her hair is braided down her back. She smiles at me and sits down beside my cot. She takes my hand.

"Some of my ladies hate ultrasounds. I promise there will only be this one."

"They always say that."

"It won't harm your baby."

"That's not true."

She smiles indulgently.

This morning, I saw that the redheaded woman's portrait had been put up onto the wall during the night. I forced myself to look carefully, then, at all of the other pictures, in case I had missed one.

I closed my eyes when I was finished. Started breathing again. No Tia Jackson.

"Shall we go then?"

So now it comes. I get up and follow the attendant down the hall, nodding at the women I've spoken to before, catching the eyes of others. I remember the long sage green corridor I walked when you had your first ultrasound, the one where I saw the fire of life course through your body. I am not afraid—or I might be afraid, but I can't feel the fear. I'm numb to everything but each instant that my footfall sounds. I brush my fingers along the smooth painted wallboard in the hallway, and although I'm clumsy, I can still climb up on the table when we get to the examining room. The dark-haired attendant sits by the door. The technician covers the end of the wand with clear gel and tells me that it will feel cold. I take deep breaths and block out Mother's voice. The technician touches out the baby's brain, clicking and moving the wand. But then she shakes the wand, frowning in irritation. The lights flicker, and the attendant leaves to investigate.

"Shit," the technician says. "The equipment, the screens, the electrical, it sucks."

"That's okay. I've had a million of these."

"I hate my job," she whispers.

"Why don't you quit?"

The lights are still dimmed out. The screen has gone entirely dark.

"I'm doing time too. I tried to bribe my way out, but nobody dares take money. They just take you here."

"How did you get caught?"

"Expired tabs."

"Maybe you'll tell me the truth. Why is it so dangerous?"

"Giving birth?"

I nod, unable to speak.

"It has to do with your immune system. You know how the danger in getting a heart transplant or whatever is tissue rejection, well it's like that. Even in your normal old-fashioned pregnancy your body dropped some immunity in order to accept the baby. For some reason—possibly because we've gone into the unknown here, biologically—your immune system mounts an attack against the baby during birth and that can become an autoimmune attack as well. We've tried putting women on medication with some success, for them. But it seems to limit the baby's chances, so . . ."

We wait a few minutes longer, and then at last she calls the attendant back to bring me to my cell. The lights are flickering all through the corridors. Any small reprieve at this point seems like a miracle, so in spite of my disillusionment I relent and thank Kateri. Maybe God has some plan for me. I crawl back onto my cot, and at the very notion of God Has a Plan, I start laughing so hard I have to stuff the edge of my blanket in my mouth.

The lights are too bright in here. The saints step away from me in the brilliant white glare. I know they're out there, but I can't see the multitude of beings, voiceless, rippling, hushed in the giant space, their tiny coughs and moans distorted by the booming of empty air. One spirit shouts, then others, then sound rises up all around me in a vast white wall. I am so blind and small in the cataract, and yes, I am alone, except for you.

DECEMBER 11

Hildegard of Bingen spent her youth locked in a stone hut. Hildegard's parents decided that she should be an anchoress, and in a funereal ceremony she entered complete enclosure, probably at the age of seven. At least she had her mentor, Jutta. There was a window for food to be given. And an opening for a waste bucket to pass in and out. No wonder Hildegard was subject to shattering visions.

Everything is penetrated with connectedness, penetrated with relatedness.

My good spirit visits me nearly every night, settling at the foot of the bed. And this time, there is a song that I also hear, and it is not the women's song. It is a baby's song, maybe Eddy's song, for it is high, repetitive, and comforting, like a lullaby. I hum it to you as we drift through the night, together now only for a short time.

There is the prison yard, an exercise area where we are allowed to walk in circles or aimlessly shift around. Estrella and I walk together, not speaking. Holding hands. Sometimes they try to stop us from holding hands with each other, or draping our arms over each other, or hugging, or touching each other's hair. But they give up. Even to the guards it feels mean to stop us. I see it in their eyes. They look away. We are all frightened children.

It surprises me, though, how even though the women are passing through with only a slim chance of survival, they have tried to make beauty. Here and there inside the prison, pots are set out, filled with plants with arrow-shaped leaves, waxy purple blossoms, bulbous stalks I've never seen before, nameless plants, all numbered with fascinated attention, as though someone has kept track of how they grow. I see that other accidental plants are pushing into the prison as well. Mold against the reinforced window glass, tiny vines creeping from the cracks in the stairs. Motelike insects sometimes spring from the leaves I brush. They are only visible as motion.

Once, as I'm walking by the window, a vibrating shadow stops me. Behind the shatterproof glass a dragonfly hovers just at eye level. Not a normal dragonfly. This one is giant—a three-foot wingspan, golden green eyes the size of softballs.

Inside, the plants are spreading from the pots of soil. Some vines are thin as threads, others are green ropes that loop against the windows and up the stairways, always toward the light. The leaves proliferate and already in some places here you can walk in the shade of the understory. A fern tree has shot up, giant leaves curling out like feathers. And segmented bamboolike poles of purple and green are rising out of the stairwells. Every day there is an ever thicker green profusion. When I walk around the yard, I see that even in December vines burst from the stomped ground and catch hold of the slightest ridge or frame to travel, almost visibly upward, thrusting skeins of waving leaves across the fences, across the razor wire, even along the glass towers of the guards, rearing into the ferocious sunlight.

I am the fiery life of the essence of God. I am the flame above the beauty of the fields. I shine in the waters. I burn in the sun, the moon, and the stars. And with the airy wind, I quicken all things vitally by an unseen, all-sustaining life.

Hildegard.

DECEMBER 12

Every so often, a woman survives her pregnancy. A few times they've let her out, but more often, they keep her. From our exercise yard we can see a vast field filling with tiny white crosses. One cross for both mother and baby. Past the field of crosses, two more fences, more razor wire. In spite of the slipshod feeling of how it is run, there is no rescue from this place, in case you wonder why I never mention it. I know that even with all of their combined ingenuity my family is not going to get me out of here. When I miss them to an unbearable degree, I sing the song for you, baby. Or I untuck a page of Eddy's manuscript from my pack. It helps.

PAGE 3034

The Pebble

I live yet because of a common pebble.

Yesterday the bubble burst. Once again, I saw into the depth of things; only it was worse because things are so much deeper now. Not one aspect of the world could appeal to me or affect me. Not the end of things and not the beginning. There were no colors. Everything was neutral. From this I know that hell is not black or fiery. It is an unvaried gray without promise. And so the morning passed with its coffee and dry cereal. By noon, I was at the Superpumper, deciding which method to use.

As I walked with a length of rope toward the woods out back of the shop, a pebble flipped into my shoe. It hurt. Each step was painful. I stopped, and removed it. The stone was a bit of ferric oxide, earthy banded hematite, strayed from the Mesabi Range, where one-third of the world's iron ore was at one time located. This piece of stone was laid down as a sediment in the Animikean sea sometime during the middle Precambrian period in Minnesota, and was probably between 2.6 and 1.6 billion years old. The pebble was a rich, deep, hot, clay red, striated and shaped like a tiny toaster.

I tossed it over my shoulder and continued down the path. Another pebble. Ouch. This time it was pointed. This, too, was no ordinary rock, but a shard of graywacke or green-stone, a basaltic lava that was perhaps shoved to the surface of the earth 3.5 billion years ago during the Keewatin. Howah! Lotta time. I dropped the stone to the side of the path and kept walking toward a particular tree I'd picked out sometime before. A good strong branch jutted from the trunk. Perfect to swing a rope over.

Oops, another. These low docksiders, whiteman's shoes, seemed to scoop the rocks right in. This pebble was a dime-sized circle of black basalt shaped by lake waves and probably poured out at one time from a deep volcanic fissure under the sea that covered us. The lava cooled and was broken into bits that washed away, eventually to the shore, changing on the way to this lovely water-stroked smoothness. This one I placed carefully upon a stump. The youngest pebble, it was probably no more than several million years old.

I had nearly reached the tree when a final rock cut me— actually cut me as I stepped down upon it. An agate, inexpli-cably shattered, it showed the grain of the fossilized wood and algae that it had once been. What colors! A light bronze, gray, black, and deep red. There was a landscape within its features. Chert surrounded by jasper. A living thing. It would make, I thought, a beautiful necklace for Sweetie, were it only polished.

I don't know why they want me here on earth, the little rocks. I don't know why they care about me as they do. I only know that by the time I reached the tree I had no choice but to fling the rope away from myself. I turned back, my fingers rubbing the little agate. All the way back to the store not a single rock slipped underfoot.

DECEMBER 14

We're in a gray spell—a week of clouded-over, indifferent weather. There isn't even a patch of blue sky to lift a person's thoughts. It feels to me like everything is sliding away. I am alone with the truth of my body—you are in it and I have to get you out.

Baby, I love you but you are huge. Your exit is supposed to stretch, but ten centimeters isn't that much wider than the mouth of a water glass. How stretchy am I? Not that stretchy. I'm rigid. I've always been a rigid thinker, and am lousy at yoga. You should stop growing right now, you are already too big, but you don't care. You continue to grow and grow.

My headaches, how I see bright spots, my spiking blood pressure, these could be signs that my body is having the allergic reaction to your presence. I tell nobody but Estrella. I'm puffing up. I push my finger into the flesh of my calf and the dent stays dented.

"Look," I say.

She touches my calf with her fingertips, and frowns.

DECEMBER 15

There are usually two doctors and a nurse in the room when I get a checkup. I go in every single day now. The ultrasound machines are still messed up. So I just get the regular sort of offhand check—my blood pressure is high, very high, which is why I'm being watched, my doctor says. There is something familiar about my doctor. Every time I see her, I feel that I've somehow seen her before, even known her, but there are always the others in the room so I never dare to ask. But then one day I am alone with the doctor for a moment. She's wearing square blue eyeglasses.

"Have I seen you before?"

She smiles at me and bends over as if to tie her shoe. When she gets up, she grips my hand as if to comfort me. I feel a tiny bit of paper in my palm. I grasp it and turn over on the examining table, which is not easy, it's a big deal at 38-plus weeks. I shake my hair as if I'm pouting, and read the paper inside the curtain of my hair. *The dust around us listens, the walls see, the air pumped into this room tastes our emotions.*

It's almost poetry. I hate to have to eat it. After a moment, I turn back over, my fist curled, my face stony. I try to still my heart, to breathe normally.

The doctor gives a tense little smile, glances around, and folds her arms and drums her fingers. She writes something else down and gives me the bit of paper.

Jessie, it says.

I stare in wonder, mouth the words. "The hospital?"

She nods.

I described Jessie once as a pale, skinny, chinless, nerdy type of woman. I said she was mousy, bland, limp-haired, and cave-chested. I called her the Dweeb, but I remember she went from noodly to rock steady. She really did have the nerves of an outlaw, not a dweeb, whatever that is. Now she has completely changed her look. She's chic, a leader, with tousled blond hair and fashionable blue eyeglasses. She has a chin. Where she got it, I don't know. I soon find out a few things. Turns out Jessie was not a nurse, she was an OB-GYN posing as a nurse in order to get women out of the hospital, disguising and hiding them, past security. Turns out she nearly blew her cover getting Agnes Starr off the birthing table, out of the hospital, in a body bag punched with breathing holes.

DECEMBER 18

I complain about the bright spots, exaggerate my headaches, and get sent back to the doctor. But this time, and the next time, the others stay in the room and Jessie can't talk. At last, there is a moment, and I find out that Agnes used a box cutter blade that Jessie taped to her upper arm as she went into labor. Jessie pretended that Agnes had died when her baby was born, and laid her into the bag. Agnes slit the bag open in the deep of night. She made her way out of the morgue.

I show a tiny note. It gives my old address, and where the money is still buried. And it asks:

What are my chances, baby's chances?

Both of you 15 to 20 percent chance survival.

Will you keep track of where they take my baby?

Yes.

DECEMBER 23

I know the Word. It is the oldest word in any language, first utterance. Ma, ah, oh, mama. Mother. Not the word uttered by God to make life, but spoken by the baby who recognizes the being on whom life depends.

I will hear that word. I will know that word. I will stay alive.

DECEMBER 24

For once in my life, I am right on time.

9:25 p.m. It begins.

DECEMBER 25

Estrella told me it was not going to matter, and it didn't matter where I was giving birth. Or who was in the room, except that there was no Jessie. No outlaw. That mattered. But I forgot. *I am the flame above the beauty of the fields.* One by one the saints entered the room. Over the next hours thousands of spirits were admitted. We were surrounded by a jungle of plants. *I shine in the waters. I burn in the sun, the moon, the stars.* The saints were silent. All that mattered was getting through each contraction. Then the next. And the next. I could see myself reflected in the stainless steel panels. I was in an ocean shooting sparks of light. The waves were pain. I was flung up, dashed down. Over and over to infinity and then when I thought I must have died, I took a breath, and I was surprised. The ocean also took a deep breath. The day was gone. The night was dark, the light softened, and I realized that thousands of candles cast this glow and the gorgeous music that I heard was the thousands of spirits and human beings singing, *The soul is not in the body. The body is in the soul.* I heard the other song, the women's song, between the contractions. I heard your baby song. And I pushed. The pushing went on forever, until, with a violence I didn't know was in me, I pushed you out.

You were blue, just a slight tinge. As you breathed you turned pinker and redder and the soft fuzz that covered your skin began to glow like copper. Your velvety limbs unfolded, tensile and strong. You tipped your head back. Your eyes were the newborn's slaty blue, but darker, already burning to live. You held my gaze and I put my finger into your hand. You stared at me, holding on with an implacable strength, and I looked into the soul of the world.

It's you, I said. *It was always you.*

The sting of the needle stole my consciousness. As I slipped away, someone pried apart your fist and I felt you lifted from my arms.

DECEMBER

Extremely weak. But still here.

JANUARY

They say my heart is damaged.

FEBRUARY

My dear son. I know you're going to read this someday. I can tell that you're going to wonder what it was like, in the *before*.

My parents would tell me things about the world, the way it was before, the way they knew it and loved it although, they always said this, We didn't know it was heaven.

I would ask them, What was it like, years ago? The real cold, the deep cold?

And they would tell me.

Sometimes when the lake froze quickly and the wind was high, volumes of moving water were trapped beneath the ice, said Sera. Then you heard muffled explosions deep down, in the center, and rending moans where the ice met the islands. Cracks like gunshots. Hollow reverberating gulps. Sometimes there were the quick staccato reports of snare drums, fading in and out, as if a marching band wound its way back and forth below the ice.

If the ice froze slowly, the lake made a different music. A delicate whisper as the frozen wave tips touched. If the cold waves drove hard, fracturing the edges of the ice sheets, the shards tinkled together or rang off-key. The lake was surrounded by haunted wind chimes. Sometimes the lake breathed a tortured sigh, its lungs full of broken glass. If the temperature dropped, 50 or even 60 degrees overnight, the lake might freeze clear, trapping leaves and even small fish. You walked out on the ice, threw yourself down in your snug nylon snowsuit, and peered into an altered world.

Glen remembered when the lake froze in linear figures. Wind-whipped waves had frozen in the air, shattered, and welded smoothly into the ice floor as they fell, creating jagged puzzles, mathematical labyrinths, furies of intersecting lines. The lake was entirely composed of crazy hatchmarks. Every inch was an original design.

And how did it change? They told me that, too.

First the cold didn't burn your lungs, said Sera. The cold didn't freeze the snot in your nose, didn't frost your eyelashes, didn't hurt, said Glen. And the snow didn't squeak underneath your footsteps or against the car's tires. Soon the cold stopped pinching, stopped running its fingers up your back, stopped numbing your face, your fingers. The snow still came down in fluffy flakes sometimes. Once or twice it was finely suspended in the wind and we tried to call it a blizzard. But it was only here a moment. Next winter, it rained. The cold was mild and refreshing. But only rain. That was the year we lost winter. Lost our cold heaven.

But I remember. The snow came one last time.

The snow is what I think about as I recover, and as I wait in my cell for my next pregnancy. The bulletin board is plastered with new baby pictures. If we starve ourselves they will force-feed us. One woman hanged herself in the stairwell, using a merciful vine. The front wall of the cafeteria is nearly filled. After Estrella's photo went up, I stopped looking at the wall. I don't know what happened to Jessie, if she's still here. No message. (I dream she has taken you away. That she's keeping you safe for me.) I sing your song. My guardian spirit has returned.

I stay quiet, alone.

And I remember how I was there the last time it snowed in heaven. I was eight years old. I can feel it now. The cold seizing my body, its clarity. The snow poured out of the sky. Come! Sera cried. Glen shouted, Snow! We ran outside and stood on the dull green lawn, transfixed. The snow swirled around us, falling and falling faster. And there were birds, excited birds, a nuthatch clicking up and down the trees. Cold robins trilling as flake by flake snow collected. The air went still and still the snow kept falling. People drifted by like white shadows and their voices were the cries of lost children. Snow filled the air and kept on coming, like ecstasy, in shifting curtains. It didn't stop. It didn't melt into the grass. The snow built up on every surface. And I can feel it now, so heavy. Each twig bore a line of snow. Each birdbath became a cake and the lattice and the dried husks of summer flowers wore white frills. It snowed on each pine needle, on the tips of pickets, on the cars. In the streets, over sidewalks, in the gutter, it snowed. And I am in it, falling down in it, shoveling snow into my mouth and throwing snow up in the air, pelting snow at my mother and my father. Whiteness fills the air and whiteness is all there is. I am here, and I was there. And I have wondered, ever since your birth. Where will you be, my darling, the last time it snows on earth?

ACKNOWLEDGMENTS

Thank you to my daughters—Persia, who listened to this book's beginnings on a road trip in 2001 and kept up with the many changes; Pallas, who read drafts, gave invaluable advice, and rescued this manuscript after I had abandoned it for years in the memory of a Mac G4 Cube (and thanks as well to Keith Kostman for resurrecting portions of this manuscript from an even older turquoise iMac); Aza, who consulted with me on the progress of this book and gave me visual ideas for Cedar's magazine, *Zeal*, which will appear at the end of the paperback edition; and Kiizh, for kindness, honesty, and startling insights.

I would also like to thank my sister Heid Erdrich and my brother-in-law John Burke for sharing speculative theories, which unnervingly came true. As ever and always, thank you to my editor Terry Karten, for critical wisdom and impeccable literary instinct. And thank you, Trent Duffy, master copy editor, for our ongoing conversation contained on tiny scraps of paper. The spirit of the whole is always in the details.

ABOUT THE AUTHOR

LOUISE ERDRICH is the author of sixteen novels as well as volumes of poetry, children's books, short stories, and a memoir of early motherhood. Her most recent novel, *LaRose*, won the National Book Critics Circle Award in fiction, while *The Round House* received the National Book Award for Fiction. *The Plague of Doves* was a finalist for the Pulitzer Prize. Erdrich has received the Library of Congress Prize in American Fiction and the prestigious PEN/Saul Bellow Award for Achievement in American Fiction. She is a Turtle Mountain Chippewa and lives in Minnesota with her daughters. She is the owner of Birchbark Books, a small independent bookstore.